Desert

JEWELS

April 2014

May 2014

June 2014

July 2014

Desert
JEWELS

SHARON KENDRICK
ABBY GREEN
ANNIE WEST

MILLS &
BOON

Published in Great Britain 2014
by Mills & Boon, an imprint of Harlequin (UK) Limited,
Eton House, 18-24 Paradise Road, Richmond, Surrey, TW9 1SR

DESERT JEWELS © 2014 Harlequin Books S.A.

The Sheikh's Undoing © 2012 Sharon Kendrick
The Sultan's Choice © 2011 Abby Green
Girl in the Bedouin Tent © 2011 Annie West

ISBN: 978 0 263 24590 5

011-0414

Harlequin (UK) Limited's policy is to use papers that are natural, renewable and recyclable products and made from wood grown in sustainable forests The logging and manufacturing processes conform to the legalenvironmental regulations of the country of origin.

Printed and bound in Spain
by Blackprint CPI, Barcelona

The Sheikh's Undoing

SHARON KENDRICK

Sharon Kendrick started storytelling at the age of eleven and has never really stopped. She likes to write fast-paced, feel-good romances with heroes who are so sexy they'll make your toes curl! Born in west London, she now lives in the beautiful city of Winchester—where she can see the cathedral from her window (but only if she stands on tiptoe). She has two children, Celia and Patrick, and her passions include music, books, cooking and eating—and drifting off into wonderful daydreams while she works out new plots!

Visit Sharon at www.sharonkendrick.com.

CHAPTER ONE

THE sound of the telephone woke her, but Isobel didn't need to see the name flashing on the screen to know who was ringing. Who else would call her at this time of night but the man who thought he had the right to do pretty much whatever he wanted? And frequently did.

Tariq, the so-called 'Playboy Prince'. Or Prince Tariq Kadar al Hakam, Sheikh of Khayarzah—to give him his full and rather impressive title. And the boss if not exactly from hell then certainly from some equally dark and complicated place.

She glanced at the clock. Four in the morning was early even by *his* standards. Yawning, she picked up the phone, wondering what the hell he had been up to this time.

Had some new story about him emerged, as it so often did, sparked by gossip about his latest audacious take-over bid? Or had he simply got himself tied up with a new blonde—they were always blonde—and wanted Isobel to juggle his early morning meetings for him? Would he walk into the office later on with yesterday's growth darkening his strong jaw and a smug smile curving the edges of his sensual lips? And the scent of someone's perfume still lingering on his skin...

It wouldn't be the first time it had happened, that was for sure. With a frown, Isobel recalled some of his more famous sexual conquests, before reminding herself that she was employed as his personal assistant—not his moral guardian.

Friends sometimes asked whether she ever tired of having a boss who demanded so much of her. Or whether she was tempted to tell him exactly what she thought of his outrageously chauvinistic behaviour—and the answer was yes. Sometimes. But the generous amount of money he paid her soon put a stop to her disapproval. Because money like that provided security—the kind of security which you could never get from another person. Isobel knew that better than anyone. Hadn't her mother taught her that the most important lesson a woman could learn was to be completely independent of men? Men could just walk away whenever they wanted...and because they could, they frequently did.

She answered the call. 'Hello?'

'I-Isobel?'

Her senses were instantly alerted when she heard the deep voice of her employer—because there was something very different about it. Either he was in some kind of post-coital daze or something was wrong. Because he sounded...*weird*.

She'd never heard Tariq hesitate before. Never heard him as anything other than the confident and charismatic Prince—the darling of London's casinos and international gossip columns. The man most women couldn't resist, even when—as seemed inevitable—he was destined to break their heart into tiny little pieces.

'Tariq?' Isobel's voice took on a sudden note of urgency. 'Is something wrong?'

From amid a painful throbbing, which felt as if a thousand hammers were beating against his skull, Tariq registered the familiar voice of his assistant. His first brush with reality after what seemed like hours of chaos and confusion. Almost imperceptibly he let out a low sigh of relief as his lashes parted by a fraction. Izzy was his anchor. Izzy would sort this out for him. A ceiling swam into view, and quickly he shut his eyes against its harsh brightness.

'Accident,' he mumbled.

'Accident?' Isobel sat up in bed, her heart thundering as she heard the unmistakable twist of pain in his voice. 'What kind of accident? Tariq, where are you? What's *happened*?'

'I...'

'Tariq?' Isobel could hear someone indignantly telling him that he shouldn't be using his phone, and then a rustling noise before a woman's voice came on the line.

'Hello?' the strange voice said. 'Who is this, please?'

Isobel felt fear begin to whisper over her as she recognised the sound of officialdom, and it took an almighty effort just to stop her voice from shaking. 'M-my name is Isobel Mulholland and I work for Sheikh al Hakam—would you please tell me what's going on?'

There was a pause before the woman spoke again. 'This is one of the staff nurses at the Accident and Emergency department of St Mark's hospital in Chislehurst. I'm afraid that the Sheikh has been involved in a car crash—'

'Is he okay?' Isobel interrupted.

'I'm afraid I can't give out any more information at the moment.'

Hearing inflexible resistance in the woman's voice,

Isobel swung her legs over the side of the bed. 'I'm on my way,' she said grimly, and cut the connection.

Pulling on a pair of jeans, she grabbed the first warm sweater which came to hand and then, after shoving her still-bare feet into sheepskin boots, took the elevator down to the underground car park of her small London apartment.

Thank heavens for sat-nav, she thought as she tapped in the name of the hospital and waited for a map to appear on the screen. She peered at it. It seemed that Chislehurst was on the edge of the Kent countryside—less than an hour from here, especially at this time in the morning.

But, even though there was barely any traffic around, Isobel had to force herself to concentrate on the road ahead and not focus on the frightened thoughts which were crowding into her mind.

What the hell was Tariq doing driving around at this time in the morning? And what was he doing *crashing his car*—he who was normally as adept at driving as he was at riding one of his polo ponies?

Her fingers tightened around the steering wheel as she tried and failed to imagine her powerful boss lying injured. But it was an image which stubbornly failed to materialise, for he was a man who was larger than life in every sense of the word.

Tall and striking, with distinctive golden-dark colouring, Sheikh Tariq al Hakam commanded attention wherever he was. Complete strangers stopped to watch him walk by in the street. Women pressed their phone numbers into his hand in restaurants. She'd seen it happen time and time again. His proud and sometimes cruel features had often been compared to those of a fallen angel. And he exuded such passion and energy that it was impossible to imagine anything inhibiting those qualities—even for a second.

What if…? Isobel swallowed down the acrid taste of fear. What if her charismatic boss was in *danger*? What would she do if he was in a life-threatening condition? If he…he…

She'd never thought of Tariq as mortal before, and now she could think of nothing else. Her heart missed a beat as she registered the blaring horn of a passing car and she tightened her fingers on the steering wheel. There was no point in thinking negatively. Whatever it was, he would pull through—just like he always did. Because Tariq was as strong as a lion, and she couldn't imagine anything dimming that magnificent strength of his.

A dull rain was spattering against the windscreen as she pulled into the hospital car park. It was still so early that the morning staff hadn't yet arrived. The whole building seemed eerily quiet as she entered it, which only increased her growing sense of foreboding. Noiselessly, she sped down the bright corridors towards the A&E department until she reached the main desk.

A nurse glanced up at her. 'Can I help you?'

Isobel wiped a raindrop from her cheek. 'I've come… I'm here about one of your patients. His name is Tariq al Hakam and I understand he's been involved in a car crash.'

'And you are?' enquired the nurse, her carefully plucked eyebrows disappearing beneath her fringe.

'I work for him.'

'I'm afraid I can't tell you anything,' said the nurse,

with a dismissive smile. 'You aren't his next of kin, are you?'

Isobel shook her head. 'His next of kin lives in the Middle East,' she said. Swallowing down her frustration, she realised that she'd crammed her thick curls into a ponytail and thrown on a pair of old jeans and a sweater. Did she look unbelievably scruffy? The last kind of person who would be associated with the powerful Sheikh? Was that the reason the nurse was being so…so…*officious?* 'I work closely with the Prince and have done for the past five years,' she continued urgently. 'Please let me see him. I'm…I'm…'

For one stupid moment she was about to say *I'm all he's got.* Until she realised that the shock of hearing he was injured must have temporarily unhinged her mind. Why, Tariq had a whole *stable* of women he could call upon in an instant. Women who were far closer to him than Isobel had ever been or ever would be.

'I'm the person he rang just over an hour ago,' she said, her voice full of appeal. 'It was…it was me he turned to.'

The nurse looked at her steadily, and then seemed to take pity on her.

'He has a concussion,' she said quietly, and then shook her head as if in answer to the silent question in Isobel's eyes. 'His CT scan shows no sign of haemorrhaging, but we're putting him under observation just to be sure.'

No sign of haemorrhaging. A breath of relief shuddered from Isobel's lips, and for a moment she had to lean on the nurses' station for support. 'Thank you,' she whispered. 'Can I *see* him? Please? Would that be okay? Just for a moment.'

There was a moment's assessment, and then the nurse nodded. 'Well, as long as it *is* a moment. A familiar face is often reassuring. But you're not to excite him—do you understand?'

Isobel gave a wry smile. 'Oh, there's no danger of that happening,' she answered—because Tariq thought she was about as exciting as watching paint dry.

He'd often described her as the most practical and sensible woman he knew—citing those as the reasons he employed her. Once, she'd even overheard him saying that it was a relief to find a woman under thirty who wasn't a *distraction,* and although it had hurt at the time, she could live with it. She'd always known her place in his life and that wasn't about to change now. Her job was to soothe his ruffled feathers, not to excite him. There were plenty of other contenders for *that* category.

She followed the rhythmical squishing of the nurse's rubber-soled shoes into a side-room at the far end of the unit, and the unbelievable sight that confronted her there made her heart skip a painful beat.

Shrouded in the bleached cotton of a single sheet lay the prone figure of her boss. He looked too long and too broad for the narrow hospital bed, and he was lying perfectly still. The stark white bedlinen threw his darkly golden colouring into relief—and even from here she could see the dark red stain of blood which had matted his thick black hair.

Waves of dizziness washed over her at the sight of the seemingly indestructible Tariq looking so stricken, and Isobel had to quash a stupid instinct to run over to his side and touch her fingers to his cheek. But the nurse had warned her not to excite him, and so she mustered up her usual level-headed attitude and walked quietly towards him.

His eyes were closed—two ebony feathered arcs of lashes were lying against a face which she could see was unusually blanched, despite the natural darkness of his olive skin.

She swallowed down the acid taste of fear. She had seen Tariq in many different guises during the five eventful years she'd been working for him. She'd seen him looking sharp and urbanely suited as he dominated the boardroom during the meetings which filled his life. She'd seen him hollow-eyed from lack of sleep when he'd spent most of the night gambling and had come straight into the office brandishing a thick wad of notes and a careless smile.

Once she'd started remembering Isobel couldn't stop. Other images crowded into her mind. Tariq in jodhpurs as he played polo with such breathtaking flair, and the faint sheen of sweat that made his muddy jodhpurs stick to his powerful thighs. Tariq in jeans and a T-shirt when he was dressed down and casual. Or looking like a movie idol in a sharply tailored tuxedo before he went out to dinner. She'd even seen him in the flowing white robes and headdress of his homeland, when he was leaving on one of his rare visits to the oil-rich kingdom of Khayarzah—where his brother Zahid was King.

But she had never seen her powerful boss looking so defenceless before, and something inside her softened and melted. At that moment she felt almost *tender* towards him—as if she'd like to cradle him in her arms and comfort him. Poor, vulnerable Tariq she thought bleakly.

Until the reality of the situation came slamming

home to her and she forced herself to confront it. Tariq was looking vulnerable because right at this moment he *was*. Very vulnerable. Lying injured on a hospital bed. Beneath the wool of her sweater she could feel the crash of her heart—and she had to fight back a feeling of panic, and nausea.

'Tariq,' she breathed softly. 'Oh, Tariq.'

Tariq screwed up his eyes. Through the mists of hammering pain he was aware of something familiar and yet curiously different about the woman who was speaking to him. It was a voice he knew well. A voice which exemplified the small area of calm which lay at the centre of his crazy life. It was…*Izzy's* voice, he realised—but not as he'd ever heard it before. Normally it was crisp and matter-of-fact, sometimes cool and disapproving, but he'd never heard it all soft and trembling before.

His eyes opened, surprising a look of such darkened fear in her gaze that he was momentarily taken aback. He studied the soft quiver of her lips and felt the tiptoeing of something unfamiliar on his skin. Was that really Izzy?

'Don't worry. I'm not about to die,' he drawled. And then, despite the terrible aching at his temples, he allowed just the right pause for maximum effect before directing a mocking question at the woman in uniform who was standing beside his bed, her fingertips counting the hammering of his pulse. 'Am I, Nurse?'

Inexplicably, Isobel felt angry at Tariq for being as arrogant as only he knew how. He could have killed himself, and all he could do was flirt with the damned nurse! Why had she wasted even a second being sentimental about him when she should have realised that he was as indestructible as a rock? And with about as much emotion as a rock, too! She wanted to tell him not to dare be so flippant—but, recognising that might fall into the category of exciting him, she bit back the words.

'What happened?' she questioned, still having to fight the stupid desire to touch him.

Bunching her wistful fingers into a tight fist by her side, she stared down at the hawkish lines of his autocratic face.

'You may not be the slowest driver in the world, but you're usually careful,' she said. And then seeing the nurse glare at her, Isobel remembered that she was supposed to be calming him, not quizzing him. 'No, don't bother answering that,' she added hastily. 'In fact, don't even think about it. Just lie there—and rest.'

Black brows were elevated in disbelief. 'You aren't usually quite so agreeable,' he observed caustically.

'Well, these aren't usual circumstances, are they?'

Isobel gave what she hoped was a reassuring smile— but it wasn't easy to keep the panic at bay. Not when all she wanted to do was take him in her arms and tell him that everything was going to be all right. To rest his cheek against the mad racing of her heart and lace her fingers through the inky silk of his hair and stroke it. What on earth was the *matter* with her?

'You've just got to lie there quietly and let the nurses take care of you and check that you're in one p-piece.'

That unfamiliar tremble in her voice was back, and Tariq's eyes narrowed as her face swam in and out of focus. Funny. He couldn't really remember looking at Izzy's face before. Or maybe he had—just not like this. In the normal progression of a day you never really stared at a woman for a long time. Not unless you were planning to seduce her.

But for once there was nowhere else to look. He could see the freckles standing out like sentries against her pale skin, and her amber eyes looked as if they would be more at home on a startled kitten. She looked *soft,* he thought suddenly. *Cute.* As if she might curl into the crook of his arm and lie there purring all afternoon.

Shaking his head in order to rid himself of this temporary hallucination, he glared at her.

'It'll take more than a car crash or a nurse to make me lie quietly,' he said, impatiently moving one leg—which had started to itch like no itch he could remember. As he bent his knee, the sheet concertinaed down to his groin and one hair-roughened thigh was revealed. And despite the pain and the bizarre circumstances he could not resist the flicker of a smile as both the nurse and Isobel gave an involuntary little gasp before quickly averting their eyes.

'Lets just cover you up, shall we?' questioned the nurse briskly, her cheeks growing bright pink as she tugged the sheet back in place.

Isobel felt similarly hot and bothered as she realised that her handsome boss was completely naked beneath the sheet. That, unless she was very much mistaken, the sheet seemed to be moving of its own accord around his groin area. She wasn't the most experienced cookie in the tin but even she knew what *that* meant. It was a shockingly intimate experience, which started a heated prickling of her skin in response. And that was a first.

Because—unlike just about every other female with a pulse—she was immune to Tariq al Hakim and his sex appeal. His hard, muscular body left her completely cold—as did those hawk-like features and the ebony glitter of his dark-lashed eyes. She didn't go for men who were self-professed playboys—sexy, dangerous men who knew exactly the kind of effect they had on women. Who could walk away from the women who loved them without a backward glance. In fact, those were precisely the men she tended to despise. The ones her mother had warned her against. Men like her own father—who could shrug off emotion and responsibility so easily...

Composing herself with a huge effort of will, she turned to the nurse. 'What happens now?' she asked but Tariq answered before the woman in uniform had a chance to.

'I get off this damned bed and you drive me to the office. That's what happens,' he snapped. But as he tried to sit up the stupid shooting pain made him slump back against the bed again, and he groaned and then glared at her again as if it was all *her* fault.

'Will you please *lie still,* Prince al Hakam?' ordered the nurse crisply, before turning to Isobel. 'The doctors would like to keep the Sheikh in for twenty-four hours' observation.'

'Izzy,' said Tariq, and as Isobel turned to him his black eyes glinted with the kind of steely determination she recognised so well. 'Sort this out for me, will you? There's no way I'm staying in this damned hospital for a minute longer.'

For a moment Isobel didn't speak. There were many times when she admired her boss—because nobody could deny his drive, his determination, his unerring nose for success. But his arrogance and sheer self-belief sometimes had the potential to be his downfall. Like now.

'Look, this isn't some business deal you're masterminding,' she said crossly. 'This is your *health* we're talking about—and you're not the expert here, Tariq, the doctors and nurses are. They don't want to keep you in because it's some sort of *fun*—I can't imagine it's much fun having *you* as a patient—but because it's necessary. And if you don't start listening to them and doing what they say, then I'm going to walk out of here right now and leave you to get on with it.'

There was a pause as Tariq's eyes narrowed angrily. 'But I have meetings—'

'I know precisely what meetings you have,' she interrupted, her voice gentling suddenly as she registered the strain which was etched on his face. 'I organise your diary, don't I? I'll sort everything out back at the office and you're not to worry about a thing. Do you…?' She found herself staring down at the white hospital sheet which now seemed to be stretched uncomfortably tight across the muscular expanse of his torso. 'Do you want me to get hold of some pyjamas for you?'

'Pyjamas?' His mouth curved into a smile which mocked her almost as much as the lazy glitter of his eyes. 'You think I'm the kind of man who wears pyjamas, do you, Izzy?'

Inexplicably, her heart began to pound with unwilling excitement—and Isobel was furious at her reaction. Had he seen it—and was that why his smile had now widened into an arrogant smirk? 'Your choice of nightwear isn't something I've given a lot of thought to,' she answered crossly. 'But I'll take that as a no. Is there anything else you want?'

Tariq winced as he recalled the blood-stained and crumpled clothing which was stuffed into a plastic bag in the locker next to his bed. 'Just bring me some clean clothes, can you? And a razor?'

'Of course. And as soon as the doctors give you the thumbs-up I'll come and get you. Is that okay?'

There was a pause as their gazes met. 'You don't really want me to answer that, do you?' he questioned, closing his eyes as a sudden and powerful fatigue washed over him. It was like no feeling he'd ever experienced and it left him feeling debilitated. Weak. The last thing he wanted was for his assistant to see him looking weak. 'Just go, will you, Izzy?' he added wearily.

Slipping silently from the room, Isobel walked until she stepped out into the brightening light of the spring morning. Sucking in a deep breath, she felt a powerful sense of relief washing over her. Tariq was alive. That was the main thing. He might have had a nasty knock to the head, but hopefully he hadn't done any lasting damage. And yet… She bit her lip as she climbed into her car and started up the engine, her thoughts still in turmoil. How *alone* he had looked on that narrow hospital bed.

The loud tooting of a car made her glance into the driving mirror, where she caught a glimpse of her pale and unwashed face. A touch of reality began to return.

Alone?

Tariq?

Why, there were innumerable women who would queue around the block to put paid to that particular myth with no more incentive than the elevation of one black and arrogant eyebrow and that mocking smile. Tariq had plenty of people to take care of him, she reminded herself. He didn't need *her*.

Arriving back in London, she spent the rest of the day cancelling meetings and dealing with the calls which flooded in from his associates. She worked steadily until eight, then went over to his apartment—a vast penthouse in a tall building which overlooked Green Park. Although she held a spare set of keys, she'd only ever been there once before, when she had delivered a package which the Sheikh had been expecting and which had arrived very late at the office, while she'd still been working. Rather than having it couriered round to him, Isobel had decided to take it there herself.

It had been one of the most embarrassing occasions of her life, because a tousle-headed Tariq had answered the door wearing what was clearly a hastily pulled on silk dressing gown. His face had been faintly flushed as he'd taken the package from her, and she hadn't needed to hear the breathless female voice calling his name to realise that he had company.

But it had been his almost *helpless* shrug which had infuriated her more than anything. The way his black eyes had met hers and he'd bestowed on her one of his careless smiles. As if he was inviting her to join him in a silent conspiracy of wondering why he was just so irresistible to women. She remembered thrusting the package into his hands and stomping off home to an empty apartment, cursing the arrogance of the Playboy Prince.

Closing her mind to the disturbing memory, Isobel let herself into the apartment using the complicated trio of keys. Experience made her listen for a moment. But everything was silent—which meant that his servants had all gone home for the evening.

In his dressing room she found jeans, cashmere sweaters and a leather jacket—and added a warm scarf. But when it came to selecting some boxer shorts from the silken pile which were heaped neatly in a drawer, she found herself blushing for the second time that day. How...*intimate* it was to be rifling through Tariq's underwear. Underwear which had clung to the oiled silk of his olive skin...

Frustrated with the wayward trajectory of her thoughts, she threw the clothes into an overnight bag and let herself out. Then she phoned the hospital, to be told that the Sheikh's condition was satisfactory and that if he continued to improve then he could be discharged the next day.

But the press had got wind of his crash—despite the reassuring statement which Isobel had asked his PR people to issue. Fabulously wealthy injured sheikhs always provided fascinating copy, and by the time she arrived back at the hospital the following morning there were photographers hanging around the main entrance.

Tariq had been transferred to a different side ward, and Isobel walked in to see a small gaggle of doctors gathered around the foot of his bed. There was an unmistakable air of tension in the room.

She shot a glance at her boss, who was sitting up in bed, unshaven and unashamedly bare-chested—the vulnerability of yesterday nothing but a distant memory. His black eyes glittered with displeasure as he saw her, and his voice was cool.

'Ah, Izzy. At last.'

'Is something wrong?' she asked.

'Damned right there is.'

A tall, bespectacled man detached himself from the group, extending his hand and introducing himself as the consultant. 'You're his partner?' he asked Isobel, as he glanced down at the overnight bag she was carrying.

Isobel went bright red, and she couldn't miss the narrow-eyed look which Tariq angled in her direction. But for some reason she was glad that she wasn't the same wild-haired scarecrow she'd been in the middle of the night. That she'd taken the care to wash and tame her hair and put on her favourite russet-coloured jacket.

Just because the Sheikh never looked at her in the way he looked at other women it didn't mean she was immune to a little masculine attention from time to time, did it? She gave the doctor a quick smile. 'No, Doctor. I'm Isobel Mulholland. The Sheikh's assistant.'

'Well, perhaps you could manage to talk some sense into your boss, Isobel,' said the consultant, meeting her eyes with a resigned expression. 'He's had a nasty bang to the head and a general shock to the system—but he seems to think that he can walk out of here and carry on as normal.' The doctor continued to hold her gaze. 'It sounds like a punishing regime at the best of times, but especially so in the circumstances. Unless he agrees to take things easy for the next week—'

'I can't,' interrupted Tariq testily, wondering if his perception had been altered by the bump on the head he'd received. Was the doctor *flirting with Isobel?* And was she—the woman he'd never known as anything other than a brisk and efficient machine—*flirting back?* He had never found her in the least bit attractive himself, but Tariq was unused to being overlooked for another man, and his mouth thinned as he subjected the medic to an icy look. 'I need to fly to the States tomorrow.'

'That's where you're wrong. You need rest,' contradicted the consultant. 'Complete rest. Away from work and the world—and away from the media, who have been plaguing my office all morning. You've been driving yourself too hard and you need to recuperate. Otherwise I'll have no alternative but to keep you in.'

'You can't keep me in against my will,' objected Tariq.

Isobel recognised that a stand-off between the two men was about to be reached—and she knew that Tariq would refuse to back down if it got to that stage. Diplomatically, she offered the consultant another polite smile. 'Does he need any particular medical care, Doctor?'

'Will you stop talking about me as if I'm not here?' growled Tariq.

'Just calm and quiet observation,' said the doctor. 'And a guarantee that he won't go anywhere near his office for at least seven days.'

Isobel's mind began to race. He could go to a clinic, yes—but even the most discreet of clinics could never be relied on to be *that* discreet, could they? Especially when they were dealing with billionaire patients who were being hunted by the tabloids. Tariq didn't need expensive clinics where people would no doubt seek to exploit his wealth and influence. He needed that thing which always seemed to elude him.

Peace.

She thought about the strange flash of vulnerability she'd seen on his face and an idea began to form in her mind.

'I have a little cottage in the countryside,' she said slowly, looking straight into a pair of black and disbelieving eyes. 'You could come and stay there for a week, if you like. My mother used to be a nurse, and I picked up some basic first aid from her. I could keep my eye on you, Tariq.'

CHAPTER TWO

'WHERE the hell are you going, Izzy?'

For a moment Isobel didn't answer Tariq's growled question as she turned the small car into a narrow country lane edged with budding hedgerows. Why couldn't he just settle down and relax—and be grateful she'd managed to get him out of the hospital? Maybe even sit back and appreciate the beauty of the spring day instead of haranguing her all the time?

It wasn't until she was bowling along at a steady pace that she risked a quick glance and saw the still-dreadful pallor of his face, which showed no signs of shifting. He was in *pain,* she reminded herself—and besides, he was a man who rarely expressed gratitude.

Already she'd had to bite back her words several times that morning. They had left by a staff exit at the back of the hospital, and although he had initially refused to travel in a wheelchair she had persuaded him that it would help elude any waiting press. Which of course, it had. The photographers were looking for the muscular stride of a powerful sheikh—not a man being pushed along by a woman. She remembered her mother telling her that nobody ever looked at people in wheelchairs—how society was often too busy to care about those who were not able-bodied. And it seemed that her mother was right.

'You know very well where I'm going,' she answered calmly. 'To my cottage in the country, where you are going to recuperate after your crash. That was the agreement we made with the doctor before he would agree to discharge you. Remember?'

He made a small sound of displeasure beneath his breath. His head was throbbing, his throat felt as dry as parchment, and now Izzy was being infuriatingly *stubborn*. 'That's the doctor you were flirting with so outrageously?' he questioned coolly.

Isobel's eyes narrowed as she acknowledged her boss's accusation. In truth, she'd been so worried about *him* that she'd barely given a thought to the crinkly-eyed consultant. But even if she *had* fallen in love at first sight and decided to slip the doctor her phone number—well, it was none of Tariq's business. Wasn't she doing enough for him already, without him attempting to police her private life for her?

'And what if I was?' she retorted.

He shrugged. 'I would have thought that extremely unprofessional behaviour on his part.'

'I hardly think that you're in any position to pass judgement on flirting,' she murmured.

Tariq drummed his fingers against one tense thigh. It was not the response he'd been expecting. A firm assertion that the doctor had been wasting his time would have been infinitely more desirable. Isobel was resolutely single, and that was the way he liked it. It meant that she could devote herself to *his* needs and be there whenever *he* wanted her.

'I thought you only told him all that stuff about taking me to your cottage to get him off my back,' he objected.

'But that would have been dishonest.'

'Do you always have to be so damned *moral?*'

'One of us has to have morals.'

His eyes narrowed. 'Is that supposed to be a criticism?'

'No, Tariq,' she answered calmly. 'It's merely an observation.'

He stared at her set profile and inexplicably began to notice the way the pale spring sunshine was picking out the lights in her hair, turning it a glowing shade of amber. Had the doctor also noticed its subtle fire? he wondered. Would that explain his behaviour? 'I don't know why you're dragging me out to the back of beyond,' he said, 'when I can rest perfectly well at home.'

'In central London?' She gave a dry laugh. 'With the press baying at your door like hounds and all your ex-girlfriends lining up to offer to come and mop your brow for you? I don't think so. You'll be much safer at my cottage. Anyway, it's a done deal. I've informed the office that you'll be incommunicado for a week, and that all calls are to come through me. Fiona in the PR office is perfectly capable of running things until we get back. I've had your housekeeper pack a week's worth of clothes, which are being couriered down. And I haven't told anybody about your exact whereabouts.'

'My brother—'

'Except for your brother,' she concurred, remembering the brief conversation she'd had earlier that day with the ruler of Khayarzah. 'I telephoned the palace and spoke to the King myself—told him that you're on the mend but that you needed to recuperate. He wanted you flown to Khayarzah, but I said that you would be fine with me.' She shot him a glance. 'That was the right thing to do, wasn't it?'

'I suppose so,' he answered moodily, but as usual she had done exactly the right thing. The last thing he needed was the formality of palace life—with all the strictures that came with it. He'd done his level best to escape from the attendant attention which came with being the brother of the King—a role which had been thrust on him when his brother had suddenly inherited the crown. A role which had threatened his freedom—something he had always guarded jealously. Because wasn't his freedom the only good thing to have emerged from the terrible isolation of his childhood?

He fixed her with a cool and curious stare. 'You seem to have it all worked out, Izzy.'

'Well, that's what you pay me for.' She glanced in the driving mirror and let a speedy white van overtake them before starting to speak again. 'Do you want to tell me what happened? About why one of the most careful drivers I know should crash his car?'

Tariq closed his eyes. Wasn't it frustrating that a split-second decision could impact so dramatically on your life? If he hadn't been beguiled by a pair of blue eyes and a dynamite body then he wouldn't be facing the rather grim prospect of being stuck in some remote cottage with his assistant for a week.

'I went for dinner with a woman,' he said.

'No—' Isobel started to say something and then changed her mind, but Tariq seized on her swallowed words like a cat capturing a mouse.

His thick lashes parted by a fraction. 'No what, Izzy?'

'It doesn't matter.'

'Oh, but it does,' he answered stubbornly.

'I was about to say no change there. You having dinner with a woman is hardly remarkable, Tariq. Blonde, was she?'

'Actually, she was.' Reluctantly, his lips curved into a smile. Sometimes Izzy was so damned sharp he was surprised she didn't cut herself. Maybe that was what less attractive women did—they made up for their shortcomings by developing a more sophisticated sense of humour. 'But she wasn't all she seemed to be.'

'Not a transvestite, I hope?'

'Very funny.' But despite the smile which her flippant comment produced Tariq was irritated with himself. He had been stressed out, and had intended to relax by playing poker until the small hours. He hadn't really been in the mood for any kind of liaison, or the effort of chatting someone up. But the woman had been very beautiful, and he'd found himself inviting her for a late dinner. And then she had started to question him. Wanting to know the kind of things which suggested that she might have done more than a little background research on him.

Tariq had some rules which were entirely his own.

He didn't like being interrogated.

He didn't trust people who knew too much about him.

And he never slept with a woman on a first date.

At heart, he was a deeply old-fashioned man, with plenty of contradictory values. For him sex had always been laughably easy—yet he didn't respect a woman who let him too close, too soon. Especially as he had a very short attention span when it came to the opposite sex. He liked the slow burn of anticipation—to prolong the ache of desire until it became unbearable. So when the blonde had made it very clear that she was his for the taking—some primitive sense of prudery had reared its head. Who wanted something which was so easily obtained? With a jaded yawn, he had declined her offer and reached for his jacket.

And that was when the woman's story had come blurting out. It seemed that it hadn't been fate which had brought her into his life, but cunning and subterfuge.

'She was a journalist,' he bit out. He'd been so angry with himself because he hadn't seen through her flimsy cover. Furious that he had fallen for one of the oldest tricks of all. He'd stormed out, wondering if he was losing his touch, and for those few seconds when his attention had wandered so had had his powerful sports car. 'She wanted the inside story on the takeover bid,' he finished.

Isobel shrugged as her little car took a bend in the road. 'Well, if you *will* try and buy into the Premier League, what do you expect? You know the English are crazy about football—and it's a really big deal if some power-hungry Sheikh adds a major team to his portfolio.'

'There's nothing wrong with being hungry for power, Izzy.'

'Only if it becomes addictive,' she countered.

'You think I'm a power junkie?'

'That's not for me to say.'

His black eyes narrowed. 'I notice you didn't deny it, though.'

'I'm glad you're paying attention to what I say, Tariq.'

With a small click of irritation, he attempted, without much success, to stretch his legs. Some lurid looking air-freshener in the shape of a blue daisy hung from the driving mirror and danced infuriatingly in front of the windscreen. Other than the occasional childhood ride on a camel in his homeland, he could never remember enduring such an uncomfortable form of transport as this. Rather longingly, he thought about the dented bonnet of his smooth and gleaming sports car and wondered how long before it would be roadworthy again.

'Is your cottage as cramped as your car?' he demanded.

'You don't like my car?'

'Not really. I don't like second-hand cars which don't go above fifty.'

'Then why don't you give me a pay rise?' she suggested sweetly. 'And I'll buy myself a newer one.'

For a moment Tariq acknowledged the brief flicker of discord which made his pulse quicken. Wasn't it strange how a little tension between a man and a woman could instantly begin to heat a man's blood and make him start thinking of…

But the smile left his face as he realised that this was *Izzy* he was about to start fantasising about. Safe and sensible Izzy. The plain stalwart of his office—and the very last candidate for any erotic thoughts. So how was it that he suddenly found his attention riveted on a pair of slender thighs which were outlined with delectable precision beneath the blue of her denim skirt?

With an effort, he dragged his gaze away and settled back in the seat. 'I pay you enough already—as well you know,' he said. 'How far is it?'

'Far enough,' said Isobel softly, 'for you to close your eyes and sleep.' *And stop annoying me with your infuriating comments.*

'I'm not sleepy.'

'Sure?'

'Quite sure,' he mumbled, but something in her voice was oddly soothing, so he found himself yawning—and seconds later he was fast asleep.

Isobel drove in a silence punctuated only by the low, steady sound of Tariq's breathing. She tried to concentrate on her driving and on the new green buds which were pushing through the hedgerows—but it wasn't easy. Her attention kept wandering and she felt oddly light-headed. She kept telling herself it was because her usual routine had been thrown out of kilter—and not because of the disturbing proximity of her boss.

But that wouldn't have been true. Something had happened to her and she couldn't work out what it was. Why should she suddenly start feeling self-conscious and *peculiar* in Tariq's company? Why couldn't she seem to stop her eyes from straying to the powerful shafts of his thighs and then drifting upwards to the narrow jut of his hips?

She shook her head. She'd been alone with Tariq many, many times before. She had shared train, plane and car journeys with him on various business trips. But never like this. Not in such cramped and humble confines, with him fast asleep beside her, his legs spread out in front of him. Almost as if they were any normal couple, just driving along.

Impatiently, she shook her head.

Normal? That was the last adjective which could ever be applied to Tariq. He was a royal sheikh from the ancient House of Khayarzah and one of the wealthiest men on the planet.

Sometimes it still seemed incredible to Isobel that

someone like her should have ended up working so closely for such a powerful man. She could tell that people were often surprised when she told them what she did for a living. That he who could have anyone should have chosen her. What did *she* have that a thousand more well-connected women didn't have? That was what everyone always wanted to know.

Deep down, she suspected it was because he trusted her in a way that he trusted few people. And why did he trust her? Hard to say. Probably because she had met him when he was young—at school—before the true extent of his power and position had really sunk in. Before he'd realised the influence he wielded.

She'd been just ten at the time—a solitary and rather serious child. Her mother, Anna, had been the school nurse at one of England's most prestigious boarding schools—a job she'd been lucky to get since it provided a place to live as well as a steady income. Anna was a single mother and her daughter Isobel illegitimate. Times had changed, and not having a father no longer carried any stigma, but it certainly had back then—back in the day.

Isobel had borne the brunt of it, of course. She remembered the way she'd always flinched with embarrassment whenever the question had been asked: *What does your father do?* There had been a thousand ways she had sought to answer without giving away the shaming fact that she *didn't actually know.*

As a consequence, she'd always felt slightly *less than*—a feeling which hadn't been helped by growing up surrounded by some of the wealthiest children in the world. She'd been educated among them, but she had

never really been one of them—those pampered products of the privileged classes.

But Tariq had been different from all the other pupils.
His olive skin and black eyes had made him stand out
like a handful of sparkling jewels thrown down onto a
sheet of plain white paper. Sent to the west to be educated by his father, he had excelled in everything he'd
done. He'd swum and ridden and played tennis—and
he spoke five languages with native fluency.

Sometimes, Isobel had gazed at him with wistful
wonder from afar. Had watched as he was surrounded
by natural blondes with tiny-boned bodies and swish
flats in Chelsea.

Until the day he had spoken to her and made a lonely
little girl's day.

He'd have been about seventeen at the time, and had
come to the sanatorium to ask about a malaria injection
for a forthcoming trip he was taking. Her mother had
been busy with one of the other pupils and had asked
Isobel to keep the young Prince entertained.

Initially Isobel had been tongue-tied—wondering
what on earth she could say to him. But she couldn't
just leave him looking rather impatiently at his golden
wristwatch, could she? Why, her mother might get into
trouble for daring to keep the young royal waiting.

Shyly, she had asked him about his homeland. At first
he had frowned—as if her question was an intrusion.
But a brief and assessing look had followed, and then he
had sat down so that he was on her level before starting
to talk. The precise words she had long forgotten, but
she would never forget the dreamy way he had spoken
of desert sands like fine gold and rivers like streams of
silver. And then, when her mother had appeared—look-

ing a little flustered—he had immediately switched to the persona of confident royal pupil. He hadn't said another word to her—but Isobel had never forgotten that brief encounter.

It had been over a decade later before their paths crossed again. She had gone back to the school for the opening of a magnificent extension to the library and Tariq had been there, still surrounded by adoring women. For one brief moment Isobel had looked at him with adult eyes. Had registered that he was still as gorgeous as he was unobtainable and that her schoolgirl crush should sensibly die a death. With a resigned little shrug of her shoulders she had turned away and put him right out of her mind as of that moment.

The new library was fabulous, with softly gleaming carved wooden panels. Tooled leather tables sat at its centre, and the long, leaded arched windows looked out onto the cool beauty of the north gardens.

By then Isobel had been a secretary—working in a dusty office for a rather dry bunch of lawyers in London. It hadn't been the most exciting work in the world, but it had been well paid, and had provided her with the security she had always craved.

There'd been no one in the library that she knew well enough to go up and talk to, but she'd been determined to enjoy her time there, because secretly she'd been delighted to get an invitation to the prestigious opening. Just because she'd been educated at the school free, it didn't mean she'd been overlooked! She'd drunk a cup of tea and then begun to look at the books, noting with interest that there was a whole section on Khayarzah. Picking up a beautifully bound volume, she'd begun to flick through the pages, and had soon been lost in the pictures and descriptions of the land which Tariq had once made come alive with his words.

She'd just got to a bit about the source of the Jamanah River when she'd heard a deep voice behind her.

'You seem very engrossed in that book.'

And, turning round, she'd found herself imprisoned in the Sheikh's curious gaze. She'd thought that his face was harder and colder than she remembered—and that there was a certain air of detachment about him. But then Isobel recalled the sixth-former who'd been so kind to her, and had smiled.

'That's because it's a very engrossing book,' she said. 'Though I'm surprised there's such a big section on your country.'

'Really?' A pair of jet eyebrows was elevated. 'One of the benefits of donating a library is that you get to choose some of its contents.'

Isobel blinked. '*You* donated the new library?'

'Of course.' His voice took on a faintly cynical air. 'Didn't you realise that wealthy old boys—particularly foreign ones—are expected to play benefactor at some point in their lives?'

'No, I didn't.'

Afterwards, Isobel thought that his question might have been some sort of test—to see if she was one of those people who were impressed by wealth. And if that *was* the case then she'd probably passed it. Because she genuinely didn't care about money. She had enough for her needs and that was plenty. What had her mother always told her? *Don't aim too high; just high enough.*

'I just wanted to know if it was as beautiful as...' Her words tailed off. As if he could *possibly* be interested!

But he was looking at her curiously, as if he *was* interested.

'As beautiful as what?'

She swallowed. 'As the way you described it. You once told me all about Khayarzah. You were very...passionate about it. You said the sand was like fine gold and the rivers like streams of silver. You probably don't remember.'

Tariq stared at her, as if he was trying to place her, but shook his head.

'No, I don't remember,' he admitted, and then, as he glanced up to see a determined-looking blonde making her way towards them, he took Isobel's elbow. 'So why don't you refresh my memory for me?' And he led her away to a quieter section of the room.

And that was that. An unexpected meeting between two people who had both felt like outsiders within the privileged walls of an English public school. What was more it seemed that Tariq happened to have a need, and that Isobel could be just the person to answer that need. He was looking for someone to be his assistant. Someone he could talk to without her being fazed by who he was and what he represented. Someone he could trust.

The salary he was offering made it madness for her even to consider refusing, so Isobel accepted his offer and quickly realised that no job description in the world could have prepared her for working for *him*.

He wanted honesty, yes—but he also demanded deference, as and when it suited him.

He was fair, but he was also a powerful sheikh who had untold wealth at his fingertips—so he could also be highly unreasonable, too.

And he was sexy. As sexy as any man was ever likely to be. Everyone said so—even Isobel's more feminist friends, who disapproved of him. But Isobel's strength was that she simply refused to see it. After that meeting in the library she had trained herself to be immune to his appeal as if she was training for a marathon. Even if she considered herself to be in his league—which she didn't—she still wouldn't have been foolish enough to fancy him.

Because men like Tariq were trouble—too aware of their power over the opposite sex and not afraid to use it. She'd watched as women who fell in love with him were discarded once he'd tired of them. And she knew from her own background how lives could be ruined if passion was allowed to rule the roost. Hadn't her mother bitterly regretted falling for a charmer like Tariq? Telling her that the brief liaison had affected her whole life?

No, he was definitely not on Isobel's wish-list of men. His strong, muscular body and hard, hawkish features didn't fill her with longing, but with an instinctive wariness which had always served her well.

Because she wouldn't have lasted five minutes—let alone five years—if she had lost her heart to the Sheikh.

She steered the car up a narrow lane and came to a halt outside her beloved little cottage. The March sunshine was clear and pale, illuminating the purple, white and yellow crocuses which were pushing through the earth. She loved this time of year, with all its new beginnings and endless possibilities. Opening the car door a fraction, she could hear birds tweeting their jubilant celebration of springtime—but still Tariq didn't stir.

She turned to look at him—at the ebony arcs of his feathered lashes which were the only soft component to make up his formidable face. She had never seen him asleep before, and it was like looking at a very different man. The hard planes and angles of his features threw shadows over his olive skin, and for once his sensual lips were relaxed. Once again she saw an unfamiliar trace of vulnerability etched on his features, and once again she felt that little stab of awareness at her heart.

He was so *still*, she thought wonderingly. Remarkably still for a man who rarely stopped. Who drove himself remorselessly in the way that successful men always did. Why, it seemed almost a shame to wake him…and to have him face the reality of his convalescence in her humble home.

Racking her brain, she thought back to how she'd left the place last weekend, and realised that there was no fresh food or milk. Stuff she would normally have brought down with her from London.

Reaching out her hand, she touched his shoulder lightly—but his eyelashes moved instantly, the black eyes suspicious and alert as they snapped open.

For a moment Tariq stayed perfectly still, his memory filtering back in jigsaw pieces. What was he doing sitting in an uncomfortably cramped and strange car, while Izzy frowned down at him, her breathing slightly quickened and her amber eyes dark with concern?

And then he remembered. She had offered to play nursemaid for the next week—just not the kind of nursemaid which would have been *his* preference. His mouth hardened as he dispelled an instant fantasy of a woman with creamy curves busting out of a little uniform which ill concealed the black silk stockings beneath. Because Isobel was not that woman. And under the circumstances wasn't that best?

'We're here!' said Isobel brightly, even though her heart had inexplicably started thudding at some dangerous and unknown quality she'd read in his black eyes. 'Welcome to my home.'

CHAPTER THREE

'CAREFUL,' warned Isobel.

'Please don't state the obvious,' Tariq snapped, as he bent his head to avoid the low front door.

'I was only trying to help,' she protested, as he walked straight past her.

Stepping into the cluttered sitting room was no better, and Tariq quickly discovered that the abundance of overhanging beams was nothing short of a health hazard. 'I've already had one knock to the head, and I don't particularly want another,' he growled. 'Why is your damned ceiling so low?'

'Because men didn't stand at over six feet when these houses were built!' she retorted, thinking that he had to be the most ungrateful man ever to have drawn breath. Here she was, putting herself out by giving him housespace for a week, and all he could do was come out with a litany of complaints.

But some of her exasperation dissolved as she closed the front door, so that the two of them were enclosed in a room which up until that moment she had always thought of as a safe and cosy sanctuary. But not any more. Suddenly it didn't seem safe at all...

She felt hot blood begin to flood through her veins—

because the reality of having Tariq standing here was having a bizarre effect on her senses. Had the dimensions magically shrunk? Or was it just his towering physique which dwarfed everything else around him?

Even in jeans and the soft swathing of a grey cashmere sweater he seemed to exude a charisma which drew the eye like nothing else. His faded jeans were stretched over powerful thighs and the sweater hinted at honed muscle beneath. Somehow he managed to make her cottage look like a prop from Toytown, and the thick and solid walls suddenly seemed insubstantial. Come to think of it, didn't she feel a little insubstantial herself?

She remembered that uncomfortable feeling of awareness which had come over her in the hospital—when she'd looked down at him and something inside her had melted. It was as if in that moment she had suddenly given herself permission to see him as other women saw him—and the impact of that had rocked her. And now it was rocking her all over again. Something about the way he was standing there was making her heart slam hard against her ribcage, and an aching feeling began to tug at her belly.

Isobel swallowed, willing this temporary madness to subside. Because acknowledging Tariq's charisma was the last thing she needed right now. Arrogant playboys were not number one on her list of emotional requirements. And even if they were…as if he would ever look at a woman like *her*.

She flashed him a quick smile, even as she became aware of the peculiar prickle of her breasts. 'Look, why don't you sit down and I'll make you some tea?'

'I don't want any tea,' he said. 'But I'd quite like to

avoid getting frostbite. It's absolutely freezing in here. Give me some matches and I'll light a fire.'

Isobel shook her head. 'You aren't supposed to be lighting fires. In fact, you aren't supposed to be doing anything but resting. I can manage perfectly well—so will you please sit down on the sofa and put your feet up and let me look after you?'

Tariq's eyes narrowed as her protective command washed over him. His first instinct was to resist. He wasn't used to *care* from the fairer sex. His experience of women usually involved the rapid removal of their clothing and them gasping out their pleasure when he touched them. Big eyes clouded with concern tended to be outside his experience.

'And if I don't?' he challenged softly.

Their gazes clashed in a way which made Isobel's stomach perform a peculiar little flip. She saw the mocking curve of his lips and suddenly she felt almost *weak*— as if she were the invalid, not him. Clamping down the sudden rise of longing, she shook her head—because she was damned if he was going to manipulate her the way other women let him manipulate *them*. 'I don't think you're in any position to object,' she answered coolly. 'And if you did I could always threaten to hand my notice in.'

'You wouldn't do that, Izzy.'

'Oh, wouldn't I?' she returned fiercely, because now she could see a hint of that awful pallor returning to his face, and a horrifying thought occurred to her. Yes, her mother had been a nurse, and she had learned lots of basic first aid through her. She had managed to convince the hospital doctor that she could cope. But what if she had taken on more than she could handle? What if Tariq began to have side-effects from his head injury? She thought about the hospital leaflet in her handbag and decided that she'd better consult it. 'Now, will you please *sit down?*'

Unexpectedly, Tariq gave a low laugh. 'You can be a fierce little tiger at times, can't you?'

Something about his very obvious approval made her cheeks grow warm with pleasure. 'I can if I need to be.'

'Okay, you win.' Sinking down onto a chintzy and over-stuffed sofa, he batted her a sardonic look. 'Is that better, *Nurse?*'

Trying not to laugh, Isobel nodded. 'Marginally. Do you think you could just try sitting there quietly while I light the fire?'

'I can try.'

Tariq leaned back against a heap of cushions and watched as she busied herself with matches and kindling. Funny, really—he'd never really pictured Izzy in a cottage which was distinctly chocolate-boxy despite the sub-zero temperatures. Not that he'd given very much thought at all as to how his assistant lived her life.

Stifling a yawn, he looked around. The sitting room had those tiny windows which didn't let in very much light, and a big, recessed fireplace—the kind you saw on the front of Christmas cards. She was crouching down in front of the grate, and he watched as she began to blow on the flames to coax them into life. He found his eyes drawn to the denim skirt, which now stretched tightly over the curves of her buttocks.

He swallowed down a sudden, debilitating leap of desire which made him harden in a way he hadn't been expecting. In five years of close contact with his highly efficient assistant he couldn't remember ever noticing her bottom before. And it was actually a rather fine bottom. Firm and high and beautifully rounded. The kind of bottom which a man liked to cup in the palms of his hands as he…

'What?' Isobel turned round and frowned.

'I didn't…' Tariq swallowed. What the hell was going on? Did bumps to the head make men lose their senses, so that they started imagining all kinds of inappropriate things? 'I didn't say anything.'

'But you made a funny sort of noise.' Her eyes narrowed as she looked at him. 'Are you all right? Your eyes have gone all glazed.'

'Are you surprised?' Shifting his position, Tariq glared at her, willing his erection to subside. 'I've just had to endure your driving.'

Isobel turned back to the now leaping flames, an unseen smile playing around her lips. If he was jumping down her throat like that, then there couldn't be very much wrong with him.

She waited until the fire was properly alight and then went into the kitchen and made his favourite mint tea—bringing it back into the sitting room on a tray set with bone china cups and a jar of farm honey.

To her relief, she could see that he had taken her at her word. He'd kicked off his hand-made Italian shoes and was lying stretched out on the sofa, despite it being slightly too small to accommodate his lengthy frame. His thick black hair was outlined by a chintz cushion and his powerful thighs were splayed indolently against the faded velvet. It made an incongruous image, she realised—to see the *über*-masculine Sheikh in such a domestic setting as this.

She poured tea for them both, added honey to his,

and put it down a small table beside him, her gaze straying to his face as she sat on the floor beside the fire. Tariq was known for his faintly unshaven buccaneering look, but today the deep shadowing which outlined the hard definition of his jaw made him look like a study in brooding testosterone.

Now it was Isobel's turn to feel vulnerable. That faint butterflies-in-the-stomach feeling was back, bigtime. And so was that sudden sensitive prickling of her breasts. She swallowed. 'How are you feeling?'

His eyes narrowed. 'Will you stop talking to me as if I'm an invalid?'

'But that's what you are, Tariq—otherwise you wouldn't be here, would you? Just put my mind at rest. I'm not asking you to divulge the secrets of your heart— just answer the question.'

For the first time he became aware of the faint shadows beneath her eyes. She must be tired, he realised suddenly, and frowned. Hadn't he woken her at the crack of dawn yesterday? Called her and known she would come running to his aid without a second thought—because that was what she always did? Safe, reliable Izzy, who was always there when he needed her—often before he even realised he did. It wasn't an observation which would have normally occurred to him, and the novelty of that made him consider her question instead of batting it away with his habitual impatience.

Oddly—apart from the lessening ache in his head and the woolly feeling which came from his having been inactive for over a day—he felt strangely relaxed. Usually he was alert and driven, restlessly looking ahead to the next challenge. He was also constantly on his guard, knowing that his royal blood made him a target for all kinds of social climbers. Or journalists masquerading as dinner-dates.

Since his brother had unexpectedly acceded to the throne it had grown worse—placing him firmly in the public eye. He was bitterly aware that his words were always listened to, often distorted and then repeated—so he used them with caution.

Yet right now he felt a rush of unfamiliar *contentment* which was completely alien to him. For the first time in his adult life he found himself alone in a confined space with a woman who wasn't intent on removing his clothes....

'I have a slight ache in my...' he shifted his position as she tucked her surprisingly long legs beneath her and he felt another sharp kick of awareness '...head. But other than that I feel okay.'

The gleam in his black eyes was making Isobel feel uncomfortable. She wished he'd stop *looking* at her like that. Rather unnecessarily, she gave the fire a quick poke. 'Good.'

Tariq sipped at his tea, noting the sudden tension in her shoulders. Was she feeling it too? he wondered. This powerful sexual awareness which was simmering in the air around them?

With an effort, he pushed it from his mind and sought refuge in the conventional. 'I didn't realise you had a place like this. I thought you lived in town.'

Isobel laid the poker back down in the grate, his question making her realise the one-sided quality of their relationship. She knew all about *his* life—but he knew next to nothing about hers, did he?

'I do live in town. I just keep this as a weekend place—which is a bit of a luxury. I really ought to sell it and buy myself something larger than the shoebox I currently inhabit in London, but I can't quite bring myself to let it go. My mother worked hard to buy it, you see. She lived rent-free at the school, of course, and when she retired she moved here.' She read the question in his eyes, took a deep breath and faced it full-on. 'She died six years ago and left it to me.'

'And what about your father?'

All her old defensiveness sprang into place. 'What about him?'

'You never talk about him.'

'That's because you never ask.'

'No. You're right. I don't.' And the reason he never asked was because he wasn't particularly interested in the private lives of his staff. The less you knew about the people who worked for you, the less complication all round.

But surely these circumstances were unusual enough to allow him to break certain rules? And didn't Izzy's hesitancy alert his interest? Arouse his natural hunter instincts? Tariq leaned back against the pillow of his folded elbows and studied her. 'I'm asking now.'

Isobel met the curiosity in his eyes. If it had been anyone else she might have told them to mind their own business, or used the evasive tactics she'd employed all her life. She was protective of her private life and her past—and hated being judged or pitied. But that was the trouble with having a personal conversation with your boss—you weren't exactly on equal terms, were you? And Tariq wasn't just *any* boss. His authority was enriched with the sense of entitlement which came with his princely title and his innate belief that he was always right. Would he be shocked to learn of her illegitimacy?

She shrugged her shoulders, as if what she was about to say didn't matter. 'I don't know my father.'

'What do you mean, you don't know him?'

'Just that. I never saw him, nor met him. To me, he was just a man my mother had a relationship with. Only it turned out that he was actually married to someone else at the time.'

He narrowed his eyes. 'So what happened?'

She remembered all the different emotions which had crossed her mother's face when she had recounted her tale. Hurt. Resentment. And a deep and enduring sense of anger and betrayal. Men were the enemy, who could so easily walk away from their responsibilities, Anna Mulholland had said. Had that negativity brushed off on her only daughter and contributed to Isobel's own poor record with men? Maybe it had—for she'd never let anyone close enough to really start to care about them.

'He didn't want to know about a baby,' she answered slowly. 'Said he didn't want anything to do with it. My mother thought it was shock making him talk that way. She gave him a few days to think about it. Only when she tried to contact him again—he'd gone.'

'Gone?' Tariq raised his eyebrows. 'Gone where?'

'That's the whole point—she never knew. He'd completely vanished.' She met the look of disbelief in his eyes and shook her head. 'It was only a quarter of a century ago, but it was a different kind of world back then. There were no computers you could use to track people down. No Facebook or cellphones. A man and his wife could just disappear off the face of the earth and you would never see them again.'

Tariq's frown deepened. 'So he never saw you?'

'Nope. Not once. He doesn't even know I exist,' she

answered, as if she didn't care—and sometimes she actually managed to convince herself that she didn't. Wasn't it better to have an absent father rather than one who resented you, or didn't match up to your expectations? But deep down Isobel knew that wasn't the whole story. There was always a bitter ache in her heart when she thought about the parent she'd never had.

For a moment Tariq tensed, as an unwilling sense of identification washed over him. Her childhood sounded sterile and lonely—and wasn't that territory he was painfully familiar with? The little boy sent far away from home to endure a rigid system where his royal blood made him the victim of envy? And, like her, he had never known what it was to be part of a 'normal' family.

Suddenly, he found his voice dipping in empathy. 'That's a pretty tough thing to happen,' he said.

Isobel heard the softness of his tone but shook her head, determined to shield herself from his unexpected sympathy—because sympathy made you weak. It made regret and yearning wash over you. Made you start wishing things could have been different. And everyone knew you could never rewrite the past.

'It is what it is. Some people have to contend with far worse. My childhood was comfortable and safe—and you can't knock something like that. Now, would you like some more tea before it gets cold?' she questioned briskly.

He could tell from the brightness in her voice that she wanted to change the subject, and suddenly he found he was relieved. It had been his mistake to encourage too much introspection—especially about the past. Because didn't it open up memories which did no one any good?

Memories which were best avoided because they took you to dark places?

He shook his head. 'No thanks. Just show me which bathroom you want me to use.'

'Right.' Isobel hesitated. Why hadn't she thought of this? 'The thing is that there's only one bathroom, I'm afraid.' She bit her lip. 'We're going to have to...well, share.'

There was a pause. 'Share?' he repeated.

She met the disbelief in his eyes. He's a *prince,* she reminded herself. He won't be used to sharing and making do. But it might do him some good to see how the other half lived—to see there were places other than the luxurious penthouses and palaces he'd always called home.

'My cottage is fairly basic, but it's comfortable,' she said proudly. 'I've never had the need or the money to incorporate an *en-suite* bathroom—so I'm afraid you'll just have to get used to it. Now, would you like me to show you where you'll be sleeping?'

Tariq gave a mirthless smile, acknowledging that it was the first time he'd ever been asked that particular question without the involvement of some kind of foreplay. Wordlessly he nodded as he rose from the sofa to follow her out into the hall and up a very old wooden staircase. The trouble was that her movements showcased her bottom even more than before. Because this time he was closer—and every mounting step made the blue denim cling like honey to each magnificent globe.

How could he have been so blind never to have noticed it before? His gaze travelled downwards. Or to have registered the fact that her legs were really very shapely—the ankles slim enough to be circled by his finger and his thumb…?

'This is the bathroom,' Isobel was saying. 'And right next door is your room. See?'

She pushed open a door and Tariq stepped inside and looked around, glad to be distracted by something other than the erotic nature of his thoughts.

It was a room like no room he'd ever seen. A modestly sized iron bedstead was covered with flower-sprigged bedlinen, and on top of one of the pillows sat a faded teddy bear. In the corner was an old-fashioned dressing table and a dark, rickety-looking wardrobe—other than that, the room was bare.

Yet as Tariq walked over to the window he could see that the view was incredible—overlooking nothing but unadulterated countryside. Hedgerows lined the narrow lane, and primroses grew in thick lemon clusters along the banks. Beyond that lay field after field—until eventually the land met the sky. There was absolutely no sound, he realised. Not a car, nor a plane—nor the distant trill of someone's phone.

The silence was all-enveloping, and a strange sense of peace settled on him. It crept over his skin like the first sun after a long winter and he gave a sigh of unfamiliar contentment. Turning around, he became aware that Izzy had walked over to the window to join him. And she was looking up at him, her eyes wide and faintly uncertain.

'Do you think you could be comfortable here?' she questioned.

Contentment forgotten now, he watched as she bit her lip and her teeth left behind a tiny indentation. He saw the sudden gleam as the tip of her tongue moistened the spot. Her tawny eyes were slitted against the sunlight which illuminated the magnificent Titian fire of her hair. Wasn't it peculiar that before today he'd never really noticed that her hair was such an amazing colour? And that, coupled with the proximity of her newly discovered curvaceous body, made a powerful impulse come over him.

He forgot that she was sensible Isobel—the reliable and rather sexless assistant who organised his life for him. He forgot everything other than the aching throb at his groin, which was tempting him with an insistence he was finding difficult to ignore. He wanted to kiss her. To plunder those unpainted lips with a fierce kind of hunger. To cup those delicious globes of her bottom and find if they were covered with cotton or lace. And then…

He felt the rapid escalation of desire as his sexual fantasy took on a vivid life of its own and the deep pulse of hunger began a primitive beat in his blood. For a moment he let its tempting warmth steal into his body, and he almost gave in to its powerful lure.

But Tariq prided himself on his formidable willpower, and his ability to turn his back on temptation. Because the truth was that there wasn't a woman in the world who couldn't be replaced.

What would be the point of seducing Isobel when the potential fall-out from that seduction could have far-reaching consequences? She'd probably fall in love with him—as women so often did—and when he ended it, what then?

When she'd told him about her father he'd seen a streak of steel and determination which might indicate that she wasn't a total marshmallow—but still he couldn't risk it. She was far more valuable to him as a member of staff than as a temporary lover.

He saw that she was still waiting for an answer to her question, the anxious hostess eager for reassurance, and he gave her a careless smile. 'I think it will be perfectly *adequate* for my needs,' he answered.

Isobel nodded. Not the most heartfelt of thanks, it was true—but who cared? She was feeling so disorientated that she could barely think straight. Had she imagined that almost *electric* feeling which had sizzled between them just now? When something unknown and tantalising had shimmered in the air around them, making her blood grow thick with desire? When she'd longed for him to pull her into his arms and just *kiss* her?

Apprehension skittered over her skin as she tried to tell herself that she didn't find Tariq attractive. She *didn't*. Her innate fear of feckless men had always protected her from his undeniable charisma.

So what had happened to that precious immunity now? Was it because they were in *her* home, and on *her* territory instead of his, that she felt so shockingly vulnerable in his presence? Or because she'd been stupid enough to blurt out parts of her life which she'd always kept tucked away, and in so doing had opened up a vulnerable side of herself?

Suddenly she was achingly aware of his proximity. Every taut sinew of his powerful body seemed to tantalise her and send a thousand questions racing through her mind. What would it be like to be held by him? To be pressed against that muscular physique while his fingertips touched her aching breasts?

Aware that her cheeks had grown flushed, she lifted

her eyes to his, wondering what had happened to all her certainties. 'Is there…is there anything else you need?'

He wondered what she would do if he answered that question honestly, and a wry smile curved the edges of his lips as he noted her sudden rise in colour. Would her lips fall open with shock if he told her that he longed for her to fall to her knees, to take him in her mouth and suck him? Or would she simply comply with the easy efficiency she showed in all other elements of their working relationship? Would she *swallow?* he found himself wondering irreverently.

His desire rocketed, frustrating him with a heavy throbbing at his aching groin. He needed her out of here. Now. Before he did or said something he might later regret.

'Leave me now, Izzy,' he commanded unsteadily. 'Unless you're planning to stay and watch while I shower?'

CHAPTER FOUR

SOMEHOW, Isobel managed to hold onto her composure until she'd closed the bedroom door, and then she rushed back down the creaky staircase to the kitchen. Once there, she leaned against one of the cupboards, her eyes squeezed tight shut as she tried not to think about the Sheikh's powerful body, which would soon be acquainting itself with her ancient little bathroom. Her heart was hammering as an imagination she hadn't known she possessed began to taunt her with vivid images.

She thought about Tariq naked. With little droplets of water gleaming against his flesh.

She thought about Tariq drying—the towel lingering on his damp, golden flesh as he rubbed himself all over.

Swallowing down the sudden lump which had risen in her throat, she shook her head. Weaving erotic fantasies about him would lead to nothing but trouble—and so would baring her soul. Taking Tariq into her confidence would only add to the vulnerability she was already experiencing. She wondered what had made her confide in him about her father, and the fact that she'd never known him.

She knew she had to pull herself together. *She* had

been the one who'd invited him to stay, and he was going to be here for the next few days whether she liked it or not. Just because her feelings towards him seemed to have changed—what mattered was that she didn't let it show.

Because Tariq was no fool. He was a master of experience when it came to the opposite sex, and he was bound to start noticing her reaction if she wasn't careful. If she dissolved into mush every time he came near, or her fingers started trembling just like they were doing now, wouldn't that give the game away? Wouldn't he guess that her senses had been shaken into life and she'd become acutely attracted to him? And just how embarrassing would that be?

She needed a plan. Something to stop him from dominating her mind with arousing thoughts.

Opening the door of the freezer, she peered inside and began to devise a crash course in displacement therapy which would see her through the days ahead. She would make sure she had plenty to occupy her. She would be as brisk and efficient as she was at work, and maybe this crazy *awareness* of him would go away.

But that was easier said than done. By the time Tariq came back downstairs she was busy chopping up ingredients for a risotto, but she made the mistake of lifting her head to look at him. And then found herself mesmerised by the intimate image of her boss fresh from the bath. His hair was damp and ruffled, and he carried with him the faint tang of her ginger and lemon gel.

Isobel swallowed. 'Bath okay?'

He raised his eyebrows. 'You didn't bother telling me that you don't have a shower.'

'I guessed you find out soon enough.'

'So I did,' he growled. 'It's the most ancient bathroom I've used in years—and the water was tepid.'

'Don't they say that tepid baths are healthier?'

'Do they?' He looked around. 'Where's your TV?'

'I don't have one.'

'You don't have a TV?'

Isobel shot him a defensive look. 'It isn't mandatory, you know. There's a whole wall of books over there. Help yourself to one of those.'

'You mean *read?*'

'That *is* what people usually do with books.'

With a short sigh of impatience, Tariq wandered over to examine the neat rows of titles which lined an entire wall of her sitting room.

The only things he ever read were financial papers or contracts, or business-related articles he caught up with when he was travelling. Occasionally his attention would be caught by some glossy car magazine, which would lure him into changing his latest model for something even more powerful. But he never read books. He had neither the time nor the inclination to lose himself in the world of fiction. He remembered that stupid story he'd read at school—about some animal which had been abandoned. He remembered the tears which had welled up in his eyes when its mother had been shot and the way he'd slammed the volume shut. Books made you *feel* things—and the only thing he wanted to feel right now were the tantalising curves of Izzy's body.

But that was a *bad* idea. And he needed something to occupy his thoughts other than musing about what kind of underwear a woman like that would wear beneath her rather frumpy clothes.

In the end he forced himself to read a thriller—grateful for the novel's rapid pace, which somehow seemed to suck him into an entirely believable story of a one-time lap dancer successfully nailing a high-profile banker for fraud. He was so engrossed in the tale that Izzy's voice startled him, and he looked up to find her standing over him, her face all pink and shiny.

'Mmm?' he questioned, thinking how soft and kissable her lips looked.

'Supper's ready.'

'Supper?'

'You *do* eat supper?'

Actually he usually ate *dinner*—an elegant feast of a meal—rather than a large spoonful of glossy rice slapped on the centre of an earthy-looking plate. But to Tariq's surprise he realised that he was hungry—and he enjoyed it more than he had expected. Afterwards Izzy heaped more logs on the fire, and they sat there in companionable silence while he picked up his novel and began to race through it again.

For Tariq, the days which followed his accident were unique. He'd been brought up in a closeted world of palaces and privilege, but now he found himself catapulted into an existence which seemed far more bizarre.

His nights were spent alone, in an old and lumpy bed, yet he found he was sleeping late—something he rarely did, not even when he was jet-lagged. And the lack of a shower meant that he'd lie daydreaming in the bath in the mornings. In the cooling water of the rather cramped tub he would stretch out his long frame and listen to the sounds of birds singing outside the window. So that by the time he wandered downstairs it was to find his Titian-haired assistant bustling around with milk jugs and muesli, or asking him if he wanted to try the eggs from the local farm.

For the first time in a long time he felt *relaxed*—even if Izzy seemed so busy that she never seemed to stop. She was always doing *something*—cooking or cleaning or dealing with the e-mails which flooded in from the office, shielding him from all but the most necessary requests.

'Why don't you loosen up a little?' he questioned one morning, glancing up from his latest thriller to see her cleaning out the grate, a fine cloud of coal dust billowing around her.

Izzy pushed a stray strand of hair from out of her eyes with her elbow. Because action distracted her from obsessing about his general gorgeousness, that was why. And because she was afraid that if she allowed herself to stop then she might never get going again.

What did he expect her to do all day? Sit staring as he sprawled over her sofa, subjecting her to a closer-than-was comfortable view of his muscular body? Watch as he shifted one powerful thigh onto the other, thus drawing attention to the mysterious bulge at the crotch of his jeans? A place she knew she shouldn't be looking—which, of course, made it all the more difficult not to. She felt guilty and ashamed at the wayward path of her thoughts, and began to wonder if he had cast some kind of spell on her. Suddenly the clingy behaviour of some of his ex-lovers became a little more understandable.

Her nights weren't much better. How could they be when she knew that Tariq was lying in bed in the room next door? Hadn't she already experienced the disturbing episode of him wandering out of the bathroom one morning with nothing but a small towel strung low around his hips?

Tiny droplets of water had clung to his hard, olive-skinned torso, and Isobel's heart had thumped like a piston as she'd surveyed his perfect physique. She'd briefly thought of suggesting that perhaps he ought to be using a bigger towel. But wouldn't that have sounded awfully presumptuous? In the end, she had just mumbled, 'Good morning...' and hurried past him, terrified that he would see the telltale flush of desire in her cheeks.

Almost overnight the cool neutrality she'd felt towards her boss had been replaced with new and scary sensations. She felt almost molten with longing whenever she looked at him—yet at the same time she resented these disturbing new feelings. Why couldn't she have felt this sharp sense of desire with other men? Decent, reliable men? The kind of men she usually dated and who inevitably left her completely cold? Why the hell did it have to be *him?*

'Izzy?' His deep voice broke into her disturbed thoughts. 'Why don't you sit down and relax?'

'Oh, I'm happier when I'm working,' she hedged, as she swept more dust out of the fireplace. 'Anyway, we're going back to London tomorrow.'

'We are?' He put his book down and frowned. 'Has it really been a week?'

'Well, five days, actually—but you certainly seem better.'

'I feel better,' he said, acknowledging that this was something of an understatement. He hadn't felt like this in years—as if every one of his senses had been retuned and polished. He was looking forward to getting back to London and hitting the ground running.

But his last night in Izzy's little cottage was restless, and the sound sleep he'd previously enjoyed seemed to elude him. Inexplicably, he found himself experiencing a kind of regret that he wouldn't ever sleep in this old-fashioned bed again, beneath the flower-sprigged linen. He lay awake, wondering if he was imagining the sound of Izzy moving in her sleep next door, her slim, pale limbs tossing and turning. Maybe he was—but he certainly wasn't imagining his reaction to those thoughts.

With a small groan he turned onto his side, and then onto his stomach—feeling the rising heat of yet another erection pressing against the mattress. It had been like this for most of the week, and it had been hell. Night after night he'd imagined parting Izzy's pale thighs and sliding his hot, hard heat into her exquisite warmth. He swallowed as the tightness increased. Was his body so starved of physical pleasure that he should become fixated on a woman simply because she happened to be *around?* Yet what other explanation could there be for this inexplicable lust he was experiencing?

In the darkness of the bedroom he heard the distant hoot of an owl in the otherwise silent countryside and his mouth thinned. He needed a lover, that was for sure—and the moment he got back to London he'd do something about it. Maybe contact that beautiful Swedish model who had been coming on to him so strong…

Resisting the urge to satisfy himself, he buried his cheek against a pillow which smelt of lavender, and yawned as he fantasised about a few more likely candidates.

But sleep still eluded him, and at first light he gave up the fight, tugged on a pair of jeans and went downstairs—still yawning. He made strong coffee in Izzy's outdated percolator, and after he'd drunk it settled down to finish his thriller.

And that was where Isobel found him a couple of hours later—stretched out on the sofa, the book open against the gentle rise and fall of his chest. The feathery dark arcs of his lashes did not move when she walked in, and she realised that he was fast asleep.

Her barefooted tread was silent as she padded across the room towards him, unable to resist the temptation to observe him at closer quarters—telling herself that she only wanted to see if he looked rested and recovered. To see whether it really was a good idea for him to go back to London later that day.

But that was a lie and she knew it. Deep down she knew she was going to miss this crazy domestic arrangement. Despite the pressure of wanting him, she had enjoyed sharing her living space with her boss. Even if it had been an artificial intimacy which they'd created between them, it didn't seem to matter. She'd seen another side to him—a more *human* side—and she couldn't help wondering what it would be like once they were back in the office.

Yet, despite her mixed thoughts, she felt a quiet moment of pride as she looked down at him—because he was certainly back to his usual robust self. If anything, he looked better than she could ever remember seeing him. Less strained. More relaxed. His olive skin was highlighted with a glorious golden glow, and his lips were softened at the edges.

But the hard beating of her heart made her realise that her new-found feelings for him hadn't gone away. That stupid softness hadn't hardened into her habitual indifference towards him. Something had changed—or maybe the feeling had always been there, deep down. Maybe it was a left-over crush from her schooldays and she'd only buried it rather than abandoning it. But, either way, she didn't know what she was going to do about it.

She continued to stare at him, willing herself to feel nothing—but to no avail. She was itching to touch him, even in the most innocent of ways. Because what other way did she know? A thick ebony lock of hair had curled onto his forehead, and she had to resist the impulse to smooth it away with the tips of her fingers.

But maybe she moved anyway—if only fractionally—because his lashes suddenly fluttered open to reveal the watchful black gleam of his eyes.

Did she suck in a sudden breath and then expel it with a sigh which shuddered out from somewhere deep in her lungs? The kind of sigh which could easily be mistaken for longing? Was that why his arm suddenly snaked up without warning, effortlessly curling around her waist before bringing her down onto his bare chest in one fluid movement?

'T-Tariq!' she gasped, feeling the delicious impact as their bodies made unexpected contact.

'Izzy,' he growled, as every fantasy he'd been concocting over the last few days burst into rampant life.

Izzy with her hair loose and cascading around her shoulders. Izzy wearing some ridiculously old-fashioned pair of pyjamas. Izzy warm and soft and smelling of toothpaste, just begging to be kissed. Reaching up, he tangled his fingers in the rich spill of her curls and brought her mouth down on his.

'Oh!' Her startled exclamation was muffled by his kiss, and it only partially blotted out the urgent clamour of her thoughts. She ought to stop him. She knew that. A whole lifetime of conditioning told her so.

But Isobel didn't stop him, and the words which her mother had once drummed into her floated straight out of her mind. It no longer mattered that Tariq was the worst possible person to let make love to her. Because her body was on fire—a fire created by the blazing heat of his. She wanted him, and she wanted his kiss. She wanted it enough to turn her back on all her so-called principles, and now she gave in to it with greedy fervour, her mouth opening hungrily beneath his.

She could hear the small moan he made as the kiss deepened. He crushed his lips against hers and a fierce heat began to flood through her body, from breast to belly and beyond.

Frantically, her fingers slithered over his chest and began to knead at the silken flesh, feeling the mad hammer of his heart against her palm. She moaned into his mouth as his hand skimmed down from the base of her throat to her breast, slipping his fingers inside her pyjama jacket and capturing the aching mound with proprietorial skill. She could feel him stroking one pinpoint nipple between finger and thumb until she gasped aloud, wriggling uselessly as she felt the flagrant ridge at his groin pressing against her belly.

Tariq groaned. She tasted of mint, and her hair tickled him as the thick curls cascaded down the side of her face. She felt *amazing*. Was that because this had come at him out of the blue? Or was it novelty value because she was the last person in the world he could imagine responding with such easy passion? My God, she was *hot*.

He kissed her until he had barely any breath left in

his lungs, and it became apparent that her narrow sofa was hopelessly inadequate for two people who were exploring each other's bodies for the first time.

'This is getting a little crowded,' he managed, pulling his lips away from hers with an effort.

He slid them both to the ground, barely noticing the hard flagstones beneath the thin rug. All that concerned him was the gasping beauty in his arms, her hair spilling out all over the floor like tendrils of pale fire and her eyes as tawny as a tiger's.

'Comfortable?' he questioned, as he smoothed some of the wiry corkscrews away from the pink flush of her cheeks.

Heart thundering, Isobel gazed up at him, wondering why she didn't feel shyer than she did. Was it because Tariq was staring down at her with such gleaming hunger in his eyes that in that moment she felt utterly desirable? As if almost *anything* was possible? 'Oddly enough, yes, I am.'

'Me too. Deliciously comfortable. Perhaps I can help make you more comfortable still, *anisah bahiya.*' Pulling open her dressing gown, he began to unbutton her pyjamas—until two rosy-peaked breasts were thrusting towards him. Unable to resist their silent plea, he bent his head to suckle one. Slicking his tongue against the tight bud, he felt the responsive jerk of her hips and heard her gasp his name. 'I've never seduced a woman in pyjamas before,' he whispered against the puckered flesh.

'Are you…are you going to seduce me, then?'

'What do you think? That I've got you down here because I want to discuss my diary for next week?'

Thinking was the last thing Isobel wanted to do— because if she did that then surely she would realise that what they were doing was crazy. Wouldn't thinking remind her that Tariq was a cavalier playboy, and that there was a reason why men like him should be avoided like the plague? Wouldn't it prompt her into doing the only sensible thing—which was to tear herself away from him and rush upstairs to her room, away from temptation?

She felt the graze of his teeth against her nipple and shut her eyes. Far better to feel. To allow these amazing sensations to skate over her skin and fill her with an urgent longing which was fast spiralling out of control.

'Oh!' she breathed, eagerly squirming her hips beneath him and feeling a warm, wild heat building up inside her. And he answered her voiceless plea by slipping his hand inside the elasticated waistband of her pyjamas.

She held her breath as his warm palm navigated its way down her belly, tiptoeing tantalisingly to the fuzz of hair which lay beyond. Still she held her breath as he stroked at the sensitive skin of her inner thigh, and then gasped as his fingertips seared over her moist heat.

'Oh!' she said again.

'You're very wet.'

'A-am I?'

'Mmm...' Tariq's mouth brushed over hers as his finger strayed to the tight bud at the very core of her desire. Her instant compliance didn't surprise him—he was capable of reducing a woman to a boneless state of longing no matter what the circumstances. But the sheer and urgent spontaneity of what they were doing made him tense—just for a moment. And that moment was enough for him to remember one vital omission.

He froze, before snatching his hand away from her. Damn and damn and *damn!*

'I don't have any protection with me,' he ground out.

For one stupid moment Isobel thought he was talking about the bodyguards he sometimes used, and then she saw the look of dark frustration on his face and realised what he meant. A wave of insecurity washed over her.

Should she tell him?

Of *course* she should tell him—they were on the brink of making love, and now was not the time for coyness.

'Actually, I'm…' Isobel swallowed, wanting his fingers back on her aching flesh. 'I'm on the pill.'

Her admission dampened his ardour fractionally. He drew away from her, his black eyes slitted in a cool question. 'The pill?'

Isobel heard the unmistakable disapproval in his voice. 'Lots of women are.'

There was a pause. 'Yes. I imagine that they are.'

Suddenly she shrank from the truth in his hard black eyes, indignant words tumbling from her lips before she could stop them. 'I suppose you think that the kind of woman who happens to have contraception covered is easy?'

Tariq shrugged. 'You must agree that it does imply a certain degree of *accessibility.*'

'Well, you couldn't be more wrong, Tariq,' she declared hotly. 'Because…because I've never had a lover before!'

He stared at her, genuinely confused. 'What the hell are you talking about?'

'I was prescribed the pill because my periods are

heavy, and that's the only reason. I've... Well, I've never had any other reason to take it.'

This commonplace and unexpected disclosure highlighted the unusual degree of intimacy between them, and Tariq frowned. He brushed a corkscrew lock of hair away from her forehead, trying to make sense of her words. 'You're trying to tell me you're—?'

'Yes, I'm a virgin,' she said, as if it didn't matter.

Because surely it didn't? What mattered was Tariq kissing her and transporting her back to that heavenly place he'd taken her to before. Just because she had waited a long time for a man to turn her on as much as this, it didn't mean that she should be treated as some kind of leper, did it?

Sliding her arms around his neck, she lifted her face to his, hungry for him. 'Now, kiss me again,' she whispered.

How could he refuse her soft entreaty? Tariq groaned as he tasted her trembling lips and a shaft of pure desire shot through him. He could feel the softness of her breasts yielding against his bare chest, their taut tips firing at him like little arrows towards his heart. Irresistibly, his fingers slipped inside the waistband of her pyjama trousers again, and he heard her little gurgle of anticipation.

For one moment he was about to peel them right off. Then his hand paused, mid-motion, as he forced himself to recall the unbelievable facts.

She was a virgin!

And more importantly...

She was his assistant!

'No!' he thundered, dragging his lips away from hers. 'I will not do this!'

Her body screaming out its protest, Isobel looked up at him in confusion. 'Will not do what?'

'I will not rob you of your innocence!'

She stared at him, still not understanding. 'Why not?'

'Are you crazy? Because a woman's purity is her greatest gift. And it's a one-off—you don't get to use it again. So save it for a man who will give you more than I ever can, Izzy. Don't throw it away on someone like me.'

For a moment he cupped her chin between his palms, looking down at her with a regret which only compounded her intense feeling of rejection. She jerked her face away—as if to allow him continued contact might in some way contaminate her.

'Then w-would you mind moving away from me and letting me get up?' she said, trembling hurt distorting her words.

'I can try.' With a grimace, he rose to his feet, the heavy throb at his groin making movement both difficult and uncomfortable.

Despite the scene he now rather grimly anticipated he couldn't help a flicker of admiration as he looked at Isobel clambering to her feet, tugging furiously at the jacket of her pyjamas. Passion always changed a woman, he mused, but in Izzy's case it had practically *transformed* her. Her hair was falling in snake-like tendrils all around her slender shoulders and she stood before him like some bright and unrecognisable sorceress. For a moment he experienced a deep sense of regret and frustration—and then he steeled his heart against his foolishness and turned his back on her.

With shaking fingers Isobel began to do up her pyjamas, realising that she had let herself down—and in so many ways. She had shown Tariq how much she wanted him and he had pushed her away, leaving her feeling guilty that she'd been prepared to 'throw away' her virginity on someone like him. How did you ever get back from something like that? The dull truth washed over her. The answer was that you didn't.

Biting her lip, she watched as he turned away to adjust his jeans, trying to ignore the sense of having missed out on something wonderful. Of having been on the brink of some amazing discovery. Inevitably she was now going to lose her job, and she didn't even have the compensation of having known him as a lover. But surely it was better to face up to the consequences of her behaviour than to wait for him to put the knife in?

'You want me to hand my notice in?' she asked quietly.

This was enough to make Tariq turn back and scrutinise her, steeling himself against the enduring kissability of her darkened lips, knowing that if he didn't get out of there soon he'd go back on everything he'd just said and thrust deep and hard inside her, tear her precious membrane and leave his mark on her for ever. He shook his head. 'Actually, that's precisely what I *don't* want. That's one of the reasons I pulled back. I value you far too much to want to lose you, Izzy.'

In spite of everything, his words took Isobel aback. In five years of working for him it was the first time he'd ever said anything remotely like that. She screwed her face up, wondering how to react to the unfamiliar compliment. 'You do?'

'Of course I do—and this week has shown me just how much. I have a lot to thank you for. You're a hardworking, loyal member of my staff, and I've come to rely on you a great deal. And believe me—I'd have a lot of trouble replacing you.'

Isobel kept her face expressionless as something inside her withered and died. 'I see.'

'And just because of this one uncharacteristic lapse...'

She grimaced as his voice tailed off. Now he was making her sound like a docile family dog which had unexpectedly jumped up and bitten the postman.

'I don't see why it should have to change anything,' he continued.

'So you want that we should just forget what has happened and carry on as normal?'

'In theory, yes.' His black eyes bored into her. 'Do you think you can do that?'

It was the patronising tone of the question which swung it. Isobel had been on the verge of telling him that she didn't think there was any going back—or forward—but his arrogant assumption that she might struggle with resuming their professional relationship made her blood boil.

'Oh, I don't think *I'd* have a problem with it,' she answered sweetly. 'How about you?'

Tariq's eyes narrowed as she tossed him the throwaway question. Was she now implying that she was some sort of irresistible little sex-bomb who was going to test his formidable powers of self-control once they were back in the office? He gave a slow smile. He thought she might be forgetting herself.

Once she was back in her usual environment, with her hair scraped back and her rather frumpy clothes in place, there would be no reoccurrence of that inexplicable burst of lust. There would be no flower-sprigged pyjamas and soft curves to send out such sizzling and mixed messages, threatening to make a man lose his head.

'I wouldn't over-estimate your appeal, if I were you,' he said coolly. 'Because that would be a big mistake. I can resist you any time I like.'

CHAPTER FIVE

How could he have been so damned *stupid?*

Tariq stared out of the window at the darkening London skyscape which gave his office its magnificent views. Stars were twinkling in the indigo sky, and in the distance he could see the stately dome of St Paul's cathedral.

He should have been on top of the world.

The doctor had given him the all-clear, his car was in the garage being painstakingly mended, and his acquisition of the Premiership team looked almost certain. Khayarzah oil revenues were at an all-time high, and he had received an unexpected windfall from some media shares he'd scooped up last year. It seemed that everything he turned his hand to in the world of commerce flourished. In short, business was booming.

He turned away from the magnificent view, trying to put his finger on what was wrong. Wondering why this infuriating air of discontentment simply would not leave him—no matter how hard he tried to alleviate it.

He gave a ragged sigh, knowing all too well what lay at the heart of his irritation yet strangely reluctant to acknowledge its source. Its sweet and unexpected source...

Izzy.

His rescuer and tormentor. His calm and efficient assistant, with all her contradictory qualities, who had somehow—against all the odds—managed to capture his imagination.

Had it been pure arrogance which had made him so certain that his lust for her would dissolve the moment they were back in the office? He'd decided that the crash had weakened him in all ways—mentally, physically *and* emotionally. He'd thought that was why he had been so curiously susceptible to a woman he had never found in the least bit attractive. An insanity, yes—but a temporary one.

But he had been wrong.

Since being back at work he'd been unable to stop fantasising about her. Or to stop thinking about those prudish pyjamas which had covered up the red-hot body beneath. His mind kept taking him back to their tangled bodies on the floor of her cottage, reminding him of just how close they'd got. If common sense hadn't forced him to call a halt to what was happening he would have... would have...

But it was more than just frustrated lust which was sending his blood pressure soaring. His desire was compounded by knowing that she was a virgin. That she had never known a man's lovemaking before and she had wanted *him*. Just as he had wanted *her*.

He swallowed. The fact that she worked for him and that it was entirely inappropriate did little to lessen his appetite. On the contrary, the thought of making love to her excited him beyond belief—perhaps because it was his first ever taste of the forbidden. And for a man like Tariq very few things in life were forbidden...

His erotic thoughts were interrupted by the cause of

his frustration as Izzy walked in, bearing a tiny cup of inky coffee which she deposited in front of him with a smile. Not the kind of smile he would have expected, in the circumstances. It was not tinged with longing, nor was it edged with a frustration similar to the one he was experiencing. No, it was a bright and infuriatingly sunny smile—a sort of pre-weekend kind of smile. As if she had forgotten all about those passion-fuelled moments back in her country cottage.

Had she?

'You aren't changing?' she questioned.

Tariq blinked at her, her question arrowing into the confusing swirl of his thoughts. 'Changing?' he growled. 'What's wrong with the way I am?'

Isobel felt her heart hammer in response. Oh, but he was edgy this evening! Even edgier than he'd been all week. Mind you, she'd been feeling similarly jumpy— just determined not to show it. Her pride had been shattered by his rejection, and she was determined to salvage what was left of it by maintaining a cool air of composure. But it was difficult trying to pretend that nothing had happened when your boss had fondled your naked breasts and part of you was longing for him to do it all over again.

She tipped her head to one side and pretended to consider his question. 'How long have you got?'

'Izzy—'

'I meant *changing* in a literal sense,' she clarified, with a quick glance at her watch. 'Aren't you due for a party at the Maraban Embassy at seven? And don't you usually wear something dark and tailored instead of…?' Her bravado suddenly evaporated, her voice tailing off as she was momentarily distracted by his physical presence. *Why* had she allowed her eyes to linger on his physique, when she had determinedly been avoiding it all week?

'Instead of what, Izzy?' he questioned silkily, for he had noticed the sudden. rapid blinking of her eyes.

'Instead of…' She realised that he must have removed his tie at some point during the afternoon, and loosened at least two buttons of his shirt. Because rather more of his chest was on show than usual—and it reminded her of his warm, bare flesh beneath her fingertips on the floor of her cottage.

She could see the lush, dark whorls of hair growing there—which added texture to the olive glow of his skin and invited the eye on an inevitable path downwards…

Keep your mind on the job, she urged herself fiercely. *You're not supposed to be lusting after him—remember?*

'It's…it's a formal event, isn't it?' she finished helplessly.

Tariq felt a brief moment of triumph as he saw her eyes darken. So she was *not* completely immune to him—despite the way she'd been behaving all week. His mouth hardened with grudging respect—for Izzy had shown herself to be made of sterner stuff than he would have thought. Since they'd been back in the office she had treated him with exactly the same blend of roguish yet respectful attitude as she'd done all through their professional relationship. As if his being moments away from penetrating her body had left her completely cold. So was that true? Or was it all some kind of act?

He let his eyes drift over her, wondering if she had decided to showcase the dullest items in her wardrobe. Maybe he'd seen that skirt before—and her pale sweater certainly wasn't new—but she looked dowdier than he could ever remember. Was that deliberate? Or was it because now he knew more about her he was looking at her more closely? Comparing how she looked now to how she'd looked when she had been writhing around beneath him? And he couldn't rid himself of the unsettling knowledge of the magnificent rose-tipped and creamy breasts which lay beneath her insipid armour.

'Yes, it's a formal event,' he drawled. 'And, to be truthful, I don't feel like going.'

'But you have to go, Tariq.'

'Have to?' He raised his brows. 'Is that an order?'

'No, of course it isn't.'

He began to walk towards her, noticing the tip of her tongue as it snaked out to moisten her lips 'Why do I have to?' he queried softly.

'Well, your two countries are neighbours, and you've just signed that big trade agreement, and it will look very b-bad if…if…'

He heard her stumbled words with a triumphant kick of pleasure. 'If what?'

Isobel swallowed. What was going on? What was he doing? The gap between them was closing, and instinct made her step backwards—away from his inexorable path towards her. But there was no escaping him despite the massive dimensions of his office. Nowhere to go until she reached a wall and felt its smooth, cool surface at her back. She stared up at him with widened eyes. Wasn't he breaking the agreement they'd made?

'T-Tariq! What do you think you're doing?'

Pushing one hand against the wall right beside her head, he leaned forward and looked deep into her tawny eyes. 'I'm wondering why you're trying to give me lessons in protocol I neither want nor need. But mostly I'm wondering whether you're feeling as frustrated as I am.'

Perhaps if he'd put it any other way than that Isobel might have given his question some consideration—or allowed her feelings to sway her. Because hadn't she been teetering on a knife-edge of wanting him and yet terrified of letting him know that? Hadn't it been as much as she could do each morning not to gaze wistfully at the sensual curve of his cynical lips? Not to wish that they were subjecting her to another of those hard and passionate kisses?

But his question had been more mechanical than emotional. No woman wanted to feel like an itch which a man needed to scratch, did she? And hadn't she told herself over and over again that no matter how much she wanted him no good would come of any kind of liaison? She *knew* about his track record with women. And only someone who was completely insane would lay herself open to an inevitable hurt like that.

'We aren't supposed to be discussing this,' she said flatly.

'Aren't we? Says who?'

'Said *you!* And me! That's what we agreed on back at the cottage. We agreed that it was a mistake. We're supposed to be carrying on as normal and forgetting it ever happened.'

'Maybe we are. But the trouble is…' And now he leaned in a little further towards her, so that he could feel the warm fan of her rapid breathing. 'The trouble is that I'm finding it difficult to forget it ever happened. In fact, it's proving impossible. I keep thinking about how it felt to have you in my arms. About how wild your hair looks when you let it down. I keep remembering what it was like to kiss you, and how your breasts felt when I was touching them.'

'Tariq,' she whispered, as his words made her body spring into instant life and her mouth dried as she stared into his darkening eyes. 'You were the one who stopped it. Remember?'

'And I did that because you're a virgin!' he said, letting his hand fall by his side. 'I decided I had no right to take your innocence from you. That you deserved a man who would cherish you more than I could ever do.'

'Well, that much hasn't changed. I haven't rushed out and leapt into bed with someone else in the meantime. I'm still a virgin, Tariq.'

'I realise that.' Their gazes clashed as he fought to do the decent thing. 'And I still don't think it's the right thing to do.'

She bit her lip. Was he playing games with her? 'So why are we even *having* this conversation?'

For a moment he clenched his fists savagely by his thighs, telling himself that he had no right to take an innocence which would be better given to another man. A man who would love her and cherish her. Who was capable of giving her the things that every woman wanted.

But the soft, sweet tremble of her lips defeated his best intentions, and a ragged sigh shuddered from between his lips. 'Because I'm finding resisting you harder than I anticipated.'

She stared into the heated gleam of his black eyes as a blend of frustration and emotion began to bubble up inside her and that sweet, terrible aching started all over again. 'And what about what *I* think?' she questioned quietly. 'What if I'm finding resisting *you* harder than I thought?'

Once again he fought with his conscience, but this time it was even more difficult because he realised that Izzy was enchantingly unique. An innocent who was up-front about her needs. A woman who wasn't playing coy games. The fists at his sides relaxed, and he lifted his hand and began to trace a light line around the butterfly tremble of her lips.

'You know I can't offer you anything in the way of commitment? That nothing long-term is going to come out of this? Three weeks is about my limit with any woman—you know that better than anyone, Izzy.'

She heard the stark warning in his words, but she wanted him too much to pay them any attention. And she was wise enough not to question him about why he was so adamant about short-term relationships. Maybe she'd ask him another time...just not now. Now she was fighting for something she wasn't prepared to give up on.

'You think that all virgins expect marriage from the first man they sleep with? Er, hello—and welcome to the twenty-first century! Aren't I allowed to do something just because I want to—the way you always seem to do? Just for the hell of it?'

Tariq felt his resistance trickling away. Nobody could say he hadn't tried—but it seemed that Izzy was intent on fighting him every inch of the way. Maybe this *was* the only solution to the otherwise unendurable prospect of the two of them dancing around each other every day, aching with frustrated need. And wasn't there something about making love to her which appealed to him on a very fundamental level? Something which he had never done with any other woman...

'For the hell of it? I think you're selling yourself short.

Why don't we try a taste of heaven instead?' he said, and he pulled her into his arms and let his mouth make a slow motion journey to meet hers.

She actually cried out with pleasure out as he began to kiss her, the taste and feel of his mouth seeming gloriously familiar. Gripping his shoulders, she dug her fingers into his suit jacket, afraid that her knees might give way if she didn't have something to cling onto. And as the kiss grew deeper she could feel the hard jut of his hips, which framed the unmistakable evidence of his arousal. Recklessly she pressed her body closer still, making no protest when he began to ruck her skirt up, urging him on with a guttural little sound of hunger which didn't sound a bit like her.

'Damn tights,' he ground out as his fingers met the least erotic piece of clothing ever designed by man. But he could feel the heat searing through them at the apex of her thighs, and the restless circling of her hips as he touched her there.

With practised ease he yanked them down, slithering them over her knees to her ankles. He knelt to slide off first one shoe and then the other—tossing them aside with the tights, so that they lay discarded. And then he rose again to take her in his arms.

Maybe he should have carried her across to one of the plush sofas which comprised the more casual meeting area of his office. Stripped her off slowly and provocatively as she doubtlessly deserved. But for the first time in his life Tariq couldn't bear the thought of delaying this for a second longer than was necessary. Her wide eyes and quickened breath were doing something inexplicable to him. He felt unaccountably *primitive*…

as if his desire to possess her was urging him along on a dark and unstoppable tide.

He touched her against her panties, heard her make some yelping little sound of pleasure and frustration as he ripped them apart. Then he unzipped himself with a shaking hand, freeing the leaden spring of his erection with a ragged sigh of relief.

She was wet and ready for him, clinging to him eagerly as he thrust into her—hard and deep and without warning. Yet it still came as a shock as he encountered a momentary resistance, and he stilled as he heard her make a little moan of discomfort.

'Aludra!' he choked out, stopping inside her to give her the chance to acclimatise herself to these new sensations. Holding her close, he bent his lips to her ear. 'Did I hurt you, little Izzy?'

She shook her head. 'If you did, then I've forgotten. Please don't stop,' she whispered back, giving a little yelp of pleasure as he began to move inside her. 'It feels…' She closed her eyes and expelled a shuddering breath. 'Oh, Tariq, it feels…*incredible.*'

It felt pretty incredible for him, too. Especially when she wrapped her legs around his back with athletic skill. But it was more than that. He'd never done it like this before. Had never felt this free. This *powerful.* Was that because it was Izzy? A woman who knew him better than any other woman? Didn't that add an extra piquant layer of desire? Or was it because there was no infernal covering of thin rubber between them? He could feel the soft squash of her buttocks as he cupped them, and the deep molten tightness of her body as it welcomed him. He could hear her soft exclamations of pleasure and astonishment, and that too reminded him of the reality.

She's never done this with anyone else.

That possessive thought only sharpened his hunger, and he shuddered with pleasure as he drove deeper and deeper inside her. He spoke to her in half-forgotten words of Khayarzahian as they moved in ancient rhythm, until he heard her make a helpless little cry and felt her begin to convulse around him.

She gasped his name and clutched at his shoulders like a woman who was drowning, and then at last he let go. And it was like nothing he'd ever experienced. One sweet and erotic spasm after another racked through him, until he felt as if he'd been wrung out and left to dry. Her head fell against his shoulder and he could feel the quiver of her unsteady breath as she panted against his neck. Her legs slipped down from his waist and he wrapped his arms around hers and held her very close.

He didn't know how long they stayed like that—just that it seemed like warm and satiated bliss. As if they were in their own private and very erotic bubble. Until he felt himself begin to harden again inside her and knew that he had to move.

Reluctantly he withdrew from her, tilting her face upwards with his hand. Her cheeks were flushed, and some of the Titian corkscrew curls had come loose and were falling untidily around her shoulders. She looked as wanton as any woman could—and light-years away from the woman who had placed a cup of coffee in front of him not long ago.

He felt...*dazed.* And for the first time in his life slightly *bewildered.* That had been *incredible.* And yet slightly perturbing too, for he could never remember being so out of control before.

Pushing away any remaining doubts, he brushed a

dancing corkscrew strand away from her lips, recognising that a latent sense of guilt would serve no useful purpose. 'Well, I don't remember *that* being in your job description,' he murmured.

Isobel took her lead from him. She was obviously supposed to keep it light. Her lips curved into a coquettish smile she'd never used before. 'And did I perform the task to your satisfaction…*sir?*'

Softly, he laughed. 'Well, there'll need to be a repeat session, of course. I can't possibly judge after just one performance.'

Performance? The word cut through her heightened senses and Isobel bit her lip, suddenly feeling way out of her depth. 'And was I…?'

'You were amazing,' he reassured her softly. 'In fact you were more than amazing.'

He stared down into her face as if he was seeing it for the first time—though this was the face that greeted him each day. This was Izzy—who told him the truth when he asked her. And sometimes when he didn't ask her. Would sex destroy some of the unique rapport which existed between them? he wondered, as even more questions began to flood into his mind.

'Let's go and sit down,' he said abruptly.

Tugging her skirt back over her naked hips, he led her over to one of the low sofas on the far side of the office. Gently, he pushed her down on it, then slid next to her, his black eyes narrowed and questioning.

'So why?' he queried softly.

She guessed she could have pretended to misunderstand him, but she knew exactly what he meant. And that was the trouble—she knew Tariq far too well to play games with him. 'Why am I a virgin, you mean?'

'Wrong tense,' he corrected acidly.

Slightly flustered, she looked at him, seeking refuge in flippancy. 'Because you make me work such long hours that I hardly ever have the opportunity to meet any other men?'

'Izzy. I'm serious. Why?'

She sighed. 'Because... Oh, Tariq. Why do you think?'

Because no man had ever come close to the way he'd made her feel. Because it had been impossible *not* to let him make love to her once they'd started down that path. He'd warned her that there was going to be no long-term or commitment, and she wasn't holding out for any. But that didn't mean she couldn't be honest, did it? Just as long as she kept it cool.

'Because nobody has ever turned me on as much as you do.'

He found himself slightly shocked to hear her talking to him in that way—but that was what he wanted, wasn't it? The fact that she could see their lovemaking for what it was and not construct some romantic fantasy about it the way that women always did?

'It was like that for me too,' he admitted softly. 'In fact...' Hot and erotic memories flooded back. Of skin on skin as she welcomed him into her hot, slick body. He swallowed, acknowledging the potency of what had happened between them. And because of her innocence he felt he owed her the truth. 'It was the best sex of my life.'

Isobel drew away from him, hating the sudden leap of her heart, angry with herself for wanting to buy into what was clearly a lie. And angry with him for feeling that she needed to be placated with a lie as whopping as that one. 'Oh, come on, Tariq—with all the lovers you've had, you're honestly expecting me to believe that?'

'But it is true.' He stared into her now smoky tawny eyes, wondering how much of the truth she could bear. 'You see, never before have I made love to a woman without protection. It is a risk that I can never take— for all the obvious reasons. But a virgin who has never known another man cannot be tainted.' He took her fingers and drifted them over his groin, enjoying seeing her eyes widen as he hardened instantly beneath them. 'And a virgin who is on the pill cannot give me an unwanted child.'

Isobel snatched her hand away. 'So you really hit the jackpot with me?'

He gave a low laugh as he recaptured her hand and brought it up to his lips. 'You wanted to know why I found sex with you more exciting than with anyone else and I've told you. Don't ask the questions, Izzy, if you can't bear to hear the answers.'

'You're impossible,' she whispered.

'And you're...' His eyes narrowed as he kissed each fingertip in turn. 'Well, right now you are looking positively *decadent.*'

Her indignation melted away as he slid her fingers inside the moist cavern of his mouth. It was as if even his most innocuous touch could weaken all her defences. 'Am I?'

'Extremely.' He drifted the now damp fingers to the faint indigo shadows beneath her sleepy tawny eyes. 'But you also look worn out, *kalila.*'

She loved him touching her like that. She loved him touching her pretty much anywhere. 'Mmm?'

'Mmm. So why don't you just relax?' He brushed

back the heavy spill of curls which had fallen down around her face. 'Go on, Izzy. Relax.'

With a little sigh, she let her head drift back against the sofa as he continued to stroke her hair, just as if she were some cat that he was petting.

Distantly, as her weighted eyelids whispered to a close, she could hear the sound of water splashing. For one crazy moment she could have sworn that she heard someone *whistling*. But then the emotion of what had just happened and the stupefying endorphins it had produced made Isobel drift off into a glorious half-world of sleep.

She was woken by the distinct smell of sandalwood and the lightest brush of lips over hers, and when she blinked her eyes open it was to see Tariq standing over her. His black hair was glittering with tiny droplets of water and he was wearing a stark and beautifully cut tuxedo. He must have showered and changed in his office's luxury bathroom, she thought dazedly.

The crisp whiteness of his silk shirt contrasted against the glow of his olive skin, and his black eyes positively *gleamed* with energy and satisfaction. He looked like a perfect specimen of masculinity, she thought— all pumped up and raring to go. As if, for him, sex had been nothing but a very gratifying form of exercise.

She stared up at him. 'What's…what's happening?'

Tariq swallowed down a surge of lust. She looked so damned sexy lying there that part of him wanted to carry on where they'd left off. To do it to her again—only more slowly this time, and on the comfort of a couch. But wouldn't some kind of natural break be better—for both of them? Wouldn't that allow them to put some necessary perspective on what had just happened—and allow her not to start reading too much into what could be a potentially awkward situation?

'You know I have to go to the party at the Maraban Embassy,' he said softly. 'You were nagging me about it before we...'

Isobel kept the stupefied smile glued to her lips. *He was still planning on going to the party!*

'Yes. Yes, of course. You must go.' She struggled to sit up a little, but Tariq made matters even worse by leaning over her and stroking a strand of hair away from her lips with the tip of his thumb. For a moment his thumb lingered, tracing its way around the sudden tremble of her lips.

'I'll get my car to drop you off home,' he said.

'No, honestly. I can get the—'

'Bus?'

'Well, yes.'

'Without your panties?' His rueful gaze drifted across the room to where her ripped knickers were lying in a crumpled little heap of silk. 'I don't think so, *anisah*. So go and quickly run a brush through your hair, and then we'll go.'

It was rather a grim end to an eventful afternoon, and one which made Isobel question the wisdom of what she had just done. Quickly she availed herself of his bathroom, dragging the Titian curls into some sort of order and straightening her clothes before they went down in the elevator to his waiting car.

There was no back seat kiss, no telling her that she was the most gorgeous woman he'd ever met and that he would spend the evening thinking about her. Instead all proprieties were observed as Tariq spent the short journey to the Maraban Embassy tapping on the flat, shiny screen of his laptop.

When the car pulled up and he looked up he seemed almost to have forgotten who he was with.

'Izzy,' he said softly.

She looked at him, aware that he looked impeccably groomed in comparison to the rumpled exterior she must be presenting. Was he regretting what had happened? Wondering how he could have allowed himself to get so carried away in the heat of the moment? Well, she didn't know how these things usually worked, but she was determined that he should have a let-out clause if he wanted one.

Batting him a quick smile, she pointed to the car door, which was already being opened for him. Let him see that she was perfectly cool about what had happened.

'Better hurry along, Tariq,' she said quickly. 'Leave it much later and you'll have missed all the canapés.'

CHAPTER SIX

'I *JUST wanted to check that you got home okay. The party at the Embassy went on longer than I thought. In fact it was a bit of a bore. I should have stayed right where I was and carried on with exactly what I was doing.*' There was a pause before the distinctive voice deepened. '*I'll see you in the office tomorrow, Izzy.*'

With an angry jab of her finger Isobel erased the message on the answer-machine and made her way out to her tiny kitchen; where the morning sunshine was streaming in. It was a strangely unsatisfying message from the man she'd given her virginity to—Tariq must have left it late last night, after she'd gone to bed. But what had she expected? Softness and affection? Tender words as an after-sex gesture? Why would he bother with any of that when she'd practically *begged* him to have sex with her?

She stared at the piece of bread which had just popped out of the toaster and then threw it straight into the bin. She wasn't in the mood for breakfast. She wasn't in the mood for anything, come to think of it, except maybe crawling right back under the duvet and staying there for the rest of the week. She certainly wasn't up for going into work this morning to face her boss after what had happened in the office last night.

She closed her eyes as a shiver raced over her skin, scarcely able to believe what she'd done. Taken complete leave of her senses by letting Tariq have wild sex with her, pressed up against the wall of his office. After years spent wondering if maybe she didn't *have* the sexual impulses of most normal women, of wondering if her mother had poisoned her completely against men, she had discovered that she was very normal indeed.

Behind her eyelids danced tormenting memories. Was that why she'd behaved as she had? Because a lifetime of longing had hit her in a single tidal wave? Or was it simply because it was Tariq and subconsciously she'd wanted him all along?

She shuddered. She'd been like a woman possessed—urging him on as if she couldn't get enough of him. It had been the very first time she'd ever let a man make love to her, and she'd been so greedy for him that she hadn't wanted to wait. She felt the dull flush of shame as she acknowledged that she hadn't even been ladylike enough to hold out for doing it in private—in a *bed!*

Yet she *knew* what kind of man he was. Hadn't she seen him in action often enough in the past? She'd lost count of the times she'd been dispatched to buy last-minute presents for his current squeeze—or bouquets of flowers when he was giving chase to a new woman.

And what about when he started to cool towards the object of his affections, so that he became positively arctic overnight, usually three to four weeks into the 'relationship'? She'd witnessed the faint frown and the shake of his head when she mouthed the name of some poor female whose voice was stuttering down the telephone line as she asked to speak to him. She'd even seen him completely cold-shoulder one hysterical blonde who'd been lying in wait for him outside the Al Hakam building. Then had had his security people bundle her into a car and drive her away at speed. Isobel remembered watching the woman's beautiful features contorted with rage as she glared out of the back window of the limousine.

Time and time again she had told herself that any woman who went to bed with Tariq needed her head examined—and now she had done exactly that. Was she really planning to join the long line of women who had been intimate with him and then had their hearts broken into smithereens?

She stared at her grim-faced reflection in the mirror.

No, she was not.

She was going to have to be grown-up about the whole thing. Men and women often made passionate mistakes—but *intelligent* men and women could soon forget about them. She would go in to work this morning and she would show him—and herself—how strong she could be. She would surprise him with her maturity and her ability to pretend that nothing had happened.

So she resisted the urge to wear a new blouse to work, putting on instead a fine wool dress in a soft heathery colour and tying her hair back as she always did.

Outside it was a glorious day, and the bus journey into work should have been uplifting. The pale blue sky and the fluffy clouds, the unmistakable expectancy of springtime, had lightened people's moods. The bus-driver bade her a cheerful good morning, and the security man standing outside the Al Hakam building was uncharacteristically friendly.

The first part of the day went better than she'd expected—but that was mainly because Tariq was away from the office, visiting the Greenhill Polo Club in Sussex, which he'd bought from the Zaffirinthos royal family last year.

She juggled his diary, answered a backlog of e-mails, and dealt with a particularly persistent sports journalist.

It was four o'clock by the time he arrived back, and Isobel was so deep in work in the outer office that for a moment she didn't hear the door as it clicked open.

It was only when she lifted her head that she found herself caught in the ebony crossfire of his gaze. His dark hair was ruffled, and he had the faint glow which followed hard physical exercise. He looked so arrogantly alpha and completely sexy in that moment that her heart did a little somersault in her chest, despite all her best intentions. She wondered if he'd been riding one of his own polo ponies while he'd been down at Greenhill, and her imagination veered off the strict course she'd proscribed for it. She'd seen him play polo before, and for a moment she imagined him astride one of his ponies, his powerful thighs gripping the flanks of the magnificent glistening animal…

Stop it, she told herself, as she curved her lips into what she hoped was her normal smile. No fantasising— and definitely no flirting. It's business as usual. It might be difficult to begin with, but he's bound to applaud your professionalism in the end.

'Hello, Tariq,' she said, her fingers stilling on the keyboard. 'Good day at Greenhill? I've had the *Daily Post* on the phone all morning. They want to know if it's true that you've been making approaches to buy a defender from Barcelona. I think they were trying to trick me into revealing whether the football club deal is still going ahead. I told him no comment.'

Tariq dropped his briefcase to the floor and frowned. He'd been anticipating...

What?

A blush *at the very least!* Some stumbled words which would acknowledge the amazing thing which had taken place last night. Maybe even a little pout of her unpainted lips to remind him of how good it had felt to kiss them. But not that cool and non-committal look which she was currently directing at him.

'I'll make you a coffee,' she said, rising to her feet.

'I don't want coffee.'

'Tea?'

'I don't want tea either,' he growled. 'Come over here.'

'Where?'

'Don't be disingenuous, Izzy. I want to kiss you.'

Desperately she shook her head, telling herself that she couldn't risk a repeat of what had happened. He was *dangerous.* She *knew* that. If she wasn't careful he would break her heart—just as he'd broken so many others in the past. And the closer she let him get the greater the danger. 'I don't want to kiss you.'

He walked across the office towards her, a sardonic smile curving his lips as he reached for her, his hand snaking around her waist as he pulled her close. 'Well, we both know that's a lie,' he drawled, and he brushed his lips over hers.

Isobel swayed, and for a moment she succumbed— the way women sometimes succumbed to chocolate at the end of a particularly rigid diet. Her lips opened beneath his kiss, and for a few brief seconds she felt herself being sucked into a dark and erotic vortex as he pressed his hard body into hers. Her limbs became boneless as she felt one powerful thigh levering its way between hers, so that she gave an instinctive little wriggle of her hips against it.

Until common sense sounded a warning bell in her head.

Quickly she broke the contact and stepped away from him, her cheeks flushing. She cooled them with the tips of her trembling fingers. 'D-don't.'

'Don't?' he echoed incredulously. 'Why not?'

His arrogant disbelief only made her more determined. 'Isn't it obvious?'

'Not to me.'

'Because…because I don't want to. How's that for clarification?'

Tariq's gaze ran over her darkened eyes and the telltale thrust of the taut nipples which were tightening against her dress. His lips curved into a mocking line as he transferred his gaze to her face. 'Really?' he questioned softly. 'I think the lady needs to get honest with herself.'

Stung by the slur, but also aware of the contradictions in her behaviour, Isobel shook her head. 'Oh, Tariq— please don't look at me like that. I'm not saying that I'm not attracted to you—'

'Well, thank heavens for that.' He gave a short laugh. 'For a moment I thought my technique might be slipping.'

'I don't think there's any danger of that,' she said drily. 'But I've been thinking about last night—'

'Me, too. In fact I have thought of little else.' His voice softened, but the blaze in his black eyes was searing. 'You're now regretting the loss of your innocence? Perhaps blaming me for what happened?'

She shook her head. 'No, of course I'm not blaming you. I'm not blaming anyone,' she said carefully. 'It's just I feel I'm worth more than a quick fumble in the office—'

'A *fumble?*' he interrupted furiously. 'This is how you dare to describe what happened between us?'

'How would *you* describe it, then?'

'With a little more poetry and imagination than that!'

'Okay. That…that amazing sex we had, pressed up against the wall of your office.' She sucked in a deep breath—because if she didn't tell him what was bugging her then how would he know? 'And you then treating me like a total stranger in the car before waltzing off to your fancy party at the embassy.'

Tariq narrowed his eyes with sudden comprehension. So *that* was what this was about. She wanted what all women wanted. Recognition. A place on his arm to illustrate their closeness—to show the world their togetherness. But wasn't she being a little *presumptuous,* in the circumstances?

'I didn't touch you because I knew what would happen if I did—and I had no intention of walking into the party with the smell of your sex still on my skin. No.' He shook his head as he saw her open her mouth to speak. 'Let me finish, Izzy. It would have been inappropriate for me to take you to the party,' he added coolly. 'For a start, you weren't exactly dressed for it.'

'You mean I would have let you down?'

'I think you would have felt awkward if you'd gone to a party in your rumpled work clothes, post-sex. Especially to a diplomatic function like that.'

'I'm surprised you know the meaning of the word *diplomatic*,' she raged, 'when you can come out with a statement as insulting as that!'

'I was trying to be honest with you, Izzy,' he said softly. 'Isn't that what this is all about?'

His question took the wind right out of her sails. She supposed it was. She had no right to be angry with him just because he wasn't telling her what she wanted to hear. If he'd come out with some flowery, untrue reason why he hadn't taken her to the embassy, wouldn't she have called him a hypocrite?

'Maybe last night should never have happened,' she said in a small voice.

Ignoring the sudden hardening of his body, Tariq thought about the mercurial nature of her behaviour. Last night she had been *wild* and today she was like ice. Was she testing him to see how far she could push him? She had turned away from him now, so that he got a complete view of her thick curls tied back in a ribbon and a dress he'd seen many times before. Nobody could accuse Izzy of responding to their lovemaking by becoming a vamp in the office. She was probably the least glamorous woman he'd ever met.

Yet the strange thing was that he wanted her. Actually, he wanted her more than he had done yesterday. The contrast between her rather unremarkable exterior and the red-hot lover underneath had scorched through his defences. The memory of how she had yielded so eagerly wouldn't leave him. But it was more than a purely visceral response. Her freshness and eagerness had been like sweet balm applied to his jaded senses. Hadn't she given him more than any other woman had ever done—surrendering her inno-cence with such eagerness and joy?

And yet what had he done for her? Taken that inno-cence in as swift a way as possible and offered her noth-ing in return. Not even dinner. He felt the unfamiliar stab of guilt.

'What are you doing tonight?' he said.

The question made Isobel turn round. 'It's my book club.'

'Your book club?'

'Six to eight women,' she explained, since he'd clearly never heard of the concept. 'We all read a book and then afterwards we sit round and discuss it.'

He knitted his brows together. 'And that's supposed to be enjoyable?'

'That's the general idea.'

'Cancel it.' The answering smile he floated her was supremely confident. 'Have dinner with me instead.'

Shamefully, she was almost tempted to do as he suggested—until she imagined the reaction of her girl-friends. Hadn't she let them down enough times in the past, when Tariq had been in the middle of some big deal and she'd had to work right through the night? Did he really expect her to drop everything now, just so he could get a duty dinner out of the way before another bout of sex?

She thought about everything she'd vowed. About not leaving herself vulnerable to heartbreak—which wasn't going to be easy now that she *had* taken such a big leap in that direction. But even if she had made herself vul-nerable she didn't have to compound it by being a total doormat.

'I don't want to cancel it, Tariq—I'm hosting in my

apartment. There's two bottles of white wine chilling in the fridge and we're reading *Jane Eyre*.'

Damn *Jane Eyre,* he thought irreverently—but something about her resistance made his lips curve into a sardonic smile.

'What about tomorrow night, then? Do you think you might be able to find a space in your busy schedule and have dinner with me then?' he questioned sarcastically.

Her heart began thundering as she stared at him. Wasn't that what she'd wanted all along? The cloak of respectability covering up the fact that they'd had sex without any of the usual preliminaries? Wouldn't a civilised meal prevent their relationship from being defined by that one rather steamy episode—no matter what happened in the future? Because the chances were that they might decide never to have sex again. Maybe in a restaurant, with the natural barrier of a table between them and the attentions of the waiting staff, they could agree that, yes, it had been a highly pleasurable experience—but best kept as a one-off.

Isobel nodded. 'Yes, I can have dinner with you tomorrow night.'

'Good. Book somewhere, will you? Anywhere you like.'

His expression was thoughtful as he walked through to his inner sanctum. Because this was a first on many levels, he realised.

The first time he'd ever had sex with a member of his staff.

And the first time a woman had ever turned him down for a dinner date.

CHAPTER SEVEN

'This is the last kind of place I'd have thought you'd choose,' said Tariq slowly.

Isobel looked up from the laminated menu, which she already knew by heart, and stared at the hawk-like beauty of the Sheikh's autocratic features. 'You don't like it?'

He looked around. It was noisy, warm and cluttered. Lighted candles dripped wax down the sides of old Chianti bottles, posters of Venice and Florence vied for wall-space with photos of Siena's football team, and popular opera played softly in the background. He could remember eating somewhere like this years ago as a student, at the end of a rowdy rugby tour. But never since then. 'It's…different,' he observed. 'Not the kind of place I normally eat in. I thought you might have chosen somewhere…'

'Yes?' Isobel raised her eyebrows.

'Somewhere a little more upmarket. The kind of place you'd always wanted to go but never had the chance.'

Isobel put the menu down. 'You mean somewhere like the Green Room at the Granchester? Or the River Terrace? Or one of those other fancy establishments with a celebrity chef, where you can only ever get a table at short notice if you happen to *be* someone? All the places *you* usually frequent?'

'They happen to be very good restaurants.'

She leaned forward. '*This* happens to be a good restaurant, too—though you seem to be judging it without even trying it. Just because you don't have to take out a mortgage to eat here, it doesn't mean the food isn't delicious. Actually, I thought *you* might like to try somewhere different and a bit more relaxing. Somewhere you aren't known, since you often complain about rubbernecking people staring at you.' She sat back in her chair again and shot him a challenge with her eyes. 'But maybe you like being looked at more than you care to admit—and anonymity secretly freaks you out?'

He gave a soft laugh. 'Actually, I'm rather enjoying the anonymity,' he murmured, and glanced down at the menu. 'What do you recommend?'

'Well, they make all their own pasta here.'

'And it's good?'

'It's more than good. It's *to die for.*'

His gaze drifted up to the curve of her breasts, which were pert and springy and outlined by a surprisingly chic little black dress. 'I thought women didn't eat carbs.'

'Maybe the sorts of women you know don't,' she said, thinking about his penchant for whip-thin supermodels and feeling a sudden stab of insecurity. 'Personally, I hate all those dietary restrictions. All they do is make people obsessed with eating, or not eating, and their whole lives become about denying themselves what they really want.'

Tariq let that go, realising that he was denying himself what *he* really wanted right at that moment. If it was anyone other than Izzy he would have thrown a large wad of notes down on the tablecloth and told the waiter that they'd lost their appetite. Then taken her back to his apartment and ravished her in every which way he could—before sending out for food.

He realised that he was letting her call the shots, and briefly he wondered why. Because he'd taken her innocence and felt that he owed her? Or was it because she worked for him and his relationship with her was about as equal as any he was likely to have?

'Perhaps we'll have a little role-reversal tonight. How about you choose for me?' he suggested.

'I'd love to.' She beamed.

She lifted her head and instantly the waiter appeared at their table, bearing complementary olives and bread and making a big fuss of her. For possibly the first time in his life Tariq found himself ignored—other than being assured that he was a very lucky man to be eating with such a beautiful woman.

As he leant back in his chair he conceded that the waiter had a point and Izzy *did* look pretty spectacular tonight. For a start she'd let down her hair, so that corkscrew curls tumbled in a fiery cascade around her shoulders. Her silky black dress was far more formal than anything she'd ever worn to work, and it showcased her luscious curves to perfection. A silver teardrop which gleamed at the end of a fine chain hung provocatively between her breasts. And, of course, she had that indefinable glow of sexual awakening…

With an effort, he dragged his gaze away from her cleavage and looked into tawny eyes which had been highlighted with long sweeps of mascara, so that they seemed to dominate her face. 'I take it from the way the waiter greeted you like a long-lost relative that you've been here before?'

'Loads of times. I've been coming here since I first started working in London. It's always so warm and friendly. And at the beginning—when I didn't have much money—they never seemed to mind me spending hours lingering over one dish.'

'Why would they? Restaurants never object to a pretty girl adorning their space. It's a form of free advertising.'

Isobel shook her head. 'Were you born cynical, Tariq?'

'What's cynical about that? It happens to be true. I'm a businessman, Izzy—I analyse marketing opportunities.'

She waited while the waiter poured out two glasses of fizzy water. 'And did you always mean to become a businessman?'

'As opposed to what? A trapeze artist?'

'As opposed to doing something in your own country. Doing something in Khayarzah. You used…'

He frowned as her words trailed off. 'Used to what?'

'At school.' She shrugged as she remembered how sweet he had been to her that time—how he'd made her feel special. A bit like the way he was treating her tonight. 'Well, I hardly knew you at school, of course, but I do remember that one time when you talked about your homeland. You spoke of it in a dreamy way—as if you were talking about some kind of Utopia. And I suppose I sort of imagined…'

'What did you imagine?' he prompted softly.

'Oh, I don't know. That you'd go back there one day.

And live in a palace and fish in that silvery river you described.'

'Ah, but my brother is King there now,' he said, his voice hardening as he acknowledged the capricious law of succession and how it altered the lives of those who were affected by it. 'And Zahid became King very unexpectedly, which changed my place in the natural order of things.'

Isobel looked at him. 'How come?'

'Up until that moment I was just another desert sheikh with the freedom to do pretty much as I wanted—but when our uncle died suddenly I became second in line to the throne. The spare.'

'And is that so bad?' she prompted gently.

'Try living in a goldfish bowl and see how *you* like it,' he said. 'It means you have all the strictures of being the heir, but none of the power. My freedom was something I cherished above everything else...' Hadn't it been the one compensation for his lonely and isolated childhood? The fact that he hadn't really had to account for himself? 'And suddenly it was taken away from me. It made me want to stay away from Khayarzah, where I felt the people were watching me all the time. And I knew that I needed to give Zahid space to settle into his Kingship in peace.' There was a pause. 'Because there is only ever room for one ruler.'

'And do you miss it? Khayarzah, I mean?'

He studied her wide tawny eyes, realising that he had told her more than he had ever told anyone. In truth, his self-imposed exile had only emphasised his feelings of displacement, of not actually belonging anywhere. Just like the little boy who had been sent away to school. As a child he'd felt as if he'd had no real home and as an adult that feeling had not changed.

'Not really,' he mused. 'I go back there on high days and holidays and that's enough. There's no place for me there.'

Isobel sipped her drink as the waiter placed two plates of steaming pasta before them. His last words disturbed her. *There's no place for me there.* Wasn't that an awfully *lonely* thing to say? And wasn't that what she'd thought when she'd seen him lying injured in hospital— that he'd looked so alone? What if her instinct then had been the right one?

'So you're planning on settling down in England?' she questioned, and then gave a nervous laugh. 'Though I guess you already are settled.'

There was brief pause as Tariq swirled a forkful of tagliatelli and coated it in sauce. But he didn't eat it. Instead, he lifted his eyes to hers, a sardonic smile curving his lips. It was always the same. Or rather women were. Didn't matter what you talked about, their careless chatter inevitably morphed into thinly veiled queries about his future. Because didn't they automatically daydream about *their* future and wonder if it could be a match with his? Weren't they programmed to do that, when they became the lover of a powerful alpha male?

'By "settling down", I suppose you mean getting married and having children?' he questioned.

Isobel nodded. 'I suppose so.'

Tariq's lips curved. She *supposed* so! 'The perfect nuclear family?'

'Well—'

'Which doesn't exist,' he interjected.

'That's a little harsh, Tariq.'

'Is it?' Black eyes iced into her. 'You experienced one yourself, did you?'

'Well, no. You know I didn't. I told you that I never knew my father.'

'And it left a gaping hole in your life?'

'I tried never to think of it that way,' she said defensively. 'Holes can always be filled by something else. It may not have been a "normal" family life, but it was a life.'

'Well, I never knew a "normal" childhood, either,' he said, more bitterly than he had intended.

'Can I...can I ask what happened?'

He stared at her, and she looked so damned sweet and soft that he found himself telling her. 'My mother almost died having me, and after I was born she was so ill that she needed round-the-clock care. Zahid was that bit older, and a calmer child than me, and it was decided that my needs were being neglected. So they sent me away to boarding school when I was seven. That's when I first came to England.'

Isobel frowned. She hadn't realised that he'd been so young. 'Wasn't there anywhere closer to home you could have gone?'

He shook his head. 'We have a completely different system of schooling in Khayarzah—it was decided that a western education would be beneficial all round.' He read the puzzlement in her tawny eyes. 'It meant that I would be able to speak and act like a westerner. More importantly, to think as a westerner thinks—which has proved invaluable in my subsequent business dealings. It's why the Al Hakam company has global domination,' he finished, with the flicker of a smile.

But, despite his proud smile, Isobel felt desperately

sad for him, even though she could see the logic behind his parents' decision. She had been the daughter of a school nurse and knew how illness could create chaos in the most ordered of lives. Sending away a lively little boy from his mother's sickbed must have seemed like a sensible solution at the time.

Yet to move a child to live somewhere else—without any kind of family support nearby—and what did that child become? A cuckoo in the nest in his adopted country. And surely he must have felt like an outsider whenever he returned to his homeland? Tariq had spoken the truth, she realised. He *didn't* have any place of his own—not in any true sense of the word. Yes, there were the apartments in London and New York, and the luxury houses on Mustique and in the South of France—but nowhere he could really call *home*. Not in his heart.

'So you don't ever want children of your own?' she questioned boldly.

At this the shutters came down and his voice cooled. 'Not ever,' he affirmed, his gaze never leaving her face—because she had to understand that he meant this. 'My brother has helpfully produced twin boys, and our country now has the required heir and a spare. So my assistance with dynasty-building is not required.'

A shiver ran down her spine as his unemotional words registered. Was that what he thought fatherhood and family life was all about...*dynasties?* Didn't he long to hold his own little baby boy or girl in his arms? To cradle them and to rock them? To see the past and the future written in its tiny features?

She looked at his face in the candlelight. Such a strong and indomitable face, she thought, with its high slash of cheekbones, the hawk-like nose and wide, sensual mouth. But behind the impressive physical package he presented she had discovered a reason for the unmistakable sense of *aloneness* which always seemed to surround him.

Yet this notoriously private man had actually confided in her. Surely that had to mean *something*? That he trusted her, yes—but was there anything more than that. And was it enough for her to face risking her heart?

She drifted her eyes over his hands—powerful and hair roughened. On the white silk cuffs of his shirt gleamed two heavy golden cufflinks. She could see that they were Khayarzah cufflinks, with the distinctive silhouette of a brooding falcon poised for flight. And somehow the bird of prey reminded her of him. Restless and seeking...above the world, but never really part of it.

Had he seen her looking at them? Was that why his hand suddenly reached out and caught hold of hers, capturing her wrist in his warm grasp and making it seem tiny and frail in comparison? His thumb brushed over the delicate skin at her wrist and he gave a brief smile as he felt the frantic skitter of her pulse.

'Stunned into uncharacteristic silence by my story, are you, Izzy?'

'It's some story,' she admitted quietly.

'Yes.' He looked down at her untouched plate. 'You're not eating.'

'Neither are you.'

'Delicious as it looks, I'm not feeling particularly hungry.'

'No.'

Across the candlelit table, their eyes met. 'Perhaps some fresh air might give us a little *appetite*.'

Isobel blinked at him in bewilderment. 'You want to go for a walk?'

His smile was wry. He'd forgotten that she had every right to be naïve, for she knew nothing of the games that lovers played... 'Only as far as the car. I thought we could go to my apartment. There's plenty of food there.'

Isobel's heart began to pound as his lazy suggestion shimmered into the space between them. She hadn't thought a lot beyond the meal itself. Somehow she had imagined that she might be going home alone to her little flat, as if the whole...*sex*...thing had been nothing but a distant dream. She'd told herself that would be the best for both of them, even if her commitment to the idea had been less than whole-hearted.

But then Tariq had opened up to her, taking her into his confidence. It had felt almost as intimate as when he'd been driving into her body. How could she possibly go home alone when she thought about the alternative he was offering her?

He was gesturing for the bill, seeming to take her silence for acquiescence, and the waiter was coming over to their table, his face creased in an anxious frown.

'You no like the food?' he questioned.

'The food is delicious,' Tariq replied, giving Isobel's hand a quick squeeze. 'I just find my partner's beauty rather distracting. So we'll just have the bill, please.'

Isobel saw the man-to-man look which passed between Tariq and the waiter, and for a moment she felt betrayed. Suddenly she had become someone else—not the woman who'd been frequenting this place for years, but someone dining with a man who was clearly way out of her league.

The waiter moved away, and Isobel tried to wriggle her fingers free. But Tariq wasn't having any of it.

'What's the matter, Izzy?'

'Just because you want to go to bed with me, it doesn't mean you have to tell lies!'

'Lies?' he questioned, perplexed.

'I am *not* beautiful,' she insisted.

'Oh, but you are,' he said unexpectedly, and then he did let go of her hand. Instead, he moved to cup her chin, running the tip of his thumb over it. 'Tonight you look very beautiful, sitting there, bathed in candlelight. I like your hair loose. I even like your eyes flashing with defiance. In fact, I can't quite remember ever seeing a woman look quite as desirable as you do right now, and it's making me ache for you. And you feel exactly the same, don't you?'

'Tariq!'

'Don't you?'

She met the mocking gleam in his ebony eyes. 'Yes,' she whispered.

'So pick up your handbag and let's get out of here— before I do something really crazy like hauling you to your feet and kissing you in front of the entire restaurant. Now, that really *would* provide fodder for the tabloids.'

She was trembling with anticipation as they went outside, where Tariq's chauffeur-driven car was sitting purring by the kerb. Climbing into its sumptuous interior, she waited for him to pull her into his arms. To kiss her as she so badly wanted to be kissed.

But he didn't. In fact he slid his body as far away from her as possible, and when he saw her turn her head he must have read the disappointed expression in her eyes because he shook his head.

'No, Izzy,' he said sternly. 'Not here and not now. I think we have demonstrated the wilder side of passion, and I think I've made it clear that once I start touching you all bets seem to be off. Tonight we will have the slow burn of anticipation and I will show you just how pleasurable *that* can be.'

Even when they reached his apartment he simply laced his fingers in hers and led her along the long corridor to his bedroom. Once there, with dexterous efficiency, he began to slide the clothes from her body. Only this time he hung her black silky dress over the back of a chair and did not tear off her panties.

When at last she was stripped bare, he peeled back the silken throw which covered his bed and laid her down on it.

'I want to see you naked,' he murmured appraisingly, as his gaze travelled slowly down the length of her body.

She watched as he undressed, the breath dying in her throat. His body was taut and magnificent—and he made no attempt to hide the heavy length of his arousal. But when at last he was completely naked, and maybe because he felt the trembling of her body, he frowned.

Smoothing back the cascade of Titian curls, he looked deep into her eyes. 'You are nervous?'

'A little.'

'But there is no reason to be, *habiba*.' He brushed his mouth over hers. 'For tonight there will be no pain— only endless pleasure.'

She gave herself up to his kiss at last, glad to lose herself in its seductive power. And grateful, too, for the clamour of her senses, which responded instantly to his expert touch and drove all nagging thoughts from her mind.

It was only afterwards that they came back to haunt her. When all passion was spent and they were lying there, Tariq's hand splayed possessively over the damp fuzz of curls at her thighs and her head slumped against his shoulder.

No pain, he had said—only pleasure.

But he had been talking about the physical pain of having surrendered her virginity to him. Not the infinitely more powerful pain she suspected might be about to be inflicted on her heart.

CHAPTER EIGHT

THE office door clicked quietly shut, and Tariq's distinctively soft voice whispered over Isobel's senses.

'So what has it been like without me, *kalila?* Did the office grind to a halt without me? More importantly... did you miss your Sheikh while he was away?'

Isobel looked up from her work, trying to steel herself against the impact of seeing Tariq for the first time in almost a week. Having to fight back the urge to do something stupid—like leaping up and throwing herself into his arms.

He'd been to New York on business, and along the way had taken delivery of a new transatlantic jet. He'd also announced the expansion of the Al Hakam Bank in Singapore, but was still refusing to confirm reports that he was in the process of buying the famous 'Blues' football team. Consequently, his face had been pictured on the front pages of the financial press—and Isobel had secretly pored over them whenever she had a spare moment. It had felt slightly peculiar to look at the hard and handsome face which stared back at her amid the newsprint. And to realise that the man with the hawk-like features and noble lineage was actually her lover.

Now he leaned over her desk, a vision of alpha-sexiness in a dark grey suit and pristine white shirt. His olive skin made him look as if he had been cast in gold, and his black eyes gleamed as they surveyed her questioningly.

'Tariq,' she said slowly, laying down her pen and putting the churned up feeling in her stomach down to his tantalising proximity. 'You know perfectly well that the office always runs smoothly in your absence. In fact, there's a quiet air of calm around the place. People are that bit more relaxed when the big boss isn't around.'

He gave a slow smile as he loosened his tie and dropped it in front of her like a calling card. She sounded as unruffled as she always did when she spoke to him in the office—her cool air of composure barely slipping. Why, nobody would guess that the last time they'd seen each other she had been giving him oral sex in the back of his darkened limousine. Demonstrating yet another new-found sexual skill which she seemed to have adopted with her usual dexterity.

And he had reciprocated by sliding his fingers beneath her skirt and bringing her to a shuddering orgasm just moments before he'd left the car to catch his flight to JFK.

Yet to look at her now she seemed light-years away from his fevered and erotic memory of her. She looked restrained and efficient—almost *prim*.

To Tariq's surprise, any fears he'd had that she would become cloying or demanding had not been realised. Despite being such a sexual novice, Izzy seemed to have no problems juggling her dual roles as his lover and PA, and was as discreet as anyone in his position could have wished for.

He frowned. The only downside was that she seemed

to be getting underneath his skin in a way he hadn't anticipated. By now he should have been growing a little bored with her—because that was his pattern. Once the gloss of new sex had worn off, predictability tended to set in—and three weeks was usually long enough for him to begin to find out things about a woman which irritated him.

But Izzy was different, and he wasn't quite sure why. Might it be because she knew him better than almost anyone? Working so closely with him over the years had given her glimpses of the private person that he would never have allowed another to see. Sometimes it felt as though she had already stripped away several layers to see the man who lay beneath. Was that what gave sex with her its extra dimension of closeness? Or was it just the fearless way she responded to him? The way she looked straight into his eyes while he was deep inside her? As if she wanted to see into his soul with those big tawny eyes of hers. Sometimes it unsettled him and sometimes it did not—but it always excited him.

He watched as she picked up his discarded tie and began to roll it into a neat silken coil. 'So, did you miss me?' he repeated.

Isobel put the tie down and looked at him. What would he do if she told him that she *always* missed him? That she wished she could suddenly become one of his ties, so that she could wrap herself round his neck all day and stay there? He would run a million miles away—that was what he would do. Declarations of adoration were not what Tariq wanted, but she could see perfectly well from his darkening eyes just what he *did* want.

She rose from her desk and walked towards him,

aware of his gaze on her and conscious of the fact that her thighs were bare above her stocking tops. She'd dressed with deliberate daring for the office this morning, knowing that he was bound to want her as soon as he arrived—and determined to feed into the fantasies he had assured her on the phone last night had been building all week.

She might be new to all this, but some survival instinct had made her turn herself into the best lover she could possibly be. Because wasn't that her default method? To do something to the best of her ability? Didn't that usually mean security? If you became so good at something then you wouldn't be replaced.

Only this wasn't a new job, or a new project which was going to enhance her life. This was all about a relationship—it was strange new territory. Her mother's often repeated warnings still came to her from time to time, but how could she take them seriously when she was looking into the glittering hunger of Tariq's black eyes and feeling the lurch of her heart in response?

'Of course I've missed you,' she said softly.

'How much, on a scale of one to ten?'

'Well…' She pretended to think about it. 'How about seven?'

'*Seven?*'

'Eight, then. Nine! *Tariq!* Okay—ten!'

'You're wearing *stockings,*' he breathed in disbelief.

'Well, you've nagged me often enough about my tights.'

'With good reason. Let me see.' He lifted up her skirt and expelled a small appraising sigh. The tops of the dark silk stockings had been embroidered with deep turquoise and green, so that it looked as if some peacock had wrapped its feathers enticingly around her thighs and left them there. 'You know that there are consequences to dressing like that?' he questioned unsteadily.

'What kind of consequences might they be?'

'Can't you guess?' he breathed, as he placed her hand on the fly of his trousers.

'T-Tariq.'

'I want you, Izzy.'

'You always want me,' she whispered back, her fingertips caressing the thick, hard shaft.

He swallowed. 'And is it mutual?'

'You know it is.'

He caught her by the shoulders and looked down into her widened tawny eyes. 'Then why don't you show me how much you've missed me?' he questioned unsteadily. 'Because I have missed you too, *kalila*.'

She savoured his unsteady words as she rose up on tiptoe to kiss him, revelling in the sheer pleasure of being in his arms again. She closed her eyes as his practised fingers began to reacquaint themselves with her body. At times like this, when he could reduce her to boneless longing within seconds, it was easy to imagine that a unique bond existed between them. Was that because they seemed to have the ability to anticipate each other's needs—despite the disparity of their experience—or was it because they simply knew each other so well?

Or was it something far more commonplace? He'd told her candidly that making love without having to wear a condom was the biggest turn-on he'd ever known. For him, that was a brand-new experience, and that was rare enough to excite a man who'd been having sex since he was a teenager. She'd tried telling herself that

Tariq's reaction to her was purely physical. Because if she looked the truth straight in the face then surely there was less likelihood of her getting hurt?

If only her own feelings were as straightforward. If only she hadn't started to care. Really care. She wondered if it was normal for a woman to become a little more emotionally vulnerable every time her man made love to her. For her to start wanting things she knew she wasn't supposed to want—things he'd specifically warned her against? Things that Tariq was renowned for never delivering—and especially to a woman like her. Stuff like commitment and happy-ever-after.

'Izzy?'

She closed her eyes, letting go of the last of her troubled thoughts, allowing pure and delicious sensation to take over instead. 'Yes,' she whispered, as he pushed her down onto the floor and sank down beside her. 'Oh, yes.'

His fingers were on her flesh now, stroking open the moist and heated flesh at the very core of her, and he was saying, *'Luloah...'* softly and fervently beneath his breath, something which Isobel had learnt meant 'pearl' in his native tongue.

'You taste of honey,' he said on a shuddered breath, his mouth high on her thigh.

'Tariq—' His tongue had reached the most sensitive part of her anatomy, and Isobel gave a little gasp of pleasure as she felt its delicate flick. Glancing down, she could see the erotic image of her boss's black head between her legs, and the sheer intimacy of it only increased the sensations which were beginning to ripple through her.

Her head fell back as an unstoppable heat began to

build, and she trembled on the brink as he teased her with his tongue.

'Tariq,' she gasped again, clutching at his shoulders, her fingers biting into him.

'What?' he drawled against her heated flesh.

Tariq, I think I'm falling in love with you!

But her passionate thoughts dissolved as a feeling of intense pleasure washed over her—strong enough to sweep away everything else in its wake. Wave after wave of it racked her trembling body—and just when she thought it couldn't get any better he thrust deep inside her.

'You feel so *good,*' he said unsteadily.

'So...do you.'

He thrust even deeper, his breaths becoming long and shuddering. 'And I've been wanting to do this to you *all week.*'

She heard his voice change and felt his body tense, watched him splinter with his own pleasure. She loved the helplessness of his orgasm, feeling in those few heightened moments of sensation that he was really hers.

Afterwards, they lay wrapped tightly in each other's arms, until Isobel lifted her head to free some of the hair which was trapped beneath his elbow.

'You know, we're going to have to stop meeting like this,' she murmured.

Tariq laughed , drawing his fingers through the spill of her curls and marvelling at how *uncomplicated* all this seemed. His mouth settled into a curve of satisfaction. He could walk in from a trip and within minutes have her writhing and compliant in his arms. There were no demands made, nor questions asked. What could be better than that?

'I think this is a very good place to meet.' He yawned. 'You've brought a whole new meaning to the expression "job satisfaction".'

But Isobel wasn't really listening. Now that her euphoric state had begun to evaporate she was remembering what she'd been thinking at the height of their lovemaking. About loving him.

She stared at the ceiling, her heart beginning to pound with fear. *Love?* Surely she wasn't crazy enough to waste an emotion like that on a man who very definitely didn't want it? Who had explicitly warned her against it? And hadn't her mother done the very same? She'd managed to convince her daughter that love was rare—and Isobel knew it was an impossibility to expect it from a seasoned playboy who shied away from commitment.

Uncomfortably, she wriggled, wanting to get away, to try and soothe her confused thoughts into some kind of order. 'Tariq, we can't lie here all day.'

'Why not? We can do anything we like.' He touched his lips to hers. 'I *am* the boss.'

She pulled away from him—but not before he had caught hold of her, his eyes narrowed. 'Something is wrong, *kalila?*' he queried softly. 'You are angry with me because we have had yet another *fumble* on the floor of the office?'

Isobel smiled. 'I can hardly blame you for wanting instant sex when I was a willing participant. I just happen to know that there's a whole pile of things which need your attention. And we *are* supposed to be working.'

Yawning, he rose to his feet and held out a hand. 'By

the way—I've brought you a present from New York,' he said as he pulled to her feet.

'Oh?' She felt her heart skip a beat. 'It's not my birthday.'

"That's a little disingenuous of you, Izzy.' Walking over to his briefcase, he slanted her a lazy smile as he withdrew a slim leather case. 'Don't you like presents?'

She wasn't sure—her feelings were pretty mixed when it came to presents from Tariq. She wanted to be the first and only woman he'd ever bought a gift for. Not to feel as if she was just one in a long line of women who smiled their acceptance of whatever glittering trinket he had bought them. *But she was. That was exactly what she was.*

She wanted to tell him that she didn't need presents. Because she knew him too well and she knew how he operated. Her counterpart in New York had probably been dispatched to choose something for her—just as she had chosen such gifts for his lovers many times before. She had probably even consulted him to find out what the budget for such a gift should be.

But she kept silent. She was curious and scared, knowing that she was in no position to make highly charged pronouncements because of what the outcome might be. Because mightn't he just shrug his shoulders and walk away?

So she took the box he handed her and flipped open the clasp with fingers which were miraculously steady. The first irreverent thought which crossed her mind was that she was pretty low down on the price scale. After five years of choosing various sparklers for Tariq's women, she could see instantly that her own offering would not have caused a stratospheric hole in his wallet. No diamonds or emeralds for *her*.

But in a stupid way she was glad. Precious jewels would have been all wrong on someone like her: they would have felt like some sort of *payment* and they wouldn't have suited her. Instead Tariq had bought her something she might actually have saved up for and bought for herself.

Lying on bed of blue-black velvet lay a shoal of opals, fashioned into in a dramatic waterfall of a necklace. Isobel drew it out of the box. The stones were dark grey—almost black—but as the necklace shimmered over her fingers she could see the transformation of each gem into a vivid rainbow.

'Do you like it?' questioned Tariq.

Isobel blinked. 'It's the most beautiful thing I've ever seen,' she whispered.

'I chose it myself,' he said unexpectedly. 'I liked the element of surprise. In some lights it looks quite subdued—while in other aspects it's amazingly vibrant.' His eyes narrowed and his tone was dry. 'A little like you, in fact, Izzy.'

Isobel suddenly became extremely preoccupied with the jewellery, swallowing down the glimmer of tears which were hovering at the back of her eyes. He'd chosen it himself. To her certain knowledge he'd never done that before—not in all the time she'd worked for him. So did that *mean* anything? She couldn't help the wild leap of her heart. Did such an unexpected gesture mean that his feelings for her might be growing and changing? Dared she…dared she *hope* for such a thing?

'You do like it, Izzy?'

His question broke into her thoughts and she lifted her head. 'I do like it. In fact, I *love* it.'

'Good.' There was a pause. 'I thought you might want to wear it tomorrow night.'

She heard the studied casualness in his voice. 'Why? What's happening tomorrow night?'

'My brother is in town.'

She blinked. 'You mean your brother, the *King?*'

'I only have one brother,' he answered drily. 'He flew my sister-in-law to Paris for their wedding anniversary. Francesca hasn't been back in England in nearly a year, so they've decided to come on to London. Our embassy is throwing a formal dinner for them tonight—which I shall have to attend. But tomorrow they want to meet up privately. You've spoken to Zahid on the phone so many times that I thought you might like this opportunity to meet him.'

Carefully, she put the necklace back in its case and smiled. 'I'd love to meet your brother,' she said.

'Good.' Tariq walked through to his private office, calling out over his shoulder, 'I'll let you have the details later.'

Isobel waited until the door had closed behind him, then stared at the jewellery case in her handbag, a strange cocktail of emotions forming a tight knot at the pit of her stomach. She might be going out of her mind, but try as she might she couldn't quite subdue the sudden flare of happiness which rose within her. Hand-picked jewels and meeting his brother were surely remarkable enough to merit a little analysis. Was it possible that, deep down, Tariq was willing to move this relationship on to something a little more tangible?

Cold reason tried to swamp her as she remembered

the emphatic way he'd told her that he didn't ever want commitment, or a family of his own. But measured against that was the terrible loneliness he'd experienced as a child. Maybe now he was coming to realise that people could change—and so could circumstances. That what they had was good. That it didn't have to peter out after a few weeks—that maybe it could endure and grow. Was that too much to hope for?

But she felt as if she was on shifting sands—her hopes quickly replaced by a strange feeling of foreboding as she remembered something she'd read somewhere.

She clicked open the box to stare at the multi-hued fire of her brand-new necklace, and frowned. Because weren't opals supposed to be awfully *unlucky?*

CHAPTER NINE

'You look *fine,* Izzy. Really.'

For the umpteenth time Isobel smoothed damp palms down over her thick mass of curls, aware that she was probably mussing her hair up instead of flattening it. She frowned at Tariq. What kind of a recommendation was that? 'Fine' wasn't the kind of description she wanted when she was about to meet the King of Khayarzah and his English bride Queen Francesca. Not when she felt so nervous that her knees were actually shaking.

'That's a pretty lukewarm endorsement,' she said.

His black eyes gleamed as he captured one of her fluttering hands and directed it towards his mouth. 'I thought honesty was our mantra?'

'Maybe it is, but sometimes a woman needs a little fabrication.'

'No need for fabrication, *kalila,*' he said. He brushed her a brief kiss as their car drew to a halt outside the glittering frontage of the Granchester Hotel, but if the truth were known he was finding this very feminine need for reassurance a touch too *domestic* for his taste. Had it been wise to extend this invitation? he wondered. Or was Izzy now reading far more into it than he'd intended her to read? Maybe he should have made it clearer that there was no real significance behind the meeting with his brother. 'You look absolutely stunning,' he drawled. 'Didn't I tell you exactly that just an hour ago?'

Yes, he had, Isobel conceded. But a man said all kinds of things to a woman when he had just finished ravishing her in the middle of his big bed...

Their spontaneous lovemaking had left her running late—but maybe it was better not to have had time to fret about her appearance when she'd been nervous enough already. She was wearing a new dress in grey silk jersey, and its careful draping did amazing things for her figure. She'd teamed the dress with high-heeled black suede shoes, and on Tariq's instructions had left her hair hanging loose. She'd wondered aloud if the wild cloud of Titian curls was not a little too much, but he had wound his fingers through its corkscrew strands and told her that it was a crime to hide it away.

Her only adornment was the opals he had brought her back from America, and they sparkled rainbow light at her throat and dominated the subdued palette of her outfit. *The gems he'd chosen for her himself...* How could such beautiful gems possibly be unlucky? she asked herself, her fingertips reaching up to touch the cool stones as a doorman sprang to open the car door.

The private elevator zoomed them up to the penthouse suite, and when the door was opened by a man who was unmistakably Tariq's brother all Isobel's expectations were confounded.

He had the same hawk-like features as Tariq—and the same knockout combination of ebony hair and glowing olive skin. But he was casually dressed in dark trousers, and although he was wearing a silk shirt he was tieless. Isobel had been expecting to be greeted by a servant, so her curtsey was hastily scrambled together and ill-prepared. But King Zahid smiled at her as he indicated that she should rise.

'No formality,' he warned. 'That is my wife's instruction, and I dare not disobey!'

'Why, Zahid—you sound as if you are almost under the thumb,' mocked Tariq softly.

'Perhaps I am. And a very beautiful thumb it happens to be,' murmured Zahid.

'You've changed,' observed Tariq, creasing his brow in a frown. 'You'd never have admitted to something like that in the past.'

'Ah, but everything changes, Tariq,' said Zahid. 'That is one of life's great certainties.'

For a moment the light of challenge sparked between the eyes of the brothers, and for a moment Isobel caught a glimpse of what the two men must have been like as children.

'Come this way,' continued Zahid, leading them into an enormous sitting room whose floor-to-ceiling windows overlooked the park.

And there, with a baby on her knee and another crawling close by on the floor, was the English Queen Francesca, her dark hair tied back in a ponytail and a slightly harassed smile on her face. She had a snowy blanket hanging over one shoulder, and was holding a grubby white toy polar bear, at which the sturdy baby on her lap kept lunging.

Isobel blinked. The last thing she'd expected was to see a queen in blue jeans, playing nursemaid!

'No, please don't curtsey, Izzy—we're very relaxed here,' said Francesca with a wide smile. 'But if you want to be really helpful you could pick up Omar before he tries to eat Zahid's shoe! Azzam has already tried! Darling, I do wish you'd keep them out of reach.'

Rather nervously, Isobel bent to scoop up the black-haired baby, aware that one of these precious boy twins was the heir to the Khayarzah throne. A robust little creature, Omar was wearing an exquisite yellow romper suit which contrasted with his ebony curls. He took one long and suspicious look at the woman now holding him, then gave a shout as he began to tug at her hair.

Isobel giggled as she extricated his tiny chubby fingers, all the nerves she'd been feeling suddenly evaporating. You couldn't possibly feel uptight when you were holding a cuddly bundle like this. He was so *sweet!* She risked a glance at Tariq, but met no answering smile on his face. In fact his expression suddenly looked so *glacial* that she felt momentarily flummoxed. But at least he was now directing the chilly stare at his brother instead of her.

'Don't you have any nannies with you?' Tariq asked Zahid coolly.

'Not one,' answered Zahid, giving his wife a long and indulgent look. 'Francesca decided that she wanted us to have a "normal" family holiday—just like other people.'

'And you agreed?' questioned Tariq incredulously.

'Actually, I find that I'm enjoying the experience,' said Zahid. 'It's useful to be "hands-on".'

'I want our children to know their parents,' said Francesca firmly. 'Not to be brought out like ornaments, for best. Zahid, aren't you going to offer our guests a drink?'

Isobel saw Tariq's face darken. Clearly he did *not* approve of the babies being present, and she noticed that he kept as far away from his nephews as possible. She wondered how he could possibly ignore such cute little black-haired dumplings, before deciding that it was *his* problem and that she was just going to relax and enjoy herself.

In fact the evening went much better than she could have hoped. She took turns cuddling both Omar and Azzam, and ended up kicking off her high-heeled shoes and helping Francesca bath the twins in one of the fancy *en-suite* bathrooms. Her dove-grey dress was soon splattered with drops of water, but she didn't care.

They grappled to dress the wriggling boys in animal-dotted sleepsuits, and then brought them in to the men to say goodnight, all warm and rosy and smelling delicious. But she noticed that Tariq's embrace was strictly perfunctory as each baby was offered up to him for a kiss.

She tried not to be unsettled by his rather forbidding body language as she and Francesca carried the babies through to the bedroom and laid them down in their two little cots. For a while they stood watching as two sets of heavily hooded eyes drooped down into exhausted sleep, and then—as if colluding in some wonderful secret—both women smiled at each other.

Francesca bent to tuck the polar bear next to Azzam, then straightened up. 'You know, we've never met any of Tariq's girlfriends before,' she said.

Isobel wasn't quite sure how to respond. She didn't really *feel* like his girlfriend—more like an employee, with benefits. But she could hardly confess that to the Sheikh's sister-in-law, could she? Or start explaining the exact nature of those 'benefits'? Instead, she smiled.

'I'm very honoured to be here,' she answered quietly.

Francesca hesitated. 'Sometimes Zahid worries about Tariq. He thinks that surely there's only so much living in the fast lane one person can do. It would be nice to see him settle down at last.'

Now Isobel felt a complete fraud, because she knew very well that Tariq had no intention of settling down. Not with her—and not with anyone. He'd made that more than clear. Because when a man told you unequivocally that he never wanted children he was telling you something big, wasn't he? Something you couldn't really ignore. And if she'd been labouring under any illusion that he hadn't meant it—well, she'd discovered tonight that he had. With his stony countenance and disapproving air, he'd made it pretty clear that children didn't do it for him.

And if Zahid and Francesca thought that her appearance here was anything more than expedient—that she and Tariq were about to start playing happy-ever-after—well, they were in for a big disappointment.

'I don't know whether some men are ever quite ready to settle down,' she told the Queen diplomatically. 'He isn't known as the Playboy Prince for nothing!'

Francesca opened her mouth as if she wanted to say something else, but clearly thought better of it because she shut it again. 'Come on,' she said. 'Let's go and eat dinner. I want to hear all about life in England—the fashion, the films. Who's dating who. What's big on TV. I get a whole load of stuff off the internet, of course, but it's never quite the same.'

And Isobel nodded and smiled, feeling an immense sense of relief that the subject of Tariq's inability to commit had been terminated.

Dinner was served in the lavish dining room which

led off the main room, its table covered in snowy linen and decorated with white fragrant flowers. Heavy silver cutlery reflected the light which guttered from tall, creamy candles, and the overall effect was one of restrained luxury and taste.

'This looks wonderful,' said Isobel shyly, realising that this was the first time she'd been given an insider's experience of Tariq's royal life.

'A dinner fit for a king!' said Francesca, and they all laughed as they took their places around the table.

The evening passed in a bit of a blur. Isobel was aware of being served the most amazing food, but it was mostly wasted on her. She might as well have been eating bread and butter for all the notice she took of the exquisite fare. She could hardly believe she was here with Tariq—meeting his family like this. It had the heady but disconcerting effect of almost *normalising* their relationship—and she knew that was a dangerous way to start thinking. Just because you really wanted something, it didn't necessarily mean it was going to happen.

So she joined in as much as she could, though she felt completely lost when the two brothers began speaking in their own language.

'They're discussing the new trade deal with Maraban,' confided Francesca.

Isobel put her knife and fork down. 'Do you speak any Khayarzahian?' she questioned.

'Only a little. I'm learning all the time—though it's not the easiest language in the world. But I'm determined to be fluent one day—just as my sons will be.'

'They're such beautiful babies,' said Isobel, a sudden note of wistfulness entering her voice almost before she'd realised.

'Not getting broody, are you?' Francesca laughed.

It was perhaps unfortunate that the brothers' conversation chose that precise moment to end and Tariq glanced up. He must have heard what they'd been saying, Isobel thought, her skin suddenly growing cold with fear. He *must* have done. Why else did he fix her with an expression she'd never seen before? A calculating look iced the ebony depths of his eyes which made her feel like some sort of gatecrasher.

'Of course I'm not!' she denied quickly, reaching for a glass of water and horribly aware of the sudden flush of colour to her cheeks. Why was he looking at her like that—with his eyes full of suspicion? Did he think she was trying to ingratiate herself with the monarch and his wife? Or did he think she really *was* getting broody?

One moment she had been part of their charmed inner circle—warmed by its privileged light—and now in an instant it felt as if she had been kicked out and left to shiver on the darkened sidelines.

By the time the evening ended her feeling of despondency had grown—though she managed to maintain her bright air of enjoyment until the car door had closed on them and they were once more locked within its private space.

She settled back in the seat, unable to shake off the feeling of having been judged and found wanting, aware that Tariq did not slide his arm around her shoulder and draw her closer to him. And suddenly she was reminded of that very first time she'd had sex with him. When she'd been driven home—knickerless and confused— after first dropping him off at the Maraban Embassy.

Back then she had been painfully aware of him keeping her at a distance, and he was doing it again now.

Even though in the intervening weeks they had been lovers it was almost like being transported back in time. Because nothing had really changed, had it? Not for Tariq. She might be guilty of concocting fast-growing fantasies about how hand-chosen pieces of jewellery meant that he was starting to care for her—but that was just wishful thinking. Like some young girl who read her horoscope and then prayed it would come true.

'You seemed to be getting on very well with Francesca,' he observed, his voice breaking into her thoughts.

'I hope I did all right?' she questioned, telling herself that any woman in her position would have asked the same question.

'I thought you carried it off superbly.'

'Thanks,' she said uncertainly.

But Tariq leaned back in his seat, unable to dispel the growing sense of unease inside him. The whole evening had unsettled him, and it wasn't difficult to work out why. Zahid in jeans—with no help for the children—and in a hotel suite which looked as if it had just been burgled.

He shook his head in faint disbelief. It was scarcely credible to him that his once so formal and slightly stuffy older brother was now like putty in the hands of his wife.

But it hadn't just been the sense of chaos which had unsettled him. Something about their close family unit had opened up the dark space which was buried deep in Tariq's heart. Watching his brother playing with his children had reinforced his sense of feeling like an outsider. Always the outsider.

He shot Isobel a glance, remembering the way their

gazes had met over the dark curly head of his nephew. Had that been wistfulness he'd read in her eyes as she'd held the baby in her arms? Was she doing that clucky thing which seemed to happen to all women, no matter how much they tried to deny it? Especially if they knew that a man was watching them...

But why *shouldn't* she long for babies of her own? That was what women were conditioned to do. The most unforgivable thing would be for a man who didn't want children to waste the time of a woman who *did*.

He saw that her eyes were now closed. Her cheeks looked as smooth as marble. Her grey dress and the new opals were muted in the subdued light of the car. Only her magnificent mane of hair provided glowing life and colour. And suddenly, in this quiet place, all the things he usually blotted out came crowding into his mind.

He hadn't given any thought to the future. He hadn't planned this affair with Izzy—it had just sprung up, out of the blue, and been surprisingly good. But sooner or later something had to give. It wasn't for ever. His relationships never were. And the longer it went on, then surely the more it would fill her with false hope. She might start seeing a happy-ever-after for them both—which was never going to happen. Wasn't it better and more honest to end it now, before he really hurt her—a woman he liked and respected far too much to ever want to hurt?

He realised that she had fallen asleep, and although a part of him wanted to lean over and wake her with a kiss he reminded himself that this wasn't a fairytale.

He was not that prince.

Gently, he shook her shoulder, and her big, tawny eyes snapped open.

'Wake up, Izzy,' he said softly.

'What's the matter?' Groggily, she sat up and looked around. 'Are we nearly home?'

It was her choice of word which helped make his mind up. Because for them there was no 'home' and there never would be. She had her place and he had his—and maybe it was time to start drawing a clear line between the two.

'I'm going to get the car to drop me off,' he said softly. 'And then the driver will take you on to your apartment.'

Isobel snuggled up to him. 'Don't be silly,' she murmured. 'I'll come home with you.'

There it was again—that seemingly innocuous word which now seemed weighted down with all kinds of heavy meaning.

'Not tonight, Izzy. I have to take a conference call very early tomorrow, and it's pointless the two of us being woken up.' Lightly he brushed his lips over hers before drawing away—before the sweet taste of her could tempt him into changing his mind—glad that the limousine was now drawing up outside his apartment. 'And, thanks to you, I got very little sleep last night.'

Feeling stupidly rejected, Isobel nodded. In a way, his explanation made things worse. It made her feel as if she was *wanting* something from him and he was withholding it.

Or was she simply tired and imagining things? Maybe it would be better all round if she *did* go home alone. She could have an undisturbed night's sleep, and tomorrow morning she would wake up bright and cheerful.

And everything would be the same as it had been before.

'Yes, we could probably *both* do with a good night's

sleep,' she said, keeping her voice resolutely cheerful.
'I'll see you in the morning.'

But as Tariq got out of the car she saw the sudden
shuttering of his face, and she couldn't shift the sinking
certainty that something between them had changed.

And changed for the worst.

CHAPTER TEN

So it was true.

Horribly, horribly true.

Isobel's fears that Tariq was *cooling* towards her were not some warped figment of her imagination, after all. She was getting the cool treatment. Definitely. She recognised it much too well to be mistaken.

She hadn't spent a night with him in almost a week even though he'd been in the same country—the same city, even. Every night there was another reason why he couldn't see her. He was eating out with a group of American bankers. Or meeting up with a friend who'd just flown in from Khayarzah. And even though his reasons sounded perfectly legitimate, Isobel couldn't shift the certainty that he was avoiding her.

These days, even when he came into the office, he seemed distracted. There was barely a good morning kiss. No smouldering look to send her pulse rate soaring and have her anticipating what might happen later. It was as if the Isobel she had been——the woman he desired and lusted after——was disappearing. She felt as if the old, invisible Isobel had returned to take her place. As if a switch had been flicked in Tariq's mind and it would never be the same again.

She tried telling herself it was because he was busy—but deep down she suspected a different reason for his distance. After all, she'd seen it happen countless times before, with other women. One minute they were flavour of the month, and the next they were like unwanted leftovers, lying congealed on the side of the plate.

The question was, what was she going to do about it? Was she going to sit back and let him push her away—gradually chipping at her already precarious self-esteem—until she was left with nothing? Or was she going to be proactive enough to reach out and take control of her life? Should she just face up to him and ask whether they were to consign their affair to memory?

Until she realised that Tariq's apparent lack of interest was the least of her worries. And that there were some things which were of far more pressing concern…

She told herself that the nausea she was experiencing was a residual from the brief burst of sickness she'd had, caused by some rogue fish she'd eaten. That the slight aching in her breasts was due to her hormones, nothing else. She was on the pill, wasn't she? And the pill was blissfully safe. Everyone knew that.

But the feeling of nausea began to worsen, and so did the aching in her breasts. And then Tariq said something which made her think that perhaps she *wasn't* imagining it…

It happened that weekend, when she was staying over at his apartment. It seemed ages since they'd spent two whole days together, and she loved being there when they didn't have work the next day. It was the closest she ever felt to him—as if she was a real girlfriend, rather than a secretary who had just got lucky.

It was early on the Sunday morning that he made his

observation. Half-asleep, he had begun to kiss her, his hands to caress her breasts, and she had given a little sigh and nestled back against the soft bank of pillows.

'Izzy?' he murmured. 'Have you put on a little weight, do you think?'

She stiffened beneath the practised caress of his fingers. 'Why?' she blurted out. 'Do you think I'm getting fat?'

'There's no need to be so defensive.' He blew softly onto the hollow of her breastbone. 'You're slender enough to carry a few extra pounds. Men like curves— I've told you that before.'

But his words only increased her sense of anxiety, and she was almost relieved when the phone in his study began ringing and he swore a little before going off to answer it. It was the one phone he never ignored—the private line between him and his brother's palace in Khayarzah.

Isobel could hear him speaking in a lowered voice, so she took the opportunity to head for the bathroom down the corridor—the one he never used. Her heart was racing as she closed the door, and the terrible taste of fear was in her mouth. And she knew that she could no longer put off the moment of truth.

She flinched as she saw the image which was reflected back at her in the full-length mirror. Her face was paper-pale and her eyes looked huge and haunted, but it was her body which disturbed her. Like most women, she was not usually given to staring at her naked self, but even she could see that her breasts looked swollen and the nipples were much darker than usual.

Was she pregnant? *Was* she?

For a moment she lowered her head, to gaze at the

pristine white surface of the washbasin. She remembered how unequivocal Tariq had been about not wanting children—and clearly it hadn't been an idle declaration. Hadn't she witnessed for herself how cold he could be when he was around them? Why, he'd barely touched Omar or Azzam the other day—he'd seemed completely unmoved by their presence when everyone else had been cooing around them.

She wanted to sink to her knees and pray for some kind of miracle. But she couldn't afford to have hysterics or to act rashly. She needed time to think, and she needed to stay calm.

Quickly, she showered and put on jeans and a shirt, feeling the slight tug as she fastened the buttons across her chest.

The silence in the apartment told her that Tariq had finished his conversation, and in bare feet she padded along the corridor to find him standing in his study. He was staring out of the window, his powerful body silhouetted against the dramatic view.

When he turned round, he didn't comment on the fact that she had showered and dressed. A couple of weeks ago he would have growled his displeasure and started removing her clothes immediately, but not now—and a wave of regret washed over her for something between them which seemed to be lost.

'Is anything wrong?' she questioned.

He stared at her, his eyes focussing on her pale skin and anxious eyes, and a heavy sense of sadness enveloped him. What had happened to his smart and wise-cracking Izzy? He felt the heavy beat of guilt, aware of the enormity of what he had done. In typical Tariq fashion he had seen and he had conquered. Selfishly, he had listened to the voracious demands of his body and taken her as his lover, refusing to acknowledge the thoughtlessness of such an action.

She had been too inexperienced to resist the powerful lure of lust when it had swept over them so unexpectedly. *He* should have known better and *he* should have resisted. But he had not. He had done what he always did—he had taken and taken, knowing that he had nothing to give back.

And now he was left with the growing suspicion that he was going to lose the best assistant he'd ever had. For how could they carry on like this, when much of her natural spontaneity seemed to have been eroded by the affair?

He could tell that something had changed. It was as if she was walking on eggshells. He noticed that she kept biting back her words—which usually meant that a woman was falling in love with him, that she was weighing up everything she said for fear of how he would interpret it. And all these negative feelings would snowball—he knew that, too. How could he possibly face her in the office if her reproachful looks were to continue and the gap between them widened daily?

'Tariq?'

Her soft voice broke into his troubled thoughts. 'What?'

'I wondered if anything was wrong.'

'Wrong?'

She looked at him questioningly, telling herself that it was her business to know what was going on his life. But deep down she wanted to clear that scary look of distraction from his face. To have him *talk* to her. Properly.

'The phone call you've just had from Khayarzah?'

she elaborated. 'I hope everything's okay with your brother?'

With an effort, he focussed on the conversation he'd just finished. 'Zahid wants my help with a relative of ours.'

'Oh?'

'A distant cousin of mine, from my mother's side,' he explained. 'Her name is Leila, and she's in trouble.'

Isobel's face blanched as she wondered if the gods were taunting her. Because hadn't that expression always been a euphemism for a particular *kind* of predicament in which a woman sometimes found herself? Was it possible that a cruel fate was about to inflict not one but *two* unplanned pregnancies on the al Hakam family?

'Trouble?' she questioned hoarsely. 'What kind of trouble?'

'It seems she's decided she wants to junk university and go off to America to be a model. Can you imagine?' He gave a grim smile. 'Zahid thinks that she needs to be shown the error of her ways, and he thinks that I may just be able to sort things out.'

'I see.' Isobel nodded. Was she imagining the relief on his face—as if he was anticipating an adventure which would fully occupy him for the foreseeable future? As if he was pleased to have a *bone fide* reason to unexpectedly leave the country? 'Why does he think that?'

'He says that my uniquely western perspective might help persuade her. That I've seen enough of that kind of world to convince her that it's all starvation and cigarettes and people who will try to exploit her.' He shrugged. 'Nothing that need concern you—but I'm going to fly out later tonight, if you could make sure the new jet is ready for me?'

Two things occurred to her at the same time. The first was that he still came and went exactly as he pleased—becoming her lover had not curtailed his freedom in any way at all. And the second was that she knew there was no way she could announce her momentous news. Not when he was about to go on some mission of mercy for his brother. Not when she hadn't even had it confirmed. And until she did then surely there was always the chance that it was nothing but a false alarm?

But her decision didn't give her any peace of mind. She was still left with nagging doubts. Tariq was leaving to go back to his homeland, and suddenly she didn't know where her place in his life should be. She struggled to a find common ground.

'Did...did your brother and his wife enjoy themselves in London last week?' she asked.

'I assume so.'

'They didn't mention it?'

He raised dark brows. 'Should they have done?'

'Just...well, I thought it was quite a fun evening, that's all.'

'Indeed it was.' He gave a brief smile, preoccupied with his forthcoming trip and pleased to have something to take his mind of the damned tension between them. 'But they have a hectic life, you know, Izzy. Pretty much wall-to-wall socialising wherever they are.'

It was the hint of aloofness in his tone which made Isobel stiffen. That and the patronising sense that she had stepped over some invisible line of propriety. As if she had *dared* to look on the King and his wife as some sort of equals, instead of people she'd been lucky enough to meet only on a whim of Tariq's.

'Silly of me,' she said lightly.

There was a pause as she forced herself to acknowledge the tension which had sprung up between them and which now seemed there all the time. She didn't know when exactly it had happened, but it wouldn't seem to go away. Like a pebble dropped into a pond, the ripples carried on for ages after the stone had plopped out of sight.

She knew what was going on because she'd witnessed it countless times before. Tariq was beginning to tire of her and he wanted the affair to be over—with the least possible disruption to *him*.

She thought of how the situation might pan out. He might decide to stay longer in Khayarzah than he'd intended. Or he might slot in lots of extra trips abroad which would seamlessly and physically separate them. And when they finally came face to face back in the office so much time would have passed that it would be easy to consign the whole affair to history.

Easy for him, perhaps—but not for her. She hadn't done this kind of thing before. Unlike him, she was *no good at pretending.*

Wasn't it better to face the truth head-on—no matter how difficult that might be? To confront reality rather than trying to airbrush it away? Wouldn't that at least go some way to restoring her pride and making sure she didn't whittle away at her self-respect until there was nothing left but an empty husk?

She forced a smile. 'Tariq, I've been thinking.'

Something in her tone made his eyes narrow. 'Oh?'

Her heart was hammering, but she forced herself to

look directly into his eyes. 'I'm due a lot of holiday—and I was wondering if I might take the chance to use up some of my entitlement while you're away? Fiona's pretty much up to speed, and she's perfectly capable of running your office.'

Tariq stiffened as he heard the sudden formality of her tone. Holiday *entitlement.* Fiona *running his office.* He met her tawny gaze and felt a brief spear of something like pain as he realised what she was doing. Izzy was clever, he conceded. Clever enough to sense that he was cooling towards her.

'Is that really necessary?' he said.

It was a loaded question. She knew it, and he knew it too. Isobel nodded her head. 'I think so. I think we need to give each other a little space, Tariq. This...*affair* has been pretty amazing, but I suspect it's run its course—don't you?' She stared at him, willing him to say no. Longing for him to pull her into his arms and tell her she was out of her mind.

Tariq looked at her and felt a wave of admiration underpinned by a fleeting sense of regret. For, although he knew that this was the perfect solution, he was going to miss her as a lover. But relationships never stayed static. Already he could sense that she wanted more from him. More than he could ever give. And if he allowed her these weeks of absence mightn't she come back refreshed and able to put the whole thing behind her? Couldn't they go back to what they'd had before? That easy intimacy they'd shared before they had allowed sex to complicate everything?

Briefly, he acknowledged the stab of hurt pride that she should be the one to end it. But why *shouldn't* he be the one on the receiving end of closure for a change? Mightn't it do him some good?

'I think you could be right,' he said slowly.

'You do?' Could he hear the disappointment which had distorted her voice?

He nodded. 'I do. Maybe it's better we stop it now before it impacts on our working relationship.'

'Oh, absolutely,' she agreed, gritting her teeth behind her smile. Wanting to lash out at him for his naïveté. Did he really think it *hadn't* impacted on their working relationship already?

'And you deserve a break,' he said, his gaze drifting over her face. 'Why don't you get some sun on your cheeks? You look awfully pale, Izzy.'

Dimly, she registered his words, and they gave her all the confirmation she needed. He thought that a short spell in the sun was all she needed to bring her back to normal. Oh, if only it was that easy. A strange dizziness was making her head spin. For a moment she felt icy-cold beads of sweat pricking her forehead and the sudden roar of blood in her ears.

'Izzy?' He was grabbing hold of her now, hot concern blazing from his black eyes. 'For heaven's sake! What's the matter?'

His fingers were biting into her arms, but she shook them off and pulled herself away. Gripping onto the edge of the desk, she sucked in deep breaths of air and prayed she wouldn't pass out.

Tell him.

'Izzy?'

Tell him.

But the words wouldn't come—they stayed stubbornly stuck at the back of her throat and she swallowed them down again. I'll tell him when I know for sure, she thought. When he gets back.

'I'm fine, Tariq. Honestly. I just feel a little off-colour, that's all. Must have been something I ate. And now, if you'll excuse me for a minute, I'd better see about your jet. And then I'll ring through to Fiona and have her sit in on our meeting.'

She waited until she'd spoken to the airfield, and then calmed an excited Fiona's nerves, telling her that of *course* she could cope with running Tariq's office.

And it was only then that Isobel slipped along to the thankfully empty sanctuary of the bathroom, where she was violently sick.

CHAPTER ELEVEN

IT WAS confirmed.

The blue line couldn't be denied any longer—and neither could the test Isobel had done the day before, or the day before that. Because all the tests in the world would only verify what she had known all along. And all the wishing in the world wouldn't change that fact.

She was pregnant with Prince Tariq al Hakam's baby. The man who had told her in no uncertain terms that he had no desire to have a baby was going to be a father.

Feeling caged and restless, she stared out of the window at the red bus which was lumbering down the road below. It was stuffy and hot in her tiny flat, but she felt too tired to face walking to the nearest park. She'd been feeling tired a lot recently…

Little beads of sweat ran in rivulets down her back, despite the thin cotton dress and the windows she'd opened onto the airless day. Somehow summer had arrived without her really noticing—but maybe that wasn't so surprising. In the two weeks since Tariq had flown out to Khayarzah she certainly hadn't been focussing on the weather.

Her thoughts had been full of the man whose seed was growing inside her—and she had a strange feeling of emptiness at being away from work. For once she couldn't even face going down to the cottage, where the memories of Tariq would have been just too vivid.

She'd always thought there was something slightly pathetic about people who haunted the office while they were supposed to be on holiday, and so she hadn't rung in to work either. Fiona would contact her soon enough if she needed her help, and so far she hadn't.

Which made Isobel feel even emptier than she already did. As if she had made herself out to be this fabulous, indispensable addition to the Al Hakam empire when the reality was that she could quite easily be replaced.

And she had heard nothing from Tariq. Not even an e-mail or text to tell her he was alive and well in Khayarzah. If anything proved that it was all over between them, it was the terrifying silence which had mushroomed since his departure.

There had been times when she'd been tempted to pick up the phone, telling herself that she had a perfect right to speak to him. Wasn't he still her boss, even if he was no longer her lover? But she wasn't a good enough actress for that. How could she possibly have a breezy conversation with him, as if nothing was happening, when inside her body their combined cells were multiplying at a frightening speed?

And what would she say? Would she be reduced to asking him whether it was *really* over between them— and hearing an even bigger silence echoing down the line?

No. She was going to have to tell him face to face. She knew that. And soon. But how did you break the news that he was going to be a father to a man who had expressly told you he didn't want children? And not just any father—because this wasn't just any baby. It was a *royal* baby, with *royal* blood coursing through its tiny veins—and that would have all kinds of added complications. She knew enough history to realise that the offspring of ruling families were always especially protected because royal succession was never certain. Wouldn't that make Tariq feel even more trapped into a life he had often bitterly complained about?

But that's only if he accepts responsibility for the child, taunted a voice inside her head. *He might do the modern-day equivalent of what your own father did and walk away from his son or daughter.*

Dunking a camomile teabag in a mug of boiling water, she heard the ring of her doorbell and wondered who it might be. The post, perhaps? Or some sort of delivery? Because nobody just dropped by in London on a weekday lunchtime. It could be a lonely city, she realised with a suddenly sinking heart—and this little flat was certainly no place to bring up a baby.

A baby.

The thought of what lay ahead terrified her, and she was so distracted that she'd almost forgotten about the doorbell when it rang again—more urgently this time. Her thin cotton dress was clinging to her warm thighs as she walked to the door, and she was so preoccupied that she didn't bother to check the spyhole. When she opened the door, the last person she expected to see on her step was Tariq.

She gave a jolt of genuine surprise, her tiredness evaporating as she feasted her eyes on him. She had thought of little else but him since he'd been gone, but the reality of seeing him again was a savage shock to the system. His physical presence dominated his surroundings just as it always did, even if the heavily hooded ebony eyes were watchful and his mouth more unsmiling than she'd ever seen it. He was wearing a shirt—unbuttoned at the neck—with a pair of faded jeans. He looked cool against the day, and the casual attire made him look gloriously touchable—the irony of that did not escape her.

'Tariq,' she said breathlessly, aware of the thunder of her heart. 'This is a…surprise.'

He nodded. A surprise for him, too, if he was being honest. He hadn't intended to come and see her, and yet he'd found himself ordering his driver to bring him to this unfamiliar part of London.

He'd spent a brutal two weeks chasing around Khayarzah looking for his damned cousin, and the office had felt strangely empty when he had returned to find that Izzy was still away. Not that there was anything wrong with Fiona, her replacement. She was a sweet girl, and very eager to please. But she wasn't Izzy. His mouth hardened.

'Can I come in?'

'Of course you can.'

Tariq walked in and she closed the front door behind him. It was the first time he'd ever been there, and he walked into the sitting room and looked around. It was a small room, and much less cluttered than her country cottage. A couple of photos stood on the bookshelf. One was of her standing in a garden aged about eight, squinting her eyes against the bright sunlight. One of those images of childhood you saw everywhere. But he had no such similar pictures of his own. There had been no one around with a camera to record his growing up. Apart from official ones, the only photos he had been in were those big group ones from school—when his darkly olive complexion and powerful build had always made him stand out from the rest of his year.

He turned round as she walked into the room behind him. Her thick red curls had been scraped back and tied in a French plait, and her eyes looked huge. She looked so fragile, he thought—or was that simply because he hadn't seen her for so long?

He frowned. 'I thought you'd have been back at work by now.'

How formal he sounded, she thought. More the time-watching boss than the man who had shown her such sweet pleasure. 'You did say that I could take three weeks. And it's only been two.'

'I know exactly how long it's been, Izzy.'

They stood facing each other, as if trying to acclimatise themselves to this new and unknown stage of their relationship. It felt weird, she thought, to be alone with him and not in his arms. To have a million questions tripping off the edge of her tongue and be too afraid to ask them.

Tell him.

But the words still refused to be spoken. She told herself that she just wanted to embrace these last few moments of peace. A couple more minutes of normality when she could pretend that there was no dreaded truth to be faced. Two minutes more to feast her eyes on the face she'd grown to love and which now made her heart ache with useless longing.

'Did you find your cousin?' she questioned, raking back a strand of hair which had flopped onto her cheek.

Tariq watched as the movement drew his attention to

the lush swell of her breasts, and he felt the first twisting of desire. 'Eventually,' he said.

'And was she okay?'

'I haven't come here to talk about my damned cousin,' he said roughly.

'Oh?' Her voice lifted in hope. 'Then what *have* you come here to talk about?'

He looked at the soft curves of her unpainted lips and suddenly wondered just what he was fighting. Himself or her? 'Nothing.'

'Nothing?' Her eyes were wide with confusion. 'Then why are you here?'

'Why do you think?' he ground out, his black eyes brilliant as temptation overpowered him and he pulled her into his arms. 'For *this*.'

Isobel swayed as their bodies made that first contact and she felt the sudden mad pounding of her heart. Conscience fought with desire as he drove his mouth down on hers, and desire won hands down. Her lips opened and she made a choking little sound of pleasure as she coiled her arms around him. Because this was where she wanted to be more than anywhere else in the world. Back in the arms of Tariq. Because when she was there all her problems receded.

'Oh, *yes!*' Her helpless cry was muffled by the hard seeking of his lips. His urgent hands were in her hair and on her cheeks, and then skating down the sides of her body with a kind of fevered impatience, as if he was relearning her through touch alone. And greedily she began to touch him back.

Tariq groaned as she began to tug at his belt. She was like wildfire on his skin—spreading hunger wherever her soft fingertips alighted. He could have unzipped himself and done it to her right there. But he'd spent too many nights fantasising about this to want to take her without ceremony—and too many days on horseback not to crave the comfort of a bed.

'Where's the bedroom?' he demanded urgently.

Tell him. Before this goes any further, you have to *tell him.*

But she ignored the voice of protest in her head as she pointed a trembling finger towards a door. 'O-over there.'

Effortlessly he picked her up, as he'd done so many times before, pushing open the door with his knee and going straight over to the bed, putting her down in the centre of it. Isobel felt the mattress dip as he straddled her, one knee on either side of her body. With fingers which were not quite steady he began to unbutton her dress, and Isobel held her breath as he pulled it open. But he seemed too full of hunger to study her with his usual searing intensity, and maybe he wouldn't have noticed even if he had, for his black eyes were almost opaque with lust. Instead, he was unclipping her bra and bending his head to capture one sensitised nipple in his hungry mouth.

'I feel as if I have been in the desert,' he moaned against the puckered saltiness of her skin.

'I th-thought you had?'

'Not that kind of desert,' he said grimly.

'What kind, then?'

'*This* kind,' he clarified, his lips on her neck, his fingers hooking inside her little lace panties. 'The sexual kind. A remote place without the sweet embrace of a woman's arms or the welcome opening of her milky thighs.'

Even if they lacked emotion, the words were shockingly erotic, and Isobel lifted her head to give him more access to her neck, her fumbling fingers reaching for the buttons of his shirt and beginning to pull them open. He had come back, hadn't he? And he still wanted her. It was as simple as that. Had he found it more difficult than he'd anticipated to simply let her go?

Hope began to build in time with the growing heat of her body. She helped him wriggle out of his jeans and then the silken boxer shorts, which whispered to the ground in a decadent sigh. His shirt joined her dress on the floor and she looked up at him, strangely shy to see his powerful olive body naked on *her* bed. He seemed larger than life and more magnificent than ever—like a Technicolor character who had just wandered into a black and white film.

He moved over her, and she drew in a deep breath of anticipation. She knew his body so well, and yet she was a stranger to his thoughts. Should she tell him now? When they were physically just about as close as it was possible to be without—

'Oh!' she moaned as he entered her. Too late, she thought fleetingly, as sweet sensation shot through her body and the familiar heat began to build. Take this pleasure that you weren't expecting and give him pleasure in return. Let him see that there can still be sweetness and joy. And then maybe, maybe…

'God, you're tight,' he moaned.

'It's because you're so big,' she breathed.

'I'm always big,' came his mocking boast.

'Big*ger,* then.'

But words became redundant as he began to move

inside her, his mouth on hers as she met his every powerful thrust with the welcoming tilt of her hips.

It was the most bittersweet experience of her life. Amazing, yes—because sex with Tariq always was—but tinged with a certain poignancy, too. She was aware that things were different between them now, that nothing had been resolved. Aware too of what she still hadn't told him. And all those facts combined to heighten every one of her senses.

She felt her climax growing. The beckoning warmth which had been tantalisingly out of reach now became a blissful reality. She felt the first powerful spasm just as he gave his own ragged cry, his movements more frantic as her arms closed around his sweat-sheened back. And she was falling, dissolving, melting. Past thinking as the world fell away from her.

Minutes passed, and when she opened her eyes it was to find Tariq leaning on one elbow, his hooded eyes enigmatic as he studied her.

'Amazing,' he observed after a moment or two, a finger tracing down the side of her cheek as she sucked in a deep breath of air. 'As ever.'

'Yes.'

'You didn't ring me, Izzy.'

'I could say the same thing about you.' She looked straight into his eyes. 'Did you think I would?'

His mouth quirked into an odd kind of smile. He'd thought that her cool evaluation of their relationship having run its course had been a clever kind of bargaining tool. Had she realised that no woman had ever done that to him before? That the tantalising prospect of someone finishing with him was guaranteed to keep him interested? 'Of course I did,' he replied truthfully.

Isobel shifted restlessly. The warmth was ebbing away from her body now, and she knew she couldn't put it off much longer. Yet some instinctive air of preservation made her want to gather together all the facts first. 'Why did you come here today, Tariq?'

He smiled. 'I thought I'd just demonstrated that—to our mutual satisfaction.'

Her own smile was tight. So that had been a *demonstration,* had it? In the midst of her post-orgasmic glow, it was all too easy to forget his arrogance. 'For sex?' she queried. 'Was that why you came?'

'Yes. No. Oh, Izzy—I don't know.' He shook his head and gave a reluctant sigh, not wanting to analyse the powerful impulse which had brought him to her door today. Couldn't she just enjoy the here and now and be satisfied with that? 'Whatever it is, I've missed it.'

'If it's just sex you can get that from plenty of other women,' she pointed out.

'Then maybe it isn't just sex,' he said slowly. He lifted her chin with the tips of his fingers and she was caught in the brilliant ebony blaze of his eyes. 'Maybe what I should have said is that I've missed *you.*'

Isobel's heart missed a beat, and all the wistful longings she had suppressed as a matter of survival now came bubbling to the surface. 'You've said that before,' she whispered. 'When you've come back from a trip.'

'Yes, I know. But it was different this time—knowing that you weren't going to be here. Telling me that it was over made me realise that I could lose you—and I don't want to.'

Her heart crashed against her ribcage. 'You don't?'

'No.' He brushed his lips over hers. Back and forth and back and forth—until he could feel her shivering response. 'What we have together is better than anything I've had with anyone else. I'm not promising you for ever, Izzy, because I don't think I can do that. And I haven't changed my mind about children. But if you think you can be content with what we've got…. Well, then, let's go for it.'

His words mocked her. Taunted her. They filled her with horror at what she must now do. *Let's go for it.* That was the kind of thing a football coach said during the half-time pep talk—not a man who was telling you that you meant something really special to him. And Isobel realised what a mess she had made of everything. Despite her determination not to follow in her mother's footsteps, she had ended up doing exactly that. She had hitched her star to a man who was unavailable. In Tariq's case it wasn't because he was married but because he was emotionally unavailable. And in a roundabout way he'd just told her that he always would be.

I haven't changed my mind about children.

So now what did she do?

Feeling sick with nerves, she sat up, her unruly curls falling over her shoulders and providing some welcome cover for her aching breasts.

'Before you say any more, there's something I have to tell you, Tariq.' She sucked in a shuddering breath, more nervous than she'd ever been as he suddenly tensed. She met the narrowed question in his ebony eyes. 'You see… I'm going to have a baby.'

CHAPTER TWELVE

THE silence in the room emphasised the sounds outside, which floated through the open window. The faint roar of traffic a long way below. The occasional toot of a car. A low plane flying overhead.

Isobel stared down at Tariq's still figure, lying on the bed, and ironically she was reminded of the time when he'd lain in hospital. When he'd looked so lost and so vulnerable and her feelings for him had undergone a complete change.

But he wasn't looking vulnerable now.

Far from it. She watched the expressions which shifted across his face like shadows. Shock morphing into disbelief and then quickly settling itself into a look which she'd been expecting all along.

Anger.

Still he did not move. Only his eyes did—hard and impenetrable as two pieces of polished jet as they fixed themselves on her. 'Please tell me that this is some kind of sick joke, Izzy.'

Izzy trembled at all the negative implications behind his response. 'It's not a joke—why would I joke about something like that? I'm…I'm going to have a baby. Your baby.'

'No!' He moved then, fast as a panther, reaching down to grab his jeans before getting off the bed to roughly pull them on, knowing he couldn't face having such a conversation with her when he was completely naked. Because what if his traitorous body began to harden with desire, even as an impotent kind of rage began to spiral up inside him as he realised the full extent of her betrayal?

He zipped up his jeans and tugged on his shirt. And only then did he advance towards her with such a look of dark fury contorting his features that Isobel shrank back against the pillows.

'Tell me it isn't true,' he said, in a voice of pure venom.

'I can't. Because it is,' she whispered.

Tariq stared at her. She had known that he never wanted to be a father. She'd *known* because he'd told her! He'd even told her just now. After they'd…they'd… 'How the hell can you be pregnant when you're on the pill?'

'Because accidents sometimes happen—'

'What? You *accidentally* forgot to take it, did you?'

'No!'

'How, then?' he demanded hotly. *'How,* Izzy?'

Distractedly she held up her hands, as if she was surrendering. 'I had a mild touch of food poisoning after I ate some fish! It must have been then.'

'Must it?'

Abruptly he turned his back on her and went over to stand beside the window, staring down at the busy London street. When he turned back his face was a mask. She had never seen him look quite like that before—all cold and empty—and suddenly Isobel realised that whatever feelings he might have had for her, they had just died.

'Or was it "accidentally on purpose"?' he said slowly. 'When did it happen?'

'It was…' She swallowed. 'It was around the time when I met Zahid and Francesca.'

'You mean the *King* and *Queen?*' he corrected imperiously, unknown emotions making him retreat behind protocol—despite his conflicting feelings towards it. He remembered the way she'd held Omar that night. The way she'd looked at him over the mop of ebony curls with that soppy soft look that women sometimes assumed whenever there was a baby around.

'What? Did you look at Francesca?' he questioned. 'See another ordinary Englishwoman very much like yourself? Did you look around you and see all the wealth and status at her fingertips and think: *I wouldn't mind some of that for myself?* After all, you also had a royal lover—just as Francesca had once done. The only difference is that she didn't get herself pregnant in order to secure her future!'

If she hadn't been naked she would have lunged at him. As it was, Isobel got off the bed and grabbed at her dress to hide her vulnerability—the outward kind, anyway. For her heart was vulnerable, too—and she felt as if he had crushed it in his fist.

'I can't b-believe you could think that!' she stuttered as she started doing up the buttons, her shaking fingers making the task almost impossible.

'I suppose I can't really blame you,' he mused, almost as if she hadn't objected, a slow tide of rage still building inside him. 'Most women seem hell-bent on marriage—and the more prestigious the marriage, the better. And you can't do much better than a prince, can you?'

'You must be joking,' she hissed back. 'You might be a prince, but you also happen to be an arrogant and overbearing piece of—'

'Let's skip the insults, shall we?' he snapped, as he tried to get his head around the fact that in her belly his child grew. *His child!* A child he'd never asked for nor wanted. A child he would never be able to love…that he didn't know *how* to love. 'I thought you were into honesty, Izzy? Except now I come to think about it you haven't been very honest all the way along, have you?'

She stared at him uncomprehendingly. 'What are you talking about?'

'Just how long have you known about this pregnancy?'

She met the accusation which blazed from his face. 'For a couple of weeks,' she admitted.

A strange light entered his eyes. He looked like someone who had been trying to solve a puzzle and had just found the last missing piece stuffed down the back of the sofa. 'When we were in bed—the morning I got the phone call from Khayarzah about Leila—you knew you were pregnant then, didn't you?'

She shook her head. 'I didn't *know.* I had my suspicions, but I wasn't sure.'

'But you didn't bother to tell me? Even today you kept quiet. You let me come here and…' She'd let him lose himself in the refuge of her arms. Lulling him into sweet compliance with the erotic promise of her body.

'We had *sex,* Tariq!' she declared brutally. 'Let's not make it into something it wasn't!'

She could see the faint shock which had dilated his

eyes, but his reaction was breathing resolve into her and
Isobel felt something of her old spirit return. Was she
going to allow him to speak to her as if she was some
worthless piece of nothing he'd found on the bottom of
his shoe? As if she counted for nothing?

'I didn't tell you because I knew how you would
react,' she raged. 'Because I knew that you'd be arrogant enough to think it was all some giant conspiracy
theory instead of the kind of slip-up that's been happening to men and women ever since they started fornicat-
ing!'

His eyes bored into her. 'I'm assuming that marriage
is what you want?'

Isobel's eyes widened. Hadn't he been listening to a
word she'd been saying? 'You must be *mad,*' she whispered. 'Completely certifiable if you think that I'd ever
want to sign up for life with a man like *you.* A man so
full of ego that he thinks a woman will get herself deliberately pregnant in order to trap him.'

'You think it's never been done before?' he scorned.

'Not by me,' she defended fiercely, closing her eyes
as a wave of terrible sadness washed over her. 'Now,
please go, Tariq. Get out of here before either of us says
anything more we might regret.'

His impulse was to resist—for he was used to calling the shots. Until he realised that this wasn't the first
time Izzy had called the shots. It had been her, after all,
who'd had the courage to end the relationship. And, yes,
he had been arrogant enough to think that she might just
be playing a very sophisticated game to bring him to
heel.

But Izzy didn't do game-playing, he realised. She
hadn't told him she thought she was pregnant because

she'd feared his reaction—and hadn't he just proved those fears a thousand times over? He looked at the haunted expression on her whitened face and suddenly felt a savage jerk of guilt.

'I'm sorry,' he said suddenly.

Her eyes swimming with unshed tears, she looked at him. 'What? Sorry for the things you said? Or sorry that you ever got involved with me in the first place?'

He flinched as her accusations hit home. 'Sit down, Izzy.'

She ignored the placatory note in his voice. He thought he could spew out all that *stuff* and that now she'd instantly become malleable? How dared he tell her to sit down in her own home? 'I'll sit down once you've gone.'

'I'm not going anywhere until you do. Because there are things we need to discuss.'

She wanted to tell him that he had forfeited all rights to any discussion with his cruel comments. But she couldn't bring herself to do that. Because Tariq was her baby's father. And didn't she know better than anyone how great and gaping the hole could be in a child's life if it didn't have one?

'And we will,' she said, sucking in another deep breath, her hand instinctively fluttering to her still-flat belly. 'Just not now, when emotions are running so high.'

Tariq watched the unfamiliar maternal movement and something tugged at his heart. To his astonishment, he found that he wanted to ask her a million questions. He wanted to ask whether she'd eaten that day, whether she had been sleeping properly at night. He'd never asked for this baby, and he didn't particularly want it, but that didn't mean he couldn't feel empathy for the woman who carried that baby, did it?

He looked at her with a detachment he'd never used before. She *did* look different, he decided. More delicate than usual, yes—but there was a kind of strength about her, too. It radiated off her like the sunlight which caught the pale fire of her hair.

He should have been gathering her in his arms now and congratulating her. Laying a proprietorial hand over her belly and looking with pride into her shining eyes. If he had been a normal man—like other men—then he would have been able to do all those things. But he knew that all he had was a piece of ice where his heart should be, and that was why they were just gazing at each other suspiciously across a small bedroom.

But this was no time for reflection. Whatever his own feelings, this had to be all about Izzy. He had to think practically. To help her in any way that he could.

'You obviously won't be coming back to work,' he said.

Impatiently, she shook her head. 'I hadn't even thought about work.'

'Well, you don't have to. I want you to know that you don't have to worry about anything. I'll make sure you're financially secure.'

Now she observed him with a kind of fury. What? Buy her off? Did he think that she'd be satisfied with that as compensation for the lack of the marriage she'd supposedly been angling for? She thought of her own mother—how she had always gone out to work and supported herself. And hadn't Isobel been grateful for that role model? To see a woman survive and thrive and not be beaten down because her hopes of love had not materialised?

'Actually, I've decided that I want to carry on working,' she said. 'And besides, what on earth would I do all day—sit around knitting bootees? Plenty of women work right up until the final weeks. I'll…I'll look for another job, obviously.'

But she was filled with dread at the thought of going from agency to agency and having to hide her pregnancy. Who would want to take on a woman in her condition and offer her any kind of security for the future?

'You don't need to look for another job,' he said harshly. 'You could come back to work for me in an instant. Or I could arrange to have you work for one of the partners, if you don't think you could tolerate being in the same office as me.'

Isobel swallowed. She thought of starting work for someone new, with her pregnancy growing all the time. She wasn't aware of how much other people at the Al Hakam corporation knew about their affair. After all, it wasn't the most likely of partnerships, and Tariq hadn't exactly been squiring her around town. Would people put two and two together and come up with the right answer? Would her position be compromised once any new boss knew who the father of her baby was?

She stared at him, wondering what kind of foolish instinct it was which made her realise that she actually wanted to work for *him*. For there was a certain kind of security in the familiar—especially when there was so much happening in her life. At least with Tariq she wouldn't have to hide anything, or pretend. Tariq would protect her. Because, despite his angry words of earlier, she sensed that he would make sure that nothing and nobody ever harmed her, or her baby.

'I think I could just about tolerate it,' she said slowly. She met his eyes, knowing that she needed to believe in the words she was about to speak—because otherwise there could be no way forward. She had thought that if she quietly loved him then he might learn how to love her back—even if it was only a little bit. She had thought that maybe she could change him. But she had been wrong. Because you couldn't change somebody else—you could only change yourself. And Tariq didn't want love—not in any form, it seemed. He didn't want to receive it, and he didn't want to give it either. Not to her—and not to their baby.

'We must agree to give each other the personal space we need,' she continued steadily. 'The relationship is over, Tariq—we both know that. But there's no reason why we can't behave civilly towards each other.'

He was aware of an overwhelming sense of relief that she wasn't going to be launching out on her own. But something in the quiet dignity of her statement made his heart grow heavy with a gloomy realisation. As if somehow there had been something wonderful hovering on the periphery of his life.

And he had just let it go.

CHAPTER THIRTEEN

'THE press have been on the phone again, Tariq.'

Tariq looked up to see Izzy hovering in the doorway of his office, lit from behind like a Botticelli painting, with her hair falling down over her shoulders like liquid honey. Although she was wearing a loose summer dress and still very slim, at four months pregnant there was no disguising the curving softness of her belly. A whisper ran over his skin. For weeks now he had been watching her. Trying to imagine what his child must be like as it grew inside her.

And now he knew.

Aware of the sudden lump which had risen in his throat, he swallowed and raised his brows at her questioningly. 'What did they want?'

Isobel stared at the brilliant gleam of the Sheikh's black eyes, and the faint stubble on his chin which made him look like a modern-day pirate. Had she been out of her mind yesterday when she'd told him that he could accompany her to the doctor if he wanted to see her latest scan? What crazy hormonal blip had prompted *that?* She'd been expecting a curt thanks, followed by a terse refusal, but to her surprise he had leapt at the opportunity, his face wreathed in what had looked like a delighted smile. A most un-Tariq kind of smile. And then he'd acted the part of the caring father as if he actually *meant* it—clucking round her as if he'd spent a lifetime looking after pregnant women.

In fact, when he'd been helping her into the limousine—something which she'd told him was entirely unnecessary—his hand had brushed over hers, and the feeling which had passed between them had been electric. It was the first time that they had touched since their uneasy truce—and hadn't it started her senses screaming, taunting her with what she was missing? Their eyes had met in a clashing gaze of suppressed desire and she had felt an overwhelming need to be in his arms again. A need she had quickly quashed by climbing into the limousine and sitting as far away from him as possible.

She sighed with impatience at her inability to remain immune to him, then turned her mind back to his question about the press. 'They were asking why the Sheikh of Khayarzah was seen accompanying his assistant to an obstetrician's for her scan yesterday.'

'They saw us?'

'Apparently.' Her eyes were full of appeal. 'Tariq, I should have realised this might happen.'

Maybe she should have done. But to his surprise he was glad she hadn't. Because mightn't that have stopped her from giving him the chance to see the baby he had never wanted? He still didn't know why she had done that—and he had never expected to feel this overwhelming sense of gratitude. Perhaps he should have realised himself that someone might notice them, but the truth was he wouldn't have cared even if he'd known that a million journalists were lurking around.

He hadn't cared about anything except what he was to

discover in that darkened room in Harley Street, watching while a doctor had moved a sensory pad over the jelly-covered swell of her abdomen.

Suddenly he'd seen an incomprehensible image spring to life on the screen. To Tariq, it had looked like a high-definition snowstorm—until he had seen a rapid and rhythmical beat and realised that he was looking at a beating heart. And that was when everything had changed. When he'd stopped thinking of Izzy's pregnancy as something theoretical and seen reality there, right before his eyes.

His heart had lurched as he'd stared at the form of his son—or daughter—and the doctor had said something on the lines of the two of them being a 'happy couple'. And that had been when Izzy's voice had rung out loud and clear.

'But we're not,' she had said firmly, turning to look at Tariq, her tawny eyes glittering with hurt and challenge. 'The Sheikh and I are not together, Doctor.'

Tariq had flinched beneath that condemnatory blaze—but could he blame her? Didn't he deserve comments and looks like that after his outrageous reaction when she'd told him about the baby? Even though he had been doing his damnedest to make it up to her ever since. Short of peeling grapes and bringing them into her office each morning, he was unsure of what else he could do to make it better. And he still wasn't sure if his conciliatory attitude was having any effect on her, because she had been exhibiting a stubbornness he hadn't known she possessed.

Proudly, she had refused all his offers of lifts home or time off. Had turned up her pretty little nose at his studiedly casual enquiry that she might want to join him for dinner some time. And told him that, no, she had no desire to go shopping for a cot. Or to have her groceries delivered from a chi-chi London store. Pregnant women were not invalids, she'd told him crisply—and she would manage the way she had always managed. So he had been forced to bite back his frustration as she had stubbornly shopped for food each lunchtime, bringing back bulging bags which she had lain on the floor of her office. Though he had put his foot down about her carrying them home and told her in no uncertain terms that his limousine would drop the bags off at her apartment.

Now, as she walked into his office and shut the door behind her, he realised that the Botticelli resemblance had been illusory—because beneath her pale and Titian beauty she looked tired.

'We're going to have to decide what to say when the question of paternity comes up,' she told him, wondering why it had never occurred to her that people would want to know who the father of her baby was. 'Because it will. I mean, people here have been dropping hints about it for ages, and that journalist was on the verge of asking me outright about it today—I could tell he was.'

His voice was gentle. 'What do you want to do, Izzy?'

She gave a short laugh. 'I don't think what I *want* is the kind of question you should be asking, Tariq.'

What she wanted was the impossible—to be carrying the child of someone who loved her instead of resenting her for having fallen pregnant. Someone who would hold her in the small hours of the morning when the world seemed a very big and frightening place. But those kinds of thoughts were dangerous. Even shameful. Because wasn't the truth that she still wanted Tariq to be that man—even though it was never going to happen?

To Isobel's terror, she'd discovered that you didn't just fall out of love with a man because he'd spoken to you harshly or judged you in the worst possible way.

'I don't know what I want,' she said quietly.

He stared at her, and a flare of determination coursed through him. He was aware that he could no longer sit on the sidelines and watch, like some kind of dazed ghost. Up until now he had allowed Izzy to dictate the terms of how they dealt with this because he had been racked with guilt about his own conduct. He had given her the personal space she had demanded, telling himself that it was in her best interests for him to do so. He had scrabbled deep inside himself and discovered unknown pockets of patience and fortitude. He had acted in a way which a few short months ago would have seemed unimaginable.

But it was still not enough. Not nearly enough. Close examination of her bleached face made him realise that he now had to step up to the mark and start taking control. That to some extent Izzy was weak and helpless in this situation—even though she had shown such shining courage so far.

He stood up, walked over to her, and took hold of her elbow. 'Come and sit down,' he said, guiding her firmly towards the sofa. 'Please.'

Her lips trembled and so did her body, responding instantly to his touch, and silently she raged against her traitorous hormones. But it was a sign of her weariness that she let him guide her over to the sofa.

Heavily, she slumped down and looked up at him. 'Well?'

He sat down beside her, seeing the momentary suspicion which clouded her eyes as, casting around in his mind, he struggled to find the right words to say. Clumsy sentences hovered at the edges of his lips until he realised that nobody really gave a damn about the words—only about the sentiment behind them. 'I want to tell you how sorry I am, Izzy. Truly sorry.'

She shook her head. 'You've said sorry before,' she said, blinking back the stupid tears which were springing to her eyes and which seemed never far away these days.

'That was back then—when neither of us was thinking straight. When the air was full of confusion and hurt. But it's important to me that you understand that I mean it. That in the cold light of day I wish I could take back those words I should never have said. And that I wish I could make it up to you in some way.'

She stared at him, thinking how strange it was to hear him sounding so genuinely contrite. Because Tariq didn't *do* apology. In his arrogance he thought he was always right. But he didn't look arrogant now, she realised, and something in that discovery made her want to meet him halfway.

'We both said things we shouldn't have said,' she conceded. 'Things we can't unsay which are probably best forgotten. I'm sorry that I didn't tell you about the baby sooner.'

'I don't care about that. Your reasons for that are perfectly understandable.' There was a pause. The heavy lids of his eyes almost concealed their hectic ebony glitter. 'There's only one thing I really care about, Izzy—and that's whether you can ever find it in your heart to forgive me?'

She bit her lip as hurt pride fought with an instinctive desire to make amends. Because wasn't this something she was going to have to teach her baby—that forgiveness should always follow repentance? And there was absolutely no doubt from the stricken expression on Tariq's face that his remorse was genuine.

'Yes, Tariq,' she said softly. 'I can forgive you.'

He stared at her, but her generous clemency only heightened his sense of disquiet. It made him realise then that if they wanted some kind of future together he had to go one step further.

But it wasn't easy—because everything in him rebelled against further disclosure. Wasn't it his ability to close off the painful experiences in his life which made him so single-minded? Wasn't it his reluctance to actually *feel* things which had protected him from the knocks and isolation of his childhood? Success had come easily to Tariq because he hadn't allowed himself to be influenced by emotion. To him, emotion was something that you blocked out. Because how else could he have survived if he had not done that?

Yet if he failed to find the courage to confront all the darkness he'd locked away so long ago then wouldn't he be left with this terrible lack of resolution? As if he could never really get close to Izzy again? As if he was seeing her through a thick wall of glass? And what was the point of trying to protect himself from emotional pain if he was going to experience it anyway?

'There are some things you need to know about me,' he said. 'Things which may explain the monster I have been.'

'You're no *monster*,' she breathed instantly. 'My baby's not having a monster for a father!'

'There are things you need to know,' he repeated, even though his lips curved in a brief smile at her passionate defence. 'Things about me and my life that I need to explain—to try to make you understand.'

He frowned. He struggled to put his feelings into words—because in a way wasn't he trying to make *himself* understand his own past?

'I've never had a problem with the way I live,' he said. 'My work life was a triumph and my personal life was…manageable. I was happy enough with the affairs I had. I liked women and they liked me. But as soon they started getting close—well, I wanted out. Always.'

Isobel nodded. Hadn't she witnessed it enough times before experiencing it for herself? 'And why do you think that was?' she questioned quietly.

'Because I had no idea how to relate to people. I had no idea how to do real relationships,' he answered simply. 'My mother was so ill after my birth that I was kept away from her. My father was run off his feet with the ongoing wars with Sharifah—so my relationship with him was pretty non-existent, too. And the nurses and nannies who were employed to look after me would never dare to show *love* towards a royal child, for that would be considered presumptuous. Children only know their own experience—but even if at times I felt lost or lonely I did not ever show it. In that strongly driven and very masculine environment it was always frowned on to show any weakness or vulnerability.'

Vulnerability. The word stuck to her like a piece of dry grass. It took her back to when she'd seen him lying injured on the hospital bed—for hadn't it been that self-same vulnerability which had made her feelings towards him change and her heart start to melt? Hadn't it been in that moment when she'd started to fall in love with Tariq? When he'd shown a side of himself which he'd always kept hidden before?

'Go on,' she said softly.

'You know that they sent me away to school in England at seven? In a way, my life was just as isolated as it had been in the palace. For a while I was the only foreign pupil—and I was the only royal one. And of course I was bullied.'

'You? Bullied? Oh, come on, Tariq! As if anyone would dare try.'

He gave a wry smile. 'There are more ways to hurt someone than with your fists. I was certainly excluded on a social level—never invited to the homes of my classmates. My saving grace was that I made every sports team going and I had first pick of all the girls.' He shrugged as he realised that was about the time when he had begun to use the veneer of arrogance to protect him. 'Though of course that only increased the feelings of resentment against me.'

'I can imagine.' She sighed as she looked at him, longing to take him in her arms but too scared to dare try. Still afraid that nothing had really changed and that he would hurt her again as he had hurt her before. And besides, if he really meant it then didn't he have to come to *her*?

He saw the fear and the pain which clouded her face, and it mirrored the aching deep inside him. A terrible sense of frustration washed over him as he looked into her tawny eyes.

'Oh, Izzy—can't you see that I'm a novice at all this stuff? That for the first time in my life I don't know what to do or what to say? I've never dared love anyone before, because I didn't want to. And then when I did—I didn't know how to.'

She blinked at him, unsure whether she'd just imagined that. Love? Who'd said anything about love?

'Tariq?' she questioned, in confusion.

But he shook his head, determined to finish what he had begun, and it was like opening up the floodgates and letting his heart run free.

'In you, I found something I'd never known with any other woman. Even before we became lovers you gave me an unwitting glimpse of what life *could* be like. Those days I spent in your cottage—I'd never felt so at peace. It felt like *home*,' he realised wonderingly. 'A home I'd never really known before. Only it took me a long time to realise what was staring me in the face.' He paused. 'Just like something else which was there all the time—only I was too pig-headed to admit it. And that's the fact that I love you, Izzy. Simple as that—I just do.'

Still she didn't dare believe him—because she sensed that there would be no coming back from this. That if she discovered his words were nothing but a sham then her pain would never heal. But the light which gleamed from his ebony eyes cut through the last of her resistance. It broke through the brick wall she had erected around her heart and made it crumble away as if it were made of sand.

She lifted her fingertips to his lips.

'I love you,' he said fiercely. 'And if I have to tell you a thousand times a day for the rest of our lives before you will believe me, then so be it—I will.'

A little awkwardly, given the bump of the baby, she scrambled to her knees and sat on his lap, facing him, her hands smoothing over his face, touching his skin with a trembling delight. 'Oh, Tariq. My sweet, darling Tariq.'

'I love you, Izzy,' he said brokenly. 'And I was a stubborn fool to have tried so hard *not* to love you.' He stared at her, willing the tawny eyes to give him the only answer his heart craved. 'Just tell me it's not too late.'

'Of course it isn't,' she whispered, as she dragged in a great shuddering breath of relief. 'I think we've managed to save it in the nick of time. And thank goodness for that—because I love you too, Tariq al Hakam, and you'd better believe it. I've loved you for a long, long time, I think. Since the time you lay injured—or maybe even before that. Maybe it just took your brush with death to show me what already lay deep in my heart. And I love the baby that grows beneath my breast—*your* baby.'

He stared at her, her soft understanding suddenly hard to take. 'You are too sweet, Izzy. Too kind to a man who has done nothing but—'

'No!' she contradicted, her firm denial butting into his words. 'I'm just fighting for what is mine—and you *are* mine, Tariq al Hakam. You and this baby are all mine.'

'*Our* baby,' he said fiercely.

She touched her lips to the palm of his hand, seeing the last of the pain and regret leave his eyes as they were eclipsed by love. And she felt her heart soar as the bitterness of the past dissolved into the glorious present. 'Our baby,' she agreed.

He caught her against him and brought her head close to his. 'Beautiful, Isobel,' he whispered against her soft cheek. 'Outside and in, your loveliness shines like the moon in the night sky.'

'Poetry, too?' she questioned unsteadily. 'I didn't know you did poetry.'

'Neither did I. But then, I could never really see the point of it before.'

'Just kiss me, Tariq,' she whispered urgently. 'Kiss me quickly—before I wake up and discover this is all a dream.'

His lips grazed hers, slowly at first, and their eyes were wide open as they watched themselves kiss. And then hunger and passion and love turned the kiss into something else, and Izzy's breath began to quicken as she pressed her swollen breasts against him.

'Wait a minute,' he said, dragging his lips away and hearing her little sigh of objection. Carefully disengaging himself, Tariq got up from the sofa and went over to his desk, where he bent over and spoke into the intercom. 'Fiona, can you hold all calls, please? Izzy and I don't want to be disturbed for the rest of the day.' He turned and dazzled her with a blazing look of love. 'Do we, darling?'

In the outer office, Fiona couldn't believe it. Sheikh Tariq al Hakam had just called Isobel Mulholland *darling* and asked that they be left alone for the rest of the day! It was the sort of *unbelievable* statement which was impossible for her to keep to herself, and she went straight down to the water-cooler to tell anyone who would listen.

But perhaps that was what Tariq had intended.

Rumours were soon spreading like wildfire through the building, and by five o'clock the evening newspapers were all carrying the news that the Playboy Prince was going to be a daddy.

EPILOGUE

IT WAS a source of enormous frustration to Tariq that Izzy refused to marry him—no matter how many times he asked her.

'Why not?' he demanded one morning, exasperated by what he perceived as her stubbornness. 'Is it because of all those stupid accusations I made when you told me—when I said you'd deliberately got yourself pregnant in order to trap me?'

'No, darling,' she replied with serene honesty—because those days of fury and confusion were long behind them. 'That has absolutely nothing to do with it.'

'Why, then, Izzy?'

Isobel wasn't quite sure. Was it because things seemed so perfect now? So much the way she'd always longed for them to be that she was terrified of jeopardising them with unnecessary change? As if marriage would be like a superstitious person walking on a crack in the pavement—and bad luck would come raining down on them?

It had become a bit of a game—which Tariq was determined to win, because he always won in the end. But winning was not uppermost in his thoughts. Mostly he wanted to marry Izzy because he loved her—with a love which had blown him away and continued to do so.

'You'll be a princess,' he promised.

'But I don't *want* to be a princess! I'm happy just the way I am.'

'You are an infuriating woman,' he growled.

'And you just like getting your own way!'

His lips curved into a reluctant smile. 'That much is true,' he conceded.

He asked her again on the morning she gave birth to a beautiful baby daughter and he felt as if his heart would burst with pride and emotion. The nurse had just handed him the tiny bundle, and he held the swathed scrap and stared down at eyes which were blue and wide—shaped just like her mother's. But she had a shock of hair which was pure black—like his. Wonderingly, he touched her perfectly tiny little hand and it closed over his finger like a starfish—a bond made in that moment which only death would break.

His eyes were wet when he looked up and the lump in his throat made speaking difficult, but he didn't care. 'Why won't you marry me, Izzy?' he questioned softly.

Slumped back against the pillows—dazed but elated—Isobel regarded her magnificent Sheikh. This powerful man who cradled their tiny baby so gently in his arms. Why, indeed? Because she was stubborn? Or because she wanted him to know that marriage wasn't important to her? That she wasn't one of those women who were angling for the big catch, determined to get his ring on her finger? That she loved him for who he was and not for what he could give her?

'Doesn't it please you to know that I'm confident enough in your love that I don't need the fuss of a legal ceremony?' she questioned demurely.

'No,' he growled. 'It doesn't. I want to give our girl some security.'

And that was when their eyes met and she realised that he was offering her what her mother had never had. What *she* had never had. A proper hands-on father who wasn't going anywhere. Here was a man who wasn't being forced to commit but who genuinely *wanted* to. So what was stopping her?

'I don't want a big wedding,' she warned.

He bit back his smile of triumph. 'Neither do I.' But her unexpected acquiescence had filled him with even more joy than he had thought possible, and he turned his attention to the now sleeping baby in his arms. 'We'll have to think about what to call her.'

'A Khayarzah name, I think.'

'I think so, too.'

After much consultation they named her Nawal, which meant 'gift'—which was what she was—and when she was six months old they took her to Khayarzah, where their private visit turned into a triumphant tour. The people went out of their way to welcome this second son and his family into their midst—and Tariq at last accepted his royal status and realised that he had no wish to change it. For it was his daughter's heritage as well as his, he realised.

It was in Khayarzah one night, when they were lying in bed in their room in the royal palace, that Tariq voiced something which had been on his mind for some time.

'You know, we could always try to find your father,' he said slowly. 'It would be an easy thing to do. That's if you want to.'

Isobel stirred. The bright moonlight from the clear

desert sky flooded in through the unshuttered windows as she lifted her eyes to study her husband.

'What on earth makes you say that?'

Expansive and comfortable, with her warm body nestling against him, Tariq shrugged. 'I've been thinking about it ever since we had Nawal. How much of a gap there would be in my life if I didn't have her. If I had never had the opportunity to be a father.'

'But—'

'I know he deserted your mother,' he said softly. 'And I'm not saying that you have to find him. Or that even if we do you have to forgive him. I'm just saying that the possibility is there—that's all.'

It was his mention of the word *forgive* which made Isobel think carefully about his words. Because didn't forgiveness play a big part in every human life—their own included? And once her husband had planted the seed of possibility it took root and grew. Surely she owed Nawal the chance of meeting her only surviving grandparent…?

Tariq was right. It *was* easy to find a man who had just 'disappeared' twenty-five years ago—especially when you had incalculable wealth and resources at your fingertips.

Isobel didn't know what she had been expecting—but it certainly wasn't a rather sad-looking man with grey hair and tawny eyes. Recently widowed, John Franklin was overjoyed to meet her and her family. His own personal regret was that he and his wife had never been able to have children of their own.

It was a strange and not altogether comfortable moment when she shook hands for the first time with the man who had given life to her over a quarter of a cen-

tury ago. But then he saw the baby, and he smiled, and
Isobel's heart gave an unexpected wrench. For in it
she saw something of herself—and something of her
daughter, too. It was a smile which would carry on down
through the generations. And there was something in
that smile which wiped away all the bitterness of the
past.

'You're very quiet,' observed Tariq as they drove
away from John Franklin's modest house. 'No regrets?'

Isobel shook her head. What was it they said? That
you regretted the things you didn't do, rather than the
things you did? 'None,' she answered honestly. 'He was
good with Nawal. I think they will be good for each
other in the future.'

'Ah, Izzy,' said Tariq. 'You are a sweet and loving
woman.'

'I can afford to be,' she said happily. 'Because I've
got you.'

Their main home was to be in London, although
whenever it was possible they still escaped to Izzy's
tiny country cottage, where their love had first been ignited. Because maybe Francesca had been right, Tariq
conceded. Maybe it *was* important that royal children
knew what it was like to be ordinary.

He didn't buy the 'Blues' football team after all. It
came to him in a blinding flash one night that he didn't
actually *like* football. Besides, what was the point of
acquiring a prestigious soccer team simply because he
could, when its acquisition brought with it nothing but
envy and unwanted press attention? He wanted to keep

the cameras away from his beloved family, as much as possible. Anyway, Polo was his game.

Real men didn't prance around in a pair of shorts, kicking a ball.

Real men rode horses.

* * * * *

The Sultan's Choice

ABBY GREEN

Abby Green got hooked on Mills & Boon® romances while still in her teens, when she stumbled across one belonging to her grandmother in the west of Ireland. After many years of reading them voraciously, she sat down one day and gave it a go herself. Happily, after a few failed attempts, Mills & Boon bought her first manuscript.

Abby works freelance in the film and TV industry, but thankfully the four a.m. starts and the stresses of dealing with recalcitrant actors are becoming more and more infrequent, leaving her more time to write!

She loves to hear from readers and you can contact her through her website at www.abby-green.com. She lives and works in Dublin.

This is for Ann K.
Thank you for everything.

CHAPTER ONE

'I'M not marrying her for her looks, Adil. I'm marrying her for the myriad reasons she will make a good Queen of Al-Omar. If I'd wanted nothing but looks I could have married my last mistress. The last thing I need is the distraction of a beautiful woman.'

Princess Samia Binte Rashad al Abbas sat rigid with shock outside the Sultan of Al-Omar's private office in his London home. He hadn't been informed that she was there yet as he'd been on this call. His secretary, who had left momentarily, had inadvertently left his door slightly ajar—subjecting Samia to the deep rumble of the Sultan's voice and his even more cataclysmic words.

The drawling voice came again, tinged with something deeply cynical. 'That she may well appear, but certain people have always speculated that when the time came to take my bride I'd choose conservatively, and I'd hate to let the bookies down.'

Samia's cheeks burned. She could well imagine what the voice on the other end of the phone had said, something to the effect of her being *boring*.

Even if she hadn't heard this explicit conversation Samia already knew what the Sultan of Al-Omar planned to discuss with her. He wanted her hand in marriage. She hadn't slept a wink and had come here today half hoping that it would all be a terrible mistake. To hear him lay out in such bald terms that he was clearly in favour of this plan was shocking. And not only that but he evidently considered it to be a done deal!

She'd only met him once before, about eight years previously, when she'd gone to one of his legendary annual birthday parties in B'harani, the capital of Al-Omar, with her brother. Kaden had taken her before she'd gone on to England to finish her studies, in a bid to try and help her overcome her chronic shyness. Samia had been at that awfully awkward age where her limbs had had a mind of their own, her hair had been a ball of frizz and she'd still been wearing the thick bifocals that had plagued her life since she was small.

After an excruciatingly embarrassing moment in which she'd knocked over a small antique table laden with drinks, and the crowd of glittering and beautiful people had turned to look at her, she'd fled for sanctuary, finding it in a dimly lit room which had turned out to be a library.

Samia ruthlessly clamped down on *that* even more disturbing memory just as the Sultan's voice rose to an audible level again.

'Adil, I appreciate that as my lawyer you want to ensure I'm making the right choice, but I can assure you that she ticks all the boxes—I'm not so shallow that I can't make a marriage like this work. The stability and reputation of my country comes first, and I need a wife who will enhance that.'

Mortification twisted Samia's insides. He was referring to the fact that she was a world apart from his usual women. She didn't need to overhear this conversation to know that. Samia didn't want to marry this man, and she certainly wasn't going to sit there and wait for humiliation to walk up and slap her in the face.

* * *

Sultan Sadiq Ibn Kamal Hussein put down the phone, every muscle tensed. Claustrophobia and an unwelcome sense of powerlessness drove him up out of his leather chair and to the window, where he looked out onto a busy square right in the exclusive heart of London.

Delaying the moment of inevitability a little longer, Sadiq swung back to his desk where a sheaf of photos was laid out. Princess Samia of Burquat. She was from a small independent emirate which lay on his northern borders, on the Persian Gulf. She had three younger half-sisters, and her older brother had become the ruling Emir on the death of their father some twelve years before.

Sadiq frowned minutely. He too had been crowned young, so he knew what the yoke of responsibility was like. How heavy it could be. Even so, he wasn't such a fool to consider that he and the Emir could be friends, just like that. But if the Princess agreed to this marriage—and why wouldn't she?—then they would be brothers—in-law.

He sighed. The photos showed indistinct images of an average sized and slim-looking woman. She'd lost the puppy fat he vaguely remembered from when he'd met her at one of his parties. None of the pictures had captured her fully. The best ones were from last summer, when she'd returned from a sailing trip with two friends. But even in the press photos she was sandwiched between two other much prettier, taller girls, and a baseball cap was all but hiding her from view.

The most important consideration here was that none of the photos came from the tabloids. Princess Samia was not part of the Royal Arabian party set. She was discreet, and had carved out a quiet, respectable career as an archivist in London's National Library after completing her degree. For that reason, and many others, she was perfect. He didn't want a wife who would bring with her a dubious past life, or any whiff of scandal. He'd courted enough press attention himself over who he was dating or not dating. And to that end he'd had Samia thoroughly investigated, making sure there were no skeletons lurking in any closet.

His marriage would not be like his parents'. It would not be driven by mad, jealous rage and resemble a battlefield. He would not sink the country into a vortex of chaos as his father had done, because he'd been too distracted by a wife who'd resented every moment of being married to a man she didn't want to be married to. His father had famously pursued his mother, and it was common knowledge that in his obsession to have the renowned beauty reputed to be in love with another he'd paid her family a phenomenal dowry for her. His mother's constant sadness had driven Sadiq far away for most of his life.

He needed a quiet, stable wife who would complement him, give him heirs, and let him concentrate on running his country. And, above all, a wife who wouldn't engage his emotions. And from what he'd seen of Princess Samia she would be absolutely perfect.

With a sense of fatalism in his bones he swept all the photos into a pile and put them under a folder. He had no choice but to go forward. His best friends—the ruling Sheikh and his brother from a small independent sheikhdom within his borders—had recently settled down, and if he remained single for much longer he would begin to look directionless and unstable.

He couldn't avoid his destiny. It was time to meet his future wife. He buzzed his secretary. 'Noor, you can send Princess Samia in.'

There was no immediate answer, and a dart of irritation went through Sadiq. He was used to being obeyed the instant he made a request. Stifling that irritation because he knew it stemmed from something much deeper—the prospect of the demise of his freedom—he strode towards his door. The Princess should be here by now, and he couldn't avoid the inevitable any longer.

CHAPTER TWO

SAMIA's hand was on the doorknob when she heard movement behind her and a voice.

'You're leaving so soon?'

It was low and deep, with the merest hint of a seductive
accent, and she cursed herself for not leaving a split second
earlier. But she'd dithered, her innately good manners telling her that she couldn't just walk out on the Sultan. And
now it was too late.

Her back was stiff with tension as she slowly turned
around, steeling herself against the inevitable impact of
seeing one of the most celebrated bachelors in the world up
close. She worked among dusty books and artefacts! She
couldn't be more removed from the kind of life he led. There
was no way he would want to marry her once he'd met her.

Every coherent thought fled her mind, though, when
her eyes came to rest on the man standing just feet away.
He filled the doorway to his office with his tall, broad-
shouldered physique. His complexion was as dark as any
man from the desert, but he had the most unusual blue eyes,
piercing and seemingly boring right through Samia. Dressed
in a dark suit which hugged his frame, he was six feet four
of lean muscle—beautiful enough to take anyone's breath
away. This was a man in his virile prime, ruler of a country

of unimaginable wealth. Samia felt slightly light-headed for a moment.

He stood back and gestured with a hand into his office. 'I'm sorry to have kept you waiting. Please, won't you come in?'

Samia had no choice but to make her feet move in that direction. Her heart beat crazily as she passed him in the wide doorway and an evocative and intensely masculine scent teased her nostrils. She made straight for a chair positioned by the huge desk and turned around to see the Sultan pull the door shut behind him, eyes unnervingly intent on her.

He strolled into the room and barely leashed energy vibrated from every molecule of the man. Sensual elegance became something much more earthy and sexual as he came closer to Samia, and a disturbing heat coiled low in her belly.

His visage was stern at first, but then a wickedly sexy smile tugged at his mouth, sending her pulse haywire. Her thoughts scrambled.

'Was it something I said?'

Samia looked at him blankly.

'You were about to leave?' he elaborated.

Samia coloured hotly. 'No…of course not.' *Liar.* She went even hotter. 'I'm sorry… I just…'

She hated to admit it but he intimidated her. She might live a quiet existence and dislike drawing attention to herself—it was a safe persona she'd adopted—but she wasn't a complete shadow. Yet here she seemed to be turning into one.

Sadiq dismissed her stumbling words with one hand. He took pity on her obvious discomfort, but he was still reacting to the jolt running through him at hearing her voice. It was low and husky, and completely at odds with her rather mousy appearance. As mousy as the photos had predicted, he decided with a quick look up and down. In that trouser suit and a buttoned up shirt which did nothing for her figure, it was imposible to make out if she *had* a figure.

And yet…Sadiq's keen male intuition warned him not to make too hasty a judgement—just as a disconcerting tingle of awareness skittered across his spine. He stuck his hands into his pockets.

Samia could feel her cheeks heat up, and had a compelling desire to look down and see where his trousers would be pulled tight across his crotch. But she resolutely kept looking upwards. She tried to do the exercise she'd been taught to deal with her blushing—which was to consciously *try* to blush, and in doing so negate the reflexive action. But it was futile. The dreaded heat rose anyway, and worse than usual.

He just looked at her. Samia valiantly ignored the heat suffusing her face, knowing well that she'd be bright pink by now, and hitched up her chin. She nearly died a small death when he broke the tension and put out a hand.

'We've met before, haven't we?'

This was it—just what she'd been dreading. And it got worse when he continued.

'I knew I remembered meeting you, but couldn't place where it was. And then it came to me…'

Her heart stopped beating. She begged silently that it wouldn't be that awful moment which was engraved on *her* memory.

'You had an unfortunate tussle with a table full of drinks at one of my parties.'

Samia was so ridiculously relieved that he didn't seem to remember the library that she reached out to clasp his hand, her own much smaller one becoming engulfed by long fingers. His touch was strong and warm and unsettling, and she had to consciously stop herself from ripping her hand out of his as if he'd stung her.

'Yes, I'm afraid that was me. I was a clumsy teenager.'
Why did she sound breathless?

While still holding her hand, he was looking into her eyes
and saying musingly, 'I didn't realise you had blue eyes too.
Didn't you wear glasses before?'

'I had laser surgery a year ago.'

'Your colouring must come from your English mother?'

His voice was as darkly gorgeous as him. Samia nodded
her head to try and shake some articulacy into her brain.
'She was half English, half Arabic. She died in childbirth
with me. My stepmother brought me up.'

The Sultan nodded briefly and finally let Samia's hand
go. 'She died five years ago?'

Samia nodded and tucked her hand behind her back. She
found a chair behind her to cling on to. Her eyes darted away
from that intense blue gaze as if he might see the bitterness
that crept up whenever she was reminded of her stepmother.
The woman had been a tyrant, because she'd always known
she came a far distant second to the Emir's beloved first wife.

Samia looked back to the Sultan and her heart lurched.
He was too good-looking. She felt drab and colourless next
to him. How on earth could he possibly think for a second
that she could be his queen? And then she remembered what
he'd said about wanting a conservative wife and felt panicked
again.

He indicated the chair she was all but clutching like a life
raft. 'Please, won't you sit down? What would you like? Tea
or coffee?'

Samia quelled an uncharacteristic impulse to ask for
something much stronger. Like whisky. 'Coffee. Please.'

Sadiq moved towards his own chair on the other side of
the desk and thankfully just then his secretary appeared with
a tray of refreshments. Once she'd left, he tried not to notice
the way the Princess's hand shook as she poured milk into

her coffee. The girl was a blushing, quivering wreck, but she looked at him with a hint of defiance that he found curiously stirring. It was an intriguing mix when he was used to the brash confidence of the women he usually met.

He almost felt sorry for her as she handled the dainty cup. Miraculously it survived the journey from saucer to her mouth. She was avoiding his pointed look, so his gaze roamed freely over her and he had to concede with another little jolt of sensation that she wasn't really that mousy at all. Her hair was strawberry-blond, with russet highlights glinting in the late-afternoon sun slanting in through the huge windows. It was tied back in a French plait which had come to rest over one shoulder. Unruly curls had escaped to frame her face, which was heart-shaped.

She looked about eighteen, even though he knew she was twenty-five. And she was pale enough to have precipitated his question about her colouring. He'd forgotten that interesting nugget about her heritage.

It surprised him how clearly that memory of her knocking over the table had come back to him. He'd felt sorry for her at the time; she'd been mortified, standing there with her face beetroot red, throat working convulsively. Another memory hovered tantalisingly on the edges of his mind but he couldn't pin it down.

Absurdly long lashes hid her eyes. He had to admit with a flicker of *something* that she wasn't what he'd expected at all. Obeying some rogue urge to force her to look at him, so that he could inspect those aquamarine depths more closely, he drawled, 'So, Princess Samia, are you going to tell me why you were about to leave?'

Samia's eyes snapped up to clash with the Sultan's steady gaze. She couldn't get any hotter, and had to restrain herself from opening the top button of her shirt to feel some cool air on her skin. He was looking at her as if she were a specimen on a laboratory table. It couldn't be more obvious that she left him entirely cold, and that thought sent a dart of emotion through her.

'Sultan—' she began, and stopped when he put up a hand.

'It's Sadiq. I insist.'

The steely set of his face sent a quiver through her. 'Very well. Sadiq.' She took a deep breath. 'The truth is that I don't want to marry you.'

She saw the way his jaw tensed and his eyes flashed. 'I think it's usually customary to be asked for your hand in marriage before you refuse it.'

Samia's hands clenched tight on her lap. 'And I think it's customary to ask for the person's hand in marriage before assuming it's given.'

His eyes flashed dangerously and he settled back in the chair. Conversely it made Samia feel more threatened.

'I take it that you overheard some of my phone conversation?'

Samia blushed again, and gave up any hope of controlling it. 'I couldn't help it,' she muttered. 'The door was partially open.'

Sadiq sat forward and said brusquely, 'Well, I apologise. It wasn't meant for your ears.'

Giving in to inner panic, Samia stood up abruptly and moved behind the chair. 'Why not? After all, you were discussing the merits of this match, so why not discuss them here and now with me? Let's establish if I am conservative enough for you, or plain enough.'

A dull flush of colour across the Sultan's cheeks was the only sign that she'd got to him when she said that. Otherwise he looked unmoved by her display of agitation, and Samia cursed herself. Her hands balled on the back of the chair. He just sat back and regarded her from under heavy lids.

'You can be under no illusion, whether you heard that

conversation or not, that any marriage between us will be based purely on practicality along with a whole host of other considerations.'

When she spoke, the bitterness in Samia's voice surprised her. 'Oh, don't worry. I've no illusions at all.'

'This union will benefit both our countries.'

Suddenly a speculative gleam lit his eyes and he sat forward, elbows on the desk. Samia wanted to back away.

'I'd find it hard to believe that someone from our part of the world and culture of arranged marriages could possibly be holding out for a *love* match?'

He said this sneeringly, as if such a thing was pure folly. Feeling sick, Samia just shook her head. 'No. Of course not.' A love match was the last thing she would ever have expected or wanted. She had seen how love had devastated her father after losing her mother. She'd had to endure the silent grief in his gaze every time he'd looked at her, because *she'd* been the cause of her mother's death.

She'd seen how the ripples of that had affected everything—making his next wife bitter. Love had even wreaked its havoc on her beloved brother too, turning him hard as a rock and deeply cynical. She'd vowed long ago never to allow such a potentially destructive force anywhere near her.

The Sultan sat back again, seemingly pleased with her answer. He spread his hands wide. 'Well, then, what can you possibly have against this marriage?'

Everything! Exposure! Ridicule! Samia's hands were tightly clasped in front of her. 'I just…never saw it in my future.' She'd thought she'd faded enough into the background to avoid this kind of attention.

And then, as if he'd taken the words out of her brother's own mouth, Sultan Sadiq said with a frown, 'But as the eldest sister of the Emir of Burquat, how on earth did you think you would avoid a strategic match? You've done well to survive this far without being married off.'

Purely feminist chagrin at his unashamedly masculine statement was diminished when guilt lanced Samia. Her brother could have suggested any number of suitors before now, but hadn't. She'd always been aware that Kaden might one day ask her to make a strategic match, though, and this one had obviously been irresistible. This one came with economic ties that would help catapult Burquat into the twenty-first century and bring with it badly needed economic stability and development.

As much as she hated to admit it, they *did* come from a part of the world that had a much more pragmatic approach to marriage than the west. It was rare and unusual for a ruler to marry for something as frivolous as love. Marriages had to be made on the bedrock of familial ties, strategic alliances and political logic. Especially royal marriages.

If anything, this practical approach which eschewed love should appeal to her. She wasn't in any danger of falling for someone like Sadiq, and he certainly wouldn't be falling for her. She was almost certainly guaranteed a different kind of marriage from the one she'd witnessed growing up. Their children wouldn't be bullied and belittled out of jealous spite.

Sultan Sadiq stood up, and panic gripped Samia again. She moved back skittishly and cursed this mouse of a person she'd become in his presence. She ruled over thirty employees at the library, and was used to standing up to her brother, who was a man cut from the same dominant cloth as the Sultan, but mere minutes in *this* man's presence and she was jelly.

He prowled around the room, as if he couldn't sit still for longer than a second, and Samia recalled that he had a well known and insatiable love of extreme sports. He'd been the youngest ever sailor to take part in the prestigious Vendée

Globe race. As a keen sailor herself, she was in awe of that achievement.

In the tradition of men of his lineage he'd studied in both the UK and the US, and had trained at the exclusive royal military academy at Sandhurst. He had a fleet of helicopters and planes that he regularly flew himself. All in all he was a formidable man. Along with that came the notorious reputation of being one of the world's most ruthless playboys, picking up and discarding the most beautiful women in the world like accessories.

And every year—not that she needed to be reminded—he hosted the biggest, most lavish birthday party and raised an obscene amount of money for charity. For years after that humiliating incident at his party, she'd been scornful of the excess he presided over. But she'd seen the evidence of how much bona fide charity work he did when time after time he was lauded for his fundraising. And how did she know all this? Hours spent researching him on the internet last night, much to her shame.

He stopped pacing and quirked an ebony brow. 'Are you going to insist on refusing my offer of marriage and force me to look elsewhere for a wife?'

Samia heard the unimstakable incredulity in his voice. Patently he hadn't expected this to be hard. It gave her some much needed confidence back to see this chink in his arrogant armour.

'What would happen if I said no?'

He put his hands on narrow hips, and Samia's gaze couldn't help but drop for a moment to where his shirt was stretched across taut abdominal muscles. She could see the dark shadowing of a line of hair through the silk and her mouth dried. The physicality of her reaction to him stunned her. No man had had this kind of effect on her before. It was as if she'd been asleep all her life and was gradually coming to her senses here and now, in this room. It was most disconcerting.

'What would *happen*,' he bit out, 'is that the agreement between your brother and I would be in serious jeopardy. I would have to look to your next sister and assess her suitability.'

Samia blanched and her gaze snapped back up to Sadiq's. 'But Sara is only twenty-two.' And she jumped at her own shadow, but Samia didn't say that. Immediately all her protective older sister hackles rose. 'She's entirely unsuitable for you.'

Sadiq's gaze was glacial now. 'Which would seem to be a running trend in your family, according to you. Nevertheless, she would be considered. I would also be under no obligation to go through with my offer to help the Emir mine your vast oil fields. He would be forced to look for expertise from abroad, and that would bring with it a whole host of political challenges that I don't think Burquat can afford at this moment in time.'

Samia tried to ignore the vision he was painting and smile cynically. But her mouth tingled betrayingly when his gaze dropped there for an incendiary moment. She fought to retain her focus. 'And you're saying that your part in this is entirely altruistic? Please don't insult my intelligence, no one does anything for nothing in return.'

He inclined his head again, a different kind of gleam in his eyes now. 'Of course not. In return I get a very suitable wife—you, or your sister, which is entirely up to you. A valuable alliance with a neighbouring kingdom and a slice of the oil profits which I will funnel into a trust fund for our children.'

Our children. Samia ignored the curious swooping sensation in the pit of her belly when he said those words.

'Burquat needs an alliance with one of its Arabian

neighbours, Samia. You know that as well as I do. On the brink of revealing to the world the veritable gold mine it harbours, it's in an acutely vulnerable position. Marriage to me will ensure my support. We will be family. You and your brother will be assured of my protection. We're also poised to sign a historic peace treaty. Needless to say our marriage would provide an even stronger assurance of peace between us.'

Every word he spoke was a death knell to Samia, and every word had already been spoken by her brother. She couldn't tell if the Sultan was bluffing about her sister or not, and didn't really want to test him. She also didn't want to investigate the dart of hurt that she should be so easily interchangeable with her sister. She didn't want him to choose her and she didn't want him to choose anyone else. Pathetic.

She could feel her life as she knew it slipping out of her grasp, but an inner voice mocked her. What kind of a life did she have anyway? Burying herself away in the library and quashing her naturally gregarious spirit after years of bullying by her stepmother wasn't something she could justify any more. Her stepmother was gone.

Even so, the prospect of moving out of that safe environment was still terrifying. Desperation tinged her voice. 'What makes you believe that I'll be a good wife? The right wife for you?'

The Sultan rocked back on his heels and put his hands in the pockets of his trousers. He was so tall and dark and forbidding in that moment.

'You are intelligent and have not lived your life in the public eye, like most of your peers. I think you are serious, and that you care about things. I read the article you wrote in the *Archivist* last month and it was brilliant.'

Samia felt humiliated more than pleased at his obvious research. An article in the *Archivist* only cemented how deeply *boring* she was. She did not need to be reminded of the disparity between her and the man in front of her. He was a playboy! The thought of the exposure she would face within a marriage to him made her feel nauseous. Because with exposure came humiliation.

Sadiq went on as remorselessly as the tide washing in. 'But apart from all of that you are a princess from one of the oldest established royal families in Arabia and you were born to be a queen. God forbid, but if something happened to your brother tomorrow you would be next in line for your throne. If we were married then you would not have to shoulder that burden alone, and I would make sure that Burquat retained its emirate status.'

Samia felt herself pale. She knew she was next in line to the throne of Burquat, but had never really contemplated the reality of what that meant. Kaden seemed so invincible that she'd never had to. But Sultan Sadiq was right; she was in a very delicate position. She might know the theory of ruling a country, but the reality was a different prospect altogether. And she knew that not many other potential husbands would guarantee that Burquat retained its autonomy. Al-Omar was huge and thriving, and the fact that the Sultan saw no need to bolster his own power through annexing a smaller country made Samia feel vulnerable—she hadn't expected this.

Afraid that he would see something of the turmoil she felt, she turned to face a window which looked out over manicured lawns—a serene and typically English tableau which would normally be soothing.

She felt short of breath and seriously overwhelmed. There was a point that came in everyone's life when a person was called to make the starkest of choices, and she was facing hers right now. Not that she really had a choice. That was becoming clearer and clearer.

But, desperate to cling on to some tiny measure of illusion,

Samia turned around again and bit her lip before saying to the Sultan, 'This is a lot to take in. Yesterday I was facing only the prospect of returning to Burquat to help oversee the refurbishment of our national library, and now...I'm being asked to become Queen of Al-Omar.' She met his blue gaze. 'I don't even know you.'

A flash of irritation crossed the Sultan's face, shadowing those amazing eyes, and inwardly Samia flinched at this evidence of his dispassionate and clinical approach to something so momentous.

'We have our lifetimes to get to know one another. What won't wait, however, is the fact that I need to marry and have heirs. I have no doubt in my mind, Princess Samia, that you are the one who was born to take that position.'

Samia tried not to look as affected by his words as she felt. He was only saying it like that because he'd decided she'd make him a good wife and wasn't prepared to take no for an answer. At another time she might almost have smiled. He reminded her so much of her autocratic brother.

She knew for a fact that there were many women who would gladly trample over her to hear him speak those words to them. And she wished right now that one of them was standing there instead of her—even though her belly did a curious little flip when she thought of it.

'I just...' She stopped ineffectually. 'I need some time to think about this.'

Sadiq's face tightened ominously, and Samia had the feeling that she'd pushed him too far. With that came a sense of panic that...what? He'd choose her sister instead? That he'd send her away and tell her to have a nice life? And why was that making her feel panicky when it was exactly what she wanted?

But an urbane mask closed off any expression on that hard-jawed face, and after an interminable moment he said softly, 'Very well. I will give you twenty-four hours. This time tomorrow evening I expect you to be back here in this room to tell me what you have decided.'

Sadiq stood at the window of his private sitting room, three floors above the office where he'd just met Princess Samia. He looked out over the city of London bathed in dusky light. The scent of late-summer blossoms was heavy in the air. He suddenly missed the intense heat of his home—the sense of peace that he got only when he knew that the vast expanse of Al-Omari desert was within walking distance.

Irritation snaked through him at the realisation that due to Samia's patent reluctance he'd be forced to spend longer in Europe than he wanted to. He could see his discreet security men in front of his house—necessary trappings for a head of state—but he was oblivious to all that. For once he wasn't consumed with thoughts of politics, or the economy, or women.

He frowned. Well, that wasn't entirely true. One woman *was* consuming his thoughts, and for the first time in his life it wasn't accompanied with the enticing sense of expectation at the prospect of bedding her. And then he had to concede that it had been a long time since pure expectation had precipitated *any* liaison with a lover—it was more likely to be expectation mixed with a lot of cynicism.

Sadiq's frown became deeper, grooving lines into his smooth forehead. Since when had he acknowledged the fact that for him bedding women was accompanied by a feeling of ennui and ever deepening cynicism? He suspected uncomfortably that it was long before he'd witnessed his close friends' weddings in Merkazad.

Seeing his friends wearing their hearts on their sleeves had induced a feeling of panic and had pushed a button—a button that had been deeply buried and packed under years of cynical block building and ice. Perhaps that was what had precipitated his decision to marry? This impulse to protect himself at all costs—a desire to negate what he'd seen at Nadim and Salman's weddings. The need to prove that he wasn't ever going to succumb to that awful uncontrollable emotion again.

Even now he could remember that day, and the excoriating humiliation of baring his heart and soul to a woman who had all but laughed in his face.

In choosing to marry someone like Princess Samia he would be safe for ever from such mortifying episodes, because he was in no danger of falling in love with her. He was also safe from falling in lust. She was too pale, too shapeless. His stomach clenched… Funnily enough, though, he couldn't get those enigmatic aquamarine eyes out of his head. And he had to concede she wasn't *un*pretty. But she certainly wasn't beautiful. He'd always accepted that the wife he picked would fulfil a role—an important one. As such, to find her attractive would be a bonus and a luxury. His responsibility to his country was greater than such frivolous concerns.

Altogether, she wasn't as unappealing as he might have feared initially. He grimaced. He'd had his fair share of the world's beauties. It was time to convert his lust into building up a country unrivalled in its wealth and economic stability. He needed focus for that, and a wife like Samia would provide that focus. He wouldn't be distracted by her charms, and clearly she was not the coquettish type, so she wouldn't waste time trying to charm him.

Sadiq's frown finally cleared from his face and he turned his attention to the rolling business news channel on the muted television screen in the background. Despite the Princess's reluctance he had no doubt that she would return the next day and give him the answer he expected. The alternative was simply inconceivable.

CHAPTER THREE

24 hours later

'I'M not going to marry you.'

Sadiq's mouth was open and he was already smiling urbanely in anticipation of the Princess's acquiescence—already thinking ahead to buying her a trousseau and getting her out of those unflattering suits. Her bottom had barely touched the seat of the chair opposite him. He frowned. Surely she couldn't have just said—

'I said I don't want to marry you.'

Her voice was low and husky, but firm, and it tugged somewhere deep inside him again. Sadiq's mouth closed. She sat before him like a prim nun, hair pulled back and dressed in a similarly boxy suit to the one she'd worn yesterday. This one was just a slightly darker hue of blue. Not a scrap of make-up enhanced those pale features or those aquamarine eyes. Disconcertingly, at that moment he noticed a splash of freckles across her delicately patrician nose.

Freckles. Since when had he noticed freckles on anyone? Any woman of his acquaintance would view freckles with the same distaste as acne. Something nebulous unfurled within Sadiq, and he sat back and realised that it was a surprise—because it was so long since anyone had said no to him. Or been so reluctant to impress him. Princess Samia's chin lifted minutely, and for a second Sadiq could see her innately regal hauteur. She might be the most unprepossessing princess he'd ever met, but she was still royalty and she couldn't hide it.

The thin line of her mouth drew his focus then, and bizarrely he found himself wondering how full and soft those lips would be when relaxed…or kissed. Would they be pink and pouting, begging for another kiss?

Samia could see the conflict on the Sultan's face, the clear disbelief. That was why she'd repeated herself. It had been as much to check she hadn't been dreaming. She was trembling all over like a leaf. She'd tossed and turned all night and had kept coming back to the stark realisation that she really did not have a choice.

But when faced with Sadiq again, and the clear expectation on his face that she was there to say yes, she had felt some rebellious part of her rise up. This was her only chance of escaping this union. She crushed the lancing feeling of guilt. She couldn't worry now about the fallout or she'd never go through with it. The thought of marrying this man was just so downright threatening that she had to do something— no matter how selfish it felt.

Sadiq's voice rumbled over her, causing her pulse to jump. 'There's a difference between *not* marrying me, and not *wanting* to marry me. One implies that there is no room for discussion, and the other implies that there is. So which is it, Samia?'

Samia tried to avoid that searing gaze. He was sitting forward, elbows on his desk, fingers steepled together. The way he said her name made her feel hot. She was already unravelling at the seams because she was facing this man again, even though the heavy oak desk separated them. Even the threat to her sister wasn't enough right now to make her reconsider. She'd cross that bridge if it came to it.

He hadn't kept her waiting today. He'd been waiting for her. Standing at his window like a tall, dark and gorgeous spectre. And now he was utterly indolent—as if they might be discussing the weather. He wore a shirt and no tie. The top button was undone, revealing the bronzed column of his throat. The sleeves of his shirt were rolled up, showing off muscled forearms more suited to an athlete than a head of state. Samia felt unbearably restless all of a sudden.

Abruptly she stood up, wanting to put space between them. She couldn't seem to sit still around this man, and she couldn't concentrate while he was looking at her like that—as if she were under a microscope. So clinically.

She went and stood behind the chair, breathing erratically. 'Discussion…' she finally got out. 'Defintely the discussion one.'

Great. Now she couldn't string a sentence together—and what was she doing, encouraging a discussion with one of the world's greatest debaters? She paced away from the chair, feeling constricted in her suit. She'd never been as self-conscious about what she wore as she had been in the last thirty-six hours. Samia had always been supremely aware of her own allure, or more accurately the lack of it, and was very comfortable with a uniform of plain clothes to help her fade into the background. Or at least she had been till now.

She avoided his eye. 'Look, I know you need a wife, and on paper I might look like the perfect candidate—'

Sadiq cut in with a low voice. 'You *are* the perfect candidate.' He stifled intense irritation. She was the *only* candidate. After carefully vetting potentially suitable brides from his world and dismissing them, she was the only one he'd kept coming back to. And once he'd set his mind on something he would not rest until he had full compliance. Failure was not an option.

Samia turned back to face him, and quailed slightly under

the glowering look he was sending her. 'But I'm not! You'll see.' She searched frantically for something to say. 'I don't go out!'

'A perfectly commendable quality. Despite what you've been led to believe, I'm not actually the most social of animals.'

Samia forced her mind away from that nugget of information. This man and a quiet evening in by the fire just did *not* compute. 'You find it commendable that I don't have a life? That's not something to applaud—it's something to avoid. How can I be your queen when the last party I was at was probably yours? You must have parties every week—you move in those circles. I wouldn't know what to do…or say.'

Samia's tirade faltered, because the Sultan had moved and was now sitting on the edge of the desk, one hip hitched up. She swallowed and wished he hadn't moved. Heat was rising, and dimly she wondered if he had any heating on.

'Of course you'd know what to do and say. You've been brought up to know *exactly* what to do and say. And if you're out of practice you'll learn again quickly enough.'

Samia choked back her furious denial. She ran a hand through her hair impatiently, which was something she did when she was agitated. She forgot that it was tied back and felt it come loose but had to ignore it.

She faced him fully. 'You really don't want me for your wife. I don't like parties. I get tongue-tied when I'm faced with more than three people, I'm not sophisticated and polished.' *Like all your other women.* Samia just about managed not to let those words slip out.

Sadiq was watching the woman in front of him with growing fascination. She *wasn't* sophisticated and polished—and he suddenly relished that fact for its sheer uniqueness. She was literally coming apart in front of him, revealing someone very different from the woman she was describing. He agreed with absolutely everything she was saying—apart from the bit about her not being a suitable wife.

'And yet,' he drawled, 'you've been educated most of your life in a royal court, and your whole existence has held within it the potential for this moment. How can you say you're not ready for this?'

Samia could feel the unfashionably heavy length of her hair starting to unravel down her back. Her inner thermostat was about to explode. With the utmost reluctance she opened her jacket, afraid that if she didn't she'd melt in a puddle or faint.

Before she could stop him Sadiq was reaching out and plucking the coat from her body as easily as if she were a child, placing it on the chair she'd vacated. Too stunned to be chagrined, Samia continued, 'You need someone who is used to sophisticated social gatherings. I've been in libraries for as long as I can remember.'

The ancient library in the royal Burquat castle had always been her refuge from the constant taunting of her stepmother, Alesha. She started to pace again, disturbed by Sadiq's innate cool.

'You need someone who can stand up to you.' She stopped and stood a few feet away, facing him. She *had* to make him see. 'I had a chronic stutter until I was twelve. I'm pathologically shy. I'm so shy that I went to cognitive behavioural therapy when I was a teenager to try and counteract it.' Which had precipitated another steady stream of taunts and insults from her stepmother, telling her that she would amount to nothing and never become a queen when she couldn't even manage to hold a conversation without blushing or stuttering.

Sadiq had stood up and come closer to Samia while she'd been talking. He was frowning down at her now, arms folded across that impressive chest. 'You don't have a stutter any more, and I'd wager that your therapist, if he or she was any good, said that you were just going through a phase that any teenager might go through. And plenty of children suffer from stuttering. It's usually related back to some minor incident in their childhood.'

Samia blinked. She felt as if he could see inside her head to one of her first memories, when she had been trying to get her new stepmother's attention and was stuttering in her anxiety to be heard. She would bet that *he'd* never gone through anything like that. But he'd repeated more or less exactly what her therapist had said. It was so unexpected to hear this from him of all people that any more words dried in her throat as he started to move around her.

Sadiq was growing more intrigued by the second. Her hair had come completely undone by now, and it lay in a wavy coil down her back. His fingers itched to reach out and loosen it. It looked silky and fragrant…a little wild. It was at such odds with that uptight exterior.

So close to her like this, for the first time he noticed the disparity in their heights. She was a lot smaller than the women he was used to, and he felt a surprising surge of something almost *protective* within him. With the jacket gone he could see that she was slight and delicate, yet he sensed a strength about her—an innate athleticism. He could see the whiteness of her bra strap through her shirt, and how her shirt was tucked into the trousers, drawing his eye to a slim waist and the gentle flare of her hips. He didn't think he'd ever seen a prospective lover so demurely dressed, and that thought caught him up short. She was to be his *wife*. Lovemaking would be purely functional. If he got any enjoyment out of it, it would be a bonus.

He came to stand in front of her and could see where she'd opened the top button of her shirt, revealing the slender length of her neck right down to the hollow at the base of her throat. It looked pink and slightly dewed with moisture. She must be hot. He had the most bizarre urge to push her shirt aside and press a finger there. His eyes dropped again, and he could see very plainly the twin thrusts of her breasts, rising and falling with her breath and fuller than he had first imagined.

To his utter shock, the unmistakable and familiar spark of desire lit within him. With more difficulty than he would have liked, he brought his gaze back up to hers and felt a punch to his gut at the way those aquamarine depths suddenly looked as dark blue as the Arabian sea on a stormy day. Tendrils of hair were curling softly around her face, and she looked softer, infinitely more feminine. In fact in that moment she looked almost...beautiful. Sadiq reeled at this completely unexpected development.

Samia was helpless under Sadiq's assessing gaze. No man had ever looked at her so explicitly, his gaze lingering on her breasts like that. And yet she wasn't insulted or shocked. A languorous heat was snaking through her veins. She was caught in a bubble. A bubble of heat and sensation. As soon as he had walked behind her she'd had to undo her top button because she couldn't breathe—she'd felt so constricted. And now he was looking at her as though...as though—

'You say I need someone to stand up to me and that's what you've been doing since yesterday.' His beautifully sculpted mouth firmed. 'It's a long time since anyone has refused my wishes. I encounter people every day who are overawed and inhibited by what they perceive me to be and yet I don't get that from you.' Before Samia could articulate anything, he continued. 'Very few people would feel they had the authority to do that, but we're the same, Princess Samia, you and I.'

Samia nearly blanched at that. If there was one thing she was sure of, it was that she and this man were *not* the same.

Not in a million years. Polar opposites. 'We're not the same,' she got out painfully. 'Really, we're not.'

He ignored her. 'I know you've got a closely knit and loyal group of friends.'

Without a hint of self-pity and vaguely surprised that he knew this, she said, 'That says more about who I am and the background I come from than anything else.' Remembering one painful episode in college, she went on, 'I could never fully trust that people weren't making friends just because they thought they could get something out of me.' When he still looked unmoved she said desperately, 'I'm boring!'

He arched an incredulous brow. 'Someone who is boring doesn't embark on a three-woman trip across the Atlantic in a catamaran made out of recycled materials in a bid to raise awareness about the environment.'

Samia was immediately disconcerted. 'You know about that?'

He nodded and looked a little stern. 'I think it was either one of the most foolhardy or one of the bravest things I've ever seen.'

She flushed deeper and couldn't stop a dart of pleasure rushing through her at the thought she'd earned this man's admiration. 'I care about the environment... The other two were old friends from college, and they couldn't raise the funding required on their own... But once I got involved...' Her voice trailed off, her modesty not wanting to make it sound as if she'd been instrumental in the project.

Sadiq rocked back on his heels. 'I have a well-established environmental team in Al-Omar that could do with your support. I often find I'm too tied up with other concerns to give it my full attention. We've both grown up in rarefied environments, Samia, both grown up being aware of public duty. If anything, your teenage and childhood experiences will make you more empathetic with people—an essential quality in any queen.'

Samia objected to his constant avowal of partnership, and the tantalising carrot of being able to work constructively for the environment, but her attempt to halt him in his tracks with a weak-sounding 'Sadiq...' made no impact.

'You might find social situations intimidating, but with time they'll become second nature. Also, you can't deny that having grown up as a princess in a royal court you are aware of castle politics and protocol. You would have learnt that by osmosis. These are all invaluable assets to me in any marriage I undertake. I don't have the time or the inclination to train someone.'

Samia blinked up at him again. She couldn't deny it. As much as she might want to. Even though she'd spent her formative years avoiding her stepmother, she knew castle politics like the back of her hand—she'd had to learn to survive. Her knowledge of the things he spoke had been engraved invisibly on her psyche like a tattoo from birth.

'I want to create a solid alliance between Al-Omar, Merkazad and Burquat. We live in unstable times and need to be able to depend on each other. Marrying you will ensure a strong alliance with your brother. I already have it with Merkazad. Your father's rule put Burquat firmly in an isolated position, which did your country no favours. Thankfully your brother is reversing that stance. I don't see how you have any grounds at all—apart from your own personal concerns—to believe that you are not fit to become my queen, and in so doing ensure the future stability of your country.'

Samia swallowed painfully, glued to his glittering blue eyes in sick fascination. He was right. She could no more stand there and deny these facts than she could deny her very heritage and lineage. She might have hidden herself away in a college and then a dusty library for the past few years, but she'd always had the knowledge of this ultimate responsibility within her.

And her concerns *were* personal—selfish, in fact. She just did not have that luxury. She wasn't the same as the average person on the street. She had obligations, responsibilities.

As if he could sense her weakening, Sadiq moved closer and Samia's breath faltered. That embarrassing heat was back, rising inexorably through her body, and for the first time she recognised it not as the heat of embarrassment or shyness but as a totally different kind of heat. The heat of desire. The fact that he was having the same inevitable effect on her as every other woman he must encounter was humiliating. She was not immune.

'I...' She had to swallow to get her voice to work. He was standing so close now that all she could see was those dark blue irises, sucking her in and down into a vortex of nebulous needs she'd never felt before. She battled her own sapping will and focused. 'I accept what you're saying. They're all valid points.'

'I know they are.'

Had his voice dropped an octave? It sounded like it. They were standing so close now that Samia could feel his warm breath feather around her, could smell the intensely masculine scent of sandalwood and musky spice. It was the memory of that scent that had kept her awake for long hours last night.

To her utter shock he reached out a hand and touched his thumb to her bottom lip, tugging it. She had the most bizarre urge to flick out her tongue and taste his finger. Her heart slowed to about a beat a minute.

'That's better. You shouldn't be so tense. You have a very pretty mouth.'

A pretty mouth? No one had ever referred to her as pretty

in her life. Instantly Samia felt as if a cold bucket of water had been flung over her. She stepped back abruptly, forcing the Sultan's hand down, breaking the spell. Clearly the man felt the need to placate her with false compliments. What was wrong with her? Believing for half a second that she was in some sensual bubble with the Sultan of Al-Omar who had courted and bedded some of the world's greatest beauties?

Her face flaming again, Samia looked away and tried to regain control, breathing a sigh of relief when she sensed Sadiq move back too.

His voice was tight. 'Samia, it's inevitable. You might as well give in now, because I won't. Not until you say yes.'

She gulped and shook her head. Words were strangled in her throat. She was more sure than ever that she couldn't do this. Especially after she'd all but sucked his finger into her mouth like some wanton groupie!

She heard him sigh expressively and sneaked a look. He was glancing at his watch and then looking at her. 'I don't know about you but I'm hungry. I've had a busy day.'

Samia just looked at him stupidly for a moment. The tension in the atmosphere diminished. And then her stomach gurgled loudly at the thought of food. She'd been so wound up for the last thirty-six hours that she'd barely eaten a thing.

As if Sadiq could see the turmoil on her face he quirked his mouth and came close again, playing havoc with Samia's hearbeat, and tipped up her chin with a finger.

'Rest assured I won't stop until you have agreed to become my wife and queen. But we might as well start to get to know one another a little better in the meantime. And eat.'

Before she knew what was happening Sadiq was leading the way from the study with her jacket over his arm. She opened her mouth to protest, but then they were in the hall and he was conferring with his butler who bowed and indicated for Samia to follow Sadiq into what turned out to be a dining room.

It was more than impressive. Dark walls were lined with portraits of Sadiq's ancestors in western dress, looking very exotic, a huge gleaming oak table dominated the room and there was a setting for two at the top of the table.

Sadiq was standing behind a chair, looking at her expectantly, and, feeling very weak, Samia went forward and sat down. There was a flurry of activity as the butler came back with more staff and they were presented with options for dinner. Samia made her choice without even thinking about what she was ordering.

When they were momentarily alone Samia bit her lip for a moment and began to speak, not even sure what she wanted to say. 'Sadiq…'

But he just poured her a glass of chilled white wine and said disarmingly, 'You made the right choice with the fish. Marcel, our chef, is an expert. He used to work for the Ritz in Paris.'

Samia took the proffered glass and felt her unruly hair slip over her shoulder. She'd long lamented the fact that her hair didn't fall in sleek and smooth waves like her younger sisters', who'd all inherited their own mother's exotic dark colouring. Kaden had inherited their father's dark looks, so she'd always been the odd one out. Her stepmother had only had to breathe air into Samia's own sense of isolation to compound it.

She felt a little naked with her hair down like this—somehow exposed, as if some secret feminine part of herself was being bared to the sun. It wasn't altogether uncomfortable, which made it even more disturbing. Sadiq sat back and smiled at Samia urbanely, making her stomach flip-flop. If he turned on the charm she didn't know how she would cope.

As if privy to her private thoughts, that was exactly what he did.

For the next hour and a half, while they ate delicious food, he managed to draw Samia out of her shell. At first she did her best to resist, but it was like trying to resist the force of a white water rapid. Something was happening—some intangible shift.

Perhaps she'd started feeling this softening, melting sensation when he'd mentioned her sailing trip? Or perhaps it had been his easy acceptance when she'd told him about her stuttering and shyness. She'd never told anyone about that before, and had done so with him purely in a bid to repel him. But it hadn't worked. He'd *empathised*. It was almost like a betrayal to witness the sudden ease with which she was finding herself talking to him now, albeit about superficial subjects.

He was disarming her enough to make her forget for a moment who he was. It was seductive evidence of a self-deprecating side, and of the undeniable bond they shared in both coming from the same part of the world, from a similar background. Everything he had already pointed out. She had not expected self-deprecation from this man, or any kind of feeling of kinship with him. She hadn't expected him to defuse the tension like this.

They were finishing their coffee when Samia looked at Sadiq, somewhat emboldened after the meal and a glass of wine. 'You're very good you know,' she said.

He quirked a brow, his eyes breathtakingly blue against the olive tone of his skin. 'Good? In what way?'

Samia had to concentrate. It was like sitting across the table from a Hollywood heart-throb, not a head of state. 'At charming people.'

He shrugged minutely, and for a second Samia saw something stern flash across his face and into those eyes.

Immediately the warm bubble of fuzziness that had been infusing her dissipated. Of *course*. How could she have been so silly? This was all an act—an act put on her for benefit and his, to get to her to acquiesce to his plans for marriage. Of course he was charming her. And she was falling for it and believing it like any other woman with a pulse would.

She made a point of looking at her watch, even though she didn't register the time, and then looked back at Sadiq, tensing herself against his effect on her.

'I have to be up early tomorrow. I'm still handing over to my successor.'

Sadiq sat forward. 'You like working in the library here?'

That rebellious streak rising again, Samia said defiantly, 'Yes. And a queen who is more at home surrounded by books is hardly the queen for *you*.'

Sadiq had to quell the sudden urge to wipe that prim look off Samia's face by kissing her. He'd had her in the palm of his hand during the meal—he knew it. She'd been more relaxed than he'd seen her. And with that had come the realisation that he had grossly underestimated her appeal. The spark of desire that had lit earlier had erupted into full-on lust as he'd watched her natural effervescence emerge.

She'd blossomed quite literally before his eyes—like a flower being exposed to heat and light after being hidden in a dark corner. It was the most amazing thing. She reminded him of a dimond in the rough. Actually, he amended, more like a dark and glowing yellow diamond. A rare jewel.

But now she'd clammed up again like an oyster shell, protecting the bounty within. Those full lips were once again a thin line, the eyes downcast. He signalled discreetly to his staff and rose smoothly to his feet once his wayward body felt more under control. A dart of satisfaction went through him at seeing Samia look confused for a moment, as if she'd expected him to challenge her. And then she rose to her feet too, somewhat less assuredly, and that protective instinct surged again. Sadiq had to clench his hands to fists to stop himself reaching out to steady her.

He couldn't understand his physical response. The last woman he'd been with had been hailed as the most beautiful woman in the world three years running. And there had never been one moment when he'd felt protective of *her*. When he tried to picture her now all he remembered was that his desire for her had waned long before he'd admitted it to himself. And yet *this* woman, whose appeal was more wholesomely pretty than beautiful, was having a more incendiary effect on his libido than he could remember.

As Samia preceded Sadiq out of the dining room, he thought of something to test her. She got to the front door and turned around. Clearly she was hoping he wouldn't challenge her again. He almost pitied her for her blind optimisim. He handed her her jacket and watched her expression closely.

'You know,' he mused, 'perhaps you're right after all. Perhaps you're *not* suitable to be my wife.'

Something suspiciously exultant moved through him as he caught the split second of a reaction she couldn't hide because her face was just too expressive.

Samia opened her mouth, but nothing came out. She stilled in the act of putting her jacket on. He'd completely surprised her. And, to her utter chagrin, instead of feeling relieved she had the absurd desire to contradict him and tell him that she *could* be a good wife for him. What was going on?

She tried desperately to hide her confusion as she continued putting on her jacket. 'You mean if I was to walk out of here right now you wouldn't stop me? Or pursue this matter?'

Sadiq smiled, but it was the smile of a shark. 'You don't really believe I'm just going to let you walk away, do you?'

Anger rose bright and rapid at the realisation that he was

playing with her. Samia grabbed for the door and tried to wrench it open, but it wouldn't budge. She turned back, exasperated at being trapped. 'If your door worked you could watch me walk out right now, and there wouldn't be one thing you could do about it.'

Samia was mortified, because she knew well that he'd caught her out. She'd shown her reaction before she could hide it. He *knew* how conflicted she was about this.

'The door works fine, Samia. I just wanted to see how you'd react if you got a sniff of freedom, and your face told me all I need to know.'

Acting on a purely animal instinct to escape a threat, Samia turned back to the door and this time it opened. She stood in the doorway, breathing deep, and almost simultaneously lights exploded all around her.

The paparazzi.

Samia heard a colourful Arabic curse behind her even as she registered big burly bodyguards materializing as if from thin air to hold the photographers back. Strong arms came around and pulled her into a lean and hard muscled body. Samia was plastered against Sadiq's length as he all but carried her back over the threshold and into the house.

It took a second for her to register that it was quiet again and the door was shut behind them. Samia's breath sounded laboured, and she realised that she was still clamped to Sadiq like a limpet. Breasts crushed to his chest. She scrambled backwards, face flaming.

Sadiq raked a hand through his hair. 'Are you okay? I'm sorry about that. Sometimes they lie in wait once they know I'm here, and the bodyguards can't do anything.'

He could still feel the imprint of her body—the firm swells of her breasts pressed against him just for that brief moment. How delicate she'd been. She'd fit into his body like a missing jigsaw piece. For someone used to women who almost matched him in height, it had been a novel sensation.

She was standing there, looking dishevelled and innocently sexy with colour high in her cheeks, and he knew that she had no idea how alluring she was—which only inflamed him more, because he was used to women being all too aware of their so-called allure.

'You *knew* about that.'

He frowned, not liking the accusatory tone in her voice. 'What do you mean?'

'You just said that you know they lie in wait. I'm going to be all over the papers with you. Leaving your house.'

Samia realised she was shaking violently. She heard another curse and felt Sadiq take her arm in a firm grip. 'Come back into the study. You're in shock.'

Once in the big stately room, Sadiq all but pressed Samia down into a chair and went to get a tumbler of brandy. He came back and handed it to her. 'Take a sip. You'll feel better in a minute.'

Hating feeling so vulnerable, Samia took the glass and a gulp of the drink, coughing slightly. She watched Sadiq pour himself a drink and come to sit opposite her on a matching chair. The lights in the room made his amazing good-looks stand out. An awful alien yearning tugged low in her belly and she put down the drink and crossed her arms across her chest defensively.

Grimly he said, 'I'd forgotten all about the paparazzi. Of course I had no intention of putting you in that situation.'

Samia gulped, her anger dissipating. She knew he was telling the truth. A man like him would not have to resort to such measures. Restless, Samia stood up. 'Look, thank you for the dinner... I—'

She stopped when Sadiq stood too, and she had to curb the ridiculous urge to look for an exit, as if she were alone with a wild animal. Samia put out her hands wide in an un-consciously pleading gesture.

'What happened just now should prove how unsuitable I am. That was my first time being caught by the paparazzi. You need someone who is used to that kind of thing—who knows how to handle it.'

Distaste curdled in Sadiq's belly. That was exactly what he didn't want. He was more sure than ever that he wanted *her*—and for reasons that went beyond the practical and mundane.

He came closer to Samia and an unmistakable glint of tri-umph shone in his eyes and she felt sick. She could talk till she was blue in the face but the game was up. He'd called her bluff. She'd shown her telltale confusion. He'd manipu-lated her beautifully. Bitter recrimination burnt her. He was so close now that all she could see were those mesmerising eyes, and all she could smell was that uniquely male scent.

'Your reaction tells me you're conflicted about this de-cision, Samia. So let me take the conflict out of it for you. Agree to become my wife because there simply is no other alternative. You are of royal blood, from an ancient lin-eage. You were born for this role, and nothing you do or say can change that. To fight this is to fight fate, me and your brother.'

From his jacket pocket he pulled out a small velvet box, and all the while his eyes never left hers. He opened it, and Samia couldn't help but look down between them. The ring was surprisingly simple. It was obviously an antique—a square-cut stone in a gold setting, strikingly unusual and beautiful.

'It's a yellow sapphire. It was my paternal grand-mother's—a gift from my grandfather on one of their wed-ding anniversaries.'

Sadiq didn't tell her that this distinctive ring had been

in his mind's eye ever since he'd met her, and that it was a lucky coincidence it had been in the family's jewel vault in London. He'd sent back the diamond ring he'd planned on using, feeling absurdly exposed in acknowledging that he hadn't been happy with a stock ring, which should have been perfectly adequate for what was essentially a stock wedding.

Samia looked up, and Sadiq took her hand in his. He looked so deep into her eyes that she felt as if she might drown and diappear for ever. She knew on some rational level that he was probably not even aware of his power. Unconsciously her fingers tightened around his as if to anchor herself, and something undefinable lit in Sadiq's eyes, hypnotising her even more.

'Princess Samia Binte Rashad al Abbas, will you please do me the very great honour of becoming my wife and Queen of Al-Omar?'

CHAPTER FOUR

AT that cataclysmic moment, while Sadiq's words hung in the air, Samia had a flashback she couldn't repress. She was hiding in the library of his castle after knocking over the table of drinks, cursing herself for being so clumsy and awkward. Her peace was shattered when a man walked into the room.

He didn't spot her because the lights were dim, and all Samia knew as she sat there barely breathing was that he was tall, dark and powerful looking. Yet she wasn't afraid. He walked over to the window which overlooked one of the castle's numerous beautiful inner courtyards and stood there for long moments, as silent as a statue, with an air of deep melancholy pervading the air around him.

He sighed deeply and dropped his head to run a weary hand back and forth over his short hair. Something about this man was connecting with Samia on a very deep level, she *felt* his pain, empathised with his isolation. Without even thinking about what she was doing, responding to some impulse to do *something*, Samia was almost out of her chair when another person entered the room: a woman, tall and blonde and statuesque, and very, very beautiful.

The man turned around and to Samia's shock she realised it was the charismatic Sultan she'd met only hours before. The melancholy and sense of isolation disappeared. She watched as his blue eyes glittered, taking in the woman's approach. In the place of the vulnerability she might have imagined was the hard shell of a supremely confident and sexual man, and she knew then that she had witnessed something incredibly private—something of himself that he would hate to know had been witnessed by anyone else.

Samia watched the woman walk straight up to him. She twined herself around him and, perversely, Samia wanted the Sultan to push this woman away contemptuously. As if he was hers! But as she watched, mesmerised, he backed the blond beauty up against a wall and proceeded to kiss her so passionately that Samia made an inadvertent sound of dismay.

Two faces turned towards her and Samia ran from the room, mortified to have been caught watching like a voyeur.

And now she was looking up into those same blue eyes, and she felt as if a hole had opened up in her belly. All she could remember was that intense vulnerability she'd seen, or *thought* she'd seen, in the Sultan that night, and the connection she'd felt.

She couldn't block out that image of the secret side of this man even as she sensed his steely determination. He would not rest until she said yes, and that made a curious sense of calm settle over her. He was right: to fight this was to fight fate, her brother and *him*. She denied to herself that that evocative memory was a tipping point, because that would mean that Sadiq was connecting with her on an emotional level, and she would deny that with every cell in her body.

This decision was about inevitability, logic and practicality, and the sheer weight of her lineage which put her in this position. She opened her mouth to speak and saw Sadiq's jaw tense, as if warding off a blow. Immediately she felt the impulse to reach up and smooth his jaw. She clenched her hand.

'I…' Her voice sounded rusty. 'Yes. I'll marry you.'

For a second there was no reaction. She wasn't even sure if she'd spoken out loud. But then Sadiq slid the ring onto her finger, bent his head and pressed his lips to it. They were warm and slightly parted, and her belly tightened with a need that was becoming horribly familiar. His head was so close to her breast…

He stood again and she saw that a shutter had come down over his expression, turning him aloof. He was the stern ruler again, and he had achieved his aim. No softness or charm now. Job done. Mission accomplished. Samia thought cynically of how he'd manipulated her emotions so beautifully. And yet she couldn't turn back now. She'd sealed her fate and chosen the path she would take for the rest of her life.

Her belly churning with the sudden realisation of what she'd just done, and a whole host of other scary emotions. She tried her best to match his dispassionate look and took her hand from his, stepping back. The ring twinkled and sparkled in her peripheral vision, and it was heavy. 'I've got to be up early, so if there's nothing else…?'

A ghost of a smile touched Sadiq's mouth and he too stepped back, letting Samia breathe a little easier. He shook his head. 'No, not right now. I'll have my assistant set up a schedule and send it over to you tomorrow. It's going to be a busy three weeks before we return to Al-Omar for our wedding.'

'Three weeks?' Samia squeaked, all pretence of insouciance gone at the terrifying thought. For some reason she'd imagined the wedding happening at some far-off distant time.

He nodded, all businesslike as he escorted her to the door. 'Three weeks, Samia. That should give you plenty of time to hand over your job and prepare for the wedding. I'll be in touch. There will be a press release issued next week. You might want to let your brother know the happy news before that happens.'

The following morning at work Samia finally found five minutes to steal away somewhere private and look at the tabloid she'd furtively bought on her way to the library. She held her breath as she took in the full glory of the lurid photo. She looked like a rabbit startled in the headlights, her eyes huge and her hair wild. And that suit! She could hear her stepmother's derisive voice in her head right now, exclaiming over Samia's general incompetence. She could have wept. Sadiq loomed behind her with a stern look on his gorgeous face, like an avenging dark angel, big hands on her waist making it look tiny. She looked more like an ill-dressed PA to the Sultan rather than his fiancée.

Fiancée. Her stomach churned as she crumpled up the offending paper. She'd left the engagement ring at home that morning and her skin prickled, as if somehow he would know and pop out from behind a corner to chastise her. She still couldn't really believe it, but a long conversation with her brother the previous night, and his palpable relief that they would have Al-Omar's cooperation, had helped reality sink in. It only eased her discomfort slightly.

The disturbing sense of equanimity that had washed over her when she'd said yes to Sadiq's proposal had long disappeared. It would be the wedding of the decade, and she would be annihilated when people realised she was nothing like his long line of mistresses. Not to mention the other aspects of their marriage—like the physical one. Samia felt a dart of despair. She was so far out of Sadiq's league in that respect that she fully expected he would have to take a mistress to stay satisfied.

The really galling thing was that she was as innocent and

pure as the virgin brides rulers like Sadiq would have expected for millenia. She'd had a bad experience in college when a boy who had been pursuing her had become very pushy after a couple of dates. Samia had turned his advances down and he'd stormed off, saying, *'I was only trying to get you into bed for a dare anyway, because of who you are, but I'm glad I didn't! Life is too short!'*

She'd repressed any hint of sexuality since then, not wanting to invite any cruel criticism or attention. Diverting her mind from the painful memory, she thought back to the phone call she'd received from Sadiq early that morning, just before she'd left for work.

'I've set up an appointment with a personal shopper this weekend. You'll need a trousseau. And wedding outfits. The festivities alone will last three days.'

Samia had sat down on the chair beside the phone, the future yawning open before her and looking scarier and scarier. 'Does it have to be three days? Why can't we just get married here in a civil ceremony with a couple of witnesses?'

He'd chuckled darkly and it had made Samia want to hit him. 'Because I'm a sultan and you're a princess about to become a queen, that's why. Also,' he'd continued briskly, 'you need to be protected. As of this morning you'll have two bodyguards, and you will be transported to and from work in one of my cars. The news may not be public yet, but enough people know, or suspect something.'

Samia's sense of personal freedom was disappearing fast, like an elusive shimmering oasis in the desert. 'But—' She'd started to protest, but had been cut off.

'That's non-negotiable. As of this moment you are under my protection. It's simply too dangerous for you to proceed as you have done. You're about to be married to one of the biggest fortunes in the world, not to mention the fact that you can also lay claim to one of the world's last remaining untapped oil bounties.'

At least, thought Samia with a hint of hysteria, she didn't have to worry that Sadiq was marrying her for her money! Any lingering sense of anonymity was a delicate thread about to break for ever.

Five days later

Sadiq was in the waiting area of one of the private dressing suites in London's most exclusive department store. Samia had been spirited away to somewhere within the labyrinthine rooms to be fitted out in a range of designer outfits, while he was waited upon hand and foot by a veritable army of beautiful women, all of whom were making their interest glaringly obvious.

The latest blonde offered him an array of newspapers and he picked one. She lingered far too long, causing Sadiq to bid her a curt thank-you. Once, not so long ago, he would have looked and decided if she was worth bedding. But not today, and never again.

That thought didn't fill him with the claustrophobia he might have expected. He had to admit that his resolve to stay faithful wasn't entirely down to the fact that he was about to be married but because curiosity and desire just weren't there.

He hadn't seen Samia again until he'd picked her up that morning. He'd told himself that he had to come with her because, after seeing her wardrobe, he couldn't trust that she would pick appropriate outfits. He conveniently ignored the fact that she'd been assigned a stylist with plenty of experience.

Samia had been waiting outside her apartment building, her hair tied back and looking pale and haunted in faded jeans, a light long-sleeved top and jacket. More unadorned than the servants who worked for him at the Hussein castle in B'harani. He'd had to quell irritation and also the disturbing flare of desire. Her jeans clung lovingly to slim legs and a pertly plump bottom. And the thin material of her top showed him again that her breasts were well shaped and more generous than he'd first assumed.

He'd reassured himself that his burgeoning desire for his fiancée was purely his head instructing his body to feel something for the only woman he would sleep with ever again, but the anticipation firing up his blood made a mockery of that assertion.

When he'd formally asked Samia to marry him after their dinner, he'd been overcome with a sense of desperation that she should agree—the first time he'd felt anything like it… or the first time in a long time. And he hadn't welcomed it.

A curious sense of fear tightened his body now, as he heard the whisper of movement which meant his fiancée was returning to parade the first of her outfits for his pleasure. He'd decided that Princess Samia would make him a good, uncomplicated wife, and suddenly the road ahead seemed paved with complications he'd not accounted for.

Samia wanted to yank the silver sheath excuse for a dress up over her bust and down over her knees, but was too intimidated by the personal shopper who reminded her painfully of her stepmother. Looking her up and down while she'd stood there in her plain underwear, she'd muttered something like, *'Well, there's not much we can do. You're too short for most of these dresses…'*

Battling back trepidation at the thought of being paraded in front of Sadiq like a slave girl at an auction, Samia fixed her gaze forward, determined not to see the undoubtedly

disappointed expression on his face. She'd not even looked
at herself in the numerous mirrors.

They emerged into the waiting room and Samia was aware
of the big, powerful body lounging indolently on a cream
sofa. Instantly her pulse quickened and that heat coiled low
in her belly. She was teetering in sky-high heels and felt as
unstable as a new foal on spindly legs.

Sadiq saw Samia emerge from behind a luxurious velvet
curtain. He automatically raked her up and down with his
eyes, as he had done with numerous women in the past—a
reflex. This was usually an erotic prequel for their mutual
pleasures later on. But never in his life had any of those
women had this immediate an effect on him. So immediate
and forcible that he had to angle his body in such a way as
to disguise its rampant response.

Samia's hair was still tied back in a bun at the nape of her
neck. He'd had to curb his urge to ask her to take it down
earlier, as if she were his mistress and she wasn't pleasing
him. Now she was avoiding his eye, and she was obviously
excruciatingly embarrassed. He could see the telling red
flush creep over her chest and up her neck and something
inside him twisted.

But she was simply the most erotic vision he'd ever seen in
his life. Far from his first impression of no curves, an almost
boyish figure, she actually possessed the body of a houri.
Without the boxy suits, jeans and unflattering top, she was
all slender limbs and curves. He couldn't take his eyes off
the full line of her bosom, like some kind of out-of-control
teenager. Her skin looked silky-soft and pale golden, and he
could imagine the contrast between his skin and hers as their
limbs entwined. The acute ache in his groin intensified.

His voice came, low and authoratitive. 'Leave us for a
moment, please.'

To his relief the stylist and her assistants melted away.

Privacy was something he'd never had to worry about before, having always managed to stay in control. It was as if some invisible barrier had existed between him and women before, keeping them at some kind of a distance, but here with Samia…there was no barrier…just heat.

The dress was totally inappropriate, but it revealed the intoxicating combination of Samia's innocence and an earthy sexuality that she clearly had no clue she possessed. He didn't expect for a moment that she wasn't experienced, but he would bet right then that any lover she'd had hadn't awoken her sensuality, and a fiercely primitive feeling swept through him.

And then he realised that Samia was still resolutely avoiding his gaze. Her reluctance for this scenario was palpable. He had an uncomfortable flashback to the way his father had used to insist on his mother parading the latest fashions from Paris he'd bought for her. He knew this was nothing like that, but his desire was doused as effectively as if he'd stepped into a freezing cold shower.

His voice was arctic. 'That dress is entirely unsuitable. Clearly we've come to the wrong place. Go and change. We're leaving.'

Sadiq saw Samia's jaw tense, and the set of her shoulders as she turned and walked stiffly back through the curtain, and had to restrain himself from stopping her and explaining…*what?* That for a second he'd been afraid that he'd turned into his father? His overweight, overbearing father, who had flaunted his women in front of his only son as if it was something to be proud of, and in front of his stoic wife like a punishment for as long as Sadiq could remember?

Distaste curdled his insides, and he got up and paced impatiently while he waited for Samia.

At least he would never subject her to what his mother had had to endure for years, despite whatever justification his father might have believed he had. Sadiq had always vowed he would do things differently. He would have nothing but respect for his wife and would treat his heirs like human beings, not pawns.

Samia took a breath and stepped back into the main suite. She was still stinging inside at Sadiq's cold condemnation of the outfit—and *her*. She hadn't looked at him once but she hadn't had to to know that his eyes had inspected every single piece of her and found it lacking. It had taken all of her strength to stand there and endure it. Even her rejection at the hands of that college boy was paling into insignificance next to Sadiq's silent but damning appraisal.

She stepped back into the suite to see Sadiq looking so broodingly at the floor that she had to battle the almost overwhelming feeling of *déjà vu* and curb the impulse to ask him if anything was wrong. She almost laughed at herself. As if she needed to ask! He was marrying *her*. And it was all wrong—if only he would agree with her.

He turned to look at her and her hands gripped her jacket. She felt shabby and more unsuitable then ever to be Queen. 'That dress—I don't think it—'

His hand slashed through the air. 'It did nothing for you because it was far too obvious and your beauty is not obvious. It's subtle. Clearly this was the wrong place to come. We'll have to go to Paris instead.'

Samia's mouth opened but nothing came out. She hadn't known what he would say but she hadn't expected that. For a moment her weak heart had fluttered to hear him describe her as beautiful, but then the *subtle* had struck home. It was just another way of saying she was plain.

Sadiq was already pacing away and speaking rapidly into his phone in fluent French, taking her arm to hustle her out of the suite and the shop. Anger was starting to bubble low in her belly at his heavy-handed behaviour, but now he was on his third phone call and she could tell from the guttural Arabic that it was about politics in Al-Omar. Samia was used to her brother switching off and becoming impossible to deal with at times like this, so she just crossed her arms and seethed silently beside Sadiq.

Within an hour they were ascending into the clear blue sky from a private airfield in the middle of London. Samia wasn't unused to private air travel—her own family had a fleet of jets and helicopters—but she and her brother only used them when absolutely necessary. Both were keenly aware of the environment and their carbon footprint, and of wanting to set an example.

She wasn't aware that Sadiq had terminated his phone call until a drawling voice asked, 'Are you going to ignore me for the entire flight?'

Samia turned to face him, instantly cowed by how gorgeous he looked with his jacket off and his shirt open at the throat. She wanted to know what he would look like in jeans and a T-shirt.

Her wayward imaginings made her snap more caustically than she would have intended, 'I could ask the same of you. And I've told you all along how unsuitable I am, so I don't appreciate your silent, cold condemnation when I don't morph into the bride you want.'

His eyes narrowed on her. 'I meant what I said back there, Samia. I don't hand out platitudes or compliments for the sake of it. It's not my style. I simply recognised that the establishment I'd chosen was entirely wrong for you.' His eyes travelled up and down her body with leisurely appraisal, and then back to her face, which was hot. 'Like I said, your beauty is subtle and needs a more…delicate approach.'

Samia still refused to believe for a second that he really meant what he'd said. This was just his way of placating her.

And now he was taking her somewhere they could camouflage her better. Stiffly she said, 'Well, I hope it's worth the expense and environmental impact of taking a private plane all the way to Paris just to dress me.'

Dark amusement made his eyes glint and Samia's heart speed up.

'Don't worry, Princess. I can assure you that our carbon footprint will be as minimal as possible. One of my own team of scientists is using this plane as a vehicle to test out more environmentally friendly fuels. So, actually, we're providing valuable research.'

Samia refused to let his humour infect her. 'You really have an answer for everything, don't you?'

He smiled properly now, and it made him look ten years younger and less cynical. 'Of course.'

Samia had to turn away. He was far too attractive at that moment, and she feared that he'd see something of the ambiguous emotions she was feeling on her far too expressive face. That she found him attractive was undeniable, but that was just pure human reaction to one of the most virile specimens of man on the planet. She denied to herself that the attraction went any deeper than that—that what she felt went beyond the physical.

'Believe me,' he said now, 'when we announce our engagement to the press on Monday you'll be grateful for the armour of suitable clothing.'

'Monday...' Samia looked around, feeling herself pale. If there was any last moment when she could try and get out of this, it was now.

She was unaware of the wistful look on her face or the way Sadiq's tightened.

'Don't even think about it, Samia. We've gone too far to turn back now. There's already been speculation in the

papers after that photo. Now they're just waiting for an an-
nouncement.'

Her eyes narrowed on Sadiq and any hope was doused
at the steely look on his face. Bitterly she said, 'It's so easy
for you, isn't it? You've had your life of hedonistic freedom,
and now you've decided to marry it'll be executed with the
minimum of fuss and maximum haste.'

Sadiq's eyes flashed. 'You've had your freedom too,
Samia. As a modern twenty-five-year-old woman you can't
expect me to assume you've led such a nun's existence that
you're still a virgin?'

Instantly reacting to his mocking tone with a visceral need
to protect herself, Samia taunted, 'You mean you don't mind
that you won't be getting a pure wife on your wedding night?
I would have thought with the amount of care you put into
choosing your oh-so-suitable bride that it would have been
part of the checklist.'

Their gazes locked. Samia was breathing far too rapidly
for her liking. And she couldn't believe she'd more or less
lied so blatantly. She was leading him to believe she'd had
plenty of lovers.

A cynical smile curved Sadiq's sensual mouth. 'It doesn't
bother me in the least,' he drawled. 'Of course I didn't expect a pure bride. I'm not so old-fashioned or such a hypocrite. I've got a healthy sexual appetite and quite frankly the
thought of sleeping with a novice is not something I relish.'

A sudden pain lanced Samia. Ever since that experience
in college she'd locked away any romantic desire that she
would one day give herself to someone who would appreciate her for unique self. She'd told herself she didn't harbour
such dreams. And now she had to face the prospect of Sadiq's
horror when he found that he had indeed bagged himself an
innocent bride on their wedding night.

Overcome with an emotion she didn't want to analyse, and

feeling terribly vulnerable, Samia scrambled inelegantly out of her seat. She felt permanently inelegant next to this man. Muttering something about being tired, she escaped to the back of the cabin, where she'd been shown a bedroom earlier, and firmly closed the door behind her. They'd be landing soon, but Samia curled up on the bed anyway and tried to block out the taunting and gorgeous face of Sadiq in her mind's eye. She wondered how on earth she'd ever been deluded enough to think he might be vulnerable.

Sadiq flung down his phone and glared out of the small oval window of the plane. All he could see were clouds upon clouds—and Samia's face, with those big wounded aquamarine eyes shimmering more blue than green against the pale skin of her face. He had already come to notice how her eyes went dark blue when she was emotional.

She'd looked close to tears just then, but he couldn't fathom what he'd said to upset her. His mouth twisted wryly. Apart from asking her to marry him. He hadn't had such a comprehensive attack on his ego ever…and he had to acknowledge at the same time that it wasn't altogether unwelcome. Being surrounded by yes people and sycophants became wearing after a while.

He thought back to what he'd said, and still couldn't see that he'd said anything untoward. Of course he hadn't expected her to be pure and untainted. He was a modern man and a modern ruler. Why would he behave one way himself and expect his wife to have lived like a nun? The important thing was that, whatever Samia had been doing, he'd seen no evidence of it.

He gritted his jaw against the pervasive memory that threatened to burst free when he thought of the words *pure* and *untainted*. A woman had said those words to him with a scathing voice a long time ago.

Analia Medena-Gonzalez. A stunningly beautiful social-ite from Europe who had come to visit Al-Omar with her ambassador father when Sadiq had been eighteen. He'd been no innocent youth then, but he hadn't exactly been experi-enced either.

Analia, who was ten years his senior, had seduced him and reduced him to putty in her hands, enslaving him with the power of her sensuality and sexuality. And Sadiq, like the young fool he'd been, had believed himself in love with her.

She'd stood in front of him the day she was leaving and looked at him as if he'd just crawled out from under a rock. 'You *love* me? Sadiq, darling, you don't love me. You are in lust with me, that's all.'

Sadiq could remember biting back the words trembling on his lips to contradict her. Even then some self-preserving instinct had kicked in—much to his everlasting gratitude.

She'd looked him up and down with those exotic green eyes and sighed. 'Darling, I'm twenty-eight and looking for my second husband. You're still a boy. The sooner you learn to harden your heart and not fall for every woman you sleep with, the better it will be for you. I know the kind of women you'll meet. They will all want your body, yes, but they will also want you because you're powerful and rich. Two of the greatest aphrodisiacs.'

She'd come close then, and all but whispered into his ear, 'Believe me, Sadiq, they won't care about the man you re-ally are—just as I don't really care. That's why you have a mother. One day you'll choose some pure and untainted local girl to be your wife, and you'll live happily ever after.'

The banal cruelty of those words hadn't had the power to shock or hurt Sadiq for a long, long time. He'd learnt a valu-able lesson, and her prophecy had turned out to be largely true.

Once he'd become Sultan on his father's death, at the age

of nineteen, he'd been catapulted to another stratosphere. For almost a year Sadiq hadn't even taken a lover, too intent on taking control of a wildly corrupted and chaotic country. But once he'd re-emerged into society women had surrounded him in droves.

He'd quickly become an expert at picking the ones who knew how he wanted to play the game. No emotional entanglement, no strings. He'd become used to seeing the glazed, avaricious glitter in their eyes when they saw the extent of his inestimable wealth and on some perverse level it had comforted him—because he never again wanted to be standing in front of a woman laying himself bare to her pity and ridicule.

He'd actually met Analia once or twice over the years, and once had even seduced her again, as if to purge the effect of that day from his mind and heart for ever. He'd looked at her as she'd dressed the next morning and hadn't felt a thing. Not a twinge of emotion. It had been a small moment of personal triumph.

Seeing the way his father had been so pathologically enraged because his wife didn't love him should have been enough of a lesson to Sadiq, but it hadn't. He wasn't about to forget either of those valuable lessons now, just because the woman he'd chosen to marry was singularly unimpressed with everything he put before her, wore her vulnerability on her sleeve and made him feel unaccountably protective.

Samia was facing another velvet drape in another exclusive shop about three hours later—albeit this time in a secluded side street in Paris, the centre of world fashion. She'd woken just before the air stewardess had come to tell her they were about to land, and Sadiq had largely ignored her on the journey into Paris. She fiddled for a moment with the chiffon overlay of the dress, and then the much friendlier French stylist appeared at her side and tugged her through the drape. 'Come on, *chérie*. We have a lot of outfits to get through.'

Samia closed her eyes for a split second and held her breath, the bright light blinding her for a moment so she couldn't see the initial expression on Sadiq's face. He was standing near the window and he lowered the ever-present smart phone from his ear.

Samia desperately felt like fidgeting in the long dress, but the stylist was already fussing around her, tweaking and pulling. Resolutely refusing to be intimidated this time, she hitched up her chin and looked straight at Sadiq—but his gaze was somewhere around her breasts. Samia's jaw clenched; he was looking *for* them, no doubt. Although she had to admit that even she'd been surprised at how voluptuous the dress made them look.

The sylist had chided her that she'd been wearing the wrong size bra for years and had quoted a size of 32C, which had had Samia protesting vociferously that she must be wrong. Until she'd given her a bra to try and it had fitted like a second skin.

Sadiq's gaze finally ascended and his face was completely expressionless. Samia thought she saw a flare of something in those blue depths, but put it down to the light and cursed the traitorous jump in her pulse.

'Much better.' His voice was cool. 'This is more like it. Well done, Simone. Keep going.'

And then Samia was whisked away, back into the dressing room, and pushed and pulled and contorted into a dizzying array of outfits. Evening wear, daywear, casual wear, beachwear. She soon affected her own uninterest as she was paraded in front of Sadiq for the umpteenth time. And then they were finished. When she went back outside Sadiq was gone, and she felt an ominous lurch where her heart was.

She whirled around when the petite Frenchwoman appeared holding out her coat. 'Um…do you know where…?'

Simone smiled and said cheerily, in her gorgeous accent, 'Your fiancé is trusting my judgement for the rest of the day. You don't really want him to see your wedding outfits before the wedding, do you? And also…' She linked her arm with Samia who felt extremely uncomfortable—never having been a *girly* girl. 'I think when he sees you in your new underwear it should be a nice surprise, *non*?'

For the next few hours, until dusk fell over Paris, Samia endured the humiliation of having an army of women parade around her, poking and prodding, and of climbing in and out of underwear so indecently flimsy that she had no earthly intention of ever wearing it for herself, never mind for someone else!

She'd been measured for her main wedding dress, which she would wear on the final day of the celebrations—the most westernised part of the wedding. The rest of the fitting for that would take place the next day, as well as her spending a few hours in a beauty salon. In a couple of weeks the dress would be brought to London for a final fitting and last adjustments before they left for Al-Omar.

So apparently they were staying in Paris for the night. An ominous fluttering started up in Samia's belly.

Simone escorted her out to the car that had been ferrying them around all afternoon and bade her goodnight, telling her that all of the clothes would be delivered to London and then on to Al-Omar. She pressed a small luxury holdall into Samia's hands and winked. 'You might need this tonight.'

Samia wasn't sure what she meant until she opened it in the privacy of the back of the car. She had no idea where she was going, and was too tired to ask, and yet felt bizarrely secure in the knowledge that Sadiq would know exactly where she was.

And then she saw what was in the bag: a selection of silky underwear and pyjamas. There was a smaller bag, with exquisite toiletries and a change of clothes for the next day. She'd lost her own favourite jeans somewhere along the way today, and was now wearing a beautifully tailored pair of designer trousers and an indecently soft cashmere jumper. Together with the new lace bra she wore underneath it all felt far too decadent, and not *her*.

By the time the car pulled up outside a very expensive looking townhouse, with the iconic Al-Omar flag flying at the entrance, Samia was feeling decidedly prickly.

CHAPTER FIVE

SAMIA walked into a hushed, dimly lit and luxurious reception hall. A huge chandelier twinkled above her and a massive winding staircase led upwards. There were exquisite oriental rugs on polished parquet floors, and small antique tables with Chinese vases which she guessed were Ming. Delicate rococco design was everywhere, and expensive looking art on the walls. One of the bodyguards closed the main door behind her softly and Samia put her leather bag down, forgetting all about her discomfort in the face of this sheer opulence.

She took a moment drinking it in before she realised that Sadiq was lounging against a wall nearby, hands in pockets, half hidden in the gloom like some dark knight. Samia put her hand to her suddenly pounding heart, knowing that it had more to do with the immediate kick of her pulse at the sight of that powerful body than fright.

That prickliness was back. 'You scared me half to death. Do you normally sneak up on people like that?'

Sadiq pushed himself off the wall and strolled towards her, half coming into the light, so his face was all dark shadows and hard planes, his white shirt making those blue eyes pop out. 'I came back to take care of some work in the office, but I left you in good hands.' His eyes flicked down and Samia felt it almost like the faint lash of a whip. 'The clothes suit you…we should have come to Simone in the first place.'

His tone of voice, as if he was talking about an inanimate object, made Samia irrationally angry. Her hands were clenched. 'My jeans are gone. I liked those jeans. Do you know how long it takes to break in a pair of jeans? And my top and jacket…they were perfectly good. How can I go for a walk in Hyde Park in *these*?'

She stuck her foot out to indicate the beautiful but impractical soft leather ankle boots with high heels. Sadiq came closer and Samia stumbled backwards, off balance for a second.

'I'm afraid your days of walking in Hyde Park unaccompanied are gone, Samia. Do you want to tell me what's really wrong? You must be the only woman on this earth who can spend the day shopping with an unlimited credit card and not emerge from the experience ecstatic with joy.'

Samia diverted her gaze, suddenly ashamed at her petulance. 'I'm sorry. I don't mean to sound ungrateful…but it's just not *me*.' She plucked at the luxurious jumper which clung so lovingly to her body and looked back up, unaware of the beseeching look on her face. 'I was never into this sort of thing. I feel like…I don't know who I am any more. I'm losing myself.'

To Samia's surprise, Sadiq came and put his hands on her shoulders and propelled her gently but firmly to a long mirror on a panel of the wall nearby. He stood her in front of it. Immediately she saw her reflection and Samia winced and looked away, but Sadiq held her fast.

'Look at yourself, Samia.'

She screwed her eyes shut and shook her head. She'd managed to avoid it so far. Too many memories of her stepmother standing her in front of a mirror and pointing out all of her failings were threatening to swamp her. She'd never felt so vulnerable. Especially with Sadiq's big warm hands on her shoulders, sending all sorts of shockwaves down her arms and between her legs where a pulse throbbed. She could feel her breasts grow heavy, and the lace bra chafed against suddenly stinging nipples.

Oh, God.

'Open your eyes, Samia. We're not moving till you do.' Recognising that steel tone, Samia knew she had no choice. With the utmost reluctance she opened her eyes and then heard a dry, 'Now, look in the mirror.'

Why was it that *this* man was the one person who seemed to have been given the unique ability to make herself face up to all her innermost demons? She'd only known him for a week, and yet he already knew more about her than anyone else. Thanks to her futile attempts to persuade him that she wasn't suitable for him which had backfired in spectacular fashion.

She turned her head and looked defiantly into the blue eyes in the dark face above hers. The heels lessened the height difference between them, but it was still substantial. He was a whole head and shoulders above her.

Sadiq arched a brow. 'You can gaze into my eyes all you want, Samia, but the object of this exercise is for you to look at *yourself.*' He smiled, and it was mocking. 'However, if you would prefer to look at me, then…'

Her face flaming, Samia quickly diverted her gaze and looked at herself—because right now that was the lesser of two evils. Somewhere along the way her hair had come down and she'd lost her clip, so now it lay in long wavy tendrils over her shoulders and down her back. The little curly pieces she could never control were framing her face. Her hair had been down more often in the past week than it had since she'd been a child. Her eyes were glittering almost feverishly in her too-pale face, with two bright spots of pink in her cheeks. She groaned inwardly; she looked as if she'd just been picking apples off a tree in an orchard. About as unsophisticated as you could possibly get.

And then she saw where the clinging material of her jumper moulded lovingly to her breasts, which suddenly seemed huge, the hard points of her nipples clearly pushing against the fabric. This should have been the point when she pulled away, made some facetious comment and broke the tension. But a heavy langour seemed to have invaded her veins, a curious lethargy, and yet there was an energy too, fizzing and jumping in her blood.

The trousers lay flat against her pelvis and then skimmed her legs, elongating them and making them look almost slender.

Sadiq's voice sounded rough, and his hands tightened marginally on her shoulders. 'Perhaps, Samia, it's about you finding yourself, *not* losing yourself at all. The image in that mirror is one of a woman who is about to become a queen, and the sooner you can see that too, the better. I can see it, so you really shouldn't doubt yourself.'

His hands were suddenly gone, and so was the warmth from his body behind her. She turned around and saw he was walking away, throwing over his shoulder carelessly, 'Helene will show you to your room. We'll eat in an hour.'

As if by magic a small wizened woman appeared and beckoned with a smile for Samia to follow her. She already had her bag in her hand. Sadiq's words about finding herself were ringing in her ears and affecting her at a very visceral level as she followed the housekeeper.

Sadiq closed the door behind him in his huge study and leant back against it for a moment, shutting his eyes. But it was no good. All he could see was the provocative fullness of Samia's breasts pushing against that flimsy top. They weren't even clothes designed to drive a man wild with desire! What would he do when she appeared in the long strapless evening dress she'd worn earlier, which had pushed the pale swells of her breasts high above the bodice?

When Samia had disappeared for another change he'd made a fool of himself by asking Simone tersely if it was entirely appropriate for any kind of function they'd be attending, and Simone had looked at him with dry amusement. '*Chéri*, that dress alone contains about three hundred more yards of material than the excuse for a dress you bought the last time you were here—so, yes, it's fine.'

His eyes snapped open again but that image of Samia— one long slender leg revealed in a thigh-high slit, bare shoulders and that enticing cleavage—was burned onto his retinas. He went and poured himself a shot of whisky and walked to the window, which looked out over the immaculate flood-lit gardens. How long had she been keeping that body hidden under those boxy suits? All her life, he'd guess, and yet for all of her apparent shyness and insecurity he was seeing more and more tantalising flashes of something much more feisty.

It had been some kind of torture today, watching her parade in front of him in a range of outfits. And he couldn't fathom it. He'd watched women parade in front of him for years and it had never had such a profound effect on him.

But with each successive fitting today Sadiq's tension had risen and risen, to the point that he'd had to leave or turn into a slavering fool in front of the impeccably cool Simone, whom he suspected had already noticed the change in his usually unflappable demeanour.

The wedding dress and underwear fittings had not come soon enough, and he'd all but run out of the salon. And now he stood here, hand clenched around his glass, wondering why he felt so threatened at facing the unexpected reality that he desired his wife-to-be. Surely this had to be a *good* thing? His wedding night would be no hardship.

Even at that thought his body hardened, and Sadiq cursed. He was reduced to being turned on—as if someone was controlling a remote mechanism from a distance! He took a deep gulp of the drink and winced slightly, chastising himself. He had nothing to fear. He was being ridiculous. It was as simple as this: he was embarking on an arranged marriage and his head was merely telling his body that he desired his wife. Biology, pure and simple, to ensure that he sired heirs.

Nevertheless, when Sadiq sat down and tried to concentrate on important correspondence trepidation skated over his nerve-endings.

A little later Sadiq sat back in his chair and twirled a wine glass in his hands, the ruby liquid catching the light. Samia was mesmerised by the play of muscles in Sadiq's forearm and had to force herself to remember what he'd just asked.

'My father remarried when I turned two. Alesha was a distant cousin of his, from the northern territory of Burquat.'

Sadiq's eyes narrowed on Samia and she looked down to her empty dessert plate.

'That's it?'

Samia shrugged minutely, uncomfortably aware of how the material of her top skated over her suddenly sensitive skin. 'She wasn't…very maternal. I think she viewed my brother and I as a threat.' She looked up at Sadiq again and tried a wry smile. 'You see, my father truly loved our mother, even though it had been an arranged marriage. And when she died…' Samia's smile faltered when she thought of the deep wells of sadness her father's eyes had been. 'He was devastated.'

Sadiq frowned. 'You said she died in childbirth with you?'

Samia nodded and swallowed, pushing down the emotion

she always thought she had no right to feel—that yawning sense of loss. 'She developed pre-eclampsia and by the time they realised why she'd gone into labour early it was too late. She slipped into a coma and died a few days later.'

Wanting to divert the attention from herself, Samia asked, 'You never had any brothers or sisters?'

He looked up, and the sudden tension in the air and in Sadiq's face warned Samia that she had strayed into sensitive territory—which made her curious.

He shook his head. 'No. Just me.' He smiled, but it was tight, and drained the last of his wine.

She'd obviously touched a nerve and was instantly intrigued. She watched the strong column of his throat work, and then flushed when she realised that he had put the glass down and was looking at her intently. Her scalp itched where a few strands of hair were pulled too tight. She'd put it up again, but instead of feeling more comfortable, it actually made her feel self-conscious.

Before she knew what was happening Sadiq had reached across the table and taken her hand in his. She couldn't pull away, and just watched dumbly as he turned it over in his palm. It looked tiny and very white cradled in his. And then he intertwined his fingers with hers, and Samia felt a pulse throb between her legs. She pressed them tight together and desperately wished for him to release her.

As if he knew exactly what effect he was having on her Sadiq smiled. 'I believe this will work, Samia. A marriage between us. You underestimate your appeal, you know.'

Her eyes met his and she bit her lip. She thought of the cool way he'd looked at her in countless different outfits all day, as if she were a brood mare. He was making her feel all hot and bothered, and sudden anger at his easy charm made her snap, 'You mean I should be grateful that you don't find me so repulsive that you won't need to be blindfolded to take me to bed on our wedding night?'

He smiled again, and it sent Samia's blood pounding through her body.

'On the contrary, Princess Samia. I think we'll be lucky if we make it to our wedding night without sleeping together. After all, we're both adults, both experienced, and I think we've established that neither one of us is bound by such romantic ideals as waiting till the night of our wedding. Introducing a blindfold into the proceedings certainly might add a little…something… But it won't be for me. I want to see every reaction that crosses your expressive face when we sleep together for the first time.'

A million things exploded in Samia's head at once, even as she registered that Sadiq's thumb was now stroking lazily across her hectic pulse point. But superseding everything was the thought of all that potent masculinity focused solely on her. It was overwhelming.

Not thinking clearly at all, beyond escaping the sudden threat he posed, Samia pulled her hand free of Sadiq and said priggishly, 'Well, I quite like the idea of adhering to tradition.'

Sadiq sat back again, and Samia wondered how someone could appear to be so relaxed and yet threatening at the same time. A dark shadow of stubble made the line of his jaw seem even harder, more defined, and the deepset blue eyes over the slightly hawklike nose should have given him a cruel aspect, but instead it all added up to one of the most beautiful faces she'd ever seen on a man. And that was including her brother, who seemed to turn any woman he encountered into a simpering bimbo.

His lower lip alone was indecent in its sensual provocation. When he spoke his voice was throaty. 'I think you're a tease, Samia. You say one thing and then you look at me as if you want to climb over this table and devour me whole. Is this what you do? Present men with an innocent, slightly gauche exterior and then reveal yourself bit by bit until they're begging for mercy?'

Her face truly flaming now, Samia looked at Sadiq. He had no idea. She was reacting to him because he was the first man who had broken through the thin veneer of control she'd believed impermeable for so long. *He* was the reason she was unravelling at the seams and revealing anything of her inner self.

She shook her head. 'I'm not teasing. Trust me.'

His face was suddenly all harsh lines and angles. 'So that little performance out there in front of the mirror was real? Are you going to tell me who was the one who made you so averse to looking at your own reflection?'

Ice entered Samia's veins. He was digging too deep, too fast. 'I don't know what you're talking about.' She felt as if her skin was being pulled back so all of her insecurities were laid bare. 'I wouldn't know how to tease my way out of a paper bag, and I never could act.'

She stood up with as much grace as she could muster and watched the way his eyes dropped to the level of her breasts before returning slowly to her face. *You're the tease!* She wanted to shout at him.

'It's been a long day, so if you don't mind I'll retire for the night.' *Brilliant. Now she sounded like a Victorian heroine.*

Sadiq stood too, and inclined his head. He looked huge on the other side of the table. 'By all means—be my guest. The car will pick you up at 10:00 a.m. tomorrow. I'm afraid I won't be here for breakfast as I've got an important conference call to take with my ministers in the morning. It'll run into a few hours. But I'll see you for dinner tomorrow evening.'

* * *

The following day Samia was grateful for the chance to lie horizontal while she had her eyelashes tinted. She'd hardly slept a wink after that conversation with Sadiq, and now she'd had the wedding dress fitting and had then deposited in this opluent beauty salon just off the Champs-Elysées, with Simone issuing a stream of incomprehensible instructions to the team of therapists assigned to her. For someone who'd never had a facial or a massage in her life, the whole experience was a little scary—if faintly pleasurable.

She wondered how many of his women had been brought to the same place, and couldn't stop a dart of something that felt awfully like jealousy from spiking in the pit of her belly.

One day in the library last week, when the others had been on a lunch break, Samia—much to her everlasting shame—had looked up archived newspaper reports about Sadiq. Of all of the women with whom he'd been associated just one name had popped up more than once, and it belonged to a well-known and beautiful European socialite. Their on/off affair seemed to stretch back to when Sadiq had been quite young, and immediately warning bells had gone off in Samia's head.

She'd witnessed her own brother change for ever and become hard after a love affair gone wrong when he was nineteen. She knew exactly how men like her brother and Sadiq could shut themselves off after feeling exposed. That memory of Sadiq in the library of the Hussein castle had taken on new significance.

A relatively recent photo of Sadiq with the same woman had said more than words ever could. They were entering an exclusive hotel in Paris and Sadiq was looking down into her perfect face. The intensity of his expression alone told Samia that if this man had once had a heart, it was long lost by now.

That evening, after their dinner had been cleared away, Samia looked at Sadiq and tried not to notice the fact that he looked tired.

In a bid to distract him from sensing her concern, she blurted out, 'How will this marriage be?' He frowned slightly, and Samia cursed herself. 'What I mean is...are you going to keep mistresses on the side?' She stuck out her chin. 'Because I won't stand for that. I won't be publicly ridiculed.'

Samia was surprised at the vehemence in her voice. Clearly she'd gone from assuming he would have to take a lover to stay satisfied to rejecting the notion with every cell in her body. The picture of him with that woman was burning a hole in her brain.

Sadiq smiled, and it was mocking enough to make Samia want to slap him.

'First of all, I've never had *mistresses*. I'm a one-woman man. At a time.'

Samia cringed. 'You know what I mean.'

'I don't currently have a mistress, as I would see it as incredibly bad taste to get engaged while entertaining another woman. And, contrary to what some people may expect— clearly all the gossips *you* were listening to—I have every intention of being a faithful husband.'

Samia flushed and said defensively. 'I wasn't listening to gossips... It's not exactly a secret that you've had plenty of...lovers.'

A look of distaste flashed across Sadiq's face. 'My own father paraded his mistresses in front of my mother, and I always vowed not to disrespect a wife like that. It turned my mother into a recluse.'

A wife. So impersonal. Did he regard her as just *a wife*? As if she even needed that question answered. Of course he did. And why did that suddenly not feel okay to her?

Wanting to avoid that line of questions and answers, she asked, 'You didn't get on with your father?'

Sadiq's mouth twisted and he looked at her coolly, some

indefinable emotion flashing across his face. 'Not exactly, no. He was an angry man for much of the time, for various reasons. And he took that anger out on my mother—and me—when it suited him.'

Samia had an immediate sense of a small boy being neglected and hated, and her heart contracted at that image. She wondered if that anger had ever turned physical. She'd got used to avoiding her stepmother's free hands and could sense that Sadiq too had become adept at getting out of harm's way. This hint of vulnerability was making all sorts of flutters take off in Samia's belly, and she longed to ask him more, but couldn't. He was already looking as if he regretted saying anything, and she was just beginning to realise how little he revealed of himself at all.

'Does your mother live with you?'

Sadiq nodded. 'She has her own quarters in the castle. You'll meet her when you come to B'harani before the wedding to settle in.'

Samia's belly tensed. Her eyes darted away from his intense gaze. That blue that seemed to sear right through her. She fiddled with the ring on her wedding finger, unused to its heavy weight.

'What if...?' She trailed off. What Samia really wanted to ask was what if she didn't please him in bed? How could he honestly say then that he wouldn't take a mistress? But instead she said, 'What if we have problems with children... getting pregnant?'

'Then I would divorce you and marry again.'

The speed of his response and its stark finality made Samia look at him again. Her mouth opened and shut. She was not sure at all how she felt about that, and was not liking the feeling. Finally she got out, 'What if it's *you* that has the problem?'

He smiled tightly. 'It won't be me.'

His insufferable arrogance made Samia sit up straight in her seat. 'Well, of course it could be you. Not even you can tell the future. You might be the Sultan but—'

'I *know*.' He cut her off. 'I've had medical tests and there's no evidence that there should be problems.'

Samia's mouth closed. 'But…why would you doubt your ability to have children?'

Sadiq sat back in his seat and a muscle twitched in his jaw. 'When you tell me who it was that nurtured your lack of confidence, and why you can't look at yourself in the mirror, then I'll tell you why I believed it necessary to get checked out.'

Stalemate. No way was Samia going to open herself up to his pity and mockery.

He was grim. 'I didn't think so.' He stood up then and loomed tall across the table. 'I have business to attend to in my study, if you'll excuse me?'

Samia half stood too, her mind whirling. He sounded accusatory, as if angry with her for bringing up these issues. 'Of course…'

He stopped at the door and turned back. 'When we arrive in London in the morning we're going to give a press conference to announce the marriage, so wear something suitable.' His mouth quirked as he obviously saw the terror dawn on Samia's face. 'Don't worry. I'll do the talking. You just have to stand there and look like you're not walking the plank.'

As they stood in front of the world's media the next morning, Sadiq's arm was tight around Samia's waist. She was tucked in to his side and tense enough to crack. Cameras flashed and questions were hurled out in about five different languages. Sadiq of course replied in kind, and with him by her side, she had to admit that this wasn't half as scary as she'd feared.

She'd be eternally grateful that Simone had called to the house that morning to drop off some photos of suggestions for accessories for the wedding. She had helped Samia pick out an outfit, and now she was wearing a plain shift dress in dark blue with a matching jacket.

Her hair was down after Sadiq had given her an express look on the private jet and said succinctly, 'Either you take it down, or I will. The hairdresser was told to leave it alone for a reason.'

To her utter relief Samia heard Sadiq announce that he would take a final question, and then a cheeky Cockney voice piped up from the back. 'Give her a kiss, will you?'

Samia hadn't really registered what he'd said until she was being turned into Sadiq's body and his hands were on her arms. He was smiling down at her, a sardonic expression on his face. 'They're looking for a public display of affection—think you can manage it?'

Samia gulped and wanted to shake her head and say no, because suddenly standing in front of a baying pack of newshounds was far less threatening than the fact that Sadiq's head was coming closer and closer and she couldn't move.

In that moment Sadiq thought how ironic it was as someone who'd never previously relished any kind of PDA, he found that he couldn't wait to kiss this woman, despite the wall of media just feet away. He pulled her into his body and knew that surprise was making her more malleable. She felt so delicate, so *small*, and instinctively he curved around her as if to protect her. She was looking up at him like a deer caught in the headlights, eyes huge.

Anticipation lasered through his veins like a shot of adrenalin, and the first taste of her mouth against his was so impossibly sweet that he groaned softly. Her lips were as soft as he'd imagined they would be. The room and all the people faded into the background as he slid his arms around her back to arch her into him even more.

He felt her hands cling on to the lapels of his jacket, but he was drowning in the sweet nectar of possibly one of the most chaste kisses he'd ever experienced. It was having anything but a chaste effect on his body—especially when he could feel the firm swells of Samia's breasts pressed into his chest.

Everything was tightening and hardening, and he knew he had to stop and pull back, try and regain some sanity. But just at that moment Samia opened her mouth. He felt the tentative touch of her tongue to his and his brain went red-hot.

It was a long second before Samia realised that Sadiq had stopped kissing her and was practically pushing her back from him, hands on her arms. She felt dizzy and disorientated and her lips were tingling. Catcalls and whistles brought her back to earth, though, and with her face flaming she let Sadiq usher her off the temporary dais and out to the waiting car. Her legs were wobbly and she prayed she would stay upright.

He handed her in to the car, but didn't follow. He was stooping at the door, looking in, and Samia felt bewildered and curiously emotional. It was as if an earthquake had just happened. But Sadiq looked so cool she wondered for a minute if they had even kissed.

His voice was as cool as he looked. 'I'm staying here to take a flight to Al-Omar. I have to return to take care of government business—I've been gone too long. You'll be well protected in the meantime, and I'll see you in two weeks.'

Samia looked at the harshly beautiful face, the pristine suit and tie, her eyes glittering. Every inch of him was the stupendously powerful ruler who had taken care of sorting out a convenient wife. He'd come into her life like a whirlwind, upending everything, and now he was leaving just as suddenly.

To avoid having him see the sudden confusion she was feeling written all over her face, she said, 'Okay…' and turned to face the front. As if she was absolutely unmoved by that kiss, and not feeling suspiciously *bereft*!

'I trust you'll have enough time to get your affairs in order?'

Samia swallowed back the lurch of emotion that came from somewhere scary. He was making it sound as if she was going to die. And *was* she going to die a kind of death? Even as she thought that she could feel the blood pumping through her veins, making a mockery of her thoughts. She'd never felt *more* alive than in this moment. Not even when she'd battled the ocean on that boat.

Aware of Sadiq waiting for a response, she vigorously nodded her head. 'Yes. It'll be fine.' She just wanted to be gone—away from his intense regard and those all-seeing eyes.

After an infinitesimal moment the door shut, and then the car was moving and she was being driven away from the tall figure. Samia didn't turn around to look at Sadiq, so she didn't see how long he stood there—long after the car had disappeared.

The shockwave that had gone through her body when Sadiq's mouth had touched hers was still there. His effect on her had been nothing short of cataclysmic, but she could imagine just how mind-numbingly unerotic that kiss must have been for him. How could it have been anything else? She remembered the way it had taken her a second to come to her senses, only to realise that he was all but prising her off him. And in front of the world's media.

Samia's emotions were all over the place. Up till now they'd been pretty straightforward: she had agreed to this

marriage because quite simply she knew she had a responsibility and a destiny to fulfil. Except now…something had
shifted inside her. Something had given way, and in its place
were *emotions* and feelings. And that kiss hadn't helped one
bit. It had put those emotions right to the forefront. The kiss
had made the desire she'd been trying to deny rise up, and
now it would not be suppressed again.

In the past couple of days she'd seen chinks in the cool
armour the Sultan wore so well. It had been easy to think
of him as just a ruthless, cynical man, determined to get his
own way. But she now knew—or at least suspected— that
he'd once been in love. She knew that he'd had a less than
perfect relationship with his father. He'd grown up alone,
with no brothers or sisters. Despite the pain her stepmother
had caused her, Samia wouldn't have survived without her
brother and sisters.

She couldn't stop an image forming in her head of a small
dark haired toddler running into Sadiq's arms, and put a hand
to her mouth in shock at her wayward imagination—and,
worse, the yearning feeling that accompanied it. She'd never
thought of herself as maternal, and it would be emotional sui-
cide to harbour such fantasies when marrying someone who
would only see children as *heirs* and *spares*. Sadiq hadn't
said as much, but he hadn't said anything, either, to discount
that view.

Samia groaned softly, and jumped when the driver asked,
'Is everything all right, Your Highness?'

She got out a garbled yes, and resolutely pushed aside
her disturbing line of thinking. She had to concentrate on
packing up her life here in London. Movers would be taking most of her stuff to Sadiq's London home, and the rest
would be shipped to Al-Omar. In two weeks she'd be meeting

her fiancé again in her new home, and her life would change for ever. But that wasn't half as daunting as the prospect of seeing Sadiq again.

CHAPTER SIX

By the end of the third day in B'harani, two weeks later, Samia knew she needn't have worried about how seeing Sadiq would affect her because he'd spent a grand total of five minutes with her.

The day she'd arrived she'd been looking around the extensive and luxurious surroundings of her private suite of rooms when a peremptory knock had come on the door. Without waiting for an answer someone had opened it. Samia's crazy heartbeat had told her that it could only be one person, as everyone else had been deferential to the point of embarrassment.

Sadiq had swept into the room, dominating the entire space immediately, resplendent in traditional white and gold Al-Omari robes. And even though she'd grown up seeing men in traditional dress he'd still taken her breath away. There had been something intensely masterful about the image he'd presented.

He'd been brusque and short, blue eyes disturbingly intense. 'I trust you had a good journey and that your rooms are to your liking?'

Samia had nodded, her mouth dry, tongue-tied in the face of his overwhelming presence and sheer masculinity. And this cool reception.

'Everything was...*is* fine. Thank you.'

'Good. I'm afraid I won't have much free time to spend with you as I'm trying to clear my schedule for the wedding and honeymoon.'

He had looked tired, dark stubble lining his jaw, and absurdly concern had risen within Samia. She had shrugged lightly, suddenly relieved that she wouldn't be the focus of his attention straight away, while trying not to think about his reference to the *honeymoon*. 'That's fine. I understand.'

He'd cracked a small tight smile and then said, with a rough quality to his voice that had resonated deep within her, 'You don't have to look so pleased to see the back of me. I'll make sure you're given tours of the castle and one of my aides will show you around B'harani. We have a public function to attend on Thursday night, before the wedding festivities start at the weekend. By Sunday we will be man and wife, and you will be Queen.'

The memory died away. Samia had just returned to her room after having dinner with Sadiq's mother, Yasmeena. She'd been kind enough to take her under her wing, and Samia had seen from where Sadiq had inherited his unusual blue eyes. The elegant older woman had shown her around the castle. She was friendly, if a little reserved, and carried an air of deep sadness that reminded Samia poignantly of her father.

Responding to the allure of the dusky view outside her patio doors now, she went out to the private terrace which also held a small lap pool, complete with a kaleidescope of coloured mosaics, and walked across to the trellised wall. The balmy heat caressed her skin like a silken touch, and Samia realised just how much she'd missed this: the heat and the open spaces and the huge sky twinkling with stars.

Laid out before her eyes was the gleaming city of B'harani, a veritable jewel in the Middle East's crown. An ancient port which had grown to become one of the most developed cities in the region. Sparkling skyscrapers soaring against the mauve sky managed not to look incongruous alongside the more ancient buildings. They looked triumphant, a shining example of ambition and success.

She'd made trips here when she was a child, and while her father might have been a guest of the Sultan she and her siblings had stayed outside the castle grounds.

Samia had always loved B'harani. It had been so much more developed than Burquat had been back then. So inspirational. And nothing had changed. It had only become even more beautiful and fantastic since then. She knew that Sadiq was a keen amateur architect and had a big hand in every building that was designed. She still loved the clean, wide boulevards with plenty of trees giving leafy shade, and the numerous liberally watered green spaces where people strolled and children played.

But her favourite place so far had been the gritty docks— the oldest part of the city. It was heaving with history, a warren of ancient markets and potent smells. Ships and boats groaning under the weight of their cargoes sailed in and out of the huge harbour all day and night. And, since she'd been last, a stunningly modern marina had come to sit very sympathetically within the old port, which Samia had already vowed to come back and visit when she had more time.

She had been invisible as she'd walked around in casual trousers and a loose top, with a headscarf hiding her distinctive hair, not wanting to draw any attention in case someone had seen the tabloids in the UK. Even though she knew well that after this week she'd become one of the most recognisable faces in the country. She would be Queen to these people. As she looked out over the sprawling city now she was daunted and scared, yes, but also for the first time a fledgling sense of something else took root. It was a sense of responsibility. Ever since she'd said yes to Sadiq, the prospect of taking on such a huge role had become less about fear and more about a burgeoning sense of excitement, which alternately scared her and made her want to see what she could start doing *now*. Something she'd never have guessed she'd feel in a million years.

Her hands gripped the wall when she imagined what the reality of marriage to Sadiq would be like. What it would be like to share a bedroom, and a *bed*. Heat flowed within her lower body and she grimaced. Perhaps he wouldn't expect to share a room at all. Perhaps they would keep separate rooms and he would come to her, do his matrimonial duty and then leave.

An ominous lurching in her chest when she thought of that was so strong that she gripped the wall even tighter. She absolutely refused to investigate that surge of sudden emotion. For someone who had always vowed not to fall in love after seeing it wreak nothing but destruction she should be ecstatic at the possibility that Sadiq might want to keep things as impersonal as possible.

All she had to do was think of the perfume her maid Alia had brought her in a distinctive Al-Omari gold-and-red box. Al-Omar was famed for its perfume production all over the world, and some bottles sold for thousands of dollars. Alia had informed her that it was a gift from the Sultan, made especially to celebrate their engagement.

But when Samia had taken a sniff she'd nearly been knocked out. It was so strong. It was way too musky and overbearing for her. Nothing like the kind of delicate scent she would favour. And it had seemed to epitomise everything about her situation and the Sultan's clear lack of interest now that his convenient wife had arrived.

Sadiq let his breath out and it was unsteady—as unsteady as the pounding of his heart. Ambition and the danger of the desert, or a challenging sailing race got his heart pounding. *Not* the sight of his wife-to-be. He had been standing on the balcony terrace just outside his office when he'd seen a movement out of the corner of his eye and looked down to see Samia standing by the wall surrounding her own private terrace. She was in profile to him but he could make out the intensity of the expression on her face.

Day was tipping slowly into night—usually his favourite time to look out over the busily winding down city. But that suddenly paled into insignificance next to the sheen of light gold from Samia's hair which flowed long and wavy down to the middle of her gently arched back.

He drank in the sight of her, slender in capri pants and a figure hugging cardigan, her breasts in provocative profile, and his whole body tightened in an instant. The slow burn of desire became faster, licking through his veins as he watched her like a voyeur. A curious dismay gripped him at this rampant response. At least he could say he now desired his fiancée. But he just couldn't fathom this attraction, which only seemed to grow stronger with each passing day.

Perhaps the real root of his ambiguous feelings was the fact that she evoked something within him that no other woman ever had. Something that was fiercely primal and at the same time protective. Not even Analia had evoked such a strong mix of reactions. His mouth twisted bitterly. No. That had been much more straightforward. She'd cruelly stepped on his heart and that would never happen again.

As the day of Samia's arrival had grown nearer and nearer Sadiq had grown more irritable, not liking the sense of anticipation one bit. It was his fear of the strength of that anticipation that had led him to be so brusque when he'd welcomed her. And he hadn't liked the feeling of spreading relief at seeing her here one little bit. When he'd said he was busy he hadn't lied, but he knew he was also using it as a convenient excuse. And for someone who'd never had to make excuses in his life it wasn't a comfortable feeling.

The day he'd said goodbye to her in London, after that kiss, when she'd turned that regal profile on him and been so cool, he'd wanted to reach in and pluck her from the back of the car, carry her to his private jet and bring her straight to Al-Omar. He'd felt like one of the nomads in the desert— raw and uncultivated.

The impulse had been so strong, but he'd told himself it was just because he didn't trust that she wouldn't get cold feet. And, telling himself it was for that reason each day in the interim, he'd instructed one of his PAs to call her body-guards and track her movements, becoming increasingly obsessed with what she was doing.

One night she'd gone to a small dinner party thrown by her work colleagues in a restaurant in Mayfair, dressed in one of her new dresses. Sadiq knew because he'd asked the bodyguard to send him pictures. It had been a perfectly mod-est dress—black V-neck with sleeves, and to the knee—but she'd worn her hair down and the curves she'd been hiding for years had been on display. For the first time in his life Sadiq had felt *jealous*. He'd precipitated that change and re-sented that other people were seeing it.

Suddenly the figure down below spun away from the wall and hurried back inside, and Sadiq realised his hands were gripping the iron railing. He consciously relaxed and looked out over the city again. His wife-to-be was proving to be a monumental distraction—something that wasn't meant to happen. The sooner he got control of himself the better. This marriage signified the next phase in development for his country. Nothing more and nothing less.

All he had to do was stop his mind straying with irritat-ing predictability to his fiancée...

* * *

The next day Sadiq was looking out of his main study window, and he cursed colourfully enough to have his chief aide go red in the face. But he was unaware of that as he took in the scene down below in the main courtyard of his extensive stables. 'What *is* she doing?' he muttered out loud.

And then, before Kamil, his aide, could intervene, Sadiq spun around and clipped out, 'This meeting is over. Get my horse saddled immediately.' And he left the room, ignoring the open-mouthed older man, to change into something more suitable.

Belatedly Kamil rushed after him. 'But, sire, you have to meet with the committee in two hours!'

'I'll be back by then,' Sadiq said grimly, and disappeared.

Samia felt mildly guilty that she'd convinced the young groom to let her take a horse out without checking with Sadiq first. But the last thing she'd wanted to do was disturb him with such a small thing. She'd decided stoutly that as he didn't want to spend time with her, that suited her fine too. And she'd been feeling increasingly claustrophobic. Even though the Hussein castle was as stunning as it was vast, with hundreds of secluded gardens and tantalising labyrinthine corridors which would take weeks to explore, its walls seemed to be closing in on Samia. Everywhere she went someone popped out to see if she needed anything.

While she appreciated their dedication, and knew they were only doing their jobs, she craved some freedom and some space, knowing very well that once she was married her sense of claustrophobia would only increase. Her every move would be accounted for and long days of back-to-back appointments would become the norm.

When she'd seen the stables a few days ago a rare excitement had kicked in her belly. She'd used to love riding when she'd been smaller, until her stepmother had seen that joy and with typical malice had announced that it was too un-ladylike and forbidden Samia from riding again.

Unbeknownst to her stepmother, Kaden had taken Samia out on covert riding excursions, so her skills were not too rusty. The powerful stallion moved restlessly beneath her, and Samia felt the power move through those huge muscles. A sense of burgeoning exhilaration flowed through her blood. From here the gates opened straight out onto castle-owned desert lands, which led in turn to the desert proper, which then stretched for many miles to the north and away from B'harani. All the way up to Burquat, in fact. When Samia realised that she felt a pang of homesickness. Spurring the horse on, she left the castle behind and they surged forward.

Sadiq saw them in the distance, where clouds of sand were being kicked up by the powerful horse's hooves. Samia looked tiny on the back of the huge black animal, her hair streaming out behind her. She wasn't even wearing a hat, and Sadiq's blood thundered in his veins as he started to close the distance between them. He could recognise that she was an excellent horsewoman but even that didn't douse his anger.

Samia only sensed another's presence when she heard a thundering sound behind her. She looked around and saw an almost mythically huge stallion bearing down on her and the livid features of Sadiq. The realisation that it was *him* behind her, chasing her, made her turn back and speed up. She knew she was reacting to something deep and primal. A fear of this man and his effect on her, how he made her feel.

But before she knew it Sadiq had pulled alongside and had reached for her reins to bring both horses to a stop. Within the space of what felt like seconds the horses had stopped and Sadiq had jumped down and plucked Samia out from her saddle. Her legs nearly gave way, they were shaking so much, and it was only his big hands on her waist that kept her standing. He was glaring down at her and looked wild and gorgeous. A long robe was moulded to his body by the desert breeze and he'd ripped away the material of the turban that had shielded his mouth from the sand. Blue eyes like chips of diamond ice stood out in stark relief. He could have been a desert nomad. A hot beat of desire went through Samia's body.

Sudden anger at that response and at his heavy-handed behaviour rose up. She ripped herself out of his hands, praying her legs wouldn't give way. 'What on earth are you doing? You could have killed us both with a stunt like that. I would have stopped.'

He was impossibly grim. 'So why did you speed up when you saw me? You little fool. Who said you could take out one of the most dangerous horses in the stables?'

Samia was still clinging on to the reins. She recalled the pleading of the young groom for her to wait for the head groom to come back before she chose a horse, but she'd blithely assured him that she would be well able for any horse.

Guilt struck her, making her defensive. 'I'm a good rider.'

Sadiq seemed to grunt something in response. 'Galloping into the desert on a powerful horse takes skill. What would you have done if he hadn't wanted to stop? You don't know this land, and you certainly don't know that this part of the desert ends on a cliff-edge about half a mile from here and drops into a deep canyon. That's why it's undeveloped.'

Samia blanched. She hadn't known that. The thought of galloping full speed towards a cliff edge was terrifying. Terrifying enough to compel Sadiq to come after her himself. No wonder he was livid. 'I had no idea it could be dangerous.'

Despite the danger that she hadn't known about, in that moment Samia feared that perhaps Sadiq was going to be exactly like her stepmother, curtailing every bit of pleasure in her life and diminishing her until she faded away again. With that came the revelatory realisation of just how much she'd changed in the past few weeks, and it shook her to her core.

A part of herself was being reawakened—a part that had been denied for a long time—and she was scared it would be taken away from her again. The reins dropped from her hands as she gesticulated. 'Look, I'm sorry for rushing out so recklessly, but I won't be kept in the castle like some bird in a cage.' With an air of desperation tingeing her voice she said, 'You can't stop me from doing what I want.'

Sadiq looked down at the woman in front of him. The adrenalin was finally diminishing and being replaced by something hot and far more dangerous. Samia's hair was loosely tied back and fell over one shoulder in a long wavy coil of russet-gold. A silk shirt was coming loose from where it had been tucked into tight jodphurs, which were in turn tucked into knee-high leather boots.

The silk shirt was damp with her perspiration and clung to breasts which rose and fell enticingly with her unsteady breaths. He was close enough to smell her delicate scent and had a sudden memory of the box of perfume he'd approved for her as a gift. He knew instantly that it had been entirely wrong. It was more suited to the kind of woman he'd known *before*.

Giving in to the twisted inarticulate desires this woman roused inside him, he said throatily as he reached for her, 'I have no intention of stopping you doing anything once you're safe. But I *can* stop you driving me crazy.'

'What do you—?' Samia didn't get anything else out in time. Sadiq had pulled her into his tall hard body with both hands and everything was blocked out as his head descended and his mouth unerringly found hers.

The desert was gone, the horses were gone, reality was gone, and in their place was red-hot desire and a need to fuse herself to this man, to lose herself in him and block out all concerns. It was immediate and all-consuming, as if there had been some build-up within her that she hadn't even been aware of. She realised that ever since that kiss in London she'd been craving to touch him again.

She clung to the material of Sadiq's robe, registering the muscles of his chest against the back of her hands. This kiss blew their first kiss out of the water. Sadiq's tongue caressed the seam of her lips and she opened to him with a deep groan of need, clasping him even tighter when his tongue delved in and met hers, stroking along it with the sure mastery of a man who knew how to kiss, and *well*.

He clasped the back of her head, holding her captive to his erotic attack, and his other hand moved down over the curve of her waist and to her bottom, pulling her up and into him. When she felt the thrillingly hard ridge of his arousal against her soft belly Samia went still. Their breath mingled. And then an even greater sense of urgency drove her and she arched herself into Sadiq as much as she could, the hot, spiralling need within her making her feel desperate. Her breasts were crushed to his chest and her arms had risen to wind around his neck. And their kiss went on and on, getting so hot that Samia almost expected to feel flames licking up her back.

After a long moment something indefinable shifted between them and Sadiq started to pull back. Without even intending it, she gave a little mewl of protest. He pulled his head back and with excruciating slowness sanity returned to Samia's brain, along with much needed oxygen.

It seemed to take an age for her to be able to open her

eyes, and when she did all she could see were two stormy blue oceans. Her arms were around his neck, one of his hands was on her head, his other hand was cupping her bottom. His erection hadn't subsided one bit, and she had to fight not to give in to the urge to rock against him with her pelvis—a completely instinctive move, seeking friction.

Along with the shock filtering into her brain was something much more nebulous and disbelieving. He'd kissed her. Why had he kissed her? He'd kissed her as if he were a drowning man in the desert who'd just found water. Or had that been her? She'd certainly been drowning.

Instantly aware of how she was clinging to him like some kind of octopus, Samia pulled back, dislodging his hands. She felt the absurd urge to apologise, her eyes darting away from that gaze which saw too much. She felt over-hot and dishevelled. *Had* she thrown herself at him? Overcome with a build-up of desire she hadn't even acknowledged?

A hand come to her chin, forcing her to look up at him again. She was undone and he looked…amazing. Her belly clenched hard with another spurt of desire.

His mouth quirked and her belly flip-flopped. 'I can see you doubting what just happened.'

Samia went pink. Was she so easy to read?

Sadiq smiled. 'I kissed you because I've thought about little else since we last kissed. I kissed you because I wanted to kiss you—because your face, your eyes—' his eyes dropped to her mouth '—your mouth is all I can think about.'

Samia gulped, wondering if she was dreaming. She could see the horses standing restlessly just feet away. She could feel the heat of the unrelenting sun on her head. She frowned, trying to make sense of this development and the burgeoning lick of excitement within her.

'But why…why haven't you wanted to spend any time with me?'

Sadiq grimaced and let go of her chin. 'Because of exactly what just happened. I'm not in control around you...'

He cursed and spun away for a moment and Samia blinked. Not in control around her? That was as fantastical a thing for her to hear as if Sadiq had just told her they were expecting a snow shower any moment.

Obeying some urge to clarify this, or to see if he was mocking her, Samia reached out to touch his arm. He turned around and she dropped her hand, the feel of those muscles through the thin material of his robe far too disconcerting to her very shaky equilibrium.

She steeled herself. 'I don't know... What you're saying is crazy.' Sanity came back, and along with it the insecurity she'd battled all her life. He had to be lying, or jesting, or something. 'I don't believe you.'

The most powerful, gorgeous man in the world could not be standing here telling *her* that she turned him on to the point of distraction.

He looked grim. 'I couldn't believe it either.'

Samia flushed. If anything, that statement convinced her. Of course he hadn't believed this. The bookish, boring wife he'd chosen was turning into something of an anomaly. No wonder he was grim.

She hitched up her chin, emotion threatening to constrict her throat. She felt as though some long-diminished part of her was being allowed to breathe again, but Sadiq clearly resented it because it didn't fit with his plans. 'It's obvious that this isn't something you expected, but as we're to be married then surely...' Her bravado crumbled. 'Surely at least it'll make things...easier?'

He quirked a brow. 'You mean in the bedroom?'

Samia's face flamed but she nodded. Sadiq moved closer again, and Samia had trouble standing her ground.

His voice was low and wickedly seductive, all grimness

gone and replaced with sensual promise. 'It'll certainly make things more pleasurable. The only problem will be keeping my mind on issues of the state rather than my wife's delectable body. I hadn't anticipated that.'

Samia had a vivid memory of his conversation with his lawyer that first day, and how he'd laid out his reasons for wanting a conservative bride: because the stability of his country came first and he wanted no distractions. Hurt at his obvious surprise and reluctance at this turn of events had her retorting waspishly, 'I'm not going to apologise for the failure of your efforts to choose a wife so unappealing that you wouldn't have to deal with the annoying complication of attraction. Clearly it's just your libido that's rampant. I'm sure any other woman standing in front of you would be having the same effect, even one as unassuming as me.'

Samia turned and walked jerkily over to her horse, gathering the reins before finding her footing in the stirrup and swinging lithely onto the horse's back. She set off back the way she'd come, not even looking to see if Sadiq was following her. When she heard him behind her she straightened her spine and fought the urge to make a gallop for it.

Sadiq looked at the tense back of the woman in front of him. He'd almost grabbed her to him when she'd whirled away just now—to do what? he asked himself. To keep kissing her until he couldn't stop and had them both on the desert ground, making love against the unforgiving sand? Because that was what would have happened if he hadn't clawed up some elusive self-control from somewhere and stopped kissing her.

She was wrong. He couldn't imagine any other woman turning him on as she just had. Some of the most beautiful women had thrown themselves at him, and one memorable time one had even been waiting naked in his bed. He'd had no problem turning his back on them.

And with the women he *had* chosen, he'd had no problem turning his back once he was done with them. He'd certainly never lost himself in a simple kiss as he just had with Samia. Something about her artless innocence mixed with that earthy sensuality made his brain turn to liquid heat.

He'd told himself that his ability to control himself with lovers had been down to the lesson harshly learnt when he'd been so young and so foolish. As if he'd consciously trained himself to control base desires. But he was realising now that the reason he hadn't lost control was because he simply hadn't felt a depth of desire so strong that it obliterated anything in its path. It was that depth of desire that made him want to ride up alongside Samia and pluck her from her saddle so that he could feel her body pressed up close to his.

Not wanting to have to think about those uncomfortable revelations, he did just that. Caution was thrown to the wind as he pulled up beside Samia. The voices in his head quietened. Reaching over, he pulled her, protesting vociferously, from the back of her horse and onto his saddle in front of him, between his legs, where his erection once again came to throbbing life. But he didn't care.

As he took the reins of her horse in one hand to lead it home he could hear her spluttering and working up to a tirade. She was tense enough to break between his legs. He bit back a smile of satisfaction and bent his head to whisper in her ear. 'Relax, Samia. And you're wrong, you know. There's not another woman on the planet right now who could induce me to lose my mind with a simple kiss.'

He snaked a proprietorial hand around her middle and felt triumphant when she relaxed against him. He could also feel when she gave up trying to articulate a reponse. He had to grit his teeth to fight the desire to move his hand down underneath those tight jodhpurs to feel if his arousal pressing

into her bottom was having as incendiary an effect on her
as it was on him.

The rest of the ride home was as torturous as it was curiously exhilarating.

A few hours later Samia stepped out of her shower to dry
off, and couldn't stop remembering how Sadiq's arousal had
felt against her bottom. By the time they'd got back to the
castle she'd been as weak as a kitten, all but slithering off
the horse into his waiting arms.

His chief aide had been hopping up and down, babbling
something about a meeting and people waiting. Sadiq had
let her go after a long moment and reminded her, 'The function is tonight. I'll come for you at seven.'

And Samia had watched him walk away, disorientated
and seriously bewildered by all the emotions he was arousing within her. She'd forgotten entirely about the function.

A knock came to her bathroom door then, and Samia
jumped, putting her towel around her firmly before opening it to see Alia outside with a long dress on a hanger. She
was dressed as all of Sadiq's servants were dressed, in impeccable white. 'I'm ready to dress you, Your Highness.'

Samia smiled at the girl, despite her sudden trepidation at
the prospect of the evening ahead. 'Okay, I'll be right out.'

CHAPTER SEVEN

An hour later Samia was waiting nervously for Sadiq. When the knock came on her door Alia opened it and stood back to let Sadiq come in, curtseying as he did so. Samia didn't notice Alia slip out, or the door close. All she saw was Sadiq in a dark tuxedo, looking almost criminally handsome, and she couldn't help but think back to that evening in the study and the singular way he'd made love to that woman. Almost as if he was looking to assuage that ennui Samia had witnessed.

He came into the room, hands in his pockets, and just looked at her for such a long, silent moment that Samia forgot about painful memories and put a nervous hand to her hair, which Alia had put in a complicated chignon. 'Alia said it was more appropriate to have it up with a dress like this.'

Sadiq quirked a small smile, making his teeth flash and heat bloom between Samia's thighs. 'You haven't looked at yourself yet?'

She flushed and shook her head, hating that he'd seen that vulnerability before.

'Come here,' he said, so softly that she almost didn't hear. But then she saw the impatience on his face and moved forward, her legs touching the silk of the dress, feeling unbearably decadent. She couldn't read Sadiq's expression, but something in it made her nerve-endings jump and sizzle. Goosebumps broke out across her skin as she stopped in front of him, and once again he took her shoulders and turned her around to face the mirror.

Reflexively Samia looked away, and heard him sigh expressively behind her. She had to get over this—so she looked back. And saw someone else standing in the mirror. For a split second she didn't actually recognise herself. The woman reflected back was a *woman*, not a girl, with her hair up and twisted into loose waves which made her neck look long and elegant.

Shadow on her eyes made them look smokily blue, the lashes long and spiky. A flush stained her cheeks and her lips looked moist and pink. Bare shoulders showed off pale skin, and when her eyes dropped they widened to see how the bodice of the silvery grey dress produced a gravity-defying cleavage.

Her eyes snapped up to Sadiq's. She brought her hands up to cover her chest. 'I had no idea—'

He smiled. 'That you had breasts?' He turned her around and kept his hands on her shoulders, burning her skin. 'Well, you do. And you look...' His gaze dropped and came back up. 'Beautiful.'

Samia opened her mouth and Sadiq put his hand over it, stopping her.

'No. I don't want to hear one word of doubt again. We will be presented to the world tonight, and you need to start believing in yourself—because if they sense even a hint of insecurity they will pounce.'

He took his hand away and Samia's mouth closed. She felt wobbly inside and all over. This whole scene was so far removed from anything she'd expected. Was he saying this just to bolster her confidence before they appeared in public? But the faint incredulity in Sadiq's tone when he'd said she was beautiful made her believe that perhaps he *had* meant it. After all, she hardly even recognised herself.

He reached into a pocket then, and pulled out a small velvet bag, opening it up to let two stunning platinum and diamond earrings fall into his hand. He handed them to Samia.

She took in a shaky breath and turned to look in the mirror to put them on. They were long and ornately elaborate, without being over the top, and swung against her neck, sparkling when she moved. She looked up at Sadiq and said huskily, 'Thank you. I'll take good care of them for the evening.'

He looked slightly bewildered by her reaction. 'They're yours, Samia. Everything I give you now is yours to keep.'

Sadiq took her hand to lead her from the room and the chaste gesture suddenly felt very intimate—because no one was there, so he didn't have to do it. *Just as he didn't have to kiss you in the desert today. But he did.*

She saw him spot the perfume bottle he'd gifted her on a table, and said hastily, while trying to block out the memory of the overpowering smell, 'Thank you for the perfume too.'

Dryly he said, 'And yet you don't wear it?'

Samia blushed behind him, cursing his powers of observation—and smell. 'I…it's lovely, but it's just a bit strong for me.'

He looked back as they reached the door, grimacing slightly. 'I realised it was all wrong for you today. I've already commissioned another scent and it should be ready for our wedding.'

'Okay,' Samia replied ineffectually as she followed him out. She was a little poleaxed at his admission that he'd realised it was wrong for her, and suddenly all those vulnerable feelings were back. She knew that if the next scent was anything close to something she'd have picked her herself she'd be in a lot of trouble.

On their walk to the main part of the castle they passed ancient stone walls with soaring ceilings, and tiny open-air courtyards where exotic peacocks stepped carefully among the plants. Burning flame lanterns lit their way, making the mosaics on some parts of the walls glint, effervescent in the light. It was truly breathtaking, and yet somehow diminished by the tall man who held Samia's hand. It was almost impossible to think of this intimidating castle as her *home*. And of this man as her husband.

Sadiq was silent until they came to the return which led to the main grand staircase leading down to the formal reception area and banquet hall. He turned and looked at her and just said, 'Ready?'

Samia was about to say, *No, and I don't think I ever will be,* but stopped herself. This was it. Her heart was beating rapidly, and jerkily she nodded her head once. 'Ready.'

Sadiq took her hand, lifted it to his mouth and kissed the inner palm, scattering Samia's brain to pieces. 'Good girl.'

And then he was leading her by the hand around the corner.

Down below there was a veritable sea of people. Women like birds of paradise in stunning gowns and glittering jewels, and men dashing in dark tuxedoes and some in more traditional robes with elaborate headdresses. Sadiq tucked her arm into his and they walked down the stairs. Samia held on tight and tried to smile, even though she felt as if she was walking into a lion-infested den.

Two hours later Samia's feet ached, her head ached and her face ached from smiling. She'd sat at Sadiq's side at dinner, and now they were mingling with the guests, who were a mix of the *crème de la crème* of Al-Omari society and visiting heads of state—like Sheikh Nadim and his wife from Merkazad.

The rest of the guests would be arriving for the wedding the following day, along with Samia's brother and sisters.

She wished Kaden could be here, but he'd been held up in London.

For a moment Sadiq was pulled away from Samia's side to speak with someone and she felt momentary panic. But just then Sadiq's mother, Yasmeena, appeared and took Samia's arm. Samia smiled. She liked the older woman.

'You look stunning tonight, my dear.'

Samia fought against her natural response to put herself down and smiled graciously. 'Thank you, Yasmeena. And you look lovely too.'

Yasmeena smiled. 'You're going to be so good for my son. I can feel it.'

Samia blushed. 'I hope I don't let him down.' And as soon as she said the words she realised that she actually meant them. Somewhere along the way her loyalties had sided firmly with Sadiq, and she felt a responsibility to him now, and to his country.

Yasmeena squeezed her arm. 'You won't. Everyone is captivated by you, Samia, you're a natural.'

Samia smiled weakly. 'I wouldn't go that far.' At that moment a movement caught Samia's eye and she looked up to see Sadiq nearby, holding court. He stood head and shoulders above everyone else, so handsome. Something inside her clenched hard.

'You like him, don't you?'

Samia's head snapped back to Yasmeena. She felt absurdly exposed. 'Well...that is, of course I like him...but it is an arranged marriage. You know that.'

She felt very defensive all of a sudden. But Yasmeena hadn't noticed. She seemed to have gone inwards to some private space, and the sadness in her amazing blue eyes was profound. She looked at Samia, smiling a little. 'I'd always hoped for more for Sadiq. I didn't want him to have the same kind of sterile marriage I had with his father. But he will be good to you. His father was…not a kind man. Sadiq is certainly not soft, but he's compassionate—which is more than his father ever was. I'm afraid we're not very close. His father guarded him jealously, and he went to boarding school so young…'

'How old was he?' Samia asked.

Yasmeena smiled sadly. 'Just eight. His father sent him to school in England—told him it would toughen him up.'

Samia's eyes were drawn back to Sadiq. He looked so composed, so sure of himself. He caught her eye and a ghost of a smile flickered across his face, making a ridiculous glow spread through her. But then his gaze fell to his mother and his smile faded. Samia shivered inwardly.

Sadiq's mother patted Samia's hand then, diverting her attention. 'You're a sensible girl. I wish I'd been so sensible at your age. I do want all the very best for you and my son.' She stopped and then started again. 'I just can't help wishing that he wasn't so cynical—'

'Mother,' came a clipped and cool voice, as a steel arm wrapped around Samia's waist, making her breath hitch, 'I need to steal my fiancée.'

Yasmeena smiled faintly, seemingly unmoved by her son's cool behaviour towards her, and then Samia was being shepherded away. She wondered why Sadiq seemed to shut his mother out, but then she was being introduced to members of Sadiq's government and she forgot about everything but surviving.

Much later Samia sent up a sigh of relief when Sadiq made excuses and led her from the room. He didn't take her hand this time as he led the way, and she tried not to be bothered, or suspect that he'd laid on the charm before the function only so that she would look suitably besotted by him. She knew that no one there would expect this marriage to be anything but an arranged match, but clearly Sadiq had his pride and wouldn't have wanted his betrothed scowling at his side.

Sadiq was waiting at the top of the stairs, and, not noticing, Samia cannoned straight into him, pitching backwards with a small cry because she had nowhere to steady herself. Quick as lightning Sadiq caught her and pulled her into his chest. Heart hammering with the sudden rush of adrenalin, Samia looked up. 'I'm sorry. I wasn't looking where I was going.'

Sadiq shook his head mock sternly. 'First you take off on a stallion, and now you're trying to throw yourself down the stairs... If I didn't know better I'd say you're still trying to get out of this marriage.'

Samia shook her head, mesmerised by the deep blue flecks in Sadiq's eyes. His arms were wrapped around her so tight that she could feel the hard strength of his chest and belly. Her breasts seemed to swell against her snug bodice.

Samia went to move back, and winced when a strand of hair caught in one of the many pins pulled sharply.

Immediately Sadiq tensed. 'Did I hurt you?'

'No.' She shook her head. 'It's just my head...my hair. It's aching.'

'Come here.' Sadiq pulled her farther along the corridor and stood her against a wall. And then he started to pull the pins out from her hair, loosening it so that it fell down around her shoulders.

Samia groaned and closed her eyes as the tension was released. 'That feels so good.'

Sadiq's voice was guttural. 'I've been wanting to do this all night.'

The last pins were out and Samia felt Sadiq's hands move through the heavy strands to her skull, where he massaged back and forth. She felt like purring. A heavy langour invaded her bloodstream and unconsciously she swayed towards him. His hands left her head and came to cup her face.

She opened heavy eyes and looked up. Her heart soared when she saw his head descend. She was ready for his kiss, mouth parted, aching to taste him again, already winding her arms around his neck and stretching up. On some level she still couldn't recognise this person she'd become, or the fact that this man appeared to find her attractive, but with each kiss it was sinking in more and more.

Sadiq gathered Samia into his arms as he drank in her sweetness. It had taken all of his restraint not to take her from that room much earlier. It had taken all of his restraint not to rip her away from perfectly banal conversations with the various men who seemed to have formed an orderly line to get to her all evening. For the first time in his life he'd been aware of only one woman in the room. *This* woman.

When he'd seen her talking with his mother he'd felt incredibly exposed. As he always did when his mother looked at him with those sad eyes.

As that realisation filtered through his consciousness Sadiq also realised that he was about to unzip Samia's dress, and that they were in one of the main corridors of the castle. He felt disorientated. But alarm bells rang loud enough to slice through the haze of desire.

Samia sensed the cool breeze of his mood-change when Sadiq pulled back. He was looking at her with something almost accusatory on his face and she quickly composed herself, hiding away her own horror at the fact that they'd been kissing like teenagers behind a bike shed. Once again she had the awful feeling that she'd thrown herself at him.

Appearing utterly in control and calm, Sadiq stood back and said, as if nothing had happened, 'I'll escort you to your room.'

Samia shook her head and tried to protest, but he was

already leading the way and Samia had to trail after him. She noticed all her hairpins spread out on the floor where where they'd been standing and went crimson. She stopped and Sadiq looked back and saw them too. A muscle jumped in his jaw when he saw Samia bend to pick them up.

'Leave them.'

She looked up. 'But—'

'I said leave them. Someone will clear them up.'

Sadiq looked so fierce for a moment that Samia quailed inside, and she straightened again, following Sadiq's tall, forbidding figure. A servant passed them and Sadiq issued a command. Samia's face burned when she thought of the state of her hair and what the servant would think when he did his master's bidding.

They reached her door and Sadiq opened it and stood back. Samia went through, childishly holding her breath as she passed Sadiq, so as not to breathe in that heady masculine scent. But it was no good, it was all around her.

'Goodnight, Samia. You did well this evening.'

She looked up at him and only saw that shuttered expression he did so well. He was a different man from the one who had been kissing her into oblivion two minutes before. She had the sensation that she was seeing tantalising glimpses of another side to Sadiq just before he clammed up again.

She smiled ruefully. 'It wasn't as excruciatingly painful as I'd expected.'

'See? I told you you'd have nothing to worry about.'

Nothing to worry about. Samia let herself be moved into yet another contortion to make it easier for the women to paint the henna tattoos on her hands and feet. It was the day before the wedding and she'd been washed, waxed and buffed from head to toe. She'd also spent an hour studying Al-Omari wedding etiquette, and Sadiq's chief aide had sat down with her to go through the exact sequence of events over the next three days. It was mind-boggling and immensely complicated.

Tomorrow would be the civil ceremony, presided over by an official. Traditionally Samia should be kept apart from Sadiq during that ceremony, as they both declared their consent to marry, but he'd told her that they would do it together, and she appreciated that nod to a more modern custom. Afterwards there would be a huge celebratory banquet.

The day after that there would be a series of appearances and lesser banquets to welcome all their guests. And the third day would be the most westernised part of the proceedings, in which she would publicly marry Sadiq in a lavish gown watched by the world's media. Followed by another sumptuous banquet and a ball.

Nothing to worry about. And yet Samia had to concede that her apprehension levels had diminished hugely since she'd weathered the function last night. She knew half of that was due in part to her preoccupation with the man she was marrying, and she shivered a little when she thought again of that kiss last night.

Hours later it was dark outside, and Sadiq was sitting at his study desk with paperwork piled high as he attempted to clear it in preparation for the wedding and honeymoon. It was impossible, though. His thoughts kept straying to one person.

Sadiq had to concede that he could see how dynamic Samia might be as Queen. He'd seen her in action last night. After she'd let go of his arm with that death grip, she'd navigated the room with an innate ease which could only have come from her background and education. More than one person had come up to him and complimented him on his choice of bride, and he hadn't been unaware of the surprise that he'd chosen someone so apparently modest and unassuming.

He'd watched how she'd put people at ease instantly with a light comment, and he'd prided himself on his initial instincts being correct. But, more than that, he'd felt *proud*. He'd also felt incredibly protective, knowing how nervous she was. But in the end she'd been quite content without him by her side, and that had left a dark emotion swirling in Sadiq's gut—to think that she didn't need him.

He sighed and pushed a hand through his hair, knowing he wouldn't get anything else done tonight. Samia had been preparing all day for the wedding, and his mind automatically visualised her naked body stepping from a steaming perfumed bath. Cursing volubly because he was thinking of her *again*, Sadiq stood up to leave the room—but his eye fell on a box on his desk. He picked it up and, telling himself that he knew exactly what he was doing, went towards Samia's rooms.

Samia was securing her dressing gown around her when she heard a knock on the door. Alia had just left, after making sure that she had everything laid out for the morning, so Samia approached the door with a smile, assuming it was her.

'Did you forget some—? Oh. It's you.'

Instantly a fine sweat seemed to break out over her skin when she saw Sadiq on the other side of the door, and she had to raise her eyeline. She felt extremely undressed in the flimsy silk night clothes.

In the same instant Sadiq silently cursed himself for coming here as he took in Samia's attire and saw how the silk moulded lovingly to the curve of her waist and breasts. He could see the dark shadow of her cleavage, the faint pink of her skin, and arousal was painfully instant. Had he really deluded himself that he would just come here and hand over what he had in his hand and then leave again?

Something within him shifted, and mentally he stepped

over a line. There was no going back now. He simply didn't have it in him to walk away from this woman.

Samia watched as some enigmatic expression crossed Sadiq's face. She felt a flutter of excitement deep in the pit of her belly.

'Can I come in?'

Samia knew she should say no and close the door in his face—for all sorts of reasons. And for all sorts of reasons she didn't. She stepped back, responding helplessly to the feral glitter in his eyes. *Lord.*

The door shut behind him and Sadiq held out a distinctive red and gold box. The new perfume. She looked from it to him and had a sudden fear of opening it. She reached out to take it, hoping he wouldn't wait for her reaction, but he lifted it high so she couldn't reach it.

Feeling utterly out of her depth, and trying to cling on to some sanity, fearing he was just toying with her, she said, 'Sadiq, what do you want? I don't think we're meant to see each other the night before the wedding.'

She was very self-conscious of the henna tattoo snaking up her hands, arms, over her feet and ankles. Sadiq's mouth curved in that slightly mocking smile she was coming to know so well.

'Those romantic notions don't apply to us.'

'Of course not.' As if she needed to be reminded. She looked down, afraid he'd see the quick dart of hurt in her chest, and then looked up again determined to make sure he was under no illusions that she harboured any such notions. 'Don't worry—I don't believe in love. I've seen how it causes bitterness and destruction.'

'Good. We're in complete agreement on that score,' Sadiq replied lightly, no expression on that harshly handsome face. 'I wanted to give you this perfume before tomorrow.'

She quashed the lancing hurt that he'd agreed so readily

with her, but she couldn't focus on that now. Her voice was far too breathless. 'So why won't you just give it to me then?'

His voice was like dark velvet. 'Because I want to show you where to place it on your body to get the most potent effect.'

'Sadiq...' she protested weakly, watching as with one hand he reached out to untie the belt around her robe. Feeling drained of all energy but the one fizzing in her blood, she half-heartedly tried to stop him. He flicked her hands away. His long fingers moving against her belly made her sway slightly, as if drunk.

With an economy of movement the belt was undone, and Sadiq gave her dressing gown a gentle pull so that it fell to the floor with a swishing sound. Now Samia was standing before him in nothing but the matching negligee, which clung like a second skin. She might as well have been naked. As she watched his eyes drift down over her body the atmosphere around them crackled with electricity. Her nipples tightened and chafed against the lace of the bodice.

Sadiq lazily took the exquisite perfume bottle out of the box and put the box on a nearby table. Without taking his eyes from hers he opened the gold top and pulled her arm towards him, placing the open end of the bottle against the hammering pulse-point of her wrist. She felt the tiniest trickle of cool liquid and could imagine it turning to steam as it hit her hot skin.

Huskily he said, 'Only a tiny amount is needed because it's so potent.'

Before the smell even hit her nostrils she just knew. This time he'd got it exactly right. It was so light it was barely discernible, and yet within seconds of mingling with her skin and pulse it became headier—a faint rose scent, winding upwards around her body. It was like the late summers she remembered in England, when the air was saturated with luxurious scents. Samia nearly closed her eyes and groaned out loud.

'I think this is more you…no?'

Samia couldn't speak. She just nodded, feeling very wobbly. Sadiq was placing some drops on the tip of his finger, and touching it to the pulse at the base of her neck, trailing that finger down over her breastbone and down farther to the cleavage between her breasts.

Samia brought up her hand to cover his and looked up at him, feeling wild with a reckless abandon and yet also not sure at all if she was ready for this. 'Sadiq, wait…we shouldn't…'

He arched that arrogant brow. 'Who says? We're our own masters, Samia. No one can tell us what to do. And I want you so badly it hurts.'

Blue eyes glittering almost feverishly, he brought the hand that covered his down and placed it over the throbbing heat of his erection. Samia looked down and saw her hand captured by his, touching him so intimately. The henna tattoo stood out like a brand, calling to her, saying, *Make this man yours.*

She lifted her gaze with an effort and it was as if nothing else outside this room mattered—only the heat between them right now. Her own voice husky, she said, 'I don't really want to stop…I want you too.'

'Good. Because I don't think I would have had the strength to turn around and walk out that door.'

The evocative scent that he'd had made for her seemed to enhance the moment, and as if in a trance Samia watched Sadiq put the bottle down on a table. He came close to her, and somehow Samia realised that they'd moved nearer to the bed. The dim lights made Sadiq's skin look golden olive. He was so beautiful he took her breath away. Completely on instinct she reached up and put her hand to his jaw, feeling the texture of his lightly stubbled skin.

She felt a muscle tense against her palm, and then Sadiq took her hand and pressed a kiss to her palm, and said with such intensity that she melted all over, *'Enough.'*

CHAPTER EIGHT

SADIQ brought her hand back down and placed it by her side. She saw him draw in a deep breath, and the thought that he had to exert control because of her made her blood sing. The thin spaghetti straps of her negligee felt incredibly flimsy as he pushed his finger under one and pulled it down her arm, and then did the same on the other side.

The thin material sank lower and lower, until it clung precariously to the fullest part of her breasts. With bated breath Samia watched Sadiq reach one finger to the valley of her cleavage to pull the material all the way down, wincing as it brushed over sensitive nipples.

She saw how the flush in his cheeks deepened, how his eyes glittered brightly. His voice was rough. 'You're so beautiful.'

For the first time Samia didn't have an immediate reflex negative reaction. But the intensity of Sadiq's expression made her come to her senses for a brief moment, and she knew she had to be honest with him before they went any further. He was reaching for her, and she stopped him by putting her hands on his. 'There's something I should tell you.'

'Yes?'

She took a breath. 'I'm not experienced.'

Sadiq smiled slightly. 'I guessed as much when we were in London.'

Samia shook her head, a little stung to think that despite her efforts to appear experienced he'd still thought her inexperienced. 'No, I mean I'm really not experienced. *At all.*'

Sadiq frowned. 'What are you saying?'

She cringed. He wasn't making this easy for her. A tinge of bitterness crept into her voice. 'I'm a virgin, Sadiq. A twenty-five-year-old virgin. Amazing as that might be to comprehend. Your analysis of my nunlike existence was accurate after all.'

Suddenly self-conscious, she pulled her nightdress back up over her breasts and turned around.

Sadiq looked at Samia's back and reeled. A virgin. How was that even possible? But all he had to do was think back to how buttoned-up she'd been when he'd first met her and he had his answer. He suspected that somewhere along the way some idiot had added to the emotional decimation carried out by the person who had made her reluctant to look at herself in mirrors.

'Who was he?' he asked now.

One of Samia's slim shoulders shrugged slightly. 'Some guy in college who'd been sent on a dare by his friends to seduce the Princess.'

Rage burnt in Sadiq's belly, and with it came a rush of something much more primal—triumphant, almost. She was his and she would be no one else's. *Ever.* He put his hands to her shoulders and turned her around, tipping her chin up so she had to look at him.

The defiantly defensive look on her face made something inordinately protective move through him. She was like a kitten, showing sharp but ineffectual claws. He twisted a long strand of silky hair around his fingers and pulled her closer. 'He was an idiot. Now…where were we?'

Sadiq had to steady his hands when he pulled the straps of her gown down again, baring those perfectly shaped breasts to his gaze. He was glad he knew she was a virgin, because he was so aroused that if he hadn't known he might have hurt her.

The way that Sadiq was so easily accepting of her innocence made her confidence bloom. Samia revelled in the way he was looking at her—as if she were the only woman in the world. She blocked out the insidious voices pointing out that every woman who'd stood before him like this must have felt the same.

That heat was building again, and with a gentle tug her nightdress fell to her waist. Sadiq reached out and cupped her breasts, testing their weight and firmness, thumbs passing over hard nipples, making them pucker even more. Samia bit her lip.

Sadiq took her hand and led her to the bed, sitting down and pulling her between his legs. With his hands holding her firm he put his mouth to one breast and then the other, making helpless sounds of pleasure come from her mouth. Her head fell back, hair tickling the base of her spine, as Sadiq sucked the peaks to stinging arousal.

She felt him pull her gown down the rest of the way until it pooled on the ground, and now all she wore was a flimsy pair of silk panties. In a move so smooth she didn't see it coming, he had Samia lying on her back on the bed, looking up at him and watching as he started to undress.

The dim light in the room highlighted his taut musculature as first his shirt came off and then his hands went to his belt. Samia sat up, her eyes drawn to the tantalising line of dark hair that led downwards underneath his trousers.

His hands stopped, and Samia heard him say, 'I want you to do it.'

Feeling gauche and nervous, Samia came up on her knees

and reached out, very aware of the henna tattoo which snaked up her arms. What she was doing felt illicit, decadent and more exciting than anything she'd ever experienced in her life.

A rush of intense longing went through her. She was all fingers and thumbs on his belt, and then the buttons and zip but then she was pushing his trousers down over lean hips, taking his underwear with them, and his impressive erection sprang free, making Samia blanch suddenly. For a moment she wasn't sure if she could do this, and doubt assailed her— the memory of baring herself before and being laughed at.

Worried, she looked up at him. 'Sadiq, I—'

He put a finger to her lips. 'Shh, don't speak.'

Sadiq kicked his clothes off and came down on the bed beside her. They lay length to length beside each other, and Samia could feel the awesome power of that arousal against her belly. Instinctively she moved, seeking friction, wanting to assuage the ache between her legs. She loved the feel of his powerful body alongside hers, all hard muscle next to her softness.

He kissed her long and luxuriously, as if they had all the time in the world. His hand drifted down over her belly to her pants. He slid it underneath and his fingers found where she was so damp and hot.

She couldn't move. She was boneless with desire as Sadiq's fingers moved in and out, alternately going faster, making her back arch off the bed towards his hand, and then slower, making her mewl with a savage frustration she'd never known before.

He pulled her panties down until she kicked them off herself. Then Sadiq pushed her legs apart until they were splayed in wanton abandonment, but Samia had gone beyond embarrassment and shame. She was this man's slave.

He slowly moved down her body, kissing his way until

he was between her legs. Samia's breath stopped altogether as with his fingers he bared her totally to his mercy, licking her with such indecent intimacy that a hectic flush rose all over her body. But that was nothing compared to the wickedly indescribable pleasure he was giving her, his mouth finding that cluster of nerves and sucking with a rhythm that was resmorseless.

'Sadiq, please...I can't...' Samia was barely coherent, her hips twitching uncontrollably as wave after wave of pleasure built and built, until Sadiq splayed a big hand on her belly, holding her down. He inserted a finger and Samia's head was almost blown off. The waves came closer together, and at a rush of pleasure almost too intense to bear Samia's entire body stilled, before falling into an ocean of exquisite aftershocks that racked every bone and cell.

Sadiq moved up over Samia's supine body. Sweat beaded his brow. It had taken more restraint than he'd thought he had not to explode before now. Especially when he'd felt the tightness of her body and the contractions of her orgasm. He'd never known a woman to be so responsive. He'd always prided himself on being a good lover, but every woman he'd been with had somehow given the impression of holding something back—as if they were too aware of themselves to let go completely. But Samia held nothing back. She was unrestrained and wild.

To think that he'd once dismissed her as plain and conservative. The thought was laughable now as he took in her luscious curves, the flush on her rosy-tipped breasts and that glorious hair spread out around her head. A light sheen of perspiration made her skin glow. Her eyes were slumberous as she looked at him. With an ominous lurch in his chest he came over her and pressed a kiss to soft lips, loving the way she opened her mouth and sought his tongue, exploring his

mouth with a studied thoroughness that had him pulling back
for fear of losing it completely.

Praying for control, he settled between her spread thighs
and with extreme care slowly slid the engorged head of his
erection along her wet folds. Samia moved her hips towards
him, causing him to slip inside her a little, and he gritted his
jaw.

'Wait…I have to take this…slowly. I don't want to hurt
you.'

'You won't…' Samia said the words but had no idea if he
would or not. All she knew was that she wanted to be joined
with this man in the most basic and primitive way.

With a groan, Sadiq thrust into Samia and at first she
wondered what all the fuss about hurting her was about. And
then he thrust again, and a more intense pain than she'd ever
felt sent shockwaves to her brain. It was blinding and white-
hot.

Instinctively recoiling from Sadiq's heavy weight and
that pain, she tried to pull back, while at the same time perversely not wanting to break the connection. She let out a
small sound of agony she couldn't hide.

'I know…' he soothed. 'I'm sorry. It'll hurt just for a bit.'

'Sadiq…' Samia sobbed in earnest, gripping his arms.
The pain was intensifying. 'I don't know if I can—'

'I know it hurts. But just trust me, okay?'

Eyes huge and watering, Samia looked up at him and nodded, biting her lip.

'You need to try and relax, *habibti*…you're so tight.'

The term of endearment struck her somewhere very vulnerable. Samia took a deep breath and concentrated on relaxing the muscles which even she could feel were like a vice
around Sadiq. And when she did that she could feel the solid
length of him slide a little deeper, as if something had given

way. Immediately, magically, the pain started to lessen, and she breathed out slowly on a shuddery breath.

'Okay?' Every sinew seemed to be pulled taut across Sadiq's chest.

Overcome with a wave of something that felt suspiciously tender, Samia nodded and Sadiq kept going, with almost excruciating slowness, deeper and deeper, until Samia felt as if he'd touch her very heart. And then he slowly withdrew, until he was almost out completely. This time when he thrust in the tightness had eased a little more, and a tremor of pleasure skated along Samia's nerve-endings. Relief was overwhelming, and she could feel her muscles relaxing even more.

She bent her legs, and Sadiq groaned as he buried himself inside her. He pressed a kiss to her mouth as he started up a slow, gentle rhythm in and out that made those tremors of pleasure turn into something much stronger.

Soon the pain was forgotten completely as she arched upwards and closer to Sadiq, chest to chest, relishing it when he slid so deep within her that she could feel no space between them. His pace quickened, his breathing grew unsteady and Samia could see the dark blush of colour staining his cheeks, the sweat on his brow.

Instinctively wrapping her legs around him, she couldn't help a deep moan escape her lips as an incredibly pleasurable tension wound inside her. It built and built like the waves had before, only this was about ten times more intense. The feel of Sadiq's powerful body moving in and out with such relentless precision finally made the tension snap, and Samia gripped him tight with her thighs as his body ground into hers and she felt the warm release of his seed inside her.

For a long moment, as the tremors of pleasure subsided in both their bodies, all that could be heard was ragged breathing and pounding hearts. Samia's legs were wrapped tight around Sadiq, binding him to her body. She loved everything about the feel of his heavy weight, on her and in her.

Eventually Sadiq moved and Samia had to let him go, reluctantly, wincing slightly as he extricated himself. He lay on his back beside her, eyes closed. Samia felt nakedly vulnerable and looked for a cover, but his voice stopped her.

'Are you okay? Did you bleed?' He sounded curiously detached, and it sent a sharp dart to Samia's heart. She looked down blankly and saw that there was indeed some blood on the exquisite bedcover. An irrational wave of guilt washed over her, and embarrassment too. A cool wind seemed to be emanating from Sadiq and she wanted to be alone, to try and make sense of what had happened. One minute she'd been about to go to bed alone, and the next...she was no longer a virgin.

'Yes, there's some blood,' she said quietly, moving to get off the bed. 'I'll get something to clean it.'

An arm held her back. 'I'll take care of it.' His voice was gruff.

Sadiq got up and walked to the bathroom, switching on a light and effortlessly highlighting the supreme perfection of his physique. He was utterly unselfconscious as he disappeared, and then steam quickly filled up the cavernous bathroom. He'd obviously turned on the shower.

With a wince as she felt how tender she was, Samia got off the bed, picking up her discarded dressing gown. She pulled it on, tying it securely with a shaking hand, and picked up her panties and nightgown too, before hovering uncertainly. She didn't know what to do.

Sadiq emerged from the bathroom again, steam billowing out behind him and as gloriously naked as the day he was born. Feeling absurdly embarrassed, Samia said stiffly, 'Can you put some clothes on?'

She averted her eyes and heard his dry response. 'It's a bit late for that now, don't you think?'

But she sighed with relief when she heard him pull up a zipper, and sneaked a look to see him finish buttoning his shirt. He picked up what she saw was a damp towel—presumably to clean the blood—and her heart beat unevenly.

She put out a hand, mortified that he was even still here, witnessing this. 'Please, I'll do that. You should go. I'm sure it wouldn't look good to be found in my room on our wedding morning.' She attempted to sound light. 'It wasn't in the etiquette book.'

It was only when Sadiq looked at Samia that he felt as if he was finally coming back to his senses. For a long moment he'd felt a little concussed. His brain numb after the onrush of too much…pleasure.

He wanted to go and pull Samia back into his arms, carry her into the shower and wash her from head to toe himself. And then he wanted to take her back to bed and pleasure her until she couldn't move a muscle. But something in her rigid stance made him stop. He might have suspected that he'd hurt her, but he'd felt the powerful contractions of her orgasm. She would be sore, though. She'd been so tight.

This intensity of feeling…it had to be because she'd been a virgin. *Had to be.* He hadn't even used protection, and as much as he wanted heirs he certainly hadn't planned on *this*. This surge of a desire so strong that there'd been no time for a rational discussion about anything.

Feeling exposed in a way that was becoming horribly familiar with this woman, he put down the towel and said, 'You should have a shower. You'll be sore.'

Samia flushed with embarrassment and silently pleaded with Sadiq to leave so she could be alone and make sense of what happened. 'Yes…I will.'

She felt rather than heard him come close, and despite

the tenderness in her body she was already melting and responding. He tipped up her chin so she couldn't avoid his eyes and she cursed him inwardly. For a moment he didn't speak, and tension coiled deep in her belly. His eyes were stormy again, and there was some emotion that made her hold her breath. Finally his mouth quirked in a tight smile. 'I don't think I handled that very well.'

Samia blinked. She would imagine he hadn't had to say anything like that to a woman for a long time—if ever. 'What do you mean…? It was…' She blushed even harder. 'It was fine.'

It had been more than fine. Sex with Sadiq had exploded the very secret fear that she might be frigid and she'd tasted paradise. *Fine* was a ridiculously ineffectual word for what had just happened.

His jaw clenched. 'I meant afterwards… I'm not the cuddly type, Samia. And I'm sorry you bled. I hope you're not too sore. But I'm not sorry we slept together. And when we return from our honeymoon you'll be moving into my rooms.'

Samia's face was stained a delicate pink that had Sadiq almost carrying her back to the bed to take her again, even though he knew he couldn't. She had to recover. She bit her lip and looked away, before looking back with such artless sensuality that his body throbbed painfully.

'I'm not sorry we slept together either…and the pain…it wasn't so bad.'

Sadiq could remember the way her eyes had watered, beseeching him to ease that pain. He gritted his jaw to stop himself from bending down to kiss those swollen lips. He backed away while he still could, because despite what he'd just said he was suddenly feeling the urge to offer to spend the night in her bed, just *sleeping*. 'Get some sleep, Samia. You're going to need it.'

It was only when Sadiq had closed her door behind him that he realised he'd not planned on sharing his rooms with his wife at all. He'd planned on keeping his own private space, anticipating that the marriage bed would be purely a functional place. But suddenly everything had changed, and there was no way he could contemplate that Samia wouldn't share his bed for the foreseeable future. He was going to find it hard enough to get through the wedding without touching her.

He reassured himself as he walked to his own room that once his desire for her diminished they would renegotiate sleeping arrangements.

Samia looked at the henna tattoo as the hot water sluiced down her body in the shower and saw that some of it had run and become smudged. She'd have to ask Alia to get the women to refresh it in the morning, and she wondered if they'd be able to tell what had happened.

Her head and heart were all over the place. She wasn't sure how she felt any more—about anything. She thought of Sadiq's stark statement that she'd be moving into his rooms, and the prospect of repeating the intensity she'd just experienced night after night was overwhelming.

The whole anatomy of this marriage was changing almost by the minute, resembling nothing close to what she would have imagined in London. She put her hands to her belly under the spray, recalling the warm rush of his release deep inside her. Her heart clenched. His obvious lack of concern about contraception said it all. Not to mention her part in that unforgivable oversight. But in all honesty she'd thought that they'd discuss things rationally before embarking on the physical side of things. There had been nothing rational about tonight.

Her hands trembled on her belly and Samia turned and

rested her forehead against the marble wall while the water sluiced down her back. She could already be pregnant with Sadiq's baby. She knew that for him it would be a mere tick on the list of his things to do after marrying his convenient wife, but for Samia the future wasn't looking so black and white any more, and she had an awful sick feeling that all her lofty notions about love were about to be seriously challenged.

CHAPTER NINE

On the final and last evening of the wedding celebrations Samia felt wrung out and extremely on edge. She was sitting alone for a rare moment, in the palatial banqueting hall where she and Sadiq had repeated their vows earlier in the day for the second time, in front of a huge crowd. The wedding band was heavy on her finger, glinting in her peripheral vision like a brand. She was now married to Sadiq. He was her *husband*.

He was just feet away, talking to her brother, his broad back to her, making her think of what it had been like to rake her fingernails down it to his muscular buttocks, when he'd shattered her in pieces the other night.

She sighed deeply. She wondered now if it had been a distant dream. Sadiq hadn't shared her bed again since then, and Samia would like to be able to say that she'd been relieved—but she couldn't deny that at every moment over the past three days she'd been acutely aware of Sadiq and had had to battle flashbacks to the sounds of their hearts beating in deafening unison and the way he'd felt between her legs.

It had felt wickedly decadent to know that they'd already been intimate, but that had quickly turned to frustration as Sadiq had seemed determined to keep Samia at arm's length—sometimes visibly flinching if she touched him, even in the rare moments they'd been alone. As a result she now felt incredibly sensitive and raw. Especially after seeing all the beautiful female guests one by one making a beeline for Sadiq. She'd had to wonder which of the more cloying ones had been his lovers.

Adding to her sense of dislocation and being on edge had been the fact that her brother had turned up with the last woman Samia would have ever expected to see him with again. The Englishwoman who had broken his heart years before. When Samia had raised an enquiring brow as Kaden had introduced Julia to Sadiq, he'd just quelled her with a fierce look, and she hadn't had a chance to question him since then.

The first ceremony had been the most understated—the two of them alone in a room with a handful of official witnesses who had listened to them pledge their vows. The stark language and lack of frills had made it somehow more moving and momentous in a way which she knew it shouldn't have been. After that, they'd been married. But that short ceremony had been only the start of the most colourful and frenetic seventy-two hours of Samia's life.

It all felt slightly unreal now, like a blur. She'd gone through the motions, saying her vows to Sadiq for a second time in the more grandiose western-style service earlier. She'd been relieved when it hadn't had the same effect as the first time round, afraid that some emotion would rise up unbidden and reveal something she wasn't ready to share with herself, never mind the vast ogling crowd.

For the first two days she'd been relatively demurely dressed, in a selection of traditional Al-Omari kaftans and veils that had been made in Paris, and had changed into more elaborate couture gowns for the evenings. She'd been absurdly happy and touched to see that Sadiq had asked Simone to come for the wedding. The no-nonsense Frenchwoman had been on hand to help her in and out of the umpteen changes all weekend, and had just helped her out of the ornate wedding gown and into a dark blue evening gown.

Her husband turned now, and those blue eyes seared right through her. Samia knew she was in a dangerous mood because she was feeling so sensitive and self-conscious. Three days of being under intense scrutiny was pushing her to her limit. He walked towards where she sat and a hush fell around the room. Sadiq was resplendent in the Al-Omari military uniform, a sword hanging by his side in a jewelled scabbard. He put out a hand and Samia placed hers in his palm. It was time for their first public dance. It would be their most intimate contact in days.

Trembling all over, from fatigue and something more volatile, she let him lead her to the dance floor. With distinct irritation in his voice Sadiq said near to her ear, 'If it's not too much trouble, do you think you can manage a fake smile at least? There are about five hundred spectators watching our every move. I know this is trying for you, but it's nearly over.'

They were practically the first words he'd directed at her since they'd exchanged vows earlier. Inexplicably it made tears smart at the back of Samia's eyes, because she felt as if she'd been playing the role of a lifetime, smiling and pretending that crowds of people didn't terrify her; the only thing keeping her going had been Sadiq's solid presence by her side. But with those few words Sadiq was letting her know that her innate discomfort in this milieu had been all too evident, and their intimacy of the other night felt even more like a distant dream.

Samia hated this rollercoaster of emotions she seemed to be on, and, feeling very shrewish, looked up, her long dress not diminishing the powerful feel of Sadiq's body one bit. 'And of those five hundred I'd suspect that at least three hundred are lamenting the loss of a lover.'

Sadiq's hold tightened almost painfully, and with a dangerous smile on his face he looked down and said, 'Jealous, Samia? There's actually only two hundred women here, so unless you're counting some of the men as conquests of mine also…?'

His cool arrogance made her want to spin out of his arms and leave the dance floor. Heat and tension surged between them, and then he uttered something guttural in a dialect that Samia didn't even recognise and he was kissing her. She wasn't aware of the tumultuous applause. She was only aware that she'd been waiting like a starving person for Sadiq to kiss her again properly. The chaste touches of their lips after the vows had been like a form of torture.

When he finally broke the kiss she was pliant in his arms, staring up at him, dazed. He looked impossibly grim.

'Do you really think I would be so crass as to invite ex-lovers to our wedding and put you in a position where people could talk or mock? And, while I'm flattered that you think me capable of it, the number of women who have graced my bed is far less than you seem to imagine. The only woman here that I want is standing right in front of me.'

Samia was stuck for words, feeling incredibly chastened even as an illicit bubble of joy rose upwards. Before she could make a complete ass of herself Sadiq continued dancing, as if the explosive moment hadn't just happened.

Somehow Samia got through the rest of the evening, buoyed up by Sadiq's words and the way he clamped her to his side.

Later, when he walked her to her room, Samia felt remorse clawing upwards. She knew the past few days had been trying for him too. She was also terrified he might read something into her jealousy. She turned to him outside her door and bit her lip before saying in a rush, 'I'm sorry…about earlier. I don't know what got into me. I'm just…a bit tired.'

Sadiq's jaw was tense. And then he sighed deeply, raking a hand through his hair. 'I'm sorry too. I didn't mean to be critical. I know how hard it must have been to have everyone staring at you like an exhibit in a zoo. And you've been amazing.'

Samia immediately felt a warm glow infusing her whole being. Shyly she said, 'Really?'

Sadiq looked tense again. 'Yes. Really.'

For a moment Samia thought he was about to kiss her, but then he stepped back and said, 'Tomorrow morning, early, we leave for Nazirat. Be ready.'

Sadiq stood outside Samia's closed bedroom door for a long moment while the waves of desire pounded through his body, not abating one bit. He'd never wanted a woman so badly. A mixture of ambiguous feelings made him wary, though. The past three days had not been the tedious ritual he might have expected. As he'd been saying his vows at that first ceremony, looking at Samia's veiled and downbent head, a completely unexpected wave of emotion had surged up. He'd put it down to gratitude that he'd found the right bride for him.

And she had been...amazing. Cool, calm, dignified. The perfect bride. More than he could have hoped for. Every atom of her being exuded her lineage and background with effortless grace. He wouldn't have believed the transformation if he hadn't seen it with his own eyes, but she was no longer the awkward woman he'd first met. It hadn't stopped him feeling inordinately protective, though, because he'd sensed it was a brittle shell hiding her insecurity.

The only time she'd shown a hint of strain had been this evening, and he cursed himself now for being so harsh on her. But when he'd seen her pale, unsmiling face, he'd thought back to how reluctant she'd been to marry him. Guilt had surged upwards. And that had brought too many unwelcome reminders of his own parents' marriage. His mother's reluctance and his father's vitriolic rage.

Sadiq kept assuring himself this was different—because he wasn't obsessed with Samia the way his father had been obsessed with his mother. And yet with an uncomfortable prickling feeling Sadiq knew that the passion he felt for Samia was close to bordering on the obsessive. He assured himself again: he respected Samia and they both knew where they stood. This *was* different.

He thought of her comment earlier on the dance floor; she'd been *jealous*. Normally when a woman exhibited that emotion it made him run fast in the opposite direction. But with Samia…it had enflamed him. Turned him on. And he'd kissed her in front of that crowd of relative strangers like a starving man falling on a feast.

He finally backed away from the door and smiled grimly when he thought of the honeymoon ahead. One week with Samia alone in an oasis paradise in the desert. One week to get this fixation out of his system so that when they returned to B'harani his desire would not be this all-consuming need and he would be able to get on with his job.

Samia realised that Sadiq hadn't been joking when Alia woke her at five the following morning. She was hustled out of bed, dressed, and was blinking in the dawn light outside when Sadiq pulled up in a Jeep, looking dark and gorgeous in jeans and a casual jumper. Instantly Samia was awake and on high alert.

Sadiq barely looked at her though, brusque to the point of rudeness, and they drove to a small landing pad where a helicopter was waiting.

After a thirty-minute journey over the undulating landscape of the desert that changed colour as the sun rose, they landed near a modest-sized castle. Sadiq took her arm in a firm grip.

Samia figured that the only possible reason for his bad mood had to be because he was dreading the idea of spending a week in the desert, alone with her. Familiar insecurity constricted her insides. How could it be anything else? She was so inexperienced; he was highly sexed. The other night had to have been a disappointment for him.

She cursed herself again for having shown that she was jealous. She'd let fatigue and tension get to her, and she couldn't let that happen again.

But as soon as they were alone in a huge and stunning bedroom which seemed to open out directly onto the vast desert he turned to her with ferocity in his eyes.

'Come here,' he ordered in a rough voice, and Samia moved to him as if in a dream, half scared at the look on his face and half thrilled.

As soon as she was close enough he pulled her to him and his eyes roved over her face as if he'd never seen her before. His hand was busy undoing her hair so that it fell in thick waves down her back.

'That's better. I was afraid to speak on the way here in case I started kissing you and couldn't stop. The last three days have been the longest days of my life.' He tipped up her chin. 'Do you have any idea how hard it's been to watch you parading around in those stunning dresses and not pull you behind a column so that I could strip you bare and make love to you until you were screaming my name and I couldn't remember who I was?'

Heat flooded Samia and confusion reigned, along with an awful burst of hope within her breast. 'But…last night you didn't…?' She bit her lip for a second and blurted out, 'I wanted you to make love to me. But I didn't want to…ask.'

Sadiq smiled, and it looked slightly pained. 'I don't know

how I walked away from you but I wanted to make sure you were fully recovered. Because I don't intend to let you out of bed for this whole week. Starting now...'

And he took her face in his hands and kissed her until she was boneless. When he picked Samia up and carried her to the bed she was trembling all over with the anticipation and build-up of the last three days.

Later, with no idea how much time had passed, Samia woke but kept her eyes closed. She was naked, face-down in a soft bed, and she'd never felt so completely and utterly—

'Good evening, *habibti*...how are you feeling?'

Samia smiled. She couldn't keep it in. But she didn't open her eyes for fear of making this dream end. Her voice sounded indecently husky. 'I feel like I won't be able to move ever again.'

A dark, sexy chuckle was accompanied by a hot kiss on her bare shoulder, and then the bed dipped and Sadiq got out. Reluctantly Samia opened her eyes and watched the impressive back view of her naked husband as he walked across the luxurious room to the *en suite* bathroom. Whatever she'd experienced that first night in Sadiq's bed had been surpassed, and she knew with a little shiver of pleasure that it was only going to get better. Never in her wildest dreams or fantasies had she imagined that sex could be so...amazing.

Samia turned onto her back and looked out to see dusk falling over the dunes in the distance through the open doorway. They'd been in bed all day. And they were utterly alone, utterly remote. No one but them and the discreet staff and some of Sadiq's security men in another lodging nearby. They were deep in the desert interior of Al-Omar, majestic in its isolation. The closest civilisation was the oasis town of Nazirat, some twenty miles away.

This ancient fortress castle had been built on a small

neighbouring oasis some three hundred years previously, but Sadiq had made improvements along the way and now it was a luxurious hideaway. Alia had told Samia that apparently one of his ancestors had built it for a favoured wife. The romanticism struck a dangerous chord in Samia.

Through the open doors she could also see the still water of their private pool, the low divans around it piled high with opulent cushions and throws. Candles flickered softly in tall glass lanterns. The gentle breeze was warm. A feeling that she'd never experienced before stole over her. Samia frowned, trying to pinpoint what it was, and with a flash realised that it was contentment. And peace.

She wondered for a moment if she was in fact dreaming, because she'd never been given to dreamy introspection before, but the tenderness between her legs told her otherwise. Just then Sadiq emerged naked from the bathroom, walking towards the bed with singular intent and a wicked gleam in his eyes. If this was a dream Samia knew she didn't want to wake up just yet.

Before she could draw breath he'd plucked her up off the bed into his arms and was striding back towards the bathroom. The steam of the huge shower enveloped them like a luxurious warm mist. Within minutes of stepping under the powerful spray Sadiq was soaping her body with a thoroughness that had a visible effect on him, and Samia was all but begging him to take her, right there.

She'd obviously spoken aloud, because he tipped her head back, cocooning her from the spray with his big body. 'Believe me, I want to, *habiba*, but you're still tender. And we need to use protection. But don't worry…I won't always be so considerate.'

It was only then that Samia realised that Sadiq *had* been careful and used protection. But before she could ask him about it Sadiq was turning her around and rinsing off her back. She felt him go still behind her.

Sounding completely shocked, he said, 'You have a tattoo.'

She'd forgotten all about the tattoo across her lower back, just above her buttocks. Something rebellious rose up within her at his shocked tone and she turned around. 'Yes, I have a tattoo. Is that so hard to believe?'

Sadiq looked at her and she found the indignant look on his face slightly funny. She could well imagine that when he'd been vetting her for her suitability he wouldn't in a million years have dreamt she'd have a tattoo.

'Where did you get it done?'

'In New York with my friends, before we sailed across the Atlantic. We all got different ones which meant something personal to us.'

Sadiq switched off the shower with an abrupt move and grabbed a towel, wrapping it around Samia.

'What is it?' she asked, more hesitantly than she would have liked. 'Are you really so shocked?'

Sadiq tried to school his features as he busied himself rubbing Samia dry, which of course was entirely too distracting in itself. It was ridiculous, but in some way he felt slightly betrayed…*by a tattoo.* Samia was looking at him expectantly, her skin soft and glowing and more seductive than she could ever know.

He forced himself to be rational and quirked a wry smile. 'A tattoo is not something I associated with the mouse who came into my study that first day in London.'

Samia flushed pinker and looked away, and perversely that made Sadiq feel comforted. He caught her chin and brought her head up so he could inspect those blue depths. Curbing his insatiable desire to rip the towel away and do what she'd just been begging him to do in the shower, he asked gruffly, 'What does it mean?'

'It's the Chinese symbol for strength.'

Sadiq saw something intensely vulnerable flash in those aqaumarine depths and had to drive down a spark of emotion. It made his voice more curt than he would have intended. 'Let's have dinner and you can tell me all about why you'd want a symbol for strength tattooed onto your skin.'

He watched Samia walk into the bedroom and dither for a moment before self-consciously pulling on the kaftan which had been left out for her, leaving the towel around her till the last minute. Clearly she was not used to this kind of intimacy, and evidently Sadiq had become too jaded from seeing lovers eager to display their naked bodies to him, because watching Samia was like watching the most erotic striptease he'd ever seen.

He saw the tattoo again just before it was covered up by the kaftan dropping over her body and had to admit it was sexy, positioned where it was just above the jut of her buttocks, where only someone intimately acquainted with her body would see it.

As he dressed himself and tried to control his insatiable libido, which was responding helplessly to that image, he had to admit to a slight feeling of disorientation. Samia was turning into something of an enigma, and this was something Sadiq had not accounted for. Nor he was even sure he particularly welcomed it.

An hour later they were sitting on an open-air terrace on the level below their bedroom. A table for two had been set with flickering candles. Chilled white wine was in beautiful goblet-style glasses. The discreet staff, dressed in the same white clothes that were a trademark of the Hussein castle, had been flitting to and fro, serving a range of delicious delicacies for them to feast on.

Samia loved the rustic nature of the dinner—the fact that the table was bare and plain, despite obviously being an antique and inlaid with mother of pearl mosaics. The feel of the raw silk of the kaftan against her skin was like an erotic caress, and she had to stop herself squirming in her seat, already wantonly wishing they were back upstairs in that huge bed with nothing between them. She was also desperately hoping that Sadiq wouldn't remember what he'd said.

But, in that uncanny way he had of honing in on her most private thoughts, he sat back, took his wine glass in his hand and looked at her. 'So...tell me. Strength. What did you need strength for?'

Samia wiped her mouth with her napkin and looked across the table at Sadiq. She'd been avoiding looking at him because in this flickering light, with a hint of stubble on his jaw, he looked so gorgeous... She sighed. He was waiting for her answer.

Why did it have to be Sadiq who wanted to hone in on the workings of her psyche? She looked down and pleated her napkin nervously. 'I told you before about my stepmother?'

He nodded. 'You said you didn't get on?'

Samia nodded and looked up, took a sip of wine for fortitude. 'I got the symbol for strength because embarking on that sailing trip I felt as if I was strong—for the first time in my life. After years of feeling weak.'

She flashed a brittle smile at Sadiq, hating how vulnerable this was making her feel.

'Alesha despised me from the moment she saw me, for all sorts of reasons, but mainly because I looked like my mother. It was common knowledge that my father and mother had shared a great love. He visited her shrine every day religiously until he died.'

She grimaced slightly. 'Alesha used to tell me from when I was tiny that because I looked like my mother it made it harder for my father to be around me, because I was the reason she died.'

'Samia—'

She cut him off, pretending not to hear him, not wanting him to think she was looking for sympathy. 'Her forte was targeting people's weak spots. She used it to chip away at my self-confidence, constantly pointing out how different I was. Things got worse when she had girl after girl and no precious male heir to counteract Kaden's supremacy and mine.'

Samia's voice had become a monotone, as if she could try and hide the emotion she felt. 'If I found anything I enjoyed doing, she'd stop me. It was a constant war of attrition and I couldn't fight her.'

Sadiq said dryly, but with a steel tone, 'She sounds utterly charming.'

Samia looked at him and was relieved not to see pity. Her heart pounded a little at the look in his eyes. 'She was, you see—to anyone on the outside looking in. She was an arch manipulator, angry and bitter because she knew my father didn't love her. I was meant to give a piano recital one day in our huge banquet hall, for my father and some important guests—' Samia stopped. What was she doing, babbling on about mundane childhood incidents?

But Sadiq inclined his head. 'Go on, Samia. I want to hear this.'

Cursing herself for bringing this up, she continued reluctantly, 'I'd practised for weeks on my mother's piano. She'd nearly become a concert pianist before she met my father, and when I played I felt somehow…close to her. Not that I had half her talent.' She blushed, feeling silly, but Sadiq was still looking at her with something unfathomable yet encouraging in his eyes.

Samia took a deep breath. 'Alesha took me aside just before I went on. I don't even remember what she said now, but when I sat down...I froze. I couldn't remember a note of the music and I couldn't move. All I can remember is excruciating terror, not knowing how to just get up and leave. Kaden had to come and physically lift me off the stool. I'd let my father down in front of his guests—but, worse than that, I felt I'd let my mother's memory down. I haven't touched a piano since.'

She grimaced at herself now. 'It's all so mundane really. My childhood was no worse than many others. Alesha was just a bully. Apart from her we had a perfectly stable and secure background.'

Almost harshly, Sadiq cut in. 'No, it's not. Nothing is mundane, when you're a child and your world is threatened. You can have the most secure background and yet within that lies any number of threats.'

Samia looked at him, her eyes growing wide. 'Why do you say that?'

His jaw clenched. 'Because it's true. My world was threatened every day when my father took his anger at my mother out on me—or her. Whoever was closest. I watched my father kick her so hard in the belly once that she lay there bleeding. But he wouldn't let me help her. I tried to, but he beat me back.'

Samia sucked in a horrified gasp. 'How could he have done such a thing? And let you watch?'

Sadiq smiled grimly. 'So that I would know how to deal with a disobedient wife. A wife who wouldn't give him any more children.'

Samia shook her head, feeling sick. 'You would never be capable of such a thing. How old were you?'

Sadiq shrugged now. He felt curiously raw at Samia's easy assertion that he was not like his father. 'About five.'

Samia shook her head. 'Sadiq, that's horrific. Is that why she didn't have any more children?'

'She didn't have any more children because my father slept with mistresses while she was pregnant with me and then passed on a sexually transmitted disease to her. She wouldn't sleep with him after that, and as a result of his pride and refusal to seek treatment he became infertile.'

The disgust he felt whenever he thought of his father was rising inside Sadiq, and he wondered wildly for a moment how on earth they'd strayed onto a subject he never discussed with anyone.

'Is that why you doubted your own fertility? Or why you can't look at your mother? Because you feel guilty that you weren't able to protect her?'

Samia's question hit Sadiq right in his gut. He saw Samia's huge, expressive eyes shimmering suspiciously and put down his napkin. 'I think we've had enough conversation for one evening.'

Samia watched Sadiq stand up to his full impressive height. Her heart ached in a very peculiar and disturbing way. He looked so remote and proud. He was obviously angry with himself for having revealed what he had, and she'd gone too far with that question.

But she'd been no less forthcoming—as if someone had injected her with some kind of truth serum. She could have made up any old cliché about why she'd got the tattoo. She wasn't meant to be feeling anything for this man. When he put his hand out now she took it gratefully, suddenly as eager as he was to change the subject.

Afterwards, when Samia's head was on Sadiq's chest with his strong heartbeat under her cheek, she thought of something and said, 'You're using protection now...'

She lifted her head and looked at him, and a wave of

shyness washed over her to think that he'd just made love to her and had done so with such passion that she was still floating in a limbo of languorous satedness. Sadness gripped her at the thought that this would not last. It couldn't. If he wasn't already growing bored with her limited range of responses, he would be very soon. And she hated the self-pity that that thought engendered.

He'd gone very still for a moment, and then he looked at her, and those eyes were unreadable and his jaw was tense. He moved then, and manoeuvred them so that Samia was on her back and he was on one elbow, looking down at her.

Her insides contracted. Lord, but he was gorgeous. It was almost intimidating. The languorous bliss in her body was dissipating slightly under the cool look in his eyes.

'I thought that it would be a good idea to give ourselves some time to get to know one another before getting pregnant.'

'Oh…' Samia said ineffectually. So that was the reason for his suddenly using protection.

Sadiq twitched back the sheet from where it covered Samia's body and she flushed under his blatant appraisal. 'But as you could already be pregnant, and part of the requirements of this marriage are heirs, I don't see the advantage any more.'

And before she could speak, or formulate a response to that, Sadiq had drawn her up over his body, legs either side of his hips, where she could feel the potent strength of him against her moist core.

Samia had the feeling he was angry about something and taking it out on her, but she was too distracted by the feel of his erection. The sensation of hot skin to hot skin was too much. With a small groan of helpless desire she slid down onto his hard length and forgot all about anything but this delicious insanity.

* * *

Sadiq couldn't sleep, and he wasn't surprised. He'd just acted like a complete neanderthal and taken his own self-anger out on Samia in a very cavalier fashion. Not that she'd complained. He'd never slept with any woman so impassioned, so responsive and so giving. His heart thumped ominously. He came up on one elbow and looked at her, skin still flushed with their lovemaking, lashes long against her cheek.

He could still see her sitting astride him, and the look of pure shocked bliss on her face as she'd realised that she could dictate the pace of their lovemaking—much to his intense torture, her evident delight and an eventual climax that had been so strong he'd blacked out for a split second. A first for him.

With a muted groan he got out of the bed and pulled on his robe, crossing to the ornately trellised wall which surrounded their private terrace. The desert lay spread out before him. *Dammit.* He brought his clenched fist down on the wall. He *had* intended talking to Samia about birth control. He *had* thought it would be a good idea to wait at least for a few months, to let her get used to life at the castle.

He was uncomfortably aware that his decision had come *after* that first night. *After* he had been driven by blind aching need and any rational thought of anything other than sating the fire in his body had precluded a sane discussion about birth control. It had only been in the sober moments during the wedding that he'd realized what a risk he'd taken.

When she'd asked the question just now, she'd reminded Sadiq uncomfortably of his own woeful neglecting to be responsible. Guilt had struck hard, and all he'd been able to think of was everything he'd just told her, which he'd never shared with another person. She'd shared something with him so had he felt obliged to spill his guts too? Once again he'd reacted from a visceral place to the threat she was posing to his once very equable life. A life he'd naively thought wouldn't suffer so much as a ripple due to his marriage.

He wasn't facing a ripple now. It was a storm of unprecedented power on the horizon. This marriage was veering wildly off the tracks from the type of marriage he'd set out to secure. He'd certainly not planned such a scenario as that dinner. His stomach clenched. When she'd told him about her witch of a stepmother he'd wanted to smash something and lift her up into his arms, cursing the dead woman for making Samia ever doubt herself, for stopping her from doing what she'd so evidently loved. He'd wager a bet now that she had been a brilliant piano player.

He turned to survey the woman in the bed again, as if space could help him keep his hands off her. He almost laughed aloud at that. He'd never been so consumed with lust for anyone, and it perplexed him and sent tendrils of pure fear through him as well. It was like a primal need to stamp Samia as his. To ensure she never wanted to look at another man.

Sadiq went back towards the benignly sleeping figure on the bed and silently cursed her for not being the placid, unexciting, convenient wife he'd thought he'd signed up for.

The following morning, when the sun was high outside, Sadiq woke up to see Samia emerge from the shower, wrapping her robe around her. Immediately he felt disconcerted. He wasn't used to sleeping while in a woman's company—it had always made him feel intensely vulnerable. Yet another thing to add to the growing list of not so welcome experiences his wife was bringing into his life.

He put out a hand. 'You're overdressed. Come here so I can rectify the situation.'

She bit her lip and blushed, and immediately that tangled knot of emotions had Sadiq tensing all over. What was it about this woman?

Samia felt ridiculously nervous, and unaccountably weak

after a long night of being subjected to Sadiq's personal brand of torture. But she had to clarify something, because it was only afterwards she'd realised how arrogant he'd been.

She ignored his autocratic decree and said, 'Look, I would have appreciated talking about birth control before we...' She blushed and hitched up her chin. 'Before we made love. I think it is a good idea. If I'm already pregnant we'll know soon enough, but if I'm not then I'd prefer to use birth control for a few months at least.'

Sadiq was up on one arm, and to Samia's shock she saw a sheepish look cross his face before he smoothly got out of the bed and crossed to her. She tried to ignore his naked state and focus.

'I owe you an apology.'

'You do?'

'I should never have acted in such a cavalier manner. It was unbelievably arrogant and disrespectful to you. And, like I said, I *had* intended speaking with you about it.'

His easy apology made something melt inside her. Samia recalled the way it had felt to slide down on top of Sadiq, skin to skin, and between her legs she grew moist. If he could see inside her head she'd die of shame.

'It's fine. There was two of us there, and if I'd insisted you stop to use protection you would have.'

Sadiq tipped up her chin and with a rueful look in his eye said, 'I think you credit me with too much control—control which I seem to be in short supply of whenever you're near me.'

Samia's heart thumped once—hard. When Sadiq's eyes darkened and he opened her robe to push it from her shoulders she didn't protest.

CHAPTER TEN

THE next day Sadiq knew he was in very dangerous territory—literally and metaphorically. Samia was at the wheel of his Jeep and looking at him with a very mischievous grin on her face. They were teetering on the top of one of the steepest dunes he'd ever seen, and with not a little fear prickling his skin he cursed himself for giving in to her wish to drive. 'You do realise that if anything happens to me the Hussein line will die out?' he said.

Her grin got wider. 'Are you telling me you're scared?'

He was terrified. 'Never.'

She looked ahead, or more accurately down, and said in a grim voice, 'Hang on tight.'

And that was all Sadiq could do as they plunged down the sheer wall of sand. When they got to the bottom and he was still intact and breathing he opened one eye. Samia was already turning to climb back up the other side of the dune. She stopped the jeep and looked at him, 'See? Piece of cake. Next time we do it you can keep your eyes open.'

'I don't think so.' With awesome strength Sadiq lifted her from the driving seat and scooted over, so he was in control again. He smiled urbanely at Samia's pink indignant face. 'You've made your point. You've demonstrated your ability commendably. If I'm ever incapacitated in the desert I'd want no-one else to drive me out.'

She spluttered ineffectually as he expertly drove the Jeep back up the dune, and then finally he saw her smile out of the corner of his eye and heard something that sounded like, 'Honestly—*men*.'

The truth was that witnessing Samia's ability to dune-drive almost as expertly as he did, was making him feel off-centre. He wondered just how many more secrets she was hiding, along with that tantalising tattoo just above her plump buttocks. The thought of her buttocks made him change the gears awkwardly, grinding them painfully, and Sadiq took great pleasure in wiping the smug grin off Samia's face as they descended once again at an even more dangerous angle.

The following evening Sadiq was waiting for Samia when she came out of the bathroom. She felt a little dazed. They'd spent most of their time in bed, apart from one or two forays into the desert. She hadn't been dune-driving since she'd been a teenager with Kaden, and it had been exhilarating to surprise Sadiq with her proficiency. She'd forgotten the sheer joy there could be in that huge silent space. She'd seen a more carefree side to Sadiq than she would have believed existed—as if the desert injected him with some sort of re-laxant—and it had only been then that she'd realised how intensely he held himself in check all the time.

He was dressed in a long traditional robe and turban now, and looked slightly fearsome against the dusk. When she remembered how expertly he'd handled his peregrine falcon earlier, and had stood behind her to show her how to hold him, she felt weak inside.

He smiled and flicked his eyes up and down, taking in the flimsy towel which was all she wore. Samia wished she had the confidence to let the towel drop and sashay over to him to seduce him, but he was indicating a box on the bed and saying throatily, 'Change into those clothes and then meet me downstairs. I want to take you somewhere tonight.'

Wordlessly Samia watched him leave the room and crossed to the bed. Opening the box, she gasped to find a gorgeous satin dress in a dark red colour. There was underwear made of a material so fine it was like silk cobwebs. With clumsy hands and a delicious sense of anticipation Samia put the underwear on and let the dress drop down over her head. Against her pale skin it looked sinful, and clung to every curve before coming to rest on her feet.

She found matching shoes and put them on. They were so high she teetered for a moment, before taking a deep breath and leaving the room. Sadiq was waiting in the impressively unadorned hall. Flame lanterns lit the ancient walls. As she came down the stairs his eyes widened and the beat of her heart got loud in her ears.

She came to a stop just feet away and he took her hand to lead her ouside. He didn't say anything, but his eyes glowed fiercely blue. Suddenly she realised something and embarrassment coursed through her.

She stopped and Sadiq looked back, impatience etched into his features. 'What is it?'

Samia touched her hair and her face. 'I never did anything…with my hair or face. No makeup.'

She could have slid right into the ground. What kind of a woman was she? What kind of woman just *forgot* parts of getting ready? Alia had put together a vanity case full of makeup and hair accessories for Samia. Samia didn't know what to do with half of them, but she could have put on some mascara, or lipstick, or something.

Sadiq came close and took her face in his hands. Samia could see his impatience up close now and trembled—

because it was an impatience that echoed through her own body. An impatience to be naked and alone.

'You are absolutely stunning exactly as you are. I don't want you to change one thing. You don't need one shred of makeup.'

And then he kissed her so thoroughly that Samia knew that even if she had remembered to put lipstick on it would be well and truly gone by now. Mesmerised by his intensity, she let herself be guided into a more luxurious Jeep than the one they'd used for the dune-driving, and Sadiq drove them for about fifteen minutes in the darkening night before she saw flickering lights ahead. She was aware of the security Jeep and bodyguards behind them, but they were discreet.

She gasped when she saw what the lights were. An ornate bedouin tent, with a single palm tree and a small shimmering pool lit by the light of the full moon and flaming torches. It was beautiful—like something out of a fantasy.

Sadiq stopped the Jeep and cast her a glance. 'It's probably the smallest oasis in the world.'

Samia was already clambering out of the Jeep. 'It's perfect,' she breathed.

She took off her shoes so she could walk in the sand, and squealed when Sadiq lifted her up into his arms. He looked down at her with mock annoyance. 'You fool. Have you forgotten how dangerous it is to walk in the sand at night in bare feet?'

Samia scowled back at him. 'You're the one that gave me six inch heels. How am I supposed to walk in them?'

He grimaced. 'You're right. That was a stupid idea. I should have got you walking boots.'

Samia giggled to think of the incongruity of boots with this dress, and wiggled her toes deliciously. She cocked her head on one side. 'No, actually, I think I prefer being carried by you. Much more satisfying.'

And then, after a look so hot she wondered how she didn't go up in flames, Sadiq took her into the tent, and she had no sense of what was about to happen.

The sheer luxurious opulence of the scene took Samia's breath away and hit her between the eyes like a sledgehammer. Her heart started thumping, hard. It was like a scene from one of her childhood storybooks. The ones with pictures of sultans and Sheikhs sitting on sumptuous cushions eating delicacies, with beautiful exotic women reclining on equally luxurious divans.

She'd never even realised she held such a vision in her head. It was as if Sadiq was seeing right inside her to a secret place she hadn't been aware of herself, where she harboured a romantic fantasy of an idyll such as this, and was reproducing it with an ease that was truly awesome.

She tensed all over against the need to believe that this was real. When of course it couldn't be. Not in the way she wanted it to be—and that was a very scary revelation. It was as if she were freefalling from a great height; this whole scene was making her feel weak with yearning when it shouldn't.

An easy intimacy had stolen over Samia in the past few days, and she'd grown used to waking entwined with Sadiq, relishing his possessive embrace. But he'd warned her that he wasn't the cuddly type. He was just doing it for her benefit, for the honeymoon. It was all an act. It had to be. The man was a consummate seducer—he knew what women wanted. Was he doing this for her because he thought she needed it? Did he see the pathetic crush she was developing on him?

He finally put her down on her feet and she felt dizzy

and a little sick. Before she could make a complete fool of herself, or have him make some teasing sardonic comment, she asked in a quiet voice, 'Why are you doing this, Sadiq? You don't have to. We're married. You don't have to seduce me like this.'

'You don't have to seduce me like this.'

Sadiq felt as if he'd just been slapped in the face. He had that awful anxiety dream sensation of standing in front of a crowd of people and suddenly forgetting what he was meant to say, with everyone looking at him expectantly.

For the past few days something had stolen over him, seducing him. An intimacy he'd never experienced before. He'd found himself wanting to go deeper into the desert with Samia. Experience the vast openess with *her*. And, without even thinking about what he was doing, he'd arranged for this tent to be set up.

And now he felt foolish, exposed, because he suddenly realised how this must look. No wonder she was wondering what was going on. Why would she expect something like this? She wasn't a mistress, expecting such grand gestures. She hadn't even thought to put makeup on earlier—and why would she? She wasn't trying to entice Sadiq. They were *married*.

Suddenly absurdly angry with himself, Sadiq said harshly, 'Let's go back, then. It was a stupid idea.'

He was turning around when he felt his arm being pulled, and looked down to find himself diving into those blue depths. 'No, wait—I'm sorry. It's so beautiful. I'm just a bit confused…that's all. I'm not sure what this is.' Before he could accuse her of thinking it, Samia said in a rush, 'This is what you do for a lover, to seduce and entice, so what's the point, Sadiq?'

Sadiq's jaw clenched hard. He never acted out of blind

instinct. He was always completely aware of what he was doing and why. The enormity of what he'd done sank into him and the urge to self-protect became paramount.

He pulled her into his body, where she could feel the hard ridge of his erection. Much to his chagrin, nothing could dampen *that*. 'That's the point,' he ground out, pressing her closer, seeing how her eyes went dark with desire.

'If it makes you feel better then I'll tell you that I've brought all my mistresses here, so really it's been no bother. I fancied a change of scenery. That's all.'

Furious at the hurt that lanced her, mixed with relief that she hadn't given herself away, Samia said caustically, 'You're right. That does make me feel *so* much better. I'd hate to think you went to all this trouble just for me.'

Within seconds they were kissing furiously. Samia heard her dress rip when Sadiq pulled it open but she didn't care. All she cared about was that this mad, heated insanity was distracting her from something that felt very painful.

Their lovemaking was fast and furious, on one of the decadently sumptuous divans. When it was over Sadiq rolled away from Samia and she realised that he hadn't even fully undressed. She felt like apologizing, but the words were stuck in her throat. She could have said nothing, but she'd been so afraid of wanting to believe that this meant *something* she'd had to prove that it didn't. And she'd got her proof. Spectacularly.

Sadiq got up and rearranged his clothing. He barely glanced at Samia, who lay in what looked like wanton disarray. With a jerk of his head he said, 'There's a washing area behind the screen. When you're ready we'll go back to the castle. This was a mistake.'

Again Samia wanted to reach out and say... What? It was useless. She gathered up her dress and went behind the screen. The poor dress was so torn that Samia had to pull on a robe instead. When she emerged Sadiq was standing dressed in the doorway of the tent, the line of his back remote. It was only when Samia was walking towards the entrance that she saw the wine bucket with a bottle of champagne, two glasses, and a range of finger food delicacies.

She cursed herself for not keeping her mouth shut. Of *course* it wouldn't have meant anything—why had she had to insist on hearing that from Sadiq himself?

The next morning Sadiq stood looking out over the dawn breaking. The sight had never failed to take his breath away but this morning it was failing. Spectacularly. For some reason the desert had lost its effortless allure and it felt flat and drained of colour. And he wanted to see the back of it, which was entirely unlike him. No matter what was going on he always managed to find solace in this place.

He closed his eyes but it was no good. All he could see was Samia, holding that torn dress in her hands, and the way she'd walked with such regal hauteur back into the castle last night. It hadn't stopped him following her into the shower, though, and making love to her. The anger had still been simmering inside him, even though he'd known there was no rational reason for it. If anything, Samia had done him a favour in questioning his motives. Reminding him of what this was: a marriage of convenience.

He felt clammy now, recalling that initial feeling of exposure. What on earth had he been thinking of, organising the tent in the first place? Had his brain been so warped by a little dune driving and the hottest sex he'd ever had? Evidently.

The ironic thing about that blasted tent was that for years he'd had it in the back of his head to create some scene of seduction in the desert for his mistresses. More than one had asked him wistfully when he was going to take her to a secret desert oasis. And he never had, because at the last moment they'd always been the wrong person to share the desert with. And now the first woman he *had* brought to a secret desert oasis had all but thrown it back in his face.

He heard a rustle of movement behind him and turned slowly to face his wife, not liking the way he had to steel himself against the inevitable effect of seeing her.

Samia woke and was disorientated to see Sadiq standing looking out over the desert, fully dressed in traditional robes. For a silent moment she regarded his impressive back, and hated the ache at the back of her throat that signalled unshed tears. She was still angry when she thought of that tent, and the fact that Sadiq had seduced hundreds of women there. And, not only that, she hadn't been able to keep up her icy disdain when they'd returned to the castle. He'd arrogantly interrupted her shower and within seconds she'd been putty in his hands, slave to his masterful touch.

As if he could feel the weight of her gaze now, Sadiq turned around. Trying to look as composed and unmoved by him as she could, she came up on one arm, pushing her tangled hair over her shoulder. Self-conscious, and hating herself for it because she desperately craved to appear insouciant, she pulled the sheet up over her breasts.

He noted the movement with a small mocking smile, and Samia longed desperately to see him unsure of himself—just once.

He was cool. 'Something's come up in B'harani that needs my attention, I'm afraid we'll have to cut our time here a little short.'

Surprise, surprise, Samia thought, and said equally coolly, 'You should have woken me.'

Sadiq crossed his arms and rested back against the wall. 'I was enjoying the view too much.'

Recalling that she'd woken with the sheet barely covering her lower half, Samia gave up any pretence of nonchalance and jumped out of the bed, wrapping the sheet around her to go to the bathroom. She heard a dark chuckle, and had to restrain herself from flinging something at Sadiq's head when he stopped at the door to inform her that he'd be waiting downstairs.

The journey back to B'harani was made largely in silence, for which Samia was grateful. She felt absurdly over-emotional. Raw. When they reached the castle she jumped out of the Jeep and only stopped when she heard her name. Tense all over, she turned to see Sadiq, with a bevy of aides and advisers descending on him from all sides.

He looked stern, and already more remote. 'I'll be working late tonight so don't wait up.'

'Don't worry, Sadiq,' she said as loftily as she could. 'I don't expect you to entertain me. The honeymoon is over.'

She turned away, but he called her name again. Softly. This time when she turned he was much closer and her heart sputtered. She looked up to see a feral glitter in his eyes and the answering effect on her body was instantaneous. 'I asked for you to be moved to my rooms Samia, so make sure you have everything you need.'

Immediately she felt threatened. She'd forgotten, and the thought of coping with Sadiq every night was suddenly too much—especially feeling as raw as she did right now. She opened her mouth. 'Actually, I'm not sure that I—'

Sadiq put a finger to her lips and said with a steel tone, 'It's non-negotiable, Samia.'

And then he turned and was swallowed up by the crowd of people.

Sadiq was burningly aware of Samia's huge eyes boring into his back as he walked down the long corridor away from her, and he had to battle the urge to turn around, pick her up and take her straight to bed. He had to control himself—quash this urge to want to punish Samia for something. For making him *feel*? For making him fearful of the passion she inspired in him because it was making him act in ways he'd never done before, becoming irrational and impulsive? Just like his father?

Sadiq immediately dismissed the notion as ridiculous. But as the rogue thought was sinking in and taking up residence Sadiq's steps quickened perceptibly, and the retinue of staff almost had to run to keep up with him.

A week later Samia was fired up and full of enthusiasm. She was determined to block out the fact that the distance between her and Sadiq since they'd returned from Nazirat seemed to be growing into a wedge. She assured herself that he was busy, catching up on work he'd had to sideline for the marriage. And what had she expected anyway? Romantic dinners *à deux* every night? Hadn't she told him in no uncertain terms in Nazirat that he didn't have to do that?

In the bedroom, however, there was no distance. She blushed now as she walked along the long corridor to Sadiq's offices to think of how passionate he'd been last night. She'd been half asleep when he'd come to bed, but had soon been wide awake when she'd felt his firm, hard body curling around hers. It scared her how a warm glow seemed to infuse every cell whenever he was near or touched her. And the way everything semed to dim when he wasn't.

She tried to tell herself that she didn't miss the way he'd pulled her close after making love those first few days in Nazirat. She tried to tell herself that it didn't hurt to know that it had all just been an act for the honeymoon. Now, when they made love, Sadiq rolled away, and Samia hated the longing she felt to snuggle close, feel his arms around her. She cursed him for ever giving her that experience, so that she could miss it. Some mornings, though, she woke with the sensation that he'd held her during the night. But invariably Sadiq would already be gone, and that was always a stark reminder that they had moved very definitely into the 'convenient' part of their marriage.

Determined to stop this dangerous line of thinking, stop obsessing over Sadiq like some groupie, Samia had got up today determined to discuss with Sadiq some ideas she had that she wanted to develop and work on. When she got to the anteroom of his office, and his secretary looked up and smiled, Samia had to quash the sudden yearning to be able to just walk blithely into his office simply because he would always want to welcome her, to see her.

Oh, Lord. She almost stumbled when the implication of what she was thinking sank in. She couldn't deal with it now. She smiled back at the efficient secretary, pristine in a long white tunic and colourful veil.

'Do go in, Queen Samia. He's got a few minutes between meetings.'

Samia knocked lightly and heard Sadiq's deep voice respond. Immediately silly little butterflies started in her belly and she cursed. Opening the door, she went in and was surprised not to see Sadiq behind a mountain of paperwork. He was standing at the window, looking very brooding.

He turned around and black brows drew together in a frown. No hint of pleasure to see her. Samia cursed herself again, and hated that she felt her old sense of insecurity come back. 'I…I'm sorry to disturb you. I wanted to discuss a couple of things with you.'

Sadiq flicked a glance at his watch and Samia felt it like a slap. He was dressed in a suit today, and it reminded Samia of when she'd first seen him in London, which felt like aeons ago. He was so remote that she almost wondered if he was the same man who had made tears of pleasure soak her cheeks last night. Who had used his thumbs to wipe them away while they were still intimately joined. As if loath to let him leave her body she had jealously gripped his hips with her thighs, as if to stop him ever leaving.

She swayed for a moment because the memory was so potent, and instantly Sadiq was at her side, his frown even more fierce, 'Are you all right?'

'Fine…' Aghast at her own wayward imagination, Samia pulled free and walked over to a chair, saying much more brightly, 'I'm fine. I know you're busy.'

Sadiq had walked back behind his desk and sat down, once more cool and remote, as if that little moment hadn't occurred. The stark reality that this would be their everyday lives made her feel slightly panicky. Which got worse when he said, 'I have ten minutes.'

Samia sat down primly. Sadiq's office was huge and unahamedly masculine. Dark wood and shelves lined with books. She blurted out. 'I'd like an office.'

'You have an office.'

Samia thought of the perfectly nice room which was essentially somewhere for her to use the internet and make phone calls. She shook her head. 'No, I mean I want a proper office—like this. Where I can put my books and work on projects.'

He arched a brow and sat back, but Samia sensed the danger in his indolence. 'Projects?'

She nodded. 'Yes. You mentioned your environmental projects before. I'd like to see how I can help. And I want to set up some kind of literacy programme. Al-Omar is like Burquat in the fact that free education was only recently introduced—when you became Sultan. It was the same with my brother. The older generations who missed out have very low literacy. I'd like to set up workshops to encourage people to come back to school.'

Sadiq was looking at her with a funny expression on his face but she decided to forge on. 'And I want to set up a crèche here in the castle. There is no facility to help female staff to continue working once they've had a child, and you employ more women than men.'

Sadiq's jaw tensed. 'Anything else?'

Samia shrugged. 'Lots of things… But I'd like to start with those for now.'

Sadiq felt immediately defensive at having things pointed out to him that he'd already been aware of but hadn't really looked at yet, due to more pressing concerns. And he was also reacting to the fact that once again Samia was proving she wouldn't be morphing seamlessly into the role he'd envisaged his wife taking. He'd seen his wife firmly in the background, merely enhancing his role and perhaps attending some social events in his place. He hadn't really seen his marriage as a working partnership, and his naivety and lack of foresight mocked him now.

Self-recrimination made his voice harsh. 'The charity circuit is a well-oiled and sophisticated machine in B'harani, and there are plenty of committees of which you will have automatically become chairperson. I think, if you look at the schedule laid out for you, you'll be kept quite busy.'

Samia had looked at that schedule at the start of the week and her heart had sunk. She'd been spurred into action, doing her own research. She stood up on a wave of hot anger. 'I don't want to sit on committees to talk about things and never do them. And, as valuable as the charity circuit is, I want to do something useful—not just be a figurehead while other people do the work. I'm perfectly prepared to put in the hours being seen, but that's not enough.'

Sadiq stood too, and put his hands on the table, not liking

the way he was thinking of Samia's insecurity around crowds and being seen, and how much it moved him to see the way she seemed so determined not to let it get to her. He felt something harden inside him, and knew he was reacting to the increasingly familiar sense of threat this woman posed.

'This is not the time nor the place for this discussion, Samia, but there is one thing to consider—what happens when we have children?'

Samia gritted her jaw, dismayed and disappointed to see this hitherto hidden traditional side of Sadiq. 'If and when we have children I would expect to be able to use the crèche facility which has been set up, and in doing so demonstrate that we're rulers of the people who do not see themselves as unapproachable. And I would continue doing as much important work as I could—just as you would.'

Samia was articulating what Sadiq himself would have agreed with on any other occasion and with any other person. But here, with *her* and all the ambiguous feelings she aroused, Sadiq was frigid. 'Tell me, have you already sought out an area for this crèche?'

Samia was determined not to be intimidated. 'I have, actually, and there is a perfect spot near to the staff entrance of the castle. It's got a green area, which could be developed into a playground, and there's a huge bright room which could be converted from the storeroom it currently is.'

Sadiq instantly knew where she was talking about, and it did have potential. But for some reason he felt compelled to shoot it all down. He was reacting viscerally again, and hated that he was, but couldn't seem to stop it. He wanted to relegate Samia to some place where he wouldn't have to deal with her. Much as he had all week. Avoiding any contact by day and then using the nights to let his already shaky control go.

Each morning he'd woken up and hoped for some sense

that clarity was returning, or her sensual hold over him was diminished, but if the way his body felt so hot and hard right now was anything to go by he was in for a long wait. 'I've been running this country on my own for well over a decade, Samia. You will fulfil the role of my queen. I don't need a wife with a busier schedule than my own. I don't want you starting something off only to grow bored with it, leaving it to overworked staff to finish off.'

Samia was shaking she was so incensed. 'I wouldn't do that. You chose *me* to be your wife and I'm not going to settle for a life of posturing and preening.' To her utter horror, she felt tears threaten. 'You *know* I'm not like that. I told you from the very start and you wouldn't listen. I can be useful and I intend to be.'

Terrified she'd start crying in front of him, and of the emotion gripping her, Samia turned around and rushed from the room. She walked with tears blurring her vision until she found a quiet spot, and then hid away and tried to stifle the gulping, shuddering breaths. She knew exactly why she was so upset. The realisation had started to hit her outside Sadiq's office. She had fallen in love with her husband, and all of those iron-clad assertions that she would never be so stupid had just crumbled to dust.

She was upset because she'd gone in there today hoping… for what? she asked herself angrily as she wiped at her stinging cheeks. That he would jump up and tell her how brilliant she was? What amazing ingenuity she had? She'd been naive to think he would just allow her free rein to do what she liked.

He was right. He'd been running the country very successfully, *alone*, for a long time. He was hardly likely to welcome a couple of bright ideas along with a rush of enthusiasm as something solid to work on. But she was hurt that he didn't know her well enough by now to know that she wouldn't be so inconsistent as to start something and not finish it.

Composing herself, Samia left her hiding place and went to find Yasmeena, whom she'd promised to have lunch with that day. She hoped that the surprisingly astute woman wouldn't notice her turmoil.

Samia reassured herself stoutly that she couldn't have fallen in love with Sadiq. She was mistaken. She was over-emotional, that was all. She nearly stumbled, though, when she thought again of the crèche and had an image of Sadiq bending down to scoop up a dark haired toddler from the sandpit.

For a moment the pain was so intense that Samia thought she might have to make up some excuse and avoid lunch, but exerting all her self-control, she pasted a bright smile on her face and kept going.

A couple of days later Samia was in her office, looking at the schedule of events, and fear was rising within her. Next week was to be the start of her official duties, as the marriage festivities and honeymoon period were formally finished. This was a schedule of daytime events, and was considered part of her queenly duties—*alone*. She wouldn't have Sadiq's solid presence by her side. She could already picture the charity/social scene brigade of women who orchestrated these events and she shuddered. They would assess her in an instant and find her lacking.

Just then her door opened and Sadiq filled the space, broad shoulders blocking out the light. Samia felt that awful rush of emotion and dampened it down. She was still angry with him. She had wanted to be able to turn her back on him when he'd come to bed the previous nights, but with awful predictability within seconds she'd been incapable of remembering her name, never mind saying no to Sadiq.

Conversation had been nil, but Samia had woken up during the night and found herself wrapped tightly in Sadiq's embrace. She'd stayed awake for a long time, relishing the contact she knew he'd break free of as soon as he woke.

She strove for cool uninterest now. 'Can I help you?'

Sadiq's mouth twitched ever so slightly and Samia flushed. Even now he was laughing at her. But then he strode in and her mind blanked. He plucked the sheet of paper she'd been studying out of her hands and perused it, before calmly tearing it in two.

Samia looked open-mouthed from it to Sadiq. 'What did you do that for?'

'Because your secretary is going to draw you up a new schedule and it'll consist only of the events that you wish to go to.'

Samia repeated stupidly, 'Secretary? I don't have a secretary.'

Sadiq indicated for Samia to get up and follow him, and said, 'You do now. It sounds like you're going to be busy enough to need one.'

Struck dumb, Samia followed Sadiq out of the room and into another one, much bigger, just down the hall. It was bright and airy, and the castle workmen who were busy putting up shelves stopped working and bowed deferentially.

Sadiq said brusquely, 'Leave us, please, for a moment.'

The men filed out and Samia turned around. There was a huge desk, complete with computer, printer, fax machine. A small anteroom was obviously the secretary's office.

She was almost too scared to look at Sadiq—afraid of what he might see on her face. 'What is this…? Why have you done this?'

He sighed and she looked up. His face was unreadable. 'The truth is that I did have a preconceived notion of the role my wife would fulfil, and was quite happy to acknowledge that it wouldn't impinge on my own role at all. Merely enhance it.' He smiled tightly. 'I should have known that you wouldn't be happy with that. I like your ideas. And I'm sorry for doubting your ability to start them and finish them. I watched my father do that for years—when he died and I took over he'd left behind him a trail of destruction and half finished projects. I vowed not to let that happen again. I've wielded control for so long that it's challenging to allow myself to hand some of it over now.'

More moved than she wanted to show, Samia said quietly, 'I thought this marriage would be a partnership...apart from everything else.'

'It is, Samia. I want you to be happy here.'

Samia's heart ached at his gesture, and ached in a different way at his impersonal words. She wouldn't be truly happy here unless a miracle happened and the block of ice in Sadiq's chest melted. But this was a start. She smiled, and her heart thumped when she saw his eyes flare. They had chemistry too, and that was something to build on.

Feeling optimistic for the first time in days, Samia said simply, 'Thank you. I appreciate this, and I won't let you down.'

Sadiq felt a physical pain somewhere in the region of his chest at the sheer happiness in Samia's face. And he felt better than he had in days. A black mood had pervaded his whole being ever since their last exchange, and his conscience hadn't allowed him to continue functioning until he'd rectified the situation.

Before Samia could see how her happiness seemed to be having a disturbing effect on him, he grabbed the two hard hats he'd left on the desk earlier and handed one to her. 'Come on. I've something else to show you.'

A few minutes later Samia couldn't stop the tears from stinging her eyes. Sadiq had brought her to the back of the castle, where construction work was already starting on a crèche and playground. That potent image of Sadiq and a little toddler rose up again and wouldn't leave her alone. It was like a taunt.

When Sadiq turned and saw her glistening eyes, and asked sharply, 'What is it?' Samia panicked and muttered something about grit getting in her eye.

To her utter surprise Sadiq immediately picked her up into his arms and, despite her heated remonstrations that she was fine, took her straight to the castle's full-time nurse. Samia was brick-red with mortification, absolutely certain that the nurse would see full well that she'd just been crying and had lied shamefully. But to her abject relief Sadiq said he had to go to a meeting and left her saying something about working late. Samia was too distracted to care.

It was only when she lay in bed alone that night that she frowned slightly, trying to remember that Sadiq had said. A little dart of emotion made her breath hitch. The fact was he'd done a great thing today, and changed the anatomy of their marriage and Samia's role within it in one fell swoop. But apart from that, the distance between them was as great as ever.

Sadiq didn't seem remotely interested in involving Samia in any aspect of his life that wasn't about sex or official duties. There was no suggestion of dinner, or meeting for lunch. No suggestion of a *relationship*. And why should there be? she remonstrated with herself. She was the one yearning for more, not him. He'd got exactly what he wanted from this marriage, even if she was demanding a bigger role than he would have expected or liked.

But she couldn't help thinking back to those few days of the honeymoon, when it had felt as if they'd really been getting to know one another. Samia had enjoyed spending time with him. They'd talked. But she didn't need to be reminded that their conversation over dinner when he'd told her about his father had been their last conversation of any depth or substance. Clearly that had been an aberration that Sadiq had no intention of repeating.

Samia finally fell asleep, and tried not to mind very much that she had no idea where Sadiq was.

CHAPTER ELEVEN

THREE weeks later Sadiq was sitting in his study with a glass of whisky in his hand. He grimaced at himself. This was becoming a habit. Work until his vision blurred, wait around, and then go to bed. Invariably when Samia was already asleep or half asleep.

Each night he told himself he would be strong enough to resist her lure, that he wasn't some animal, a slave to his base instincts, but when he pulled back the covers and saw those delicate curves…that long hair…fire consumed him and he jumped into the pit. Every night. And she gave with the wild abandon he'd grown addicted to every night.

He grimaced again. Since when had his shy wife grown so *un*-shy that she felt comfortable sleeping naked? The thought of her now, naked in the bed, made him grip the glass so tight that it cracked in his palm. Sadiq saw the trickle of blood fall on his robe, and for a moment pain blocked out the ever-present awareness, and he had an insight into why people might seek pain as a sort of anaesthetic.

He smiled at his own bleak humour and got up to tend to his cut. The good mood he'd been in for days after showing Samia her new office, telling her that she had *carte blanche* to do pretty much whatever she liked, was wearing off and being replaced with something much darker and more insidious.

It didn't help that he was well aware that he was doing his utmost to avoid spending any time with his wife. Because whenever he was alone with her he couldn't think straight. All rational thought went out of the window and he found himself filled with bizarre longings that had nothing to do with lust—although that was ever-present—and more to do with something more intangible. Like the urge he'd had in Nazirat to take Samia deep into the desert.

It was too reminiscent of the moods he'd seen grip his father. What more evidence did he need than the fact he was breaking glasses in his hand just thinking of Samia? She was dangerous.

Sadiq patched up his hand and caught a glimpse of his reflection in the mirror. His eyes were glittering as if he had a fever. His jaw was stubbled with a day's growth of beard. He looked a little wild. He suddenly realised that this situation was untenable, and a surge of anger at Samia and her innocently sleeping presence made him switch off the light and stride from his study.

The following evening Samia was looking at her pink face in the steamed-up bathroom mirror. She knew it was crazy to feel disappointed—the chasm that currently existed between her and Sadiq was no place to be bringing a baby. If she'd thought that his *volte-face* about her involvement in their marriage had signified a change, then she'd been mistaken. If anything, Sadiq was growing even more distant. She put her hand to her flat belly and bit her lip. She'd just seen the spotting which signified that she wasn't pregnant.

She heard him moving in the bedroom outside and tensed. They were going to a function being held in the castle that evening—an acknowledgement of Sadiq's fundraising for charities. Taking a deep breath, she tightened the robe around her body and went out. Sadiq was stripping off his shirt and immediately Samia's pulse went into overdrive.

He caught her look and his mouth curled. 'Don't look at me like that, *habiba*. We don't have time to make something of it.'

Samia flushed, and flushed even harder when she thought of how their lovemaking last night had been imbued with something almost desperate. She'd only noticed the make-shift bandage on Sadiq's hand afterwards, and the red stain of blood. Her heart clenching, she'd asked, 'What happened?'

He'd taken his hand back and said brusquely, 'Nothing. Just a glass that broke.'

And, practically jackknifing off the bed, he'd then informed her that he'd just remembered a speech he had to work on, and pulled on some clothes and gone back to his office. Samia knew he'd only returned to their bedroom to shower that morning. So he must have slept in his office.

She thought of that now, and wanted to feel relief as she said, 'There's something I should tell you.'

He looked at her, naked now apart from form-fitting boxers that held a distinctive bulge.

Samia swallowed. She had to get sex off her brain. 'I'm not pregnant.'

For a long moment Sadiq was silent. She couldn't read his reaction. And then he just calmly pulled on his pants and said, 'Good. That's good. Thank you for letting me know.' His eyes flicked her up and down and she felt it like the lash of a whip. 'We're leaving in twenty minutes.'

Chin hitched up, Samia said, 'I'll be ready.'

And she was—with not a hint of her reaction on her face to his emotionless response to the news that she wasn't pregnant.

An hour later Sadiq was still coming to grips with the fact that he'd felt disappointed to hear that Samia wasn't pregnant—as if something elusive had slipped out of his grasp. He'd had an almost primal urge to make love to her when she'd said that, as if to ensure that she *did* get pregnant when she'd expressly told him she didn't want that.

He felt weak, at the mercy of something he had no control over. She'd taken his injured hand in hers last night, and the feel of those small cool hands had provoked an urge to put his head on Samia's breast and have her hold him. It had been strong enough to make him run. And he'd spent the night on the couch in his office, waking with a dry mouth and in a foul humour that was getting fouler by the minute.

Especially when he saw Samia across the room, laughing up into the face of a handsome man whom Sadiq recognised as one of his scientists involved in environmental research. He knew Samia had been having meetings with them last week, and to think she was cultivating a relationship—no matter how innocent—with this man was enough to propel him across the room in seconds. He took Samia's arm in his hand, relishing the feel of the delicate muscles. She was *his*. The other man backed away hurriedly, as if Sadiq had just snarled at him like an animal.

He heard Samia's husky voice. 'Sadiq? Is everything okay?'

He looked down at her and something solidified inside him. 'No,' he bit out grimly. 'Everything is not okay.'

Samia watched him locking the door behind them. He'd all but marched her into an empty anteroom, and the fierce look on his face scared her slightly. 'What's going on, Sadiq?'

'What's going on is that I leave your side for two minutes and you're flirting with another man.'

She gaped at him. 'Flirting? I can assure you that I was

not flirting. Hamad was telling me about his two-year-old son, if you must know.'

Sadiq rocked back on his heels, hands in his pockets. He said almost musingly, but with a dangerous undercurrent, 'When we first met you would have had me believe that you'd be quaking in your shoes in a situation like that, and yet you're remarkably eager to leave my side and talk to relative strangers.'

Hurt scored Samia's insides. She wasn't about to let him know how vulnerable she still felt in those situations, or why the only reason she felt she could deal with them was because he was by her side, or nearby. Even just to see him across a room was enough.

She tossed her head, knowing she was playing with fire. 'Are you accusing me of lying, Sadiq? Pretending that I was shy and insecure? And am I not *meant* to leave your side? I thought part of my brief as your queen of convenience was to *work*.'

She couldn't stop now. 'Because that's what this marriage is, isn't it, Sadiq? It's just a job, with a bit of sex thrown in. You can't even be bothered to pretend it's anything else and have *one* evening meal with me. We have nothing to discuss.'

Sadiq moved fast enough to shock Samia. He was right in front of her, saying harshly, 'You've certainly shown me intriguing facets to your personality that weren't in evidence when we first met.' His eyes were bright with a feral glitter as they dropped down and took in where her cleavage was revealed in the silk of the simple dress. 'And there's *plenty* we could discuss, Samia.'

She took a step back, railing against the evidence that he resented the aspects of her that had started to emerge as if from a long hibernation, and fought the dismayingly familiar lure to merge with this man. 'I'm not talking about sex,

Sadiq. I'm talking about the fact that you want an identikit wife and that's not what I am.'

Her voice was bitter. 'Obviously you'd prefer it if I'd stayed shy and gauche, but you're the one who has been encouraging me to overcome that shyness. You can't have it both ways, Sadiq. Perhaps there's no point to this marriage if you can't see that?'

He went very still. 'What are you saying? That you want out?'

Samia blinked. It felt as if they had jumped about three levels up from where she'd thought they were. For the first time in years she stuttered. 'N-no. I mean, I d-don't know. I didn't mean that. I just mean that we don't seem to have anything—' she blushed '—but the sex.'

The stutter got him right in the gut. That glaring sign of vulnerability underneath the thin veneer of bravado made something break inside Sadiq. His anger was defused and he saw in an instant how hard she was trying. He also recognised that she was all of the things she'd been that first day she'd met him and yet was also the emerging strong woman who had been repressed for so long.

She was the woman who still clung on to his hand with a death grip for the first few minutes in a crowded room until she was comfortable enough to leave his side. She was the woman with the tattoo above her buttocks, who could dune-drive and throw herself into the building of a crèche with so much enthusiasm that only last week he'd found her in dusty overalls, making sweet tea for the workers and laughing with them.

And she was the only woman he'd ever wanted to take deep into the desert and seduce in a bedouin tent erected just for her.

Panic and a feeling of constriction so strong that Sadiq had to stop himself undoing his bowtie forced him to speak the words that had just formed in his head from somewhere deep and dark inside him. 'If you want to leave this marriage, I'll give you a divorce.'

Samia looked at Sadiq, shock numbing her from the inside out. 'If *I* want to leave, you'll give me a divorce?'

He nodded, his face once again a mask of inscrutability.

Samia had the urge to slap him—hard. Feeling slightly desperate, she said, 'But I've committed to this marriage, to you. I'm learning to find my feet…I'm happy here.'

A voice mocked her. *Really? You're happy to be in this relationship with a man who doesn't love you and never will?*

Suddenly insecure in a way she hadn't felt for some weeks now, Samia looked at Sadiq, even though it was hard. '*You* want to divorce *me*.'

He shook his head. 'That's not what I'm saying. I'm offering you the choice. I'd be quite happy to stay married, but I don't think you're happy.' *Liar*, a voice mocked him. *You're going slowly insane.*

Samia wanted to sit down. 'Why?' she asked.

Sadiq sighed deeply and ran a hand through his hair, leaving it dishevelled. The muted chink of glasses and the hum of conversation from outside went unnoticed. 'Because you never wanted this marriage, and because I all but railroaded you into it. I don't relish the prospect of a wife who is going to feel she's in a situation she can't leave and grow to resent the feeling of being trapped. I watched my mother go through that and I won't be responsible for the same thing. I don't want to bring a child into that environment. Needless to say, if you do want to leave it won't affect my relationship with Burquat.'

'You've thought about this,' Samia said dully, the pain of that making her want to curl up somewhere.

Sadiq curbed the urge to contradict her. It seemed to be

a very simple equation in his head—hand Samia every tool or reason she might need to leave and she would leave. And he would feel sane again.

'What if I don't want to leave?'

There was something slightly defiant in her tone, and it made Sadiq alternately panicked and euphoric. Angry at the fact that she was once again confounding his expectations, he said, 'You'll have to come to terms with what this marriage is, Samia. Unless things have changed for you this is still an arranged marriage, and we are together for many reasons—none of which is about love. So I can't guarantee to be more invested than I already am.'

Every word landed on Samia like a little bomb. It was as if she'd asked silently for him to really spell it out, because she wasn't quite sure what he meant. To save herself from the final humiliation, she said coolly, 'I know what the parameters of this marriage are, Sadiq, but I'd hoped that within that we could find some balance where we at least communicated beyond the bedroom.'

Sadiq gritted out, 'We're communicating now.'

'Yes, and it's very clear. Can I have some time to think about this?'

Sadiq felt unsteady for a moment, unsettled by Samia's composure. 'Of course. This isn't something that has to be decided any time soon.'

'It's good to know there's no pressure.'

Sadiq heard the sarcasm dripping from her voice, and watched as his wife walked straight-backed to the door, turned the key and went back outside. He felt all at once light-headed, panicky and as if something incredibly precious was slipping away.

When he got back to the main ballroom, though, and saw Samia standing talking to the same man he'd seen her with before, Sadiq cursed himself for giving her an option to leave at all. He should be divorcing her point-blank—because that was the only solution to this madness.

CHAPTER TWELVE

SADIQ paced impatiently in his office and checked his watch again. Where the hell was she? Samia had told him that morning that she would come and talk to him this afternoon. As the days had passed during the past week, and Samia had gone about her business as serenely as if nothing had happened, his control had become more and more frayed. Nerves wound to breaking point.

The self-enforced sleepless nights on his couch in his study had provoked some much needed introspection. At first Sadiq had tried to block it out with alcohol, but in the end, disgusted with himself, he'd lain there and thought—really thought—about what he would do if Samia wanted to divorce, and why he'd offered it up as an option in the first place.

And then something his mother had said had hit home uncomfortably. Sick of trying to pace away his sexual frustration in his office, one morning he'd sought some air and space and had come across his mother, sitting in a quiet courtyard in the shade. He'd had that immediate reflex to leave, but in a firmer voice than she usually used she'd asked him to join her, so he had.

For the first time in a long time they'd sat in companionable silence, and finally she'd said, 'This place is changing by the day. Can't you feel it?'

He'd cast her a glance and she'd gone on, not looking at him. 'Your Samia—she's a breath of fresh air. Just what we've needed for a long time.'

The way the words *your Samia* had impacted on Sadiq had been nothing short of a block landing on his chest.

And then his mother had said quietly, 'It is possible, you know, to feel passion for someone and for it *not* to be a negative thing that has to be controlled. The difference is love. I had that once—before your father. The memory of it was the only thing that kept me sane. As well as you, of course.'

And with those engimatic words she'd got up, pressed a kiss to his head and left him sitting there, reeling. Finally seeing things clearly for the first time in weeks.

The phone rang on Sadiq's desk now, and he snatched it up, answering curtly, 'Yes?' He couldn't hide his impatience, but went very still as he listened to the voice on the other end.

After a pause he said, distractedly, 'Yes…thank you…I will.'

He put down the phone. A mixture of emotions was making him feel dizzy, but the paramount one was abject relief. Samia couldn't leave him now, even if she wanted to. He would deal with the matter of whether she wanted to or not when he found her.

Samia knew she should have been in Sadiq's study ages ago, but she couldn't see him while she was still a sniveling, quivering wreck. Ever since she'd discovered the reason for her persistant nausea all week the tears hadn't seemed to stop.

She groaned out loud as she blew her nose again. She had to get it together so that she could stand before Sadiq's cool, sardonic presence and not crumble. She'd been so strong all week—numbing herself to the pain, alternating between thinking that she would tell Sadiq she'd stay in the marriage because the prospect of not seeing him was too hard to bear, and vowing to herself that there was no other option but to divorce him and run. Before her heart broke into tiny pieces and could never be put back together.

He'd even stopped sleeping with her, so evidently he was already getting used to single life again. That provoked a fresh bout of weeping, because it was futile thinking of this. It was all beside the point now.

She heard a noise behind her and whirled around to see Sadiq, leaning against the closed library door.

'How did you know where I was?'

'I figured you'd be in the one place you feel safest.'

Samia went pink. *Why* had she told him so much about herself? 'If you've come to accuse me of pretending to be something I'm not again, then—'

He moved forward, frowning. 'You're crying.'

'No, I'm not,' she lied, looking away.

But Sadiq kept coming until he was right in front of her, tipping her chin up so he could see her face. She gritted her jaw. He was so damned arrogant. But that familiar scent wound around her and she had to stop herself closing her eyes and drinking it in deeply.

Hating his effortless effect on her, when he could be so unmoved, Samia jerked away and wrapped her arms around herself. She was dressed in a long tunic and matching tight pants.

She wasn't prepared for what Sadiq said next. 'Are you upset because of the pregnancy?'

Shocked, Samia just looked at him. 'How do you know?'

'The doctor thought you had come straight to me to give me the news, so he rang with congratulations.'

'Oh...' Samia bit her lip.

He would now know that there was no way she could leave

the marriage. Afraid to see the trapped look in his eyes, she stared down at the carpet.

'I'm not upset because of the pregnancy.' She looked up again, steeling herself for whatever Sadiq's reaction would be. 'When the doctor told me, I was happy. Apparently spotting is common in the early days. My periods have always been light…that's why I assumed I wasn't pregnant.'

Sadiq's voice was firm. 'But you are. And that changes everything.'

Samia nodded miserably, and saw something flash in Sadiq's eyes. 'Are you upset because this means you can't leave our marriage?' he asked.

Samia blinked back the onset of more tears. She half shrugged, half nodded, and shook her head. 'No… I mean… yes. But not because of what you probably think.'

The enormity of discovering about the baby had stripped Samia's soul bare. She didn't have the energy to be anything less than completely honest now, and she would just have to cope with Sadiq's indifference as best she could. She had a baby to think about, and that was more important. She felt instinctively that Sadiq would be a good father.

'I'm upset, Sadiq, because I've fallen in love with you. I don't know what I would have told you today, but I would have chosen whichever option would make my heartbreak marginally less. I hadn't yet figured out if that meant leaving you or staying here. But now…' She put her hand on her belly. 'Now I don't even have the illusion of choice, and you're just going to have to deal with the fact that, even though you've given me every opportunity to dislike you intensely, I love you.'

Samia watched several expressions cross Sadiq's face: sheer disbelief, shock, wonder and something like the sun breaking out from behind stormy clouds. Her pathetic heart started to thump but she had to ignore it.

He came close to her again and she backed away, but hit a wall of books. He was smiling, but Samia felt like scowling. He put his hands on either side of her head and leant in, trapping her. Samia had a flashback to when she'd seen him kissing that woman in this very room all those years before. She couldn't believe she hadn't remembered it straight away.

'You're remembering, aren't you?'

Samia's eyes widened. 'Remembering what?' He couldn't possibly be talking about—

'That night—in here, at my party. When you were sitting in a chair in the dark, like a scared little mouse in glasses.'

'I—' Heat was pulsing through Samia. She'd been about to deny it. 'I was already here and you came in. And then that woman.'

Sadiq grimaced. 'Don't remind me.'

Samia was finding it hard to concentrate. She'd just told Sadiq she loved him and he hadn't responded. And now his pelvis was against hers and she could feel his burgeoning response. And he remembered her from that night.

His eyes were bluer than she could ever remember seeing them, and something imperceptible had softened in his face. It reminded her of when she'd seen him smile after dune-driving, with sheer exhilaration and joy.

'Sadiq—'

'Do you know why I remember that moment now?'

She shook her head. He took a long strand of her hair that had fallen over her shoulder and wound it round his finger. 'Because seeing you here in this room brought it back. I saw your embarrassed reaction to knocking over the table of drinks that night and in a split second you'd shown more emotion than I'd seen anyone show in years. It made me feel restless, unsatisfied. I was searching for something elusive that I'd never managed to find with any woman. A depth of passion. A depth of emotion. And the only person I have ever found that with is *you*. As soon as I walked in just now and saw your eyes I remembered that you'd been the silent witness to my isolation that night…' His smile faded slightly and his eyes were intense on hers. 'And the catalyst.'

Samia was wondering if she was dreaming. 'I wanted to come and say something, and then…*she* came in.'

Sadiq nodded. 'I felt like someone was watching me, and then when I turned around it was *her* and it felt all wrong. But then when we heard you…and I saw those big eyes just before you ran…I knew it had been you, and I sensed a kinship, a connection.'

Samia looked away. She wasn't dreaming. She was about to be humiliated. 'No, you didn't. You don't have to say that.'

He caught her chin and gently brought it back. He was deadly serious. 'Yes, I did. And, yes, I do have to say that— because from the day you walked into my office in London that connection was there. I have done my absolute best from that day to avoid acknowledging it. When the explosive chemistry between us became apparent I concentrated on that, determined not to admit that there could possibly be any emotional depth too.'

Feeling very shaky and exposed, Samia said, 'What are you saying, Sadiq?'

'What I'm saying, my love, *habibti*, is that I've been fathoms deep in love with you for weeks, but I've been too afraid to admit it to myself. The more you revealed your true self, the more I fell in love with you—and the more threatened I felt. It's been a perfect law of physics. The more you captured my heart, the more I had to push you away.'

Not wanting to believe this for a moment, because it was too huge, Samia said, 'You don't have to say this just because of the baby.'

Sadiq looked fierce enough to make her tremble. He put a possessive hand on her belly. 'From the moment the doctor told me about your pregnancy all my preconceived notions flew out of the window. I've never felt such pure joy. I want to bring this child up with love. It'll be my heir, yes, but he or she will be *ours*, first and foremost, and can do whatever they want. I was coming to find you to tell you exactly what I'm telling you, but then I found you crying and assumed you were upset because it meant you were trapped with me for ever.'

He shook his head. 'Forgive me for last week. I was so confused about how I was feeling I seriously believed for all of about twenty-four hours that encouraging you to divorce me was the solution. It was only when I stayed away from you and forced myself to see what that future would be like that I had to face up to myself.'

Samia felt very wobbly, and tears were pricking her eyes. 'Sadiq, I love you so much. If you're just saying this—I don't think I could cope if you don't really mean it.'

He took her face in his hands, concern in his eyes. 'Samia, I can't live without you. It's that simple. The power of what I feel for you overwhelms me. I thought it was just passion—physical passion—and I'd seen what that did to my father. I thought I was displaying all of his crazy possessive and destructive traits. But the difference was that he never loved my mother. And love is the difference.'

If was as if there was some final brick in the wall that was guarding her heart—which was pathetic because Sadiq already had the power to crush her to pieces if he so wished. But something was holding her back from letting go. Perhaps it was her own fear of love, after seeing how it had destroyed those closest to her.

Sadiq could see it in her face, and suddenly he took her hand and tugged her after him. 'I'll show you something. Maybe then you'll believe.'

Samia wiped at her wet cheeks, almost stumbling after

Sadiq because he was walking so fast. He stopped outside a door that was on the same corridor, and took a deep breath before opening it.

It was a beautiful room, with blue and green wallpaper and sumptuous divans piled high with cushions. A window opened out onto a small private terrace and B'harani glittered in the distance. But the thing that Samia noticed most was in the centre of the room, in pride of place.

She let go of Sadiq's hand. She could feel his tension as she walked towards the piano, running her hand reverently over the bittersweetly familiar lines. With silent tears running down her face she turned back to Sadiq. 'My mother's piano. You brought it here.'

He nodded. 'I arranged with your brother to have it sent here the night after you told me what had happened to you.' He looked disarmingly unsure of himself. 'I wanted to do something... But if you don't want it...'

Samia shook her head, and the last piece of the wall fell apart. She walked back to Sadiq and stretched up to take his face in her hands to kiss him. She felt his relief, and exulted in the brief moment of insecurity he'd shown.

When she could stop kissing him she pulled back and said, 'How long has it been here?'

Sadiq smiled ruefully. 'About two weeks. But every time I thought I'd tell you I came up with an excuse, because I knew damn well that the minute you saw it you'd know exactly how I felt...'

Samia kissed him again, her heart singing. 'You're an idiot, but I love you.'

Sadiq started to pull her from the room and Samia looked back at the piano wistfully. Sadiq said fondly, 'You can come back. But I want to take you to one more place.'

Samia was floating on a cloud of bliss. She would have gone anywhere on the earth with Sadiq, and she followed him obediently to his Jeep, then a helicopter. Her heart started to pound when she saw the familiar lines of the castle at Nazirat. But they were flying over the castle, and when Samia saw where they were landing something dark pierced her haze of happiness.

If there was one place on the earth she could have avoided, it would have been the bedouin tent.

Sadiq picked up on her tension and took her hand as they got out of the helicopter. He took her face in his hands once it had lifted away into the skies again, leaving them utterly alone.

'Just trust me, okay?'

Samia nodded and bit her lip. It was almost excruciating to remember that night, and the thought that he'd been here with all those other women.

The sun was setting and painting everything a gorgeous burnished gold as she followed Sadiq into the tent again. She gasped with shock when she saw that it had been completely redecorated. Nothing remained from that night.

He pulled her around in front of him and said carefully, 'Samia, I've never brought any other woman here. Only you. This tent didn't exist until I had it built for us when we were in the castle. But that night…' He shook his head in disgust at himself. 'I think that was the start of it. I'd brought you here and suddenly you were questioning me. I couldn't believe how transparent I'd been.'

Joy was infusing every cell of Samia's body. She smiled. 'I thought I had to let you know straight away that I wasn't seeing it as a romantic gesture, but all I wanted was to believe that you'd done this for *me*.'

Sadiq pulled her close, where she could feel how badly he wanted her, and the last few nights of sleeplessness and aching and wanting rose up within Samia like a forest fire. Much like the last time, but in completely different circumstances, they were on the bed, making love with an intensity that made Samia cry out over and over again.

Much later, when their bodies were just a tangle of limbs, dark against pale, Sadiq was trailing Samia's hair through his hand and he said quietly, 'Now I know why I was so freaked out when I saw Nadim and Salman get married.'

Samia lifted her heavy head and came up on one elbow to look at her husband. 'What do you mean?'

Sadiq brushed her hair back over her shoulder, and the tender look on his face and in his eyes made Samia feel extraordinarily blessed. She caught his injured hand and kissed it.

'Because I knew that I was terrified of being as emotionally exposed as they were in those moments. And then you came along, and any hope of protecting myself from a similar fate flew out the window.'

Samia grumbled good-naturedly, 'You took long enough to come around to the idea…'

Sadiq flipped up to hover over her, covering her sensitised breasts with his chest, making her squirm against him deliciously. He smiled. 'And I'm going to spend our lifetimes paying you back for taking so long to recognise what was in my own heart. It'll be a long and slow and infinite process…'

Samia wound her arms around his neck and arched even closer, exulting in his rapidly recovering arousal. 'I like the sound of long and slow, Sultan…so what are you waiting for?'

* * * * *

Girl in the Bedouin Tent

ANNIE WEST

Annie West spent her childhood with her nose between the covers of a book—a habit she retains. After years preparing government reports and official correspondence she decided to write something she *really* enjoys. And there's nothing she loves more than a great romance. Despite her office-bound past she has managed a few interesting moments—including a marriage offer with the promise of a herd of camels to sweeten the contract. She is happily married to her ever-patient husband (who has never owned a dromedary). They live with their two children amongst the tall eucalypts at beautiful Lake Macquarie, on Australia's east coast. You can e-mail Annie at www.annie-west.com or write to her at PO Box 1041, Warners Bay, NSW 2282, Australia.

With thanks and love to Andrew, who has
been an inspiration. What a guy!

CHAPTER ONE

GRAVEL crunched under Amir's boots as he strode across the starlit compound to the tent provided for him. It had been a tedious evening in poor company. Playing guest to the renegade tribal leader in a neighbouring state was *not* how Amir chose to spend his time. Especially since he had important personal business to conclude when he returned to his own country.

'Highness.' Faruq hurried after him. 'We need to consult before the negotiations begin.'

'No.' Amir shook his head. 'Get your sleep. Tomorrow will be a long day.' Especially for Faruq. Amir's aide was city-bred, not used to this wild, remote region, where old ways held sway and diplomacy was rough and ready.

'But Highness...' The protest died as Amir gestured to Mustafa's guards stationed around the tent. Ostensibly for Amir's protection, but undoubtedly to spy if possible.

Faruq ducked his head, then murmured, 'There's also the girl.'

The girl.

Amir's pace slowed as he recalled the woman Mustafa had given him tonight with such ostentation. Blonde hair that shimmered in the lamplight like fluid silk framing a pale face. Luminous violet eyes that stared boldly back, holding Amir's gaze in a way few men and no women in this region of traditional values would dare.

The unexpected combination of beauty and defiance had for an instant stalled the air in his lungs.

Until he'd remembered his taste ran to sophisticated women. Not dancing girls, or whores in gaudy make-up presented by their master to pleasure a visiting dignitary.

Amir had his pick of gorgeous women on six continents. He chose his own bed partners.

And yet…something about her had snared his interest. Perhaps the haughty way she'd arched her delicate blonde eyebrows in a look that would have done an empress proud.

Fleetingly that had intrigued.

'You doubt my capacity to handle her?'

Faruq smothered a chuckle. 'Of course not, Sire. But there's something…unusual there.'

Unusual was right. In Monte Carlo, Moscow or Stockholm her colouring wouldn't warrant a second glance. As for those eyes—that particular shade surely indicated the use of coloured contact lenses. But here, in rough border country inhabited by nomads, brigands and subsistence farmers?

'Don't concern yourself, Faruq. I'm sure she and I will come to some…accommodation.'

Amir nodded dismissal and entered the tent. He removed his boots in the small anteroom, his feet sinking into layered carpets.

Would she be on the bed waiting for him, her skirts spread about her? Or perhaps she'd be naked. No doubt she'd offer herself with the finesse of a professional.

Despite his distaste, Amir's pulse hummed at the memory of a lush, sultry mouth at odds with the fire in her blazing eyes. That mouth promised sensual pleasure enough to interest any man.

Amir thrust aside the heavy curtain.

One step in and he registered the dimmed lamp on the far side of the room.

No sign of the girl.

He checked, senses suddenly alert, his nape prickling.

An instant later he threw up a blocking arm as someone

leapt at him out of the gloom. Something heavy hit him a glancing blow and he swung round, grabbing his assailant.

He caught at a voluminous cloak that fell as he clutched it. A jingle of clashing coins at her belt warned him of her identity just in time. He pulled back sharply to avoid felling her with a single knockout blow.

Amir caught her arm and twisted it behind her back. His movements were controlled, precise, despite the way she threshed and fought. He'd learned to wrestle with full-grown heavyweights. He couldn't use those tactics on a woman, even a woman who ambushed him in his own chamber.

Still she fought. She was like a tigress, alternately trying to wrest herself free or disable him with vicious kicks to the groin.

'Enough!' His patience was at an end. He reached to grab her free arm. But before he could catch it she twisted, rose and brought her arm down in a desperate slashing motion.

Instinct saved him. Instinct honed by years perfecting a warrior's skills and others learning less honourable ways to survive. He pivoted and snapped an arm around her wrist, just as a blade pricked the base of his neck.

'Wild cat!' He squeezed and the knife clattered to the floor. Without compunction he hooked his foot around her legs and brought her down, slamming into her as she collapsed. She landed heavily on her back, his full weight on her, his legs surrounding hers.

An instant later he'd captured both her slender wrists and pinioned them on the carpet high above her head.

She was spent, so still that for a moment he even wondered if she breathed. Then he felt the tremulous rise of full breasts beneath him and heard a raw, shuddering gasp as she drew in air.

Slowly he raised his hand to his throat. A thin trail of wetness slid down from his collarbone.

She'd stabbed him!

Reflexively his hold on her hands tightened and she cried

out—a sharp mew of pain, quickly stifled. Immediately he eased his grip.

Jaw set, he reached for the blade on the floor. Her breath hitched and she froze rigid, but he barely noticed as he balanced it in his hand. Small, sharp and beautiful. An antique paring knife. Keen enough to peel fruit, or inflict serious injury on the unwary.

The blade caught the lamplight and she flinched. What? Did she think he'd use it on her?

With a curse he tossed it to the far side of the room.

'Who sent you to do this? Mustafa?'

It didn't make sense. His host had no reason to wish him dead. Nor could he think of anyone who'd resort to royal assassination. Yet the trickle of blood across his skin was real.

This was one hell of a way to spice up a distasteful duty visit!

Curiosity and fury vied for dominance as he surveyed those lush, scarlet lips now parted to drag in air. The impossibly violet kohl-rimmed eyes, huge beneath thick purple eyeshadow.

'Who *are* you?' He leaned over her, his face bare inches from hers, but her expression was blank, as if schooled to show no fear no matter the threat.

Cursing, he rose on one arm. The movement pressed his groin harder against her body and part of his brain registered her satisfying softness, an innate invitation he couldn't quite ignore despite his scorching anger.

He forced his mind into action. This was no time to be distracted.

If she had one knife there might be others. He rolled to one side, careful to keep her thighs pinioned with one of his and her hands imprisoned.

Her breathing shallowed as he surveyed the expanse of bare skin revealed by her belly dancer's outfit. Her breasts rose and fell rapidly, threatening to pull free of the skimpy bodice. Surely there was no room for a lethal weapon there.

His gaze dropped, skimming her smooth, pale torso, past the dip to her neat waist accentuated by a decorative chain and the flare of her hips. The old-fashioned coin belt sitting low on her hips might be wide enough to conceal something, but her side-slit skirt was too filmy for a hiding place.

Amir lowered his palm to her belly, registering the flinch of her velvet soft skin. He paused. In all his years he'd never touched an unwilling woman. His mouth flattened in distaste. This had to be done—it wasn't sexual, just self-preservation.

Deftly he slid his hand under her belt.

Instantly she erupted in convulsing movement. Her hips bucked and writhed, her torso twisted, her legs scrabbled fruitlessly for purchase.

'No! Please, no!' The words rang hoarsely. Not in any of the local dialects but in a language rarely heard here.

'You're English?'

Amir whipped his head round and froze as he saw the expression in those wide violet eyes.

Sheer terror.

It was his stillness that finally penetrated Cassie's panic. That and the fact he'd slipped his large hand free of her clothes and held it, palm outward, as if to placate her.

Her heart thudded high in her throat and clammy sweat beaded her brow as she stared up at him. She couldn't get her breath, though she gulped in huge, racking breaths.

'You're English?' he said again in that language, and his black eyebrows drew down in a scowl that accentuated the hard, sculpted lines of his face. He looked fierce and frightening and aggressively male.

Would it matter if she was English? Frantically her mind scrabbled to work out if her nationality would make a difference. Was one nationality safer than another in this place where travellers were abducted and imprisoned?

'American?' His head tilted to one side and tiny lines of concentration wrinkled his brow.

He didn't look angry now, but the weight of his solid thigh, the firm grasp that bound her wrists, reminded her she was still at his mercy. He could subdue her with ease.

Her eyes flicked to the scarlet dribble of blood at his throat and she shuddered, fear rising anew. She'd thought to save herself with a pre-emptive attack, knocking him out with the brass pot, but he'd been too quick for her. Too quick, too strong, too dangerous.

'Please.' It was a hoarse whisper from a throat tight with dread. 'Don't do this.'

Every muscle and tendon in her body tensed as she waited for his response.

His sensual mouth lifted at one corner in a snarl of displeasure and his eyebrows shot up. 'You want me to release you? After this?' He gestured to his wound.

Cassie let go a quivering breath. His deep voice with its crisp English and just a hint of an exotic accent had broached her defences. And sharpened the nightmare horror of her situation.

This couldn't be happening. It just couldn't!

'I'm sorry,' she said. 'I just…' Her eyelids fluttered as the world began to dip and swirl about her.

Desperately she clawed back to full consciousness. Fear and fury had kept her strong through the last twenty-four hours. She refused to faint now! Not when she sensed she'd be safe only as long as she kept him talking.

Cassie snapped her eyes open to find he'd bent closer. She saw the slight shadow darkening his strong jaw, a pale scar to the side of his mouth, the way his nostrils flared as if scenting her. The gleam of eyes so dark and so close they looked black and fathomless.

'Please,' she choked. 'Don't rape me.'

Instantly he reared back, letting cool air rush between them. His eyes widened and his fingers tightened convulsively around her wrists. She bit her tongue rather than cry out her pain.

'You think…?' He gestured to her skirts with his free hand and suddenly it was distaste she read in his expression. 'You *really* think…?' He shook his head slowly and said something under his breath in Arabic.

She flinched at the violence in his tone but refused to look away. She was already at his mercy. To appear weak could be a fatal mistake.

His mouth snapped shut, his eyes zeroing in on her face. She felt the intensity of his stare like the burn of ice on bare flesh.

He drew a breath that expanded his chest impressively. Sickly she realised she had no hope if he forced her.

Memories swirled. The metallic tang of terror filled her mouth again as she recalled being pinioned against a door by a man twice her size and three times her age. She'd been only sixteen, but even now she remembered the feel of his meaty hand thrusting inside her shirt, his other hand bruising her thigh, his weight suffocating as he tried to—

'I would not stoop to such an act. No matter what the provocation.' The stranger's voice rang clear with outrage, shattering the past.

Cassie blinked up at a face carved of stone. His jaw clenched as if she'd offered him the worst imaginable insult and he tilted his head, looking down at her as if he'd never seen her like.

'I prefer my women willing.'

His headscarf had come off in the tussle. Glossy black hair was cut close to his well-shaped head. His eyes flashed and emotion drew the skin tight over an impressive bone structure for which any of the leading men she'd performed with would give their eye teeth.

This man would have no trouble finding willing women.

'Then let me go.'

Lying half-naked beneath him, she couldn't trust his word no matter how indignant he looked. She was too aware of his big, hard body, all heavy muscle and bone, imprisoning her. Of his callused hand encircling hers with almost casual dominance. Of the intrinsically male scent of his skin in her nostrils.

'When I'm sure you're not hiding another weapon.'

Cassie's eyes bulged. That was what he'd been doing? Looking for concealed weapons? If she'd had something other than that little knife they'd left beside the fruit platter she'd have used it as soon as he walked through the door. When she'd felt his hand thrusting down into her skirt she'd been sure—

She choked as a bubble of desperate mirth rose from tight lungs. She tried to force it away but the idea was ludicrous. As if there was space in her skimpy clothes to hide anything! Her vision blurred as she gasped for breath over the ragged, sickening laughter she couldn't stifle.

'Stop it! Now!' Firm hands shook her shoulders.

The off-key laughter died abruptly.

He sat on his heels, his eyes fixed on her. This close they looked like black velvet. His skin was golden, his brows dark as sin. A hard angular jaw and strong nose gave him an air of purpose.

His big hands clasped her shoulders, a reminder of his latent strength. A wisp of something shimmered in the air between them for a second. Something new. Her dazed brain tried to grab at it but it vanished as he withdrew his hands and she drew another breath, less ragged this time.

Her wrists throbbed as blood surged through them again. Slowly, each movement painful, she dragged her hands down to cradle them at her chest.

He'd let her go! She could scarcely believe it.

'Thank you,' she whispered, swallowing hard.

Yet, free of his hold, exhaustion engulfed her as the manic surge of adrenalin ebbed.

Twenty-four hours living on the edge of terror had sapped her reserves of strength. It took a few moments to gather herself and find the energy to stir.

Conscious of his gaze assessing every movement, of his tense body still far too close, she rolled to her side and braced her hands against the carpet, ready to get up. Each action took so much energy, and she still felt winded from the impact of what surely must be six feet three of powerfully muscled man tumbling her to the floor.

'What's that?' His voice was sharp.

Cassie looked over her shoulder, eyes wide.

'What?'

'On your back.' He gestured towards her bare back but thankfully didn't touch. 'Down low, just above your skirt, and there, on your thigh.'

Cassie's lips compressed as she pushed herself to her knees.

'Bruises, I expect. The guard likes to exert his authority.' Her lips twisted as she remembered the sadistic glitter in the big man's eyes as he'd laid into her. She'd made the error of defying him. How soon would she have to return to face his tender mercies?

Another burst of Arabic sounded and she swung her head around.

The expression in those dark eyes was ugly.

Instinctively she raised clenched hands in defensive fists.

'Don't look at me like that!' If anything, he scowled more ferociously. Finally he breathed deep, as if searching for calm. 'You have nothing to fear from me.'

It took a moment to realise his gaze had moved to the chain circling her waist and the longer, heavier one connected to it. The one that tethered her to the wide bed on one side of the room.

Cassie had spent fruitless hours trying desperately to prise one of the links open. But nothing had worked, not even the knife. Her fingers were raw and her nails torn from the attempt.

Heat surged into her cheeks as she followed his stare. The symbolism of that chain, securing her like a slave to the bed, was too blatant to be missed.

She was here for his pleasure, to service his needs. As she watched expressions flit across his stark features, Cassie was sure she spied fleeting masculine speculation there.

Defiance flared in her belly.

Cassie knew the brutal power imbalance between a man and a woman kept solely for his amusement. Even if her own society dressed it up as something a little less blatant, it was a role she'd vowed long ago to avoid. Given her background, the thought of being any man's sexual plaything made her break out in a sweat.

It was an appalling cosmic joke that she of all people should find herself in this situation!

'Where's the key?'

Cassie lifted her chin. She injected insouciance into her tone to counteract the ridiculous shame she felt. As if she'd had a say in this! 'If I knew *that* I wouldn't still be here.'

Silently he surveyed her, his skimming glance making her hyperaware of every bare inch of skin and of the weight of encircling metal at her waist.

He sprang to his feet and retrieved her cloak from the floor.

'Here. Cover yourself.' The order was brusque, as if the sight of her offended him.

Looking up at his spare, powerful face, half averted, Cassie wondered if it were true. That he wasn't interested in…

'Thank you.' The words were muffled as she snatched the material and dragged it close. Its scratchy warmth settled around her but didn't counteract the cold welling inside. Suddenly her skin was covered in goosebumps and her teeth chattered. She slumped back on her heels, wrapping her arms around herself for warmth. The mountain air was cold at night, but Cassie knew it was shock finally taking its toll.

She watched him busy himself lighting another lamp and the brazier. The warm glow and cheering crackle of the fire reached her, yet still she felt frozen.

'Come. There's food. You'll feel better after you've eaten.'

'I won't feel better till I'm out of here!'

She glared up, all her resentment focusing on the man towering above her: tall, dark and far more compelling than mere handsome could ever be.

How could she notice that at a time like this?

Was shock affecting her ability to think?

He paced forward, extending a hand, and a tremor rippled through her at the thought of touching him again. His powerful body was still imprinted on hers.

Instinct shrieked that touching him was dangerous.

Cassie pretended not to notice his gesture and scrambled up, feeling the worse for wear. Acting kept her fit and agile, but being crash-tackled to the floor by a man with the hard body of an athlete was not something she trained for.

Breathlessly she stood, swaying only a little, determined not to reach for support.

If possible, his expression hardened even more, his jaw set like stone.

'Who are you?' Her voice emerged strident and challenging.

'My name is Amir ibn Masud Al Jaber.'

He inclined his head in a smooth gesture of introduction and waited, as if expecting a reaction.

'I know your name.' Cassie made a frustrated gesture, trying to remember how she knew his name. She'd never seen him before. That face, that presence was unforgettable.

'I am Sheikh of Tarakhar.'

'Sheikh? Do you mean…?' No, it was preposterous.

'Leader, in your language.'

Cassie's eyes bulged. No wonder she'd known his name! The Sheikh of Tarakhar was renowned for his fabulous wealth and for the absolute power he wielded within his kingdom.

It was his country she'd travelled through yesterday.

Why was he here? Was he in league with the men who'd done this to her?

Fear crowded close again. Cassie wrapped her arms tighter round her torso and began to sidle out of reach.

'And you are?' He didn't move but his deep voice stopped her in her tracks. She braced herself to meet his gleaming gaze.

'My name is Cassandra Denison. Cassie.'

'Cassandra.' The familiar syllables joined in an unfamiliar, exotic curl of sound. She told herself it was his hint of an accent that made her name sound different, so seductive.

She swayed a little—or was that the flickering light?

'Come! You need sustenance.' He didn't quite click his fingers, but his abrupt gesture made her step automatically towards a low, brass-topped table.

Her instant response to his command infuriated her, but she had more important things on her mind. Cassie's eyes rounded. The knife was back where she'd found it, beside a platter of fruit and almonds.

He trusted her with the blade? Or was it a trick to lull her into relaxing?

She eyed the entrance to the vast room, the heavy material that blocked the cool night air. Were the guards still on duty around the tent, making it impossible to escape even if she could break the barbaric chain that marked her as his possession?

A hand closed around her elbow and she jumped, alarm skittering through her. She whipped round to find impenetrable dark eyes fixed on her. His scowl had gone. In its place something like sympathy softened his features.

'You cannot run. Mustafa's guards would seize you before you got ten metres. Besides, you'd stand no chance alone in the mountains, especially at night.'

Cassie sucked in a desperate breath. Were her thoughts so obvious? She tilted her chin. 'Mustafa?'

'Our host. The man who presented you to me.'

Holding her arm, he half pushed, half supported her till her legs gave way and she plopped onto a pile of cushions. Instantly he released her.

A moment later, with an easy grace that held her unwilling gaze, he sank to face her across the low table.

Even seated he loomed too big for comfort. He crowded her space, dominating her senses. Cassie registered his scent: sandalwood and spicy male. Her nostrils flared and reaction feathered through her, jangling her nerves with something other than alarm. She sat straighter, making herself meet his gaze head on.

The flickering light of the brazier accentuated the strong lines of his face. A face that surely belonged in a storybook tale of Arabian nights and proud princes.

His deep voice broke across her hectic thoughts.

'Now, Cassandra Denison, you can explain what's going on.'

CHAPTER TWO

CASSIE'S eyes flicked from his flattened mouth to the tiny trickle of blood drying on the burnished skin of his neck. She drew a slow breath as he picked up the paring knife, but relaxed with a shiver of relief when he merely wiped it clean on a snowy cloth and began to pare an orange. Mesmerised, she watched the precise way he sliced the peel, the supple flick of strong wrists and the deft movements of his long fingers.

'I'm not accustomed to waiting.' Steel threaded his smooth voice and she started.

'And I'm not accustomed to being abducted!'

Straight black brows winged up. 'Abduction? That changes things.' He stilled, his eyes on her.

Cassie had the feeling he saw deep, beyond the overdone make-up, the decorative henna on her hands and feet and the dark cloak. That he saw right down to the woman trying desperately to conquer fear with bravado.

The silence lengthened. She should be pleading, demanding help. Persuading him with her eloquence. Words were her stock in trade, after all. Yet something in his steady, assessing gaze dried the words on her tongue. Her agitated pulse slowed a fraction.

When at last he spoke again his tone was light. 'You must forgive my curiosity. Being attacked with a knife is something of a novelty. It makes me inquisitive.'

His lips quirked up at one side and Cassie's heart gave a tiny jump of surprise.

She wanted to trust him, but could she?

Was he in cahoots with her abductors?

'You mean the chain didn't give it away? The fact that I might be here against my will?' Cassie lifted her chin. If only anger could melt the hard metal that kept her captive!

'I'm afraid I had other things on my mind.'

She felt an unwilling flicker of appreciation at his self-deprecating humour. He was a cool customer. Being attacked by a desperate woman wielding a knife hadn't ruffled his composure one iota!

Nor had it affected his exquisite manners. With another graceful movement he reached for a ewer and bowl and silently invited her to wash her hands. Despite her dire situation, or perhaps because of it, his old-fashioned courtesy soothed her shredded nerves.

Slowly Cassie extended her hands over the bowl. He poured water over her fingers, waited till she rubbed them clean, then poured again.

He passed her a towel of fine cotton, careful not to touch her. Cassie drew in a quick breath of relief and dried her hands, trying not to notice that even his hands were attractive—strong and well shaped.

Instead she concentrated on the soft comfort of the towel. How different the luxury here compared with the Spartan tent where she'd been held!

Only the best for a royal sheikh.

'Besides,' he continued as if uninterrupted, 'the chain could have been a ploy.'

'A ploy?' Cassie's voice rose and her body froze in outrage. 'A ploy? You think I'm wearing this thing for *fun*? It's heavy and uncomfortable and…inhuman!'

And it made her feel like a chattel, a *thing* rather than a person.

Cassie pulled the thick cloak tighter round herself, seeking comfort in its concealing folds.

The abduction had been shocking and terrifying, but being

tethered with a chain like an animal plumbed the depths of her darkest fears. It put her captors' intentions on a new and horrible level.

Even her mother, whose life had revolved around pleasing a man, had never faced a reality so brutal.

'As you say. Even in this lawless part of the world, I didn't expect to find kidnap and slavery.'

At her wide-eyed stare he went on. 'In the old days, centuries ago, slaves were held that way.' He nodded curtly to the chain that snaked across the floor towards the bed. 'It's a slave chain. I thought it possible Mustafa had used it symbolically, rather than seriously.'

'You thought I might have *agreed* to this? That I *chose* to dress this way?' Cassie snapped her mouth shut, remembering her struggles as the women had stripped her clothes away. The horror when they'd produced this gaudy outfit that barely covered her breasts and drew attention to every curve.

She remembered too the searing look, quickly veiled, in this man's eyes when she'd been brought before him in the communal tent. It had heated her as no fire could.

'I didn't know what to think. I don't know you.'

Cassie drew a calming breath. Finally she nodded.

He was right. He knew as little of her as she did of him. The chain *could* have been a stage prop worn for effect—there to spice the jaded appetites of a man who got turned on by the idea of a woman totally at his mercy. A woman with no function but to please him.

Was Amir that sort of man?

Without warning that ancient memory broke through her weary brain's defences again. The one memory she usually kept locked tightly away. Of Curtis Bevan, who'd been her mother's lover the year Cassie turned sixteen. How he'd strutted around her mother's apartment with condescending pride, knowing everything there was bought with his money. Even his lover. How he'd turned his proprietorial eyes on Cassie that day she'd come home for Christmas—

'Cassie?'

The sound of her name in that soft-as-suede voice shattered the recollection. She looked up into a cool obsidian gaze that she would swear saw too much. Her breath snared and for a moment she foundered, caught between her nightmare past and the present.

Deliberately she straightened her shoulders.

'For the record, I don't want to be here! When you came in I thought…' Her words dried at the recollection of what she'd thought. That he'd come here for sex. That it wouldn't matter if she was unwilling.

'You thought you had no choice.' His voice was low and his expression softened. 'The pre-emptive strike was a good move. A brave one.'

Cassie shook her head. 'Just desperate.'

It had become clear within seconds she had no chance against him. He'd subdued her so quickly, lashed her threshing limbs into immobility and toppled her with an ease that merely reinforced his physical superiority.

Whatever happened now she had more sense than to try to overcome this man physically. She needed him fighting for her, not against her.

'Who is this Mustafa? What makes him think he has the right to give me to you like this?'

Amir shrugged, his wide shoulders drawing her unwilling gaze. She told herself her fascination with his sculpted features, his aura of power, was because he was her only hope of getting out of here.

'Mustafa is a bandit chief. He rules these mountains down to the border with Tarakhar. We're in his camp.'

Silently he offered her a plate of orange segments and dates. It was her first food in over twenty-four hours.

Yet she hesitated, wondering at the possibility it had been tampered with. That fear had kept her from devouring it earlier while she waited alone, frantically trying to break the chain.

But he had no need to drug her. She was already at his mercy.

Determined, Cassie forced her mind from the insidious thought.

Carefully she reached for a piece of orange. Its flavour burst like sunshine in her mouth, stinging like blazes where she'd bitten her tongue during their skirmish. Her eyes almost closed in sheer bliss despite the pain. She swallowed and reached for another piece.

'You were going to tell me how you got here.' The dark voice jerked her attention back to the man seated opposite her.

His hooded eyes gleamed with an expression she couldn't name. Was it curiosity, as he'd said? Had she imagined that flash of predatory male interest when he'd first seen her and again as she lay beneath him?

Cassie recalled his touch on her bare skin and shivered. Anxiety swirled in her stomach, and a flutter of something else she couldn't put a name to.

'I was travelling through Tarakhar by bus.'

'By yourself?' Was that disapproval in his tone?

Cassie's spine stiffened. 'I'm twenty-three and more than capable of travelling alone!'

Circumstances had forced Cassie into independence early. She'd never had the luxury of relying on others. Besides, her destination—a rural town near the border—wasn't on the tourist route. She'd had to travel overland for the last part of the journey.

'Visitors are welcomed and treated with respect in Tarakhar. Yet it's advisable not to travel alone.'

'So I've discovered.' Cassie shot him an eloquent look, her ire rising. Anger, she'd found, was preferable to fear. How dared he blame her for what had happened? She was the innocent party!

'A travel warning for foreign visitors might be useful. Perhaps you could have one issued since you're in charge?' Her voice dropped to saccharine sweetness. 'Maybe something about travellers being fair game for kidnappers?'

His eyes narrowed, yet she couldn't read his expression.

Finally he nodded. 'You're right. Action must be taken.'

Cassie watched the grooves deepen around his mouth and wondered what action he had in mind. Despite his stillness and his relaxed pose, she sensed he wasn't nearly as laid-back as he appeared.

Finally she asked the question she'd been putting off. 'You said Mustafa rules these mountains.' She paused, delaying the inevitable. 'Aren't we in Tarakhar any more?'

'No. We're no longer in my country but in the neighbouring state of Bhutran. It's Mustafa's tribal territory and he rules with an iron fist.'

Cassie's heart plunged. She'd already experienced the iron fist. But she'd hoped, prayed, they were still in Tarakhar, where help might reach her. Where Sheikh Amir had authority. Bhutran was a lawless state—notoriously so.

Despair threatened to swamp her but she fought it. Her only hope lay in not giving up. She still had to find a way out of here.

Cassie forced herself to reach for the fruit platter. She needed energy to escape.

Amir watched her devour the fruit with delicate greed. The combination of feisty opponent, all flashing eyes and quick tongue, with soft femininity intrigued him. More than he could remember being intrigued in a long, long time.

In repose her lips were a soft pout of invitation, glistening with fruit juice. The tip of her pink tongue appeared now and then to swipe the excess moisture. Amir realised her sensuality was innate, not contrived.

Yet it wasn't anything as simple as sexual magnetism alone that intrigued him.

The moment Mustafa had presented her in a flourish of generosity her sparking gaze had sizzled across the space between them, piercing Amir's boredom at the gathering's false bonhomie and crude revelry.

Later, through his fury at her attack, he'd still registered her pliant body cushioning him and her delicate scent: desert rose and warm woman.

He'd known women, *had* women in all sorts of circumstances. It had become rare for one to quicken his pulse.

She reached for a date and her cloak slipped enough to reveal the smooth, pale skin of her collarbone, her cleavage. The cloak slid again to show straining midnight blue silk. The material scooped indecently low, revealing far too much of one full, perfect breast.

He recalled how she'd looked in the skimpy dancing costume. She was all lush curves, with a slender waist accentuated by what he'd thought at the time was merely a decorative chain.

Amir yanked his gaze away. He needed to focus!

'Why were you travelling in this region?' The border country wasn't a sightseeing area.

Violet eyes clashed with his before she looked away, hurriedly securing the gaping front of her cloak.

'I've been accepted on to a volunteer programme, teaching English to adults for a couple of months.'

'You're a teacher?' He tried not to let his surprise show. Obviously these weren't her normal clothes. Look at the way she'd just covered up. Yet still he found it difficult, imagining her in a classroom.

'It's not my field back home in Australia, but they were eager for volunteers and it sounded…fulfilling.'

This woman grew more interesting by the moment. He could picture her at home in a bustling, lively city. She was so full of energy and opinions. Teaching in a provincial school was the last place he'd imagine her. 'How did you get here?'

One neat hand clutched the coarse fabric of her cloak and her jaw hardened.

'The bus broke down in the foothills near the border.

Apparently it was a major mechanical problem, something that couldn't be fixed quickly. All the passengers headed off across country to their own homes. There was just me and the driver left, and then...' She shrugged, a jerky little movement that belied her show of casualness. 'Then we heard a sound like thunder.'

She flashed a look at him. Behind the defiance he detected a shadow that might have been fear.

Instinctively Amir leaned towards her, only to straighten abruptly when she recoiled.

It wasn't a reaction to which he was accustomed.

'Horsemen came galloping down from the mountains. They grabbed me.' Her voice flattened to an emotionless pitch that anyone less observant might mistake for insouciance. 'I lost sight of the driver in all the dust and milling horses.' She paused. 'He'd been kind to me. I...don't know what happened to him.'

'You needn't fear for him. A report of the raid came through as I travelled here. The driver is recovering from concussion in hospital.'

Anger ignited in Amir's belly. For Mustafa to have led a violent raid and the abduction of a foreign national inside Tarakhan's borders the day before Amir's visit was little short of a direct insult.

Yet it wasn't Mustafa's arrogance that rankled. It was what had been done to this remarkable woman. Terrified, abducted and abused, she still managed to hold her own, challenging him and giving no ground even when it was patently clear she was dependent on his goodwill.

Was it her vulnerability or her courage that sliced straight through the diffidence he wore like a second skin?

Long dormant emotions stirred uneasily.

It was understandable he'd feel pity. Yet when had he truly cared on a personal level about anyone? Cared for anything but work or his own pleasure?

His lips twisted. *He hadn't.*

Amir was self-sufficient and glad of it. He'd never experienced love, even as a child. Nor had friendship been permitted with the other boys who, with him, had learned the ways of a Tarakhan warrior under his uncle's stern eye.

With the ease of long practice Amir turned his mind to more important matters.

Tonight he'd been the polite guest, playing the game of diplomacy and courtesy to the hilt. He'd allowed Mustafa to bask in the honour of hosting a man far more powerful than he could ever hope to be. Tomorrow his host would find a change in his revered guest.

Mustafa might live in a chaotic nation where the rule of law barely existed, but he'd soon discover the Sheikh of Tarakhar was no pushover. Earlier Amir had been impatient at the need for slow negotiations when an all-important personal arrangement required his attention at home. Now he looked forward to making Mustafa squirm.

'The driver's really OK?'

Amir saw concern on her pale features and felt a stab of admiration. Despite her own situation she was worried for the driver.

'He'll be fine. He was knocked unconscious, which would be why he didn't raise the alarm about your kidnap.'

A tide of impatience rose that he was sitting talking when every nerve screamed for action. Amir was about to surge to his feet when her expression caught his notice.

She pretended strength and insouciance, yet her posture was a little too perfect. Instead of lounging on the comfortable cushions she sat erect, as if ready for anything, even sudden attack. She'd flinched earlier at his exclamations of outrage. Obviously she still didn't trust him. How could she?

Amir subsided onto the banked cushions.

'You've been with Mustafa's men since the abduction?'

She nodded slowly, and he couldn't help but read significance into the fact that this time she didn't elaborate. He'd already learned she wasn't afraid to express her opinion.

What had they done to her?

His stomach clenched at the possibilities.

Cassie watched him pour juice into a chased goblet that looked as if it dated from the time of the crusades. Who knew? Perhaps it did.

His hand, the colour of dark honey, looked strong and capable as he held it out to her.

'Thank you.' She reached to take it from him, careful only to touch the cool metal. She remembered the heat of his skin on hers, the curious sensation when he touched her, and knew better than to risk further contact.

He was too disturbing, even now when he sat with easy composure, drawing out her story, each movement measured and non-threatening. She couldn't forget her sense of peril as she'd stared into fathomless dark eyes and that grim slash of a mouth.

What disturbed her most was the conviction the danger lay not only in his physical strength, his ability to subdue her bodily. It lay in that indefinable aura that tugged at her consciousness. The way her senses, though battered by kidnap and confinement, stirred when he gave that rueful half smile. When he apologised for being distracted, fighting for his life. When his eyes met hers and something unnamed sizzled through the air.

That didn't stop her covertly noticing the slight shadow along his jaw that made him look like a sexy bandit, and the way his full lower lip and mobile mouth turned severe features into something far too appealing.

Cassie blinked, shocked. Her mind was wandering. She clasped her hands tight and leaned closer.

'Now you know I'm here against my will, you'll be able to get me away from here.' Even outside his realm surely he'd be able to help her.

The silence lengthened. Her confident smile grew ragged.

The hastily stitched fabric of her defences began to unravel.

Each second that ticked past shredded her nerves. The thud of her heart, so fast she felt dizzy with it, almost deafened her.

He *must* help!

He couldn't *ignore* what had happened to her.

Finally he spoke. 'Unfortunately it's not that simple.'

'Not simple?' Her stunned voice echoed hoarsely. She felt betrayed. She'd counted on his assistance.

'I'm afraid not. You need to be patient.'

Stiffening her spine, Cassie stared at the man sitting so imperturbably. Shadows from the lamps cast elongated shadows across the strong lines of his face, accentuating the way his hooded eyelids veiled his expression.

Didn't he understand her desperation?

Unless he'd decided it was in his own interests not to help her.

Had she been gulled into a false sense of security by his calm questions and his mellow tone?

Breathing slowly, trying not to hyperventilate, Cassie told herself the Sheikh of Tarakhar couldn't be interested in her. She had none of the sultry allure or seductive experience she imagined his lovers possessed. Despite the stark austerity of his clothes, he looked like a man who'd only settle for the best.

If it came to sexual skills, Cassie wasn't in the running.

But then experience wasn't always required. She knew that from bitter experience.

Surreptitiously she slid her hand under cover of her cloak to where he had carelessly abandoned the knife, holding his gaze unblinking all the while.

'Sheathe your claws, kitten. You have no need of a blade now.'

Kitten! Indignation swamped doubt as her fingers clenched convulsively on the hilt of the fruit knife.

'No?' She tilted her chin.

'No. I do not harm women.' The glint in his gaze spoke of pride and outrage.

But she'd take no chances. 'In the circumstances I know you'll understand if I reserve the right to protect myself.'

Not by so much as a flicker of his eyelids did he move. Yet his features grew taut, the grooves beside his mouth deepening, the angle of his jaw becoming razor-sharp.

Amir regarded her with stunned curiosity. His word was not enough? He wasn't to be trusted?

Surely she couldn't believe him to be cut from the same cloth as Mustafa and his cronies?

It seemed she could.

She lifted her chin, revealing a slender throat that reminded him of her fragility despite her bone-deep defiance. Luminous skin caught his eye, so at odds with her gaudy make-up.

Something stirred inside. Respect for this woman who didn't realise she had no need to keep fighting.

He thought of the long years he'd spent proving himself again and again, fighting against doubt, scorching disapproval and ever-present prejudice. That determination to keep fighting had got him where he was today. Who was he to insist she give up?

'If it gives you comfort, then by all means keep the knife.'

He paused and smiled, expecting acknowledgment of his gesture. After all, to bear arms in the presence of royalty had been till recently a capital offence.

She remained stony-faced and he was torn between exasperation at her distrust and approval of her determination.

Amir gestured towards the outer wall. 'But don't try attacking one of Mustafa's guards with it. They're trained warriors. They won't hesitate to use maximum force if attacked. You'll come off worst.'

'Tell me something I don't know.' Her eyes sparked fire. 'You call them warriors? Kidnapping an unarmed woman? I thought the men here would have more pride.'

'You're right. Their behaviour blemishes honour.'

The mark branded him too. She'd been in *his* kingdom

when abducted. It sickened him that she'd been plucked from
his country and subjected to this.

'Mustafa's men will do what Mustafa tells them to.'

'And you?'

She went too far this time.

'Ms Denison.' His voice rang with hauteur. 'I give my word
you have nothing to fear from me. The first I knew of your
presence was when you were brought to me at the feasting
tent.'

'I…' She faltered and her gaze dipped. 'I see. Thank you.'

Like a balloon pricked by a pin, she seemed to deflate
before his eyes. Instantly, regret lashed him. Where was his
control? Strive as he might to reassure, his reactions to Cassandra Denison were too raw and unpredictable.

How to gentle her and win her trust?

He had a lifetime's experience in pleasuring women. His
lovers were well satisfied. But since adolescence females had
pursued him. All he'd had to do was reach out and select the
one he wanted. He treated them well, but he'd never had to
exert himself to win a woman's trust.

How was he to deal with this woman who defied yet intrigued him? A woman so reluctantly dependent on him?

CHAPTER THREE

'WHY isn't it so simple?'

'Pardon?'

Cassie struggled to sound calm. 'Getting me away from here. You said it's not that simple.'

'That's right.' He poured himself a drink, then raised a golden goblet to his lips.

Frowning, Cassie looked away to the table between them. There was something disturbingly intimate about watching the strong muscles of his burnished throat as he tipped his head back to drink.

Was it the stress of her situation that made her so hyperalert? Or the intimacy of this quiet lamplit haven, so peaceful after her recent trauma?

Slowly he lowered the goblet, and she had the unnerving feeling he was preparing to break bad news.

'I've just arrived and I won't be leaving for a week.'

Cassie nodded. 'And...?'

'And you will have to remain here till then.'

'No way!' On surging outrage she rose, only to subside again when he held out an arm to bar her way. He didn't touch. His hand stopped centimetres from hers. But his expression had its effect. 'If you expect me to wait around here a whole week—'

'That's exactly what I expect, Ms Denison. When my negotiations are over I'll escort you to safety. In the meantime, so long as you remain in this tent, you are under my protection. No one will touch you while you are mine.'

Cassie's eyes rounded. *His.*

A bolt of electricity zapped her.

It wasn't news. That scene in the other tent had been brutally clear, despite the language barrier. Yet to hear him spell it out was too much.

'I'm not yours.' Her voice rose. 'I'm not *any* man's.'

He shook his head. 'As far as Mustafa and everyone else in this camp are concerned you belong to me.'

'That's barbaric!'

What century did he think this was?

He shrugged. 'Of course it is. Mustafa thinks to shore up his position by acts of bravado and posturing.' Dark eyes dropped for a moment to her voluminous cloak, but she suspected it wasn't coarse wool he pictured in his head. A tremor ran through her as she remembered his gaze on her bare skin. 'The man has no subtlety.'

Out of nowhere heat washed her. She only just stopped herself wondering what sort of subtleties the Sheikh of Tarakhar preferred.

'But you can't expect me to stay here!'

'I cannot cut this visit short.'

'Not even to rescue a woman in distress?' Cassie never thought she'd play the helpless female, but her situation was dire.

He spread his hands, drawing her gaze to long, capable fingers and strong wrists.

'I'm here to put an end to the sort of border raid to which you fell victim. If diplomacy fails force will be needed. I'm sure you'll understand my preference not to risk the lives of my citizens unless absolutely necessary.'

At his words she raised her head and found her gaze captured.

'I cannot risk what's happened to you happening to anyone else.'

Cassie sat back on her heels. She applauded his purpose. Yet she had to fight to suppress a demand that he take her away from here now—this instant!

'But even if you're staying here I could—'

'What?' His eyebrows arrowed down and his lips thinned. 'Find your own way to safety?'

Did he have to sound so dismissive? She wasn't that naïve. 'Perhaps some of your people could take me.'

Already he was shaking his head. 'I only have a small staff with me and all are required here.' He paused. 'I regret it, but your only option is to leave when I do.'

Cassie clamped her mouth shut and looked away, lest he see the desperation in her eyes.

'This isn't as I'd wish it either.' His voice dropped. 'But it's the only way. Look at me, Cassandra.'

Startled by the sound of her name on his lips, she swung round. 'Cassie.'

'Cassie, then.' Eyes as black as the midnight desert sky bored into hers. She had the unnerving sensation he looked deep into her soul. 'You will forgive my need for absolute honesty?'

'I'd prefer it.' Knowledge was strength. She needed to know where she stood.

He nodded. 'It's essential the camp believes I am content with this arrangement. And that you accept it.'

Her eyes widened as his meaning sank in.

'Should they believe otherwise, Mustafa will give you to someone else and find me a replacement companion. Or keep you for himself.' Dark eyes pinioned hers. 'Do you want to risk that?'

Dread coursed through her veins and she shuddered, remembering the avid faces of the all-male crowd who'd watched as she was presented like some trophy to this man.

Reluctantly she shook her head. She'd stay. For now.

* * *

Half an hour later Cassie stood rigid, eyes fixed on a wall hanging of a courtyard garden with fountains and ornamental trees and beautiful ladies. One played a stringed instrument, one brushed the long, dark hair of another who lifted a cup daintily to her lips. Yet another picked a blossom with delicate fingers.

'It's a garden of pleasures,' the voice, low and rich, murmured. His breath was a puff of warmth on her bare arm and her skin contracted as if brushed by soft suede.

Cassie cleared her throat. 'Really?' She tried not to notice the way his body heat seemed to inflame her bare skin when he stood so close. Whenever his fingers brushed her bare torso she felt a curious trembling.

'Absolutely. In countries like this a garden is a paradise, a place of bountiful water, of green growing things and beauty.'

Cassie knew he only spoke to keep her mind off the fact that he was having trouble unlocking the long lead to the chain around her waist. Yet she found herself lulled by the tantalising burr of his low voice.

Half an hour of kindness, of reassurance, and her terror had abated. Enough for the rigid tension to seep away and anxiety to drop to a barely there undercurrent.

Now she registered other things. A growing awareness of the man beside her, and of her own body.

Perhaps it was the aftermath of stress that made her so sensitive to his nearness. And to his touch.

'And the women in the picture?' She searched for a way to keep him talking. She told herself it was to keep her mind off the worry that the ancient padlock on the chain would never open. Not because she needed distraction from the feel of his large hands brushing her skin with a delicacy that sent whorls of sensation through her.

'Steady, now. This lock is very stiff. You need to be still.'

Cassie sucked in her breath as he insinuated his fingers beneath the chain at her waist and tried to ease the lock free.

'The women represent the pleasures of the senses. Soothing

music, the scent of blossom, the taste of sweet nectar, the pleasure of touch and the sight of beauty.'

He tugged, then moved, adjusting his hold, and she hurried
into speech. 'That's fascinating. I just thought it was a nice
design.'

'It's far more than that. It can be read on several levels.'

She felt the soft brush of his hair on her bare skin as he bent
close over the old lock. 'Really? What other meanings does it
have?'

One hard shoulder shrugged against Cassie's hip. There
was a sound of grating, then at last a click. A moment later he
straightened, holding up one end of the long lead chain and its
ancient padlock.

He grinned, a three-cornered smile that creased his face
in unfamiliar lines and made this autocratic lord of the desert
suddenly look younger, more approachable and devastatingly
attractive.

Cassie's heart thudded to a quickening pace.

Because the loathsome chain was off. That was all.

'The picture is also a metaphor for the pleasures to be
found in a lover.' His eyes held hers and Cassie's breathing
shallowed. 'The feel of her soft skin, the sound of her sighs,
the feminine scent of her, the pleasure to be found in the sight
and the taste of her.'

His gaze dropped to her lips and a tingle of effervescence
shot through her blood.

An instant later he'd stepped away, his attention on the
chain in his hands. Cassie drew a deep breath, telling herself
she was glad he'd moved. Her gaze dropped to the chain and
she wrapped her arms around her torso. To be tethered like an
animal had been degrading.

'You'll be more comfortable without this.' Anger coloured
his voice and his knuckles tightened on the ancient links
before he let it fall with a dull thud. 'I will have it removed in
the morning.'

Her stomach clenched hard and hope flared at the sense

this man really did take her part. Always she'd fought her battles alone. This time she was grateful for help.

'Thank you, Your Highness.' Was that her voice, so breathless?

His head jerked up and their gazes collided. 'In the circumstances we can drop the formalities. You may call me Amir.'

Cassie swallowed. After all she'd been through why did this simple, sensible offer touch her to the core? Was she so desperate for a friendly face? A gentle tone?

She still felt so…vulnerable.

'Thank you, Amir.' She paused, listening to the sound of his name on her tongue.

'What about this?' She hooked a hand through the finer chain encircling her waist. He followed her gesture, his gaze dropping to her almost bare body. Heat coursed through her. 'Can you get this off?'

He shook his head and slowly lifted his eyes. 'I'd need tools to remove it. Tools I don't have with me.'

Dismay filled her. She'd have to keep wearing it? Unlike the other one, this wasn't heavy but it was a potent reminder of her untenable situation. A slave chain.

Her heady sense of freedom disintegrated as harsh reality returned.

'When we return to Tarakhar it will be a quick matter to remove it.'

Silently Cassie nodded, telling herself she was grateful for what he'd achieved. Suddenly exhaustion crept into her limbs and she felt the last of her energy seep away.

Amir gestured to the massive old-fashioned hip bath the servants had filled with hot water. Curls of steam rose languidly from the surface.

'I'll leave you now to wash.' He turned and was almost out through the door before pausing. 'Call if you need anything.'

By his watch not much time elapsed before she emerged from the bathing room. But it seemed like hours. Hours in which

Amir had soothed his fury by planning suitable punishment for Mustafa and those involved in the kidnapping. Yet Amir's thoughts strayed continually to Cassie Denison's vibrant face, her courage and determination. Her lush body.

Those long minutes working the ancient padlock free of the chain at her waist had been torment. He guessed she'd steeled herself against his touch. He hadn't questioned her yet on how badly she'd been abused by her kidnappers, and bile rose in his throat at the thought of any of Mustafa's rabble laying hands on her.

That was what had made his hands unsteady: anger.

He'd been eager to get the job done, to give her the privacy she needed. Yet he'd been curiously fumble-fingered. It hadn't just been the old lock that had been the problem. His unsteady hands had been as much to blame.

Her innocent questions about the old wall hanging, no doubt scavenged by Mustafa in some raid on an ancient stronghold, had channelled Amir's thoughts in directions that were too intimate for comfort.

He knew the look, scent, sound and feel of her. In one moment of heady madness he'd wondered how she'd taste on his tongue, till he'd pulled himself up short and focused on the lock.

His celibacy these past months told against him, letting his thoughts easily stray to sexual pleasure. It had been too long since he'd taken a woman into his bed.

He breathed deep. His advisors were right. The sooner he married the better.

Mistresses were well and good, but he grew tired of their demands and their grasping eagerness. How long since the pleasure of having beautiful women vie for his attention had begun to pall?

A wife wouldn't cling. A wife would be busy with the royal household, with raising their children. But she'd be there for his comfort too.

He smiled, enjoying the notion.

Till he realised the woman in his imaginings had eyes of deep violet and hair like tumbled corn silk.

The bedroom was still, almost dark but for the dimmed light of a single lamp. Yet Cassie paused on the threshold, her heart thumping.

The bed was massive. Low and wide enough for four. Yet it looked far too full with just one man occupying it.

No matter that he'd given his word. That he'd assured her she was safe. Cassie couldn't share his bed.

A shiver spidered its way down her backbone, drawing her skin taut at the idea. Silently she crept across the carpeted floor to gather up her black cloak. Holding her breath, she reached her other hand to the bed and slid a massive pillow towards her.

He remained oblivious, his chest rising and falling slightly with each breath.

A spurt of indignation filled her that he should be so unaffected by her presence, her story of abduction and ill use, that he'd fallen asleep. Yet it made this easier.

With quick, efficient movements Cassie wrapped the cloak around herself and curled up on a silk carpet beside the bed. She nestled her head on the plump pillow and almost sighed her pleasure. Every bone ached with tiredness.

'You can't sleep there.' The crisp voice came out of the darkness. Instantly she stiffened.

'I prefer to sleep alone.'

'We've been through this, Cassie.' Was that a sigh she heard? 'Still you do not trust me?'

'It's not…' Of course it was. A matter of trust.

But how could she trust this stranger as completely as he expected?

A stranger whose touch had been gentle yet soothingly impersonal as he'd removed that hated lead chain. A stranger whose deep voice and efficient, unfussy care had eased her frayed nerves and given her support when she needed it.

Still—

Her thoughts disintegrated as warmth surrounded her. Strong arms lifted her tight against his solid form.

Terror engulfed her, obliterating her tentative sense of well-being. Cassie fought to escape but could get no purchase on the smooth, hard muscle of his bare torso. Not when his body seemed made of unbreakable steel beneath the warm silk of his skin.

A whoosh of air was expelled from her lungs as he dropped her onto the bed. Cassie barely touched the mattress before she was scrabbling to escape, but he sat beside her, his hip hard against her own, his hold firm as he captured her flailing hands in one of his.

'Enough!' The single word broke through her panicked struggles. 'Enough. You are quite safe.'

Safe? Cassie stared up at a broad, muscled torso dusted with dark hair, to a dangerously angled jaw accentuated by the shadow of stubble. Her heart gave a single lurch. Of fear or something else?

'You can't sleep on the floor. You will sleep here, with me, and you will give the impression, when the servants arrive in the morning, that you are well content. Is that understood?'

Eyes like glittering black jade met hers. 'Cassie? Do you understand? It must appear we spent the night as lovers. For your own safety. Unless you wish to be taken away.'

Cassie swallowed, the movement like scratching sandpaper in her throat. Through the manic pounding of her heart the only sound was her ragged breathing. Fury, she assured herself.

He leaned a fraction closer and the scent of sandalwood tickled her nostrils. 'All right?'

'You give me no choice!' She had no doubt he'd bring her back if she shifted from the bed.

'I'm glad you understand.' Amir moved then, bending away from her and reaching out to something beside the bed.

Cassie froze, wary and at the same time mesmerised by the

shift and bunch of muscles in his torso. She'd never realised how imposing a naked male could be up close.

'Here.' He closed her fingers around something cold. 'My gift to you.' He straightened.

Frowning, Cassie turned from him to look at the heavy object in her hand.

'Hold it like this.' His hand closed around hers and he drew from the scabbard a lethal-looking blade that gleamed wickedly in the lamplight.

'You're kidding!' Cassie's breath sucked in on a hiss of disbelief.

'Keep it with you till I return you to safety. It's far more effective than the paring knife you dropped.'

Stunned, she looked at his smiling mouth, then up to grim eyes that belied his light-hearted tone.

Suddenly she believed. She trusted.

'Sleep with it, Cassie. And if anything frightens you in the night, remember you have this.' On the words he lifted her hand and pressed the tip of the dagger against his chest.

His hand fell away and still the deadly blade rested on his bare, bronzed skin.

Holding the heavy knife took all her strength. Yet within, something surged as she watched him watching her from beneath hooded lids. As she saw the blade glint with every slow rise and fall of Amir's chest.

Her heart squeezed. He gave her not just words, but the power that had been taken from her. The power to protect herself.

The knife wobbled dangerously in her fist and he closed a gentle hand around hers, lowering it to the cool cotton sheet near her shoulder.

'Rest now. No one will harm you.' He released her, his hand hovering a moment as if to stroke her cheek. Then his hand dropped.

His lips thinned and abruptly he stood, towering above her,

his wide square shoulders and tapering waist perfect male symmetry outlined by the single lamp.

Before she could respond he pulled the coverlet over her, and she couldn't help but tense. He stood a moment watching her, then with an abrupt movement bent to tuck in the bedding. A moment later he was striding to his side of the bed.

Cassie's eyes followed him. She took in the power of his lean torso and the powerful buttocks and thighs encased in pale drawstring pants that rode low on his hips. She'd never known a man to look so elemental. So…male.

Heart in mouth, she watched him lift the coverlet on the far side of the bed and slip beneath it. Without a word he turned away from her.

How long she lay there, staring at the golden expanse of his back, Cassie didn't know.

Eventually, despite her determination to remain watchful, her eyelids flickered and her fingers loosened their hold on Amir's knife.

As exhaustion finally claimed her she was aware of a growing sense of peace.

She was almost asleep when her drowsy brain registered why it was she felt so safe. Not because of his words. Nor the concern she'd read in his eyes. Nor the blade he'd given her to defend herself, even against him.

It was the cursory, almost unthinking comfort of that one final action.

How many years had it been since anyone had tucked her into bed for the night? Had showed her such tenderness?

Her heart clutched at the memory, then warmth filled her as she slipped into a dreamless sleep.

She was totally oblivious to the man who turned in the bed and propped himself up to watch her through the night, his brows drawn together in a frown.

CHAPTER FOUR

THE moon rose as Amir rode with Mustafa and his followers through the winding gully back to the encampment.

They'd been out since dawn, occupied by a full day of hawking and riding events designed to entertain and display the prowess of the tough mountain men who gave Mustafa their allegiance. A day designed to exhaust anyone not born to the gritty life of a fighter.

It had been a ploy to give Mustafa the upper hand in the negotiations to come.

He'd miscalculated.

Mustafa knew, of course, about the scandals that had dogged Amir. Who his parents were, his early years of luxury in foreign lands where men weren't men but had grown soft and lazy. Unpromising beginnings for a prince in a land where uncompromising grit and honour were prized.

But his host, like so many before him, hadn't done his homework thoroughly. He'd assumed that old story summed up the Sheikh of Tarakhar.

He hadn't bothered to discover that although Amir's past had shaped him into the man he was today it had made him tougher, stronger, more determined, more focused than any of the so-called warriors surrounding them.

It was Mustafa who sat swaying in his seat, surreptitiously wiping his forehead and growing ill-tempered while Amir rode easily, shoulders straight and mind keen. He could have ridden through the night, still alert and more than capable of dealing with an overblown bully like Mustafa.

He had little respect for the man as anything more than a power broker in an unstable territory. After last night's revelations it had taken all Amir's control not to reveal his fury. The time for that would come. Though Mustafa had received a taste today of the cool hauteur that was a royal sheikh's prerogative.

An image of huge violet eyes flashed into Amir's head.

She'd been asleep when he left. Dead to the world and looking far too pale. In the dawn light, her face free of make-up, she'd looked young and lovely. Even, if that could be believed, innocent.

Till Amir noticed the way her fingers curled around the hilt of her dagger even in sleep.

Emotion surged through him. Something fierce that rippled like a predator on the hunt. Something that craved blood for what had been done to her.

Yet there was also a disturbing sense of frustration. Of helplessness. Feelings he hadn't experienced since boyhood. For, though he wished it otherwise, he couldn't save Cassie Denison yet from the terror that haunted her.

He had obligations to fulfil here. To move precipitately would risk the peace talks and her safety.

Amir's hands tightened on the reins and his horse broke into a canter. Mustafa slowly followed suit, lumbering along like a sack of potatoes instead of the valiant leader of men he styled himself.

Effervescence fizzed in Amir's blood as they rounded a mountain spur and the camp came into view. Soon he'd be able to rid himself, for a while at least, of this unpalatable company.

He assured himself it wasn't eagerness he felt at the prospect of seeing Cassandra.

How many hours had he lain awake watching her? Sifting her words for truth? Letting his gaze trail over skin that he knew was soft as rose petals, hair like rays of sunlight, a delicate jaw that also spoke of obstinacy, and the most passionate mouth he'd ever seen?

Amir stopped his thoughts in an instant, recognising them as weakness.

He did not cultivate weakness. From the age of eleven he'd had to be better, stronger, tougher than his peers. It hadn't been good enough to succeed—he'd had to excel. That had required absolute commitment and focus.

The women in his life, pleasing through they were, fulfilled a very specific role. He couldn't remember ever being kept awake by the need simply to watch one sleep.

He'd opened his mouth to suggest to Mustafa that they commence discussions after dinner when a shout rent the air. There was a flurry of movement. Figures converged in the direction of his guest quarters, set away from the rest of the camp.

Instantly Amir was galloping out of the darkness towards the compound, his sixth sense urging speed.

Streaking ahead of the rest of the party, he thundered down, drawing his horse to an impossible shuddering stop metres from his tent, where cloaked figures surged and writhed.

'Enough!' The command cut the night air, clearing the space before him. Startled faces peered up and were quickly averted as the men of the camp bowed their way backwards.

Yet the tussle before him continued. Two figures, unevenly matched, grappled right up against his tent. The smaller one fought like a demon, aiming vicious kicks and cleverly leveraging the other's vast weight against him in a sudden move that almost felled the bigger man. But the hulking guard saved himself at the last moment. There was a gasp of pain and a hoarse chuckle as the smaller of the figures bowed back as if stretched taut.

'Release her. *Now*!' Amir was off the horse and striding forward as the larger of the pair raised a whip in one beefy arm.

Fury boiled in Amir's veins. He came in hard, bringing the

big guard down with a sharp punch to the jaw and another to the solar plexus.

Quick. Contained. Lethally effective. Though Amir retained enough control to do no more than stop the aggressor in his tracks. It was more difficult than he'd expected to stifle the urge for violent retaliation. The need to avenge Cassie was a roaring tide in his blood.

The man was easily recognisable as the one who'd led Cassie into the feasting tent last night. The gaoler she'd flinched from. The man who'd left his mark on her skin.

Anger scythed through Amir's belly.

He gathered Cassie to him. Despite the enveloping cloak it could be no other. Her size and proximity to his tent made it inevitable. Who else would have the temerity to keep fighting so desperately against the biggest, most brutal guard in Mustafa's retinue?

As he drew her in, close within the curve of his arm, every sense confirmed her identity.

How could a woman he barely knew feel so familiar? It wasn't merely that she fitted perfectly, tucked under his chin, her arms snaking around his waist as if for support. It was something indefinable that stirred unaccustomed sensations.

A need to protect. A desire to comfort.

'Are you all right?'

'Yes.' Her voice was a hoarse gasp that tore at his control. He felt the heat of her heavy breathing through the fine cotton of his clothes and pulled her in tighter.

Nevertheless she stood stiffly, as if poised to repel further attack, every straining muscle tense.

This woman was brave to the point of being foolhardy.

'What possessed you to leave the tent?' She *knew* there were guards. That she'd be stopped if they saw her.

'It was so late I thought you weren't coming back.'

Guilt punched his gut as he thought of the desperation that must have driven her from the tent. *Because of him.* Had she believed he'd gone and left her for Mustafa?

By now the rest of the riders had poured out of the darkness around them.

A low groan sounded from the figure sprawled before them, drawing all eyes as Mustafa dismounted.

'Your guard is overzealous, Mustafa.' Amir projected his voice to carry. It resonated with the weight of his authority. 'He raised his hand to the woman who is mine.'

Cassie peered beneath the hood of her cloak at the throng of riders around them. The smells of sweat, dust and horses filled her nostrils, and in an instant she was back on the deserted road, when raiders had swarmed around the broken-down bus, their eyes hard and their hands rough as they'd yanked her off her feet and away with them.

Fear warred with anger. These were the scum who'd abducted her days ago. Who'd treated her as a possession to be bartered for royal favour!

Despite knowing defeat was inevitable in her tussle with the guard, there'd been a sliver of satisfaction in proving she wasn't quite as defenceless as they'd assumed. One on one it hadn't been the easy victory her captor had thought. She'd seen the surprise and pain in his eyes as he realised his mistake.

But now the defiant surge of adrenalin ebbed and she faced the dangerous consequences of her attempt to escape.

Her arms tightened around Amir. He seemed the one solid point of safety in this dangerous, violent world. His warmth and the muscled solidity of his body anchored her.

Yet she guessed nothing could save her from this mob.

At their head was the man Amir called Mustafa. A tough-built man whose cold eyes had fed her fear last night. He took in the fallen guard, moaning at Amir's feet, then flicked a contemptuous stare in her direction.

Cassie stiffened, refusing to shrink away, though she sensed the rage roaring in him, perilously close to the surface. Retreating from a bully was asking for trouble.

Amir's hand squeezed hers, then he pried her fingers loose and stepped forward. Before she knew what was happening he'd shoved her behind him.

Cassie stared, dumbfounded, at his broad back, his shoulders shielding her from the crowd.

Automatically she moved. She needed to see what was happening, to be ready to put up what fight she could. Her hackles rose at being pushed out of the way.

Yet his hold tightened, forcibly restraining her.

She opened her mouth to object when logic finally reasserted itself. Where were her wits? She had no chance against this crowd. She couldn't fight them all, and she couldn't speak their language to reason or plead.

Cassie's only option was to rely on Amir. He, at least, had their respect.

It was unprecedented to have a champion take charge for her. She wasn't sure how she felt about it. Lost, as if he'd snatched something away from her, yet at the same time touched by the gesture.

There was surprising comfort in Amir's large, warm body shielding her as her heart hammered and her body stiffened from the blows that had rained down.

Staunchly she refused to think of the retribution to come. Because of her, Mustafa's lackey lay writhing in agony.

For a moment she was almost grateful for Amir's broad shoulders blocking the view. His wide-legged stance that spoke of strength and a readiness for action.

The idea of a man putting himself between her and danger seemed impossible. Yet there Amir was: solid and real, drawing all eyes to himself and away from her.

A strange sensation filled her chest—a spreading warmth that countered the chill of dread.

She heard the jingle of a harness and the restless snorts of the horses, but not a whisper from the crowd as Amir and Mustafa talked. Their voices weren't raised. They could have been discussing the weather for all the emotion she heard. But that didn't stop a shiver tripping down her spine.

That look in Mustafa's eyes... Cassie had no doubt he'd make her pay in spades for the damage done to his minion.

She tucked her hand into the sash Amir wore over his robe. To offer silent support or gain comfort?

Still they talked.

Eyes closed, head tilted forward, almost touching Amir's back, Cassie was struck by the beauty of his voice as it flowed, deep and smooth through the night, turning the unfamiliar sounds and rhythms into something arrestingly beautiful.

Finally there was a lull in the discussion and Amir spoke quietly in English. 'Go now. Walk directly to the tent and wait for me inside.'

Her brain numb after standing so long, lost in thought, Cassie opened her eyes and stared at his back. Had he really spoken or was that wishful thinking?

'Cassie!' It was a low hiss of sound. 'Go now. Quietly. Don't run. You're quite safe.'

She swallowed a mirthless laugh at the idea of being safe *here*. Yet without further thought she slid her hand free of his belt and adjusted the cloak more tightly around her. Steeling her nerve, she turned and forced herself to walk slowly towards the tent's entrance.

She'd just got inside when she met the man she'd seen last night at Amir's side, coming the other way. In his hands he carried the long chain Amir had taken off her.

Cassie shrank against the wall of the tent, heart hammering at the sight of it.

The man paused. 'Don't concern yourself, Ms Denison,' he said in fluent English. 'You won't have to worry about this again. His Highness will see to it.' Then he sketched a rapid bow and left before she could find her voice.

Ms Denison.

The title in her own language seemed incongruously formal

after a fight in the dark with a guard and the threatening crowd outside.

It reminded her of the safety she'd left behind in Australia. The foreignness of this wild place.

And her total dependence on the Sheikh of Tarakhar.

Cassie grabbed a tent pole for support as she absorbed the stunning reality of what had just happened.

Amir had done what no man ever had. He'd stood on Cassie's side. He'd done more, literally fighting her battle for her.

The memory of him putting her behind him and facing down that threatening mob made something twist inside.

The men she'd known hadn't been models of virtue. They'd been self-absorbed and anything but honourable. As a result she'd learned self-reliance and distrust young. Cassie never let any man close enough to find out if he had an honourable streak. She no longer believed such a man existed.

It worried her to discover how much she wanted to believe Amir was such a man. He'd come back for her, protected her, putting himself in danger in the process. He'd won her gratitude and respect.

But the hard lessons of youth couldn't be ignored. Would he expect recompense for his protection? Her mouth twisted at the thought, and she knew a twinge of unfamiliar regret that suspicion was so ingrained.

'Cassie?' Amir's deep voice skimmed like hot velvet over her body. 'What's wrong? Are you hurt?' An instant later strong arms enfolded her, sweeping her up against his tall frame.

Her eyes rounded in surprise. She opened her lips to demand he put her down. But she closed them as an unfamiliar sense of wellbeing filled her.

'I'm perfectly fine. I was just thinking.' She told herself she wanted to stand on her own feet despite feeling battered and bruised. Yet his embrace was insidiously comforting. Something she could get too accustomed to.

She needn't have worried. He sat her on the edge of the wide bed and stepped back, well out of arm's length.

Out of sensibility for her situation? The possibility was intriguingly novel. The bud of warmth inside her swelled.

'Thank you,' she murmured, forcing herself to sit straight despite new aches.

'Are you hurt?'

'No.' She lifted her head, meeting a dark gaze that seemed to bore right through her attempt to gloss over her injuries. 'I'm OK.'

Amir's brows arched eloquently, as if he knew just how much pain she'd borne, but he said nothing.

'How about you? Are you injured?' She hadn't seen exactly how he'd taken down the guard.

His mouth turned up at one corner in a lazy smile that tugged something in her chest tight. 'Never better.'

'Good.' She clasped her hands, unsure of the expression in those dark eyes. As an actress she prided herself on her knowledge of body language, but this man was so hard to read!

'Thank you for coming to my rescue.' The words emerged primly, as if she thanked him for a trifling favour, when they both knew that without his intervention she'd have been—

'I told you I'd look after you. Why didn't you believe me?'

Cassie spread her hands. No point saying she'd learnt never to take anyone's promises at face value.

When she'd woken, rested and unharmed in that massive, empty bed, she'd almost wondered if she'd dreamed Amir's presence. But his dagger in her fist had been real. His belongings further proof he'd been there.

'I couldn't be sure. Besides, I've been alone so long I'm used to looking out for myself.'

'You've had a traumatic experience.'

Cassie nodded. She hadn't been talking about just that, but there was no point revealing her isolation had taken a lifetime to grow.

'When I didn't see anyone all day I—'

'No one?' Amir scowled. 'What about servants bringing food and water?'

Cassie shook her head and watched as the lines bracketing his mouth grew deep and fire lit his eyes.

'Go on.' His voice was grim.

'There's nothing more to say. At first it was OK. I felt safe and…comfortable.' Even though she'd chafed at the inaction, waiting for his return when all she wanted was to get away.

'Then, as evening drew in, I started to worry.' She looked away from his sharp scrutiny. No need to tell him she'd thought he'd decided to leave her to her fate. 'I wondered if something had happened to you.'

'And about what would happen to you if it had?'

Quickly she nodded, not wanting to think about it, remembering the savage blows that had rained down on her. She drew a deep breath and shifted to ease the aches in her back and side. 'Finally I gave up waiting. I took your knife and tried to slip out the back of the tent.'

If only she'd done as he'd said—trusted in his word to protect her and stayed where she was. She'd tried. She really had. But as the hours had ticked by it had become increasingly difficult to believe he would return. To believe she could trust him.

'I don't like to think what would have happened if you hadn't rescued me.'

'You are my responsibility.' His tone was matter-of-fact, but there was no mistaking its grim edge. Amir wasn't happy about this situation either.

'I'm…' Cassie shut her mouth before she could blurt out that she was no one's responsibility. She looked after herself! But in her current situation independence was an illusion, possible only with the concurrence of this man. The knowledge ate at her like acid.

Stoically she repressed a shiver.

'You're cold.' He took a step forward, then halted. Cassie

was glad of his distance. This man could crowd her with just a look.

'Your dagger!' She started, suddenly remembering the knife she'd dropped as she'd wriggled from under the tent.

'We'll look for it later.'

'No!' She couldn't have that on her conscience.

In the darkened room last night she'd noticed nothing but the fact he'd trusted her with a blade against his bare skin. That he'd given her the means to protect herself. But today she'd examined the knife and been stunned to discover what looked like an antique heirloom.

The scabbard was encrusted with rubies cut in old-fashioned cabochon style. The blade, wickedly sharp, bore a flourish of exquisite calligraphy near the hilt. The handle was a work of art: an emerald the size of an egg embedded in precious metal.

The thing was probably a national treasure!

Cassie shot to her feet, then paused, a hand going to her lower back as pain slammed through her. That guard had pulled no punches.

'Cassie?'

She forced a taut smile as she turned towards the edge of the tent. 'I'm just a bit stiff.'

'Are you always this stubborn?'

'Always.' What he called stubborn she called getting on with life.

She sensed him just behind her as she searched for the place where she'd wriggled out of the tent. The heat of his big frame so close to her should have disturbed and intimidated after the events of the past few days. Yet strangely she found his nearness comforting. As if nothing could harm her while he was there.

Nonsense! It was absurd wishful thinking. Dangerous thinking.

Yet as she crouched down and investigated the layers of

carpet at the place she'd escaped Cassie found herself grateful for his reassuring presence.

'There.' A long arm reached round her and grabbed the gleaming hilt, half hidden beneath an edge of carpet.

Cassie froze, her pulse rocketing. The sense of being surrounded was suddenly too real and not at all reassuring.

But instead of pressing home his physical advantage Amir stood, then extended his hand to her. 'Here.'

It was on the tip of Cassie's tongue to refuse his help. But grappling with the guard had taken its toll. She felt as if she'd had a run-in with a herd of wild horses.

'Thank you.' Her voice was husky as his hand engulfed hers and he pulled her up. Strange how the touch of that callused hand seemed so much more real than the smooth handshakes of the men she met and worked with in Melbourne.

His was the touch of a hard-working man. A man of decision. Of strength.

Cassie blinked and withdrew her fingers, disturbed at the trend of her thoughts.

'I wouldn't have forgiven myself if anything had happened to it.' She forced herself to turn and meet his enigmatic gaze. 'It must be worth a fortune.'

'Far more than a fortune. Its value is in the fact it's been passed through my family for centuries.'

'Yet you gave it to me?' Cassie frowned, snapping her gaze from his arresting features to the weapon in his hand.

'Your need was greater than mine.'

He made it sound so simple. Yet to trust a stranger, even for a short while, with such an heirloom seemed crazy.

'Here.' He extended his hand, palm open. Light reflected off the gem in the hilt and dazzled her. 'Keep it till you're free.'

For an instant Cassie knew an insane urge to push his hand away and say she felt utterly safe here, with him.

Until she remembered the guards surrounding the tent. The

malice in Mustafa's eyes. She reached for the weapon, her
fingers closing around its solidity.

She concentrated on its weight, the protection it represented, and tried to ignore the ripple of sensation that coursed
through her when her hand touched Amir's.

CHAPTER FIVE

AMIR was reading a report on a new gas pipeline when he sensed her enter. Her bare feet made no sound on the carpet, and without the jingling coin belt there was no obvious sign of her presence.

Yet he sensed her. *Felt* her here, in his domain.

Deliberately Amir forced himself to read another long paragraph. The pipeline was far more important to him, to his plans for Tarakhar, than the woman who'd finally emerged from the bathroom.

Yet the words ran together, jumbling into incoherence as he pretended not to notice her. Finally he thrust aside the papers and looked up. His breath seared his lungs.

She stood defiantly, as if daring him to comment. Her chin was up, her eyes narrowed, and her feet planted a little apart.

In other circumstances Amir would have warned her that the spark of challenge in her eyes, far from dousing male interest, only heightened the delicious temptation of the picture she made.

Gone was the dancing girl outfit. Instead she wore a collarless white shirt of his.

Whatever misguided sympathy had possessed him to offer his clothes for her to wear after her bath?

But how could he have known that Cassie wearing his shirt would be one of the sexiest sights he'd ever encountered?

Heat coiled low as his eyes flicked over her.

The cotton covered her almost to the knees. She'd rolled

the sleeves up and the material hung loose around her. Yet the slit neck dived to her cleavage. The hint of a shadow there intrigued him as she moved restlessly.

Worse, the cotton clung to her breasts, firm and high even without the bustier. As he watched, her nipples peaked, thrusting against the fine material.

Amir swallowed, his mouth drier than the great interior desert, as he dragged his gaze down to shapely legs and dainty feet.

Less is more.

It was true. The dancing costume had been blatantly sexy, designed to appeal to the basest of male hungers.

Yet the simplicity of what she wore now was more erotic than anything he could recall. Or was that because he knew beneath his shirt she was naked?

Quickly Amir looked away.

'I have something for you.' His voice was husky and he reached for water, telling himself he was dry after a day in the saddle.

'A pair of shoes?'

His lips curved at her undaunted humour. 'I'm afraid even I can't conjure a pair small enough to fit you.'

He shoved aside the realisation that he liked her barefoot in his rooms. No doubt the sight appealed to some deeply buried primitive instinct for dominance.

'Though I could arrange a smaller shirt if you like.' Faruq was much smaller than he. Surely one of his shirts—?

'No. Thank you. This is fine.'

Amir nodded and put the goblet down. Even as he'd suggested it part of him had protested at the idea of her wearing another man's clothes.

What sort of crazy possessiveness was that?

Cassie Denison evoked primal responses no civilised man should feel.

Amir frowned. He'd had lovers since his teens. Beautiful,

accommodating women who gave him everything he desired. He couldn't recall feeling possessive about a woman before.

'What is it? The thing you have for me?' She sounded tentative and Amir smiled.

'Liniment.' He let himself turn back to her, careful to keep his gaze on her face. Bare of make-up, her cheeks pink from a steamy bath and her hair pulled back in a long, gleaming plait of gold, she looked impossibly alluring.

His mouth tightened.

'Liniment?' Her head tilted to one side.

He nodded. 'You're bruised. This will help. One of my aides provided it.' Ever prepared, Faruq had brought it for his own use, knowing that this time diplomacy entailed days of hard riding to which he, unlike Amir, wasn't accustomed.

'I just rub it in?'

Amir nodded slowly, the glitch in his plans only now dawning on him. 'You may need help.'

'I'm sure I'll manage,' she said hurriedly, reaching out a hand.

His fingers closed around the small pot. 'Where are you hurt?' He watched her eyes dip. 'Cassie?'

She shrugged. 'My hip. I told you, I can manage.'

'And your back.' He remembered the way pain had streaked across her features when she'd suddenly risen and how her hand had shot to her lower back.

He dragged in a deep breath, reviewing the few staff members he'd brought with him and discounting each in turn. To confront her with a man she'd never met was asking too much. There must be women in the camp somewhere, but he didn't trust any of Mustafa's people to care for Cassie.

Lead settled in his gut as he realised he had no choice. So much for his altruistic gesture!

'Get into bed, on your stomach. I'll see to it.'

'I told you I'll be fine. I—'

'Don't try my patience, Cassie.' He didn't raise his voice. He didn't need to. He'd perfected the voice of authority long ago. 'You'll feel worse without treatment and this will allow you to sleep.'

He met her wide eyes and a jolt of pure energy arced through him. 'It's just liniment, Cassie. Nothing else.'

She drew a slow breath, then another, and Amir kept his eyes trained on her face. Finally her gaze slid away. As if she was the one whose thoughts betrayed a baser self!

Without a word she slipped into the bed.

Out of the corner of his eye he saw a flurry of pale legs, and heat exploded through him, slicing through his good intentions.

He waited a full minute before getting to his feet, gathering himself. His lips twisted in a travesty of a smile. When had touching a beautiful woman become an ordeal?

Since he'd become responsible for her.

He knew the old traditions. The belief that if you saved a life that person belonged to you. For a second he lingered over the notion of Cassie as *his*, available to gratify his every pleasure. Yet it wasn't so simple. His responsibility for her weighed on his conscience.

Slowly he paced to the bed. She lay with her head turned away, the covers just reaching the dip at the small of her back.

'Lift the shirt higher.' His voice was gravel, and swallowing was painful as he watched her wriggle under the covers and then tug the cotton high enough to reveal a narrow strip of pale skin.

'Good.' Amir kept his tone brisk as he sat on the edge of the bed and took the lid off the pot.

He turned his mind to massages he'd received, the placement of hands, the pressure on tight muscles, hoping to dredge up enough knowledge to do this right.

The only trouble was, in his experience, such hands-on treatment usually led to other, utterly sensual pleasures.

Cassie caught her lip between her teeth as she waited, every sense achingly aware, for him to touch her.

Was she a fool, trusting him like this?

Yes, he'd been her protector, her saviour. Even now her heart tumbled over itself as she remembered the way he'd faced that mob, putting himself between them and her.

But to place herself in a position of weakness before any man was anathema to her.

She remembered Curtis Bevan's hand thrusting into her school shirt, only minutes after he'd left her mother, and bile rose. She recalled the last slimy proposition she'd received from a director eager for her to have a 'private audition'. The salacious expressions on Mustafa's men just yesterday as she'd stood before them, more than half naked.

No matter how much those new injuries ached, she was a fool! No way could she put her faith in any man to—

Her instinctive movement stilled as something warm and wet was slapped onto her bare skin.

'I've changed my mind. I don't—'

'Just relax.' His voice was a low rumble from above, but it was his hand at her waist that stopped her moving. Large, gentle, almost tentative, it shaped the curve of her lower back, smoothing ointment from side to side.

Each muscle tensed. She was too aware of his hip against her thigh, separated only by the bedcover, the fact that beneath the cotton of his shirt she was naked.

'Stop tensing your muscles or this will hurt.'

'I don't know how.'

Was that a sigh she heard? 'Never mind. Just try to clear your head. Think of something pleasant.'

Pleasant? Desperately she tried to relax and conjure the memory of her last encore at a live performance.

Two hands caressed her back now, moving in tandem, thumbs pressing and palms pushing in a rhythmic movement that suddenly had her thinking instead of chocolate. Lush, soft truffles that melted on your tongue. Liquid dark chocolate that swished lusciously when stirred.

His touch gentled at the place where the pain was worst,

then smoothed in again where she'd felt the strain of muscle spasm on one side.

Cassie's eyes flickered shut as the steady swirl of his fingers deepened and a puff of breath escaped her.

'Oh.'

Instantly he stilled. 'I hurt you?'

'No.' Cassie stretched, her body weighted yet limber from his ministrations. 'It's…good.'

Liar. It was fantastic. So fantastic that when she felt his hands on her again Cassie was hard put to ignore the delicious swirling sensation in her belly, the trembling effervescence in her blood, the way she wanted to arch into his touch and purr her delight.

'Which hip?' He sounded different. Curiously strained.

'Right.'

A moment later he slid the sheet down a fraction on one side, but not enough to reveal her buttocks.

A hiss of air made her stiffen.

'What is it?'

'You'll be sore for a while. That's a nasty bruise.' This time there was no massage, just a whisper-soft caress as he stroked ointment over her injury.

'Where else?'

For a moment Cassie debated, then gave in. It was clear Amir had no ulterior motives. To him this was a chore. Not by a centimetre had his touch strayed.

'If you wouldn't mind…a little higher up my back?'

Wordlessly he lifted the shirt over her shoulderblades. Instinctively Cassie pressed her breasts further down into the bed.

Then his hands were on her, working magic into muscles tense with days of strain. There was a little pain as he worked the stiffness free, but above all there was lovely, drugging pleasure. She could lie here all night if only he'd keep doing this.

'You're very good with your hands.'

'Thank you.' He sounded terse. Obviously he'd had enough of playing the masseur.

'You can stop now.' Yet even as she said it Cassie found herself arching her spine and pressing her forehead into the pillow in response to the lush waves of pleasure radiating from his capable hands.

'In a minute.' Slowly he worked his way down, past the chain encircling her waist to her lower back.

A strange hollow ache began deep in her abdomen, an edginess that made her shift her hips and legs restlessly. She sought for distraction.

'Why did that man take the chain from the tent tonight?'

'Faruq?' Once more Amir's hand barely skimmed her sore hip, gently smoothing in ointment before returning to massage her back. 'He's here with me. He came to fetch the chain for the guard who attacked you.'

'Why? What's happened to him?'

'Nothing yet. Though it seems he's still in a lot of pain.'

No mistaking the satisfaction in Amir's voice. She was human enough to feel it too, knowing the man who'd tormented and hurt her suffered for what he'd done.

'And later?'

'He'll come with us. Mustafa has handed him to me for punishment.'

'Mustafa wouldn't have liked that.' Cassie recalled the raw fury on his face as he'd seen his henchman writhing at her feet.

'What Mustafa likes is of no consequence. The man attacked my woman. He must pay.'

Strangely this time Cassie didn't feel the same blistering anger at being labelled Amir's woman. Probably because she was melting in a puddle of sheer pleasure.

'What will happen to him?' She shivered, thinking of the barbarous world she'd entered. 'Will he be beaten?'

'Nothing so simple or quick.' Amir's voice was like honed steel. 'There's a huge construction project on the outskirts of my capital. It's all high-tech building processes, but there's scope for old-fashioned hard labour under strict supervision. Your friend will be up before dawn every day, digging, carrying, cutting stone. He'll stop only after the sun goes down. He will learn the hard way that violence against women is not to be tolerated.'

Cassie swung her head round to look into the dark face above her.

Amir's eyes glowed with a heat she hadn't seen before. Anger at the guard, she told herself.

Yet something in his scrutiny made her gaze slide away, warmth rising in her cheeks. She stared at the throb of Amir's pulse strong and fast at the base of his throat. She watched, fascinated, as the grimness left his mouth, his lips relaxing into sculpted sexiness.

Her breath snagged as the idea hit that his focus wasn't on the guard. It was on her.

A trembling started deep inside.

She licked dry lips. 'You're going to a lot of trouble with him.'

Amir shrugged. 'He harmed you. Deliberately. He did far more than just stop you escaping.' Amir's fingers splayed at her waist, insinuating themselves under the chain, a tangible reminder that as far as the rest of the camp was concerned she was here to please Amir.

Startled, she looked up again.

A flash of something lit his eyes. A flash that reverberated through her, drawing her nipples into tight buds and shooting a wire of tension through her abdomen, right down to the juncture of her thighs.

'What will he be building?' Her voice sounded thready, as if coming from a long distance away.

'A hospital for women and children.' Amir's mouth tilted up into a smile that suddenly dispersed the tension clogging the air between them. 'Fitting, don't you think?'

* * *

She shouldn't feel so relaxed and content. Her overwrought brain tried to remind her danger was all around, not least in the man prowling across the room to the far side of the vast bed.

But it was no good. Amir's touch, his massage, his words of reassurance and above all his presence, made her feel…safe.

Her gaze followed him. She assured herself it was natural to be curious. As for the way she followed each sleek line of that bare, powerful torso, the play of light over shifting muscles, the contrast between broad, straight shoulders and the bunch of tight buttocks beneath those loose trousers… Cassie swallowed. There was nothing wrong with acknowledging a rare example of prime masculinity, was there?

Yet a niggle of disquiet stirred.

She'd never been one to ogle a good-looking man. Not just because in her experience most of them were utterly self-absorbed.

What was it about Amir that awakened dormant feminine responses? That made her pulse quicken watching his loose-limbed stride, seeing the smattering of black hair across his broad chest as he turned?

Dark eyes snared hers across the width of the bed and her heart stuttered.

'Do you want the lamp left on again tonight? Would you feel safer?'

The jitter of response in her belly eased at his prosaic words.

She'd been mistaken. There was nothing in his look but concern. Cassie strove to smother a twinge of illicit disappointment.

She didn't *want* his interest! She was *grateful* he saw her merely as a responsibility!

'I'm OK. You can turn the light off.' She hadn't even realised he'd slept last night with the light burning. Again, his consideration for her struck home.

'If you're sure.' He turned away and a moment later the room was plunged into blackness.

Cassie blinked, as if that would let her see, but there was nothing—only the sound of Amir putting something on the small table beside the bed. She heard the whisper of the covers being drawn back, then the rustle of sheets as he slipped into bed.

Her heart hammered as reality hit her anew. She was sharing a bed with a stranger. A virile, powerful man. Surreptitiously her fingers slid under the pillow till they touched hardness, the golden hilt of that magnificent dagger.

Strangely that didn't ease Cassie's agitation. She couldn't imagine needing a weapon to protect her from Amir. What concerned her was her unwanted awareness of him. The fact that she was torn between a desire to curl up on the far side of the tent, as far away as possible, and to snuggle into him, letting his strong arms encircle her and keep her safe.

'Are you sure this is necessary?' She kept her tone prosaic.

'There were no servants here today. No one will know if we don't spend the night together in the same bed.' Cassie drew a shallow breath. 'I could sleep over—'

'No.' The single word silenced her. 'From now on you will be served as an honoured guest. I've made that clear to Mustafa. Besides…' He paused. 'You might as well be comfortable. After your ordeal you need rest.'

Silence engulfed them. Cassie focused on slowing her breathing, trying to relax. But meditation was impossible when even in the darkness she could picture with perfect mouth-watering clarity the honed power of Amir's form.

'Cassandra?' His voice came out of the darkness, low and soft, a burr that brought every sense alert.

'Yes?' She frowned, wondering at Amir's use of her full name.

'I *will* punish that man for beating you.' Amir paused long enough for Cassie to wonder if he sought the right words. 'If there is anything else he needs to be brought to account for you must tell me.'

Cassie frowned. How was she to know what other crimes the guard had committed? She'd be surprised if he hadn't assaulted others. The man was a bully.

'Cassie?'

'I don't know…'

'Or the others who brought you here. If they have harmed you in any other way they will be made to pay.' The lethal softness of his tone finally penetrated. It was a voice that, for all its control, spoke of barely contained fury.

Cassie was grateful for the enveloping darkness that hid her fiery cheeks as his meaning became clear. 'They didn't touch me like that.'

'You mustn't be ashamed.' His voice curled around her, warm and considerate. 'If they forced—'

'No!' she gasped. 'No, they didn't.' She paused, but the urge to talk outweighed her embarrassment. Here in the inky stillness it was easier to spill her fears. Easy to take comfort in Amir's presence, just out of reach.

'I was sure they'd rape me.' Her breath stalled on remembered terror. 'I expected it every hour. Whenever the guard came to the tent. When he looked at me like that…'

Cassie's words petered out as her mind filled with an image of the man's knowing smirk, the way just a look could make her feel unclean.

'And when they took me to the big tent last night I thought…'

'Of course you did.'

Cassie heard what sounded like swearing under his breath, heartfelt and violent. Yet this time it didn't make her cringe. His anger on her behalf was balm to her lacerated soul.

'You were brave last night, Cassandra. A lot of women would have been too terrified to defend themselves, much less attack.'

'Cassie,' she said. When he called her by her full name an unsettling frisson channelled through her.

'Cassie.'

She loved the way he said her name. It seemed to vibrate across her skin in his impossibly deep, soft tones.

'I'm sorry I hurt you.' She'd never properly apologised. She'd been so busy focusing on herself that she'd let him tend to her injuries when all the time his had been potentially lethal. 'If the knife had gone in further...' She shuddered at the enormity of what she'd almost done.

'It didn't. It wouldn't have.' He sounded so matter-of-fact.

Her lips twisted. 'It came close.'

'Yes. You're a woman to be reckoned with.'

Cassie's heart skipped. Of all the things he could have said *that* was the nicest compliment of all to a woman who'd spent her early years being dismissed or excluded. Who'd had to fight for everything she had and was.

'Does it hurt?'

'I'd forgotten about it.'

Sure. He'd been too busy tending to her hurts and felling bullies with just a punch to be concerned about a dagger cut to his throat.

'Remind me never to anger you when we're sharing fruit.'

A gurgle of laughter bubbled in Cassie's throat, easing her tension. It was the first time she'd felt light-hearted in days. It seemed a lifetime and it felt so good.

'Thank you, Amir.'

Silence. 'There's no need for thanks, Cassie.'

She slid her hand out from under the pillow and flexed her fingers where they'd stiffened around his knife. 'There's every need.'

CHAPTER SIX

CASSIE savoured the crisp mountain air and the spicy scent of fresh vegetation. After being cooped up in a tent, however luxurious, the freedom of being outdoors was magic. Even though the freedom was illusory.

She glanced at the rocks to her left. Somewhere hidden from sight were the guards, there to protect their royal guest and, no doubt, to ensure *she* didn't escape.

'You like the view?' Amir's voice came from beside her, and inevitably heat spooled through her veins. That low, sexy rumble undermined every barrier she tried to maintain.

She turned, noticing how, as usual, Amir kept his distance. More than necessary for propriety. Clearly he sent a message. That despite their forced proximity he had no interest in her person.

Had he recognised the dangerous laxness that had invaded her body at his massage? The heady longing for more?

'It's magnificent,' she said quickly, cutting off that line of thought. 'Thank you for bringing me here.'

He spread his hands. 'Your confinement must be difficult to bear.' His eyes met hers and she felt that familiar jolt. 'I only wish I could do more.'

The grim lines around his mouth accentuated what she already knew. Amir was a man of action, used to resolving problems and no doubt getting his own way. It must gall him that he couldn't get her away from the camp immediately.

'I understand. Time looking after me is time away from

your negotiations. The more delays, the longer before we leave.'

A slight lift of dark eyebrows signified his surprise.

Had he thought she didn't understand the situation? She'd little to do but think about it through the long, lonely hours.

'I appreciate the trouble you've taken to arrange this.' Not only Mustafa's guards but Amir's men were on duty for this short excursion. 'But, believe me, the sooner you finish your work here the happier I'll be.' Despite Amir's protection Cassie wouldn't be truly safe till she was in Tarakhar.

She let her gaze drift to the magnificent vista, like a 3D map before her. 'So where's the border?'

Amir pointed to the foot of the escarpment. 'Beneath this range. All that—' his sweeping hand encompassed a vast plain of patchwork fields '—is Tarakhar.'

'It looks prosperous.' She recalled the route her bus had taken. 'I'd expected it to be arid.'

'Further south is the Great Interior Desert. One of the harshest environments in the world, yet still nomads exist on its fringes.'

Amir described his country, from its fertile valleys to its deserts and rugged mountains, with an enthusiasm that made her almost jealous. She enjoyed Melbourne, its bustle and vibrant arts culture, but she'd never experienced this love of place so clearly evident in Amir.

Gilded by the sun, what she could see of Tarakhar looked idyllic.

'What's that, crisscrossing the plain? They're not roads, are they?' Cassie caught the glint of water.

'Irrigation channels. That's the secret to the region's prosperity. Water from the mountains is fed through channels, some of them underground, in a system that's hundreds of years old.'

Amir led her to the comfortable folding chairs his staff had set out. Nearby a table groaned with food.

* * *

Faruq had excelled himself, Amir noted, eyeing delicacies to tempt the most jaded appetite.

Not that Cassie's appetite was jaded. She wasn't greedy, but her enjoyment of local dishes pleased him. Or maybe it was that he liked watching her eat. The way she savoured each taste. Her neat economy of movement.

She looked up to find him watching. A hint of colour tinted her cheeks and she turned away. Proof that she had no interest in him sexually. It was a timely reminder.

'I hadn't expected it to be so beautiful,' she said, looking at the distant view.

'You really do like it then?' Strange how her simple praise delighted him. He'd imagined her experiences would prejudice her. That she wouldn't see the beauty he did. But Cassie wasn't the sort to let bitterness take hold. She resented the wrongs done to her, but at core she seemed positive, vibrant and surprisingly strong.

'I enjoyed the little I saw from the bus too. And the people are very friendly.'

'Hospitality comes naturally to the Tarakhans.'

Cassie looked at the massive feast spread between them and laughed, a short peal that seemed to scintillate in the dusky air. It drew a reluctant smile from him and threatened to shatter the formality between them.

Amir walked a fine line. He needed to put her at ease and remedy as far as possible the trauma of her abduction. Yet getting close was dangerous. Already they were too intimate for comfort. Safer by far if he kept their dealings on a casual yet slightly distant footing.

Grudgingly he stifled the urge to hear that laugh again. To discover more about his fascinating companion.

So...nothing else personal.

'Let me tell you about those canals...'

* * *

Amir lay on his side, watching another dawn filter through the tent walls.

Another night without sleep, his mind in turmoil.

He shifted slightly and winced at the brush of cotton against his heated skin. Silently he cursed the need to wear loose trousers. But preserving Cassie's modesty and her sense of security was paramount.

Besides, it wasn't the restriction of fine cotton against aroused flesh that tortured him. It was Cassie.

Bad enough when she lay in the dark on the far side of the bed, her chuckle like the ripple of cool oasis water against hot skin, her breathless husky voice like the whisper of a zephyr through palm trees on a sultry night.

Each word, every action, reinforced the courage in her, commanding his respect.

Yet he had no difficulty picturing her smooth pale limbs, her forbidden curves and hollows. His fingers flexed at the memory of her skin under his hands as he massaged her. So supple, inviting and responsive. Had she realised she'd curled into his touch like a cat arching into a caress?

But he'd withstood temptation. It was this torture that had him at the edge of his tether.

In her sleep Cassie had abandoned her side of the bed and sought his warmth. She lay spooned behind him, her breasts cushioning his back, the heat at the juncture of her thighs warming his buttocks, her legs aligned with his. Her fingers splayed possessively over the taut muscle of his abdomen.

He fought the impulse to flex his hips, tilt his groin so her hand slipped and he felt her fingers *there*, where he wanted her most.

How had curiosity turned to fascination, fascination to desire in a few short days?

Amir drew a shuddering breath and tried to focus on something else. But Cassie chose that moment to sigh and wriggle closer, her warm breath hazing his back, her lips moving in innocent caress against his skin.

There was nothing innocent about her mouth. Even bereft of make-up she had the most sinfully sexy lips. Full, pouting, slightly downturned at the edges, giving her mouth a sulky look that stirred all sorts of libidinous thoughts.

Amir shuddered as desire racked him.

How many more nights of this would he have to endure?

It did no good to rationalise his reaction by remembering he hadn't taken a lover in months. He wanted to roll her over, tug her beneath him and give free rein to the hunger that ravaged him.

But he wouldn't. He couldn't. She'd been traumatised and was under his protection. She trusted him. *That* was what gave him strength to withstand temptation.

Strange that even the thought of his approaching nuptials did nothing to douse his need.

CHAPTER SEVEN

Amir slammed to a stop in the doorway between the entrance and the main chamber of the tent.

He hadn't allowed himself time today to dwell on Cassie, keeping himself busy with the intricate give and take of negotiations with a wily opponent and the slow pace of formal hospitality.

Yet he hadn't been able to rid himself of that sizzle of awareness. The knowledge that when he returned to his quarters *she'd* be there.

For days he'd behaved impeccably, honourably, despite the arousal twisting him in knots. Despite the lack of sleep that, instead of fatiguing him, focused his brain more sharply on Cassie.

And now—this!

His eyes widened as he saw her in the centre of the room. She wore again that skimpy dancer's outfit as she stretched and twisted in a show of supple strength that made his unruly brain imagine another form of exercise altogether.

He tried to clear his throat, watching as she straightened, turned, then dropped to the ground, her legs opening in perfect splits before she leant to one side, hands around her foot, forehead to her knee.

Desire surged. He wanted her wrapped around him, those pale legs locking tight and her head thrown back in abandon.

He wanted—

'Amir!' A smile lit her face, pleasure making her remarkable eyes glitter before she ducked her gaze to focus on his collarbone.

That still intrigued him—the way a woman so feisty and strong, who'd faced him down like a haughty empress when she'd been brought to him in chains, had for days avoided his gaze.

As if despite her physical courage and her impressive independence there lurked a woman unsure of herself with a man.

Or a woman aware of his unspoken tension.

He paced into the room, letting the curtain drop behind him.

Cassie scrambled to her feet, acutely aware these clothes revealed too much flesh.

Conscious too that something was wrong. Amir's jaw was sharply defined, his shoulders rigid, as if every muscle drew tight. The way his eyes glittered, bright with a fierce light she couldn't name, sent her pulse racing.

'What's happened?'

He shrugged and moved further into the room. 'Nothing. More talk. Offer and counter-offer. Courtesy and ritual.' He flexed his shoulders and a fleeting smile lit his face. 'It's a tedious business. But necessary.'

Cassie frowned. She was conscious of the burdens Amir carried. But he shouldered them with an ease that made her forget sometimes he was ruler of a wealthy kingdom, responsible for the wellbeing of millions.

With her here he couldn't even enjoy privacy after a long day.

She reached for her voluminous cloak, for the first time truly registering the inconvenience she was to him and wishing she could spirit herself away. Grateful as she was for his protection, she'd been too wrapped up in her own fears to consider how little he must want her here.

She spent her time fighting boredom and the inevitable anxiety, knowing the tent was surrounded by armed guards—some of them men who'd abducted her. She spent too much time thinking about Amir. But her thoughts hadn't been about the inconvenience she caused him.

'Are you a dancer?' His question jerked her head up.

For days they'd kept their conversation impersonal, centred on the needs of the moment. As if by mutual agreement their difficult situation would be made easier if they kept their distance. Cassie was sure that was why he spent so little time in his quarters.

Yet despite that Amir was the focus of her waking thoughts as well as her dreams. Her heart quickened in his presence and a hot, unsettled feeling flickered low inside if she inadvertently caught his eye.

'No, I'm not a dancer.' Apart from a lack of talent she wasn't built for it. Cassie had too many curves. But she wasn't about to draw Amir's attention to her overripe dimensions. Bad enough that he'd had an eyeful just now.

The thick cloak settled around her shoulders, scratchy but concealing.

'They looked like dance exercises.' He stopped in front of her and Cassie looked up into his bold, gorgeous face.

A white-hot sizzle of awareness sheared through her. It grew stronger, this discomforting reaction, every time he looked at her. She just hoped he had no inkling of what she felt whenever he drew close.

'I did a little dance years ago, but there's pilates and yoga thrown in. I need something to keep me occupied. I'm climbing the walls with nothing to do.'

Amir had brought no books or papers in English that she could use to occupy herself. Alone each day, the time dragged. She'd written long letters on paper Amir had provided to send to friends when she got away from here. But she'd finished those. Today she'd found herself counting the tassels on the silk wall hangings.

She was going stir crazy. Was it any wonder her thoughts circled back to him?

Amir didn't say anything. The way he surveyed her made Cassie look away, tension ratcheting up.

'I'm an actress,' she blurted out to fill the silence. 'It's important I keep limber. You'd be surprised how much performing takes out of you.' Besides, with her weakness for sweets, and her tendency to gain weight on the hips just looking at a block of her favourite dark chocolate, she knew the importance of exercise.

'An actress?' One dark brow arched high. 'What do your parents think of that?'

She almost smiled at his reaction to her profession. 'It's a respectable job, you know.' When he didn't respond she shrugged. 'I have no parents. My mother died last year.'

'I'm sorry.' He paused, his brow puckering. 'You must have lost your father young.'

It was on the tip of Cassie's tongue to agree and end the conversation, but looking up into Amir's concerned expression she found the lie died on her lips.

Cassie had spent a lifetime perfecting the art of keeping her private life private, her thoughts a closed book. Yet something about this man with the penetrating eyes had her spilling all sorts of things. Like the night she'd admitted her fears and felt ridiculously comforted by his response.

'My father…' She shrugged and looked over Amir's shoulder. 'We're estranged.' That was a polite way of putting it. He'd never wanted to know about her.

'But he has an obligation to care for you. To protect you.'

Cassie turned away, her movements stiff. She settled herself on a cushion by the low table.

'Cassie?'

She looked up to find him scowling. He'd seemed worn and

tense when he'd arrived, and all she'd done was make things worse.

'It's all right. Really. Water under the bridge.' She reached out and plucked a dried apricot from the earthenware platter a servant had brought.

In a single smooth movement Amir dropped cross-legged beside her. His knee grazed her thigh and she had to force herself not to shuffle away lest he realise how his nearness affected her.

'Tell me.'

Cassie looked at the apricot and knew its sweetness would turn sour in her mouth. She put it on the edge of the platter. 'My father's idea of caring was to pay for me to attend boarding school as early as possible to get me out of the way.'

'Perhaps he sought a good education for you.'

She flashed Amir a hot glance and shook her head. 'He never wanted me. I was an inconvenience. It was easier for him if I wasn't underfoot.'

Silence. Amir reached for the apricot she'd rejected and bit into it. She tried and failed not to let her gaze linger on his strong white teeth, the movement of his jaw. His lips. Were they soft as she imagined?

'Men aren't renowned for showing affection.'

She laughed then. A bitter little chirrup of sound that revealed too much of the hurt she'd thought she'd buried years ago. She snapped her mouth shut.

'Cassie? What is it?'

Cassie tilted her head and met his eyes. They were impossibly dark, yet she could swear she read sympathy there. She felt its impact like a missile blasting apart her carefully constructed defences. In all her years there'd been precious little sympathy or understanding. It wasn't something she expected. It made her feel...vulnerable.

Cassie didn't do vulnerable. Survival depended on being decisive and independent.

That was why she kept herself busy. Always looking for the next challenge, throwing herself into new projects as a way of ignoring the emptiness that threatened. That was how she'd got into teaching drama at a community centre. That in turn had sparked her interest in volunteering abroad.

'It's kind of you to be concerned, but it's all in the past.'

His steady gaze told her he didn't buy that.

She drew a slow breath. 'My parents weren't married. My father already had a family and he had no intention of advertising my presence.'

'I see.'

Cassie doubted it. But she wasn't about to mention the fact that her mother had lived as mistress to Cassie's father for years while he stayed with his wife and legitimate family. Neither had wanted a kid in the way to cramp their style. Cassie had been an encumbrance, an accident that shouldn't have happened.

'So there's no one to worry about my choice of career. I make my own decisions.'

'And who is there now, worrying what's become of you?' Amir's voice, like an undercurrent of silk, cut through her bravado.

She pasted on a bright smile. 'The school I'm going to isn't expecting me for another week. But my landlady's expecting a postcard from Tarakhar, and my girlfriends are looking forward to hearing all about my adventures when I get back. I'll have plenty to tell them, won't I?'

He didn't smile. 'So there's no one special?'

Cassie swallowed. 'No.'

She'd been alone all her life. Why, now, did that suddenly seem so momentous? She blinked, mortified at the emotion welling out of nowhere.

'What about you?' Is there someone waiting at home? Someone special?' It wouldn't surprise her to discover he had a girlfriend patiently waiting. Or perhaps a wife.

Why hadn't she thought of that before? Her stomach plunged into icy distress at the thought she'd shared a bed with a married man, dreamt of him touching her in ways she'd never let any man touch her.

Cassie's stomach churned at the idea of Amir with another woman. That had to be a bad sign, surely?

'No one special.' He didn't smile, just held her eyes with an intensity that made every nerve stir.

Something unspoken lay between them. Something portentous that she couldn't put a name to.

The silence between them stretched beyond companionable. Her pulse beat a quickening tattoo as she tried not to respond to the scent of sandalwood and warm male skin that invaded her nostrils and darted her thoughts in prohibited directions.

She strove for a change of subject, flustered as she hadn't been since that first night.

'Do you enjoy acting?' He came to her rescue, slanting his gaze down at her hands, threading together in her lap.

Instantly Cassie stilled. 'I love it. Most of the time.' Drama had been a refuge and an escape.

'But not always?'

She shrugged. 'Like everything, it's got its ups and downs.' There were too many men who believed actresses, particularly ones who looked like her, were either dumb or easy or both. 'But I make a living…most of the time. I wait tables and do whatever else I have to in order to make ends meet. It took me ages to save up for the fare here.'

'It was so important that you work here as a volunteer?'

'It's something I want to do.' She lifted her shoulders in a casual shrug, unwilling to try explaining the importance of this opportunity. With Amir she found herself revealing too much and this was…private.

Though she loved acting, increasingly she felt a need for something more in her life. Despite the bonhomie she'd found

in her profession, there was a focus on individual careers—
every man and woman for themselves.

All her life Cassie had felt adrift and alone. Time and again
she'd tried to connect with her mother without success. Her
mother had blamed Cassie for her break-up with the one man
she'd claimed to care for: Cassie's father. Having a kid underfoot, she'd said, had destroyed the romance. After that she'd
shut everyone out emotionally—especially Cassie—never
displaying anything like true caring again.

Cassie had forged that experience into self-reliance and
decisiveness. Yet she yearned for something more solid. Stability, purpose, community. A sense of contributing.

These months in Tarakhar would help her decide if she
wanted more permanent changes in her life.

Avoiding Amir's penetrating gaze, Cassie reached for an
apricot, inadvertently colliding with him as he leaned forward.
Amir jerked violently away as if scalded.

Stunned, Cassie watched his features grow taut, the
grooves bracketing his mouth carving deep. A frown pleated
his brow as he yanked his hand back from the table.

He looked forbidding, as if she'd trespassed into private
territory.

Which she had. He was royalty, used to the best of everything, and here he was sharing his private accommodation
with an unwanted guest. A guest who normally would be far
beneath his notice.

She waited for him to make some light remark, change the
subject and put her at ease as he did so often.

He remained silent.

In a flurry of movement Cassie made to rise.

'Stay!' It wasn't a request. It was a command.

Amir reached out as if to prevent her rising, but his hand
halted a telling distance from her arm. As if touching her
tainted him. Unbidden, she recalled him holding her behind
him as he faced the dangerous mob. His fingers stroking

ointment on her bruised skin. Had he felt distaste then at the need for contact?

The look on his face was grimly remote. Vanished was their easy camaraderie. Had she imagined approval in his eyes? Or had it just been a mask for disdain?

It wasn't fair or reasonable, but out of the blue the old sense of inferiority swamped her. Worse this time, because Amir was the catalyst. The man from whom she'd come to expect support.

She'd lost count of the times people had pulled away, distancing themselves when they learned the truth about her parents. About why her father had paid the bills at the elite school where she'd never felt welcome. There'd been the girls who'd made her life hell. The teachers who'd watched her with prurient curiosity or distaste. The parents who'd looked down their noses at her, as if fearing she might contaminate one of their precious darlings.

A lifetime's hurt shuddered to the surface as she looked from his hand into his set face.

Try as she might she could read nothing in his stern expression but rejection and disapproval.

'If you'll excuse me.' She needed all her dramatic skill to keep her voice cool, as if pain didn't cramp her vocal cords and frozen lungs. 'I know when I'm not wanted.'

Cassie scrambled to rise, hampered by the long cloak. She'd rather sit in the bathroom than remain here.

A hand clamped around her wrist and tugged so hard she plopped back down to the cushions, her breath escaping in a whoosh of disbelief.

Amir didn't release her. His long fingers encircled her, firm and warm. Darts of sensation shot through her from his touch and she silently berated herself—because even now she revelled in the feel of his skin against hers.

Cassie stared at him, furious, hurt and, despite herself, curious.

He gave nothing away. His features might have been carved centuries ago, by a sculptor with an eye for beauty and character. Strong nose, purposeful jaw, deeply hooded eyes that hinted at secrets well kept. A mouth that drew her gaze and made her blood rise and effervesce.

'You are.'

Cassie was so absorbed in studying his face, trying to read his thoughts, that the words didn't penetrate.

'Sorry?' With an effort she dragged her reluctant gaze from his lips, over his face of dark gold, to eyes suddenly revealed in blazing glory.

'You are…wanted.'

The words hung between them and it seemed they both held their breath. Nothing moved.

Her brain crashed into gear. That look in his eyes…

Cassie swallowed. Her pulse jumped under his long fingers. She remembered the sensation of his touch, his breath on her bare midriff when he'd worked on that ancient padlock. She felt the hard muscle of his thigh against hers and her mouth dried.

'There's no need to spare my feelings.' Indignation lingered.

His mobile mouth quirked up at one side in an expression that could have signalled wry amusement or possibly pain.

'I'm not given to platitudes, Cassie. I say what I mean.' He drew a breath that expanded his chest mightily. His fingers slid down till he held her hand. 'You are welcome in my tent. *More than welcome.*'

'It's kind of you to—'

'It's not kindness.' His voice was rich and dark like treacle, swirling languidly around her senses. 'I'm not a kind man. I have no experience of it. But I am truthful. Believe me when I say I want you.'

The breath whooshed from Cassie's lungs as she finally allowed herself to read the meaning in his glittering gaze.

Want in the physical, sexual sense.

Want in the way she'd avoided all her life. From the day she'd understood what being a 'kept woman' meant. The day she'd understood her mother survived by pandering to the sexual needs first of Cassie's father and then, when he dumped her, of a string of equally wealthy, demanding men who had precious little respect for her.

Yet, reading the stark hunger in Amir's eyes, feeling the loose grasp of his hand around hers, it wasn't the usual revulsion Cassie felt.

It was a thrill of excitement.

Only days ago the thought of Amir looking at her with desire had made her reach for a knife. But now…

The continual restless undercurrent, the hum of awareness and edginess when she thought of Amir or when he drew near, finally made sense.

For the first time in her life Cassie *wanted*. Wanted a stranger she barely knew. A stranger who'd cared for her with more genuine tenderness than anyone she'd known.

A tremor rippled through her, making her hand shake in his. His fingers wrapped more tightly around hers.

'Don't look so stunned, little one. Is it so surprising? You're a beautiful woman. A fascinating woman.'

His gaze lingered warmly—not on her curves, but her face. Almost as if it was more than her body that appealed.

'I don't… I can't…' Stunned, she shook her head. She was bereft of words. She, the expert at deflecting propositions with a light-hearted quip! Who'd sashayed unscathed past the minefield of sexual relationships with never a backwards glance.

This was different. With Amir for the first time Cassie experienced the compelling desire for intimacy. It was in the gnawing sensation deep in her womb, the need to touch him and snuggle up against his hard body. No wonder she'd been stir crazy these past days! It wasn't just her confinement; it was Amir getting under her skin.

His grip loosened and his fingers slid away. Bereft, she watched his hand bunch on his thigh. She wanted to reach out and stroke him, wrap her hand around his.

'Don't worry, Cassie. You don't have to do anything.'

Her head jerked up and she met his gaze, once more unreadable, all trace of incendiary heat banished. He looked distant, as if that moment of unbridled desire had never been.

'I want you, but you are safe under my protection. Even from me!'

Once more his mouth tilted in that one-sided smile, and this time she'd swear it was pain she read there.

Cassie opened her mouth to blurt out what she felt. That she'd been going slowly mad these past days, trying to battle the uncharacteristic need to be with him. Not just share that wide bed, but share herself.

She shook her head, innate caution intervening. They'd never even kissed, had barely talked, yet the force of her tumultuous feelings was undeniable.

The force of this yearning scared her.

She'd grown up despising her mother's lifestyle, so bitterly cold-hearted beneath the surface gloss. Despising the men who'd used her mother to satisfy their egos and sexual appetites. That had tainted Cassie's dealings with men and she'd never felt anything like this urgent attraction.

It left her floundering, torn between excitement and fear.

Could it be because of their forced proximity? Some strange version of Stockholm Syndrome? Did the danger and isolation make her fancy herself falling for not her kidnapper but the man who would rescue her?

How could she believe what she felt was real?

Yet it felt blood-pulsingly real: urgent and demanding.

She dared to reach out and touch his fist, only to see it turn white-knuckled.

'Don't touch me, Cassie.' At his sharp tone she snatched her hand back. 'This is already a test of willpower. Don't make it more difficult to keep my word.'

He spoke so coolly she was tempted to believe it was all a hoax. That for some reason he played with her, pretending to desire. But, touching him, she'd felt the tension shimmer through him, an unseen vibration.

Amir desired her.

And Cassie wanted him!

Yet surely she'd be a fool to give in to this dangerous desire, no matter how intense, no matter how tempting.

CHAPTER EIGHT

'YOU'RE a talented chess player.'

Cassie's face lit with pleasure. Then she looked away hurriedly, as if guilty at enjoying the compliment.

The light flickered in a caress over her lovely features. Cassie grew more vibrant, more engaging, with each hour. It was as if a fire had been lit within her, giving her a glow that drew him like a moth to raw flame.

How was a man to resist?

It should be easy. Though he'd spelled out his desire for her she hadn't reciprocated, hadn't encouraged.

That guaranteed she stayed off-limits. No matter the provocation of too many sleepless nights, his body taut with the need for restraint.

The abduction had made her vulnerable. Was it any wonder she had no interest in pursuing what he guessed would be a combustible passion between them?

He shouldn't have revealed his feelings. Yet her revelations had thrown him off balance. He'd been stunned by the searing hurt he'd felt on her behalf, hearing about her neglectful family and reading the vulnerability behind her bravado.

Amir had grown up distanced from everyone, especially his family. It was that isolation, that need to prove himself against doubts and scorn, that had made him successful and self-sufficient. He'd never had time for regrets. Emotion was something he eschewed.

Yet hearing snippets of Cassie's story something inside

him had cracked. He'd wanted to make someone pay for the distress she tried so valiantly to hide. Comfort her.

As if *he* had experience in providing comfort! Pleasure, yes—that was easy. But he sensed Cassie needed far more.

'I used to play chess a lot.'

'So I can see.'

She collected his rook in a daring move. 'But I'm a bit rusty,' she admitted as he captured her knight.

'Check.'

She nodded and bit her lip, her brow puckering in concentration. Amir wanted to stroke her soft lips, then press his mouth there, taste her sweetness on his tongue.

His grip tightened on the captured knight. Three more days and they'd be out of here. Three more days and he could give Cassie space till she was ready to be persuaded.

For the first time Amir discovered no other woman would do. It was *Cassie* he wanted. Not one of the many women so eager for his attention.

Cassie alone tortured him every hour. Even when he closed his eyes she was there, waiting to tempt him. She was becoming a fixation.

'Who taught you to play?'

She raised her eyes and instantly he was lost in those wary violet depths.

'A teacher at school. The same one who taught me debating and drama.'

'You were busy.'

Her luscious mouth pursed into a sultry bow and she lunged forward, moving a piece seemingly at random.

'I was the poster girl for extracurricular activities.' Her smile was perfunctory. 'I did them all—from badminton to archery, baking, French conversation, a dozen crafts, and later even motor mechanics. I could play the piano and the saxophone before I got to high school, but I had to quit violin to save everyone's ears.'

'A high achiever.' Amir could relate to that.

Again and again they'd given him new tasks to master, new skills they'd been sure he'd fail. He'd forced himself to master them all, to excel, especially at the traditional skills of a Tarakhan warrior. His uncle and the rest had been so certain Amir could never take his place among them. Their contempt had driven him to prove them all wrong.

Cassie shook her head. 'I'd rather have been playing a game or reading a book, but I wasn't given a choice. After-school lessons kept me away from home. Much more convenient than having me underfoot. Then when I was boarding it was easier to keep me occupied rather than pestering to come home.'

Again that shaft of anger mixed with regret and pain speared him. She spoke so matter-of-factly, not lingering in search of sympathy, yet she had it.

What was it about Cassie Denison that made him *feel* so much? Empathise, where in the past he'd had no difficulty retaining a discreet, unbreachable distance from those who, since his accession, wanted to get close?

'How about you? Did your father teach you chess?' She looked up at a point near his ear, then lowered her gaze. He found that almost-collision of eyes infuriating. Unsatisfactory. He wanted...what he couldn't have.

'Hardly.' The word emerged more brusquely than he'd intended and she looked up sharply. 'A palace servant taught me.'

'Really? Like an old family retainer?'

'Something like that. My uncle was horrified that I didn't know the basics of the game when I came to live in Tarakhar. He ordered one of the staff to instruct me.'

'You weren't born in Tarakhar? How did you become Sheikh?' She tilted her head in curiosity, then hurriedly turned to focus on the board.

'The Council of Elders chose me as the most suitable leader from the members of my extended family.' Amir's lips twisted derisively.

How times had changed. Once they wouldn't have given

him the time of day, much less bestowed the nation into his safekeeping.

'What is it?' She peered up at him again, obviously seeing the emotion he usually kept to himself. Why did he find himself letting down his guard with her more and more?

'Nothing. Just that when I came to Tarakhar I wasn't well regarded. I would have been last on the list to be given a public role.'

'Why? What had you done?'

She stirred, and Amir caught her skin's warm fragrance, fresh and tempting. 'I hadn't done anything. I was only eleven.' He watched her brows furrow in that tiny frown she wore when thinking, and repressed the impulse to stroke it away.

He sat straighter.

'I don't understand.'

Clearly Cassie didn't read the gossip columns. Or perhaps it was such old news the press didn't bother to dig up scandalous snippets any more. It had been years since he'd bothered to read what they printed about him.

Amir moved a piece, surprised to find she'd begun to turn the tables and attack.

'My father was youngest brother to the old Sheikh, so I was a member of the ruling family. But we didn't live in Tarakhar.'

'You were raised with your mother's family?'

'Hardly!' There'd been no family at all on his mother's side. His mother hadn't even known who her own father was. On her birth certificate 'unknown' had been inserted instead of a father's name. His uncle had made sure Amir learned that, as well as a lot of other facts he'd have preferred never to know. 'My parents moved around. They didn't have a home but stayed in hotels and resorts. One day the Caribbean, the next, Morocco or the South of France.'

'It sounds exotic.'

He shrugged, feeling a strange tautness in his shoulders. It reminded him of the tension that had gripped him as a kid, when he'd borne the weight of others' expectations—not their hopes, but their certainty he'd fail.

'I suppose it *was* exotic.' He moved a chess piece in a strategy to corner her. 'To me it was just a blur of hotel rooms and unfamiliar faces.' They'd never stayed in one place long enough for him to make friends, and his parents had had a habit of sacking the nannies hired to look after Amir just as he was beginning to know them.

Not that he'd seen much of his parents. They'd had no time for their son. They'd been too engrossed in pursuing the increasingly elusive 'good times' they had lived for.

'Why weren't you well regarded?' Cassie's soft voice tugged him back to the present.

Amir looked into searching eyes and felt a surprising urge to talk. His personal life was a topic he never discussed, even though much of it was on public record.

'I was surrounded by scandal from the moment I was born. No, before I was born.' He watched her move and pretended to survey the board when it was Cassie he wanted to watch. 'My father was the black sheep of the family. You name it, he tried it, from squandering his fortune through gambling to embezzling public funds.'

'You're kidding!'

Amir shook his head. 'He relied on his older brother to bail him out of strife and cover up for him. And he was right—the old Sheikh would have done anything to ensure he didn't face imprisonment. That would have brought shame on the family. In the end my father lived on a very generous stipend provided by his brother.'

'So he could afford the resorts?'

'And more. He was a womanizer, a party animal. The only reason he married my mother was because she was pregnant with his baby.'

'At least he married her.'

Amir watched something flicker in Cassie's eyes and

remembered what she'd said about her parents not being married. About her father living with his other family.

It sounded hard, but if her father had been like his perhaps her experience was the better option.

Slowly he nodded. 'It was the one responsible thing he did in his life. To his family's horror, though, he married a lingerie model with a slum upbringing and a reputation for kiss-and-tell affairs.' His smile was a tight twist of the lips. '*Not* what the Tarakhan royal family had hoped for.'

'I'll bet not.' Cassie sat back, the chessboard forgotten.

'The fact that they died together from an overdose of illegal drugs at an out-of-control party only made things worse.'

'Oh, Amir! I'm so sorry.'

He leaned across to take another of her pieces. He didn't need sympathy. He'd barely known his parents and hadn't missed them. If anything, the move to Tarakhar had been a blessed relief, despite his uncle's rules and regimen.

'It was a long time ago. But the point is when I arrived everyone looked sideways at me. My uncle expected me to turn out like my father—unstable and irresponsible. Everyone else followed his lead.'

'That's *so* unfair!'

'Who said life was fair?' He paused. 'Maybe knowing everyone expected me to fail was what gave me to strength to keep trying. To succeed.'

Amir kept his voice light, but memories reinforced the promise he'd long ago made to himself. No children of his would suffer as he'd done, because of his parents' scandalous behaviour. They wouldn't wear the badge of shame for something they couldn't change.

He would protect them as he'd never been protected. He had it all mapped out. Nothing would be left to chance.

He watched Cassie's slim fingers move a chess piece rather than let himself seek out her gaze.

'Surely your uncle could have given you the benefit of the doubt? You were just a kid.'

'My uncle was a decent man, but after a lifetime bailing his brother out of trouble his patience had worn thin. He spent years waiting for me to show the same traits as my father.'

'But you didn't.'

She said it with such certainty that Amir lifted his gaze to her still face. Something gleamed in the depths of her eyes. Something warm and reassuring. Something that, crazily, for this moment, he wanted to hang on to.

'I'm no saint, Cassie. I haven't always stuck to the straight and narrow.'

Cassie looked away from his dark eyes. They discussed him, yet she felt he saw too much of what she usually kept to herself.

Like the shiver of excitement inside when their eyes met. Like the feeling of connection to this man who was still virtually a stranger.

Yet, hearing about his childhood, she couldn't help but notice the similarities between them. Neither had been wanted as children—definitely in her case, and reading between the lines she'd guess in Amir's as well. Both were children of parents intent on their own pleasure. Both shadowed by the shame of their parents' behaviour. Both ostracised by others because of that.

Both alone.

'I'm not surprised you rebelled. It's a natural response.' She watched him move again, closing the trap around her king.

His movements were mesmerising. Or was it that she'd fallen under his spell? She hung on his words, addicted to the deep timbre of his voice. She watched him move whenever she could, enjoying his lithe grace and athleticism.

She'd bet anything part of his rebellion had been seducing women. Was he a playboy like his father?

Amir had charm when he wanted to exert it, and that dry, self-deprecating humour was far too attractive. Not to mention the sizzle in his eyes when he'd spoken of wanting her. Her pulse revved at the thought.

But most of all it was his aloofness, the sense that he stood alone, that intrigued. It made Cassie want to wrap her arms around him and draw him close. Learn what lay behind that guarded expression and comfort him.

Surely if anything was needed to prove her reaction to him was foolish that was it? As if Amir wanted comfort! She'd never met anyone so self-contained.

Despite what he'd said about desiring her, he'd been nothing but honourable. Protective. A man to rely on.

'Did you rebel too?' His voice came soft and low, feathering across her senses.

'Not so much rebel as escape. Acting was how I got away when things were difficult. I could escape to another world, be who I wanted to be. I could be funny or tragic. I could act out my emotions and blot out what was happening around me.'

'Sounds like it was tough.'

Cassie looked up and found he'd leaned closer, his look intent. Her skin drew tight in a flurry of tingles and she had to concentrate on not gulping in air too fast. When he looked at her like that all she could think of was him saying he wanted her.

It became difficult to remember why she should hold back.

'I got by. I grew strong.'

It took all her willpower to break his gaze and look down at the board. For a moment she couldn't make sense of it, had lost track of the strategy she'd chanced against him. Then, in a moment of clarity, she remembered.

Cassie couldn't prevent the tiny smile that curled her lips as she moved her queen, then looked up into his stunned face. 'Checkmate.'

Cassie stretched voluptuously, in her half-asleep state enjoying the hazy sensation of bone-deep comfort. Had she ever felt this relaxed, this cosy?

She rubbed her cheek against the pillow, warm and cushioned and so slightly abrasive.

Frowning, she pulled herself higher.

Pillows should be soft, shouldn't they?

No matter. This was deliciously warm and—

'Cassie.'

She felt Amir's voice rumble through her. How did he do that?

'Hmm?'

'I think you should move.'

She shook her head, burrowing closer into the spice-scented heat of the bed. She didn't want to move. Didn't want him to talk and wake her fully.

Lying here half dreaming was bliss.

'Cassie.' This time she felt the word like a purr passing through her torso.

'No.' Fretfully she turned her head, clinging to the remnants of sleep. She had nowhere to go, had she? He was the one who left this wonderful bed each morning to go out, leaving her prey to boredom and worry.

'You need to move.'

'Why?' Just a few minutes more. Just—

'Because...' He muttered under his breath and Cassie felt the last vestiges of sleep slide away. 'Because of this.'

Large hands settled on her upper arms and hauled her higher. Startled, she snapped open her mouth to protest, opening her eyes at the same time.

She had a moment's confused impression of a heated black gaze and then something brushed her mouth. Something soft and warm and inviting.

Instantly realisation hit. She was in bed with Amir. Not *in* bed, safely curled on the far side of the wide mattress, but in bed, lying sprawled over him!

It was his bare chest beneath her that generated the heat she'd snuggled into.

His lips slid against hers again in a gentle caress. Her eyes flickered shut as he slipped the tip of his tongue into her mouth in a light foray that made every sense leap.

She clung tight as he thrust further, bringing delight with every slow, lush move of his tongue against hers. Heat coiled inside as rivulets of sensation spread through her, merging and rising into a floodtide of pleasure.

She shouldn't enjoy this. She shouldn't respond. But she did. It was what she'd experienced in those fitful dreams these past few days, and so much more.

With a sigh she sank down into Amir, tilting her head to allow better access to her mouth, answering his kiss with her own demands.

His broad chest was beneath her own, his hot skin bare to her touch. She lay half across him, her right leg on his right, his bunched muscles exciting. The long cotton shirt she wore was no barrier between them. The sensation of skin on skin, of her softness against his hardness, incited a heady thrill she'd never experienced.

He moved, wrapped one arm around her waist, cupped her face in his splay-fingered hand, and she almost moaned her pleasure aloud. His touch was proprietorial and she revelled in it.

Of its own volition her mouth mimicked his, her tongue dipping into his mouth and discovering his delicious taste.

Deeper, deeper the kiss grew. Her senses swirled in heady delight as she fell into the sensuous give and take.

Cassie had been kissed before. On stage she'd scored more than her fair share of kisses, from quick pecks to lavish seductions. Away from the stage there'd been men too. Some she'd even encouraged as she'd tried to shake off her fears and her ingrained distaste. But it had never worked. No one had broken through the mental barriers she'd erected and strengthened with every passing year.

Those barriers had kept her from giving herself to a man. No one had ever swept her away on a wave of pleasure till her mind refused to engage and all she could do was feel. Until now.

Amir's taste, spicy and dark and male, filled her senses. It mingled with the fresh, clean scent of his skin. Not like hers but intriguingly different and desirable. Unique.

His touch was tender but his body was hard, inciting a terrible longing that made Cassie shift restlessly and lean closer.

His hand moved up, threading through her hair, and she thought she'd die of pleasure. It was a massage so seductive, attuned to the deepening rhythm of their kiss and the rising need within her.

Cassie wanted more. She spread her hands over Amir's shoulders, stroking the hot silk of his skin over rigid muscle and bone. She lifted a hand to his jaw, fascinated by the tiny abrasive film of stubble that felt so satisfyingly rough to her palm and tickled the corner of her mouth.

He shifted and the friction of his solid chest against her breasts notched tension within her. An urgency built, making her move fretfully, demanding more.

Amir gave it. In a single surge he gripped her close and rolled her onto her back. Cassie revelled in the sense of him propped half over her, blanketing out the world. His mouth worked magic, making her head spin.

His hand strayed to her jaw, her throat, and a delicate shudder ripped through her at his butterfly-light caress.

Her heart hammered to a new, urgent tattoo as she willed his hand lower, for the first time wanting, *needing* a man's touch on her breast.

Her skin tingled and her blood roared. Deep inside something loosened: a tightness, a constriction she'd never noticed. Cassie felt free, wonderfully alive, breathless with anticipation.

'Please,' she whispered against his mouth, hardly knowing what she wanted except that it was *more*.

A moment later his warm hand cupped her breast. Delicious heat shot through her. She moved restlessly and his hold tightened. A deep growl of masculine pleasure vibrated through her and he shifted his weight.

His fingers flexed again, but this time Cassie felt no pleasure, only a sudden suffocating fog.

A flutter of unease stirred and her eyes snapped open. He loomed huge above her in the half-dark.

The tantalising pleasure of Amir's kiss bled away. In its place erupted choking fear.

She was helpless against the strength of this big, powerful man. Abruptly, from the depths of her subconscious, came the memory of being pinioned to a door, fondled by the man who'd just emerged from her mother's bedroom. She could almost hear his hoarse chuckle as she writhed in his hold.

Somehow the hot, clean scent of Amir's skin was obliterated by the sour tang of sweat, wine and musky aftershave.

Bile rose and Cassie's stomach cramped in fear.

She had to get out, draw breath. But she couldn't break his hold.

A sob of terror rose in her throat as she shoved at those rigid shoulders. She kicked fruitlessly, hampered by the unyielding form above her.

Suddenly she was free. She scrambled to the far side of the bed, gasping desperate breaths as she pulled her knees high and wrapped her arms around them.

Finally, when the miasma lifted, she turned her head. Amir sat hunched on the other side of the bed, one hand thrust through his crisp dark hair. His shoulders rose and fell as he dragged in deep breaths and she spied tiny crimson marks there. Scratches where she'd dug her nails in as she'd frantically tried to shift him.

Cassie's breath froze.

What had happened? One moment she'd been eager for Amir. The next, claustrophobic fear had risen and flung her into panicked resistance.

'Are you all right?'

He'd swung round. Dark eyes full of concern held hers.

Silently she nodded, unable to find her voice.

She trembled all over, suddenly cold though seconds ago she'd been burning with desire and the heat of Amir's body against hers.

'I...' His hand slashed through the air—in a gesture of frustration or anger? She couldn't tell. 'Don't look at me like that, Cassie!'

He surged to his feet and strode across the dimly lit room away from her. A moment later he'd grabbed a long cloak and whirled it round his shoulders.

When he turned his face was set like stone, though his eyes held a febrile glitter.

'I apologise.' He took half a step towards her then stopped. 'That won't happen again. I thought you wanted—' He shook his head. 'You are safe.'

Guilt rose in Cassie. She *had* wanted. She'd wanted so badly.

'It's not your fault.' Her voice emerged husky from her constricted throat. 'I...'

The words died as he turned away, the cloak flaring around him.

'Sleep now, Cassie. No one will disturb you.' Then he marched from the room, barefoot but impossibly regal.

Cassie was left alone with her thoughts.

She'd never craved company more.

CHAPTER NINE

GRAVEL bit into his bare feet as he stalked across the dawn-lit compound but Amir barely registered the pain.

Instead it was the recollection of Cassie's fear that gripped him. The glazed horror in her eyes when he'd broken their kiss had shocked him.

How had he got it so wrong?

Yes, she'd been barely awake when he'd tried to make her move.

Yes, he'd been aroused, and all too ready to let his body do the thinking as he'd lain, tormented, beneath her sumptuously feminine body.

Yes, he'd known he shouldn't, but he'd been unable to resist kissing her, deepening the kiss as she'd responded.

He'd read her plea as an invitation to pleasure, believing she felt the same simmering desire that had short-circuited his brain. He'd deluded himself into thinking she wanted him as much as he wanted her.

How had he not heard instantly the desperation in her voice? How had he misinterpreted what must have been a plea for escape as a throaty-voiced request for seduction?

Bitter recriminations filled his head and guilt slashed a jagged slice through his belly.

He reached an outcrop of bare rock on the edge of camp and stood, watching the fingers of dawn light spread down from the mountain towards Tarakhar.

If only they were there now. Cassie would be cared for and

comfortable as she recuperated from her ordeals. She wouldn't have to share accommodation with a man who, despite his vaunted control, had almost taken far more than he should have.

Amir was sick to his stomach at the thought of what he'd almost done.

He recalled Cassie's desperation that first night. The fear in her voice as she'd related how she'd expected to be assaulted at any moment. How he'd reassured her she was safe with him.

A bitter laugh escaped him.

Safe?

The horror in her wide eyes moments ago told its own tale.

Two more days till their scheduled departure. Two days during which she'd fear he'd make a move on her. Two days in which he wouldn't sleep for fear of waking again to a situation he couldn't control.

He couldn't do it.

He swung round and strode back across the camp. With a supreme effort he might just be able to finalise the work he'd come here to do in one day. Then they'd only have one night to get through. Surely one more night was possible?

Cassie lay in the massive bed, unable to sleep.

She hadn't seen Amir since dawn.

Now she heard laughter and music on the night air. There must be a feast in the main tent tonight. As guest of honour Amir would attend.

Why did it hurt so much that he'd avoided her all day?

She was frantic to explain he wasn't to blame. To wipe away the guilt she'd read on his face as he'd looked at her with shock pinching his features.

The soft brush of his lips had been an invitation to pleasure, not a demand. It had been *her* plea for more that had galvanised him into action, as she'd thought she wanted.

Cassie pummelled the pillow. She needed to explain. She needed...

Cassie shied from the thought filling her head. Yet it wouldn't disappear. She knew what she *wanted*.

She wanted Amir.

Wanted him as she'd never wanted any man.

For days she'd tried to convince herself what she felt was an aberration caused by their bizarre circumstances. That, once she was free of this place, he'd lose his allure.

It wasn't true. She'd been too scared to face the truth.

Why shouldn't she desire him? He was strong, handsome and honourable. He respected her.

Then she forced herself to face another truth.

Her reaction this morning had been anything but normal. She'd wanted Amir, begged him for more. And when he'd obliged she'd frozen with terror at the memory of something that had happened in her teens.

Curtis Bevan hadn't raped her all those years ago. But he'd made her feel unclean, tainted by his touch and his lascivious intentions. After that she'd been only too glad to return to boarding school, away from the man who thought that paying for her mother gave him rights to Cassie too.

Now she glimpsed the possibility that that event, coupled with the stigma of her mother's way of life, had affected her more than she'd thought.

Was she celibate because she hadn't met the right man? Or had her emotional scars made her afraid to give herself?

Cassie had thought herself a survivor. She'd withstood bullying and ostracism. She'd been strong in the face of her mother's neglect and occasional vitriolic outbursts, her father's avoidance. She'd carved a career through talent and hard work.

Cassie had scrimped and saved to make this trip even when supporting herself was a struggle.

When her mother died Cassie had given away her few valuables rather than accept anything bought by her mother's keepers. Even the diamond brooch of which her mum had been so proud. How powerful Cassie had felt donating it to a charity shop, walking out through the door into the sunshine and feeling free of her mother's murky past.

But she wasn't free.

And she wanted to be. As much as she wanted Amir.

It was past midnight when Amir entered the sleeping chamber. He'd stayed as late as possible, though the entertainment hadn't been to his taste. Yet a lamp burned, bathing the wide bed in golden light.

His gaze was riveted on the still form there, her blonde hair flaring on the pillow.

She was asleep. He wouldn't have to face her anxiety.

Nevertheless, he didn't trust himself to sleep with her. Not after that taste this morning had awakened such hunger. He could recall it now: the flavour of her ripe lips, the scent of her honeyed skin, the need he hadn't been able to stop.

A tremor ripped through him and he clenched his hands.

He'd take the floor instead.

Quickly he disrobed and shoved his legs into light trousers. He hefted a bracing breath and reached for a pillow.

'Don't go.'

He froze, pillow in hand, as Cassie broke the silence. He whipped his head around to find her violet gaze on him. Instantly heat shimmered through him, an unholy combination of lust and remorse.

He straightened abruptly. 'I didn't mean to wake you.'

'You didn't.'

Of course she hadn't been asleep. She was probably a bundle of nerves, anxious about sharing that bed.

'Don't worry.' His attempt at a reassuring smile felt tight. 'I'll take the floor tonight.'

'That's not necessary.' She propped herself on one elbow and the covers slid down a fraction.

Amir didn't let his eyes drop to the shadow of her cleavage visible through the slit neck of his shirt. Yet every cell throbbed with awareness.

'It's better this way.' He turned from the bed, loosening his watch. A man knew his limits and Amir had reached his!

'No, Amir.'

Startled, he turned slowly.

Her face was flushed and her eyes glittered with an expression he couldn't read.

'I want to sleep with you,' she said, a defiant note in her voice.

His body locked down as shock and desire tensed every muscle. He couldn't be hearing what he thought he heard. He shook his head.

'I'm sorry about this morning—'

He raised one hand. 'You have nothing to apologise for.'

'But I do.' Cassie sat higher, her hair tumbling round her shoulders like a glossy invitation to touch. 'You did nothing wrong. I wanted your kiss. I wanted more.'

Her eyes dipped and she drew an unsteady breath. Despite his best intentions Amir was transfixed by the sight of her unbound breasts rising tremulously against the fine fabric of his shirt. Her nipples peaked as he watched.

Heat poured over him. He clamped the pillow close to cover his arousal.

'You changed your mind. That's all right.' Amir lifted his shoulders in a gesture of dismissal, but the movement was jerky and uncoordinated, as if his body didn't function properly.

Determined to end this difficult conversation, he wrenched off his watch and reached over to put it on the bedside table.

The expensive timepiece fell from suddenly nerveless fingers with a clunk onto the inlaid surface.

'I didn't think you'd mind.' Cassie's words were rushed, slightly breathless. 'I noticed them in your toiletries bag when I borrowed your comb.'

His eyes rounded in disbelief as he surveyed 'them'.

A neatly stacked pile of condoms.

Amir's heartbeat took up a new rhythm, like the gallop of

hooves across the desert. He stared, and still the sight didn't make sense. He carried condoms like he carried soap or tooth-paste. They'd stayed in the bag since his last trip. He certainly hadn't expected to use them here.

'Say something, Amir.'

Say what? That he couldn't trust himself to stop if she changed her mind again? That he was a man of flesh and blood and all too real appetites?

'This is a mistake, Cassie. You were terrified this morning.'

He turned to find she'd edged closer, her eyes solemn and huge. Then he made the mistake of looking at her mouth, the way her lips were parted as if in expectation, the sultry shape of them beckoning.

'It wasn't you. It was just that I suddenly remembered...'

'I can guess.' It must have been terrifying, the sense of helplessness when she'd been abducted. 'But sex with me isn't a cure for your fears.'

He couldn't believe he was talking her out of this!

In dealing with women Amir's allegiance had always been to Amir. Though he'd never consciously harm any woman, self-interest had always dictated his dealings.

Cassie was different. Vulnerable, yet so feisty and deter-mined. He couldn't help but be drawn to her, and want to protect her.

'You know nothing about my fears!' Typically, her chin angled high as she held his eyes, and he was struck again by the fierce independence in her. That strength of character drew him as much as her luscious body.

'In the morning you'll be relieved that we haven't—'

'I won't!' Her voice was strident. 'I know what I want, Amir, even if I didn't this morning. I want you.'

How many times had Amir heard those words, or others like them? How many times had women, silk-clad sirens or glamorous sophisticates, invited him to share their bed? Too many to count. Yet never before had he sensed the raw hon-esty he saw in Cassie's eyes.

There was a gravity about her, a consciousness of herself and of him, that for a moment locked any words in his throat.

She had such pride, such passion!

And he wanted her so very badly.

His grip tightened on the pillow as he turned away. It was the hardest thing he'd ever done, rejecting Cassie, but he couldn't risk her changing her mind again. Clearly the kidnap still traumatised her. She probably didn't know what she wanted. And if she pulled back from him again he didn't know he had the strength to stop.

'Don't tempt me, Cassie.'

A small hand touched the back of his, lightly, but it was enough to stop him stepping away.

'I *want* to tempt you. Don't you understand? This isn't like this morning. I know what I'm doing.'

Her fingers slid up to his wrist, delicately caressing, and he shuddered. It was all he could do not to move when his inner self screamed for him to pull her to him and finish what they'd begun this morning.

Before he could stop her she'd pulled the pillow from his slackening grip.

He watched as she looked down and caught her breath. She blinked, and her mouth rounded in an O of surprise that impossibly made him harden more.

He really had a thing for those sultry lips. Fire threaded his veins and exploded in his belly as he envisaged those lips on his body.

'You *do* want me.'

'Of course I want you!' Wasn't that the point? He wanted her too much to keep control.

Her mouth curved in the tiniest of satisfied smiles. An instant later she crossed her arms and tugged off the shirt she'd been wearing.

He was lost.

Strong as he was, no power on earth could save him now. Or her.

Amir swallowed hard, his throat dry as the arid mountains, his gaze anchored by her breasts.

In her dancer's clothes she'd looked voluptuous, but it was surprising how much the satin had concealed. The natural tip-tilted lushness of firm breasts. The delicate rosy hue of nipples that puckered invitingly.

Amir's palms itched with the need to touch. He longed to taste and savour.

A low groan filled his chest and spilled into the hushed silence. He stepped up to the edge of the bed and ripped back the covers.

Only the sight of her, fully uncovered, made him pause long enough to enjoy the view. Now he saw not only Cassie's breasts, but her pale thighs, the inviting arc of her hips...

He eyed the dip of her waist where the hated slave chain glinted. Yet this time, in a flash of unrepentant masculine possessiveness, exhilaration sparked at the way it accentuated her feminine shape. At the way it signified she was *his* to possess.

A moment later he was in the bed, drawing her to him.

She came easily, sliding against him in a flurry of soft flesh so tantalising he almost winced at the pleasure of it. Pleasure so intense it bordered on pain.

Unerringly his lips caught hers, his hands slid over her pale, silken skin, learning texture and shape. He gathered her close, breast to chest, and the exquisite rightness of Cassie in his arms stole his breath.

This time her mouth was as hungry as his, urgent as she shaped her lips to him, sucked his tongue in deep and clamped his head between her hands.

She trembled all over, a tiny, delicate tremor that made his chest lurch in a tumble of rare emotion.

Amir forced his hands to slow as they swept her shoulders and back, replacing urgency with a weighted, deliberate caress. Cassie arched into him. Her budded nipples grazed him and sent blood rushing low.

He hooked one leg over hers, holding her in place against

him, and pushed his hips forward. The sensuous pleasure of her soft belly, the feel of skin on skin, shot stars through his vision.

'You're certain?' he groaned, forcing himself to break the kiss and pull back enough to look at her.

He wanted to smile at the dazed delight he read in her eyes. Even now he wasn't sure he could release her if he needed to.

Her palm slid over his cheek, past his chin, to skim in the lightest of caresses over his throat. He swallowed convulsively as her hand moved further, to flatten and swirl over his chest.

'Absolutely certain.' Her eyes were serious, almost grave, but her lips were plump and soft from his kiss. Her smile was the sweetest he'd ever seen. 'Let me help you.'

She pushed his shoulder till he lay on his back and she leaned over, reaching for the side table. Her breasts brushed him teasingly, her legs slid against his, and the heat at the apex of her thighs warmed him.

'Don't!'

Startled, she stared down into what he guessed was a face full of pain. He wanted Cassie so badly each casual touch was like an incendiary flare, burning his needy body.

How would he last long enough to get a condom fitted if it was Cassie rolling it on him?

Amir gritted his teeth and nudged her backwards.

'I'll do this.'

Without waiting for a response he rolled over, stripped open a packet and sheathed himself.

He turned back, hauled her close and kissed her till he was lost in her heady sweetness and control was a fragile filament. His pelvis rocked hard against her, mimicking the thrust of his tongue in her mouth.

To his delight Cassie curved her body against his, aligning herself to his movements and clutching at him as if she'd never let go.

Amir traced the line of her ribs, rejoicing in her telltale

shiver as he cupped one pouting breast. It was the perfect size for his hand. Gently he swiped his thumb over her nipple and was rewarded with a gasp of shocked pleasure. He did it again, and her whole body bowed back as she pushed her breast deeper into his hold.

He smiled, relieved and delighted at her responsiveness. A moment later he slid down her body, rubbing his cheek against her breast.

Cassie's arms coiled tight round his head, holding him to her. He looked up, caught a flash of wonder in those eyes that had darkened now to indigo. For a moment he could almost believe this was a new experience for her, despite her offer to fit the condom.

Then he ceased thinking as he took her nipple in his mouth and sucked hard, feeling her legs wrap round him in an urgent lock that sent blood roaring through him in a cataclysmic tide.

He wanted. How he wanted.

And so did she.

Amir slipped his hand between their bodies till he zeroed in on the centre of her desire. She was hot and wet, moving urgently at his touch.

Dimly he thought about the need for foreplay. About the need to ensure Cassie's pleasure before his own. But his years of experience fell silent before the compulsion to make her his. Now.

He surged higher, pausing only to bestow a lingering kiss on her other breast, letting it turn into a tiny nip that made the breath hiss between her lips and her hips buck needily.

Then Amir was over her, propped on his elbows. Her eyes held his and there was no spark of fear. Their bodies met and slid together, eager for completion.

Using his knee, Amir nudged one leg aside, then the other. He moved, shifting his weight carefully, to settle in the cradle of her hips.

Was that a flicker of doubt in Cassie's eyes? A shadow?

Amir paused, his breath thundering in his lungs, fists clenched so hard his fingers grew numb from the pressure.

She couldn't say no. He'd die if she did.

But the size and weight of him over her must reinforce her latent fears. Was that what had gone wrong this morning?

Instinct more than reason had him rolling to his side, tugging her with him till he lay on his back with her above him.

'Kiss me,' he ordered, before she had time to think.

Their mouths melded and this time Cassie set the pace, her lips demanding and hungry. Her hands were restless on his face and shoulders, and she shifted against him as if wanting more but not knowing how to get it.

He smoothed his hands down her back, past the chain at her waist, up the curve to her firm buttocks. Slipping further, he took the backs of her thighs in his hands and pulled them wide, so her body opened over his, her knees planted on either side of him.

Yes!

Amir rocked beneath her, exultant at the sensation of flesh against flesh.

Cassie lifted her head, her lips open in a gasp of what he hoped was approval. When she showed no inclination to move he grasped her shoulders.

'Sit up, Cassie. Yes, like that!' The words ended on a deep groan of approval as she slid over the full length of his erection, drawing every nerve to aching arousal.

The sight of her above him, breasts swaying, lips curved in an answering smile, excited him as never before.

With one swift movement he grabbed her hips, lifted her high and centred her over him. His eyelids flickered in anticipated ecstasy at the feel of her heat all around him.

He pulled, slow yet firm, and she slid down, opening for him.

She sheathed him so tightly, so perfectly, it took a moment for him to realise she'd stopped and held herself rigid above him. He felt the muscles in her thighs stiffen, her fingers tighten on his shoulders. Through the rough beat of blood in his ears he thought he heard a gasp. Of discomfort?

'Cassie? Am I hurting you?' She was far smaller than he, and the sensation of pressure around him was intense. For him that meant pleasure, but for her...

'I'm fine.' She blinked and drew a deep breath, then looked down at his torso, as if absorbing every detail for later consideration. A tremor rippled through her legs. Tension or delight? 'It's just...'

'It's been a while?' Amir lifted his hands and smoothed them up her arms, trying to stroke away the tension he felt within her.

'Something like that.'

Fighting the primitive urge to drag her down the rest of the way, he let his hands move to her breasts, lazily cupping and sliding, circling and massaging.

Cassie's head lolled back and he felt her muscles relax as she grew languid under his touch. Her fingers softened against him and he risked a single tiny thrust.

She slid lower, enveloping him in a wall of heat. Another thrust and she moved with him, till finally they were one.

It was everything he'd expected. More.

With her head thrown back she was the image of wanton abandon. His hands moulding her pale breasts was the most erotic thing he'd ever seen. Unless it was the way her lips parted in a soundless sigh as she moved.

She drew out sensations of such exquisite pleasure Amir felt himself sweeping towards ecstasy.

His hands slid down, past the links at her waist, to anchor on her hips. His fingers gripped her smooth flesh, holding her steady as he bucked up, his movements more and more urgent.

Her eyes snapped open and indigo fire burned his retinas as she held his gaze.

Something sizzled through him at her look—something more than the seductive friction of two bodies moving together in harmony and complete abandon.

A wave of pleasure hit him, rolling through him to circle tighter and tighter. Incredulous, he realised there was no time for more, that the climax was upon him.

Amir had opened his mouth to apologise when it took him, racking his body in pleasure so intense he almost blacked out. A galaxy of stars whirled around him, but none eclipsed her deep blue eyes. They held him as he gasped for breath, groaning his ecstasy, shuddering as his body pumped its climax and he held her as if he'd never let her go.

CHAPTER TEN

CASSIE clung on tight as Amir heaved and rocked beneath her. Her untutored body began to respond with tiny ripples of pleasure.

Fascinated, she watched him lose control, as if plucked up by a force of nature and set spinning on another plane.

Excitement had escalated after the initial shock. When he'd touched her breasts that lovely melting sensation had filled her again, like chocolate swirled with cream and her favourite liqueur, and her body had softened around him.

Now the delicious feel of them moving together abated, and with it the tiny thrills that had begun spreading through her. Amir lay unmoving but for the way his chest rose and fell like bellows pumping. He was lax except for the hands that gripped her.

Tentatively she moved. He groaned and clamped her hips into stillness. 'Not yet,' he gasped.

Seconds ticked by and Cassie began to feel the strain where her thighs stretched, feel the little flurries of chill night air around her naked body. Began to feel…exposed, sitting above Amir who, eyes closed, seemed lost in another world.

A world she'd been denied entry to.

With a sudden movement he rolled, tipped her gently onto her side. A moment later he withdrew, and Cassie clamped her lips on the protest that welled as sensitive nerve endings stirred anew. She wanted—

He didn't even look at her, simply turned away, got up and strode to the bathroom.

Helplessly Cassie watched the play of light and shadow on his naked back, the lithe grace of his powerful body, and wished he didn't still take her breath away.

She felt…cheated. After the gloriously intense pleasure of their coupling, surely she'd been right to expect more.

Cassie grimaced and rolled away, pulling the covers high as she slid to her own side of the bed. What had made her think Amir different? Of course he'd put his own pleasure first. If she hadn't quite reached the pinnacle of ecstasy he had, then that, apparently, wasn't his problem.

But he hadn't even *looked* at her! Amir had avoided her eyes as he'd disengaged himself and hurried away. Almost as if he was ashamed of her.

Perhaps he was, now he'd taken what he wanted.

Sly dark shadows stirred, and Cassie felt the murky undercurrents of the past reaching out to her. She felt the tug of shame and anger, and a guilt she couldn't do anything to assuage. Emotions she'd carried all her life.

No! She wasn't her mother. Amir had no right to make her feel tainted.

Or was it Cassie herself making her feel that way?

She clutched a pillow close and set her jaw. At least there was a bright side. For all the disappointment, she'd managed to break through the frozen terror that had filled her earlier at the idea of intimacy. She'd learned it could be electrifying, exhilarating, wonderful! Surely by this act she'd managed to begin healing part of the unseen hurt she'd carried too long?

Next time she'd make sure she chose a man who wouldn't turn his back on her the moment he had what he wanted.

'Cassie?' His breath hazed her neck, and heat surrounded her as he slid naked behind her.

She started, and her breath seized as his arm roped her waist, pulling her towards him so his hair-roughened thighs cradled her and his solid form pressed close.

Every nerve ending shuddered into awareness and the curl of excitement in her womb twisted into life. It wasn't fair! She was angry and disappointed, yet her body betrayed her with its eagerness.

She stiffened and tried to pull away, but he held her. Temper rose at how easily he controlled her.

'I'm sorry, Cassie.' His breath on her ear made her shiver as tendrils of sensation unfurled and spread. 'I couldn't help it. I lost control.'

Dimly she wondered how often that was used by men as an excuse for selfishness.

'You're angry.'

'I—' She shrugged. Maybe her anger was out of proportion with the situation. This was her first experience of sex, and she had a horrible suspicion she was letting the past colour her judgement. 'I didn't like it when you turned away from me like that.'

It had made her feel cheap.

His hand on her shoulder pulled her round till she lay on her back. His face loomed above her like that of a reverently carved idol: beautiful yet remote. His eyes were dark as night and equally impenetrable.

He trailed his fingertips over her collarbone, up her throat to clasp her jaw. The air left Cassie's lungs in a whoosh at the implicit intimacy of his touch.

'I apologise, Cassie. It's a long time since I've had so little control.' Was that the hint of a blush colouring the high angles of his cheekbones?

Cassie frowned, trying to read his precise meaning. 'You were embarrassed?'

His mouth firmed, and if anything his sculpted face grew tauter. 'Only raw youths and selfish lovers take without giving. A certain amount of control is necessary.'

Her eyes widened. Had Amir stepped from a world completely different from the one she'd known? She'd misread him. Instead of casual thoughtlessness, he'd been too ashamed to meet her eyes.

The novel idea stunned her.

'You have a real problem with losing control.'

Amir's eyes glinted and his hand slid tantalisingly low over her breast. 'That makes two of us. I've never met a more fiercely independent woman in my life.'

Cassie gasped as trailing fingers circled her nipple. Dormant pleasure burgeoned. She wanted to savour his words, but instead it was his cheeky caress, now plucking at one rosy tip, that filled her thoughts.

'I—'

'Yes, Cassandra?' This time when he drawled all three syllables of her name in that deep, knowing voice it sounded perfect.

His hand moved lower and she opened her mouth to protest—till she felt his fingers tickle the soft hair between her legs.

'You wanted to say something?'

He didn't smile, but the glint in his eyes told her he knew what effect he had on her.

Sensation hummed through her, coalescing in a single powerful shock of pleasure when he touched her just so.

Amir watched her closely, as if able to gauge what she felt by the blush searing her cheeks and throat. Now it was her turn to feel embarrassed. She wasn't the subject of some scientific study!

Desperately she reached up and hauled his head down, kissing him open-mouthed as he touched her again. This time the bolt of power ignited ecstasy and sent it reverberating through her body. All she knew was his mouth, tender on hers, his touch, and the shock of delight as her whole body turned into a conflagration of scintillating sparks and fiery explosions.

Her hands shook as she held him. She gasped for air but refused to break the kiss that plastered him to her. She wanted to cradle him closer, hold this magic for as long as she could. Hold *him* till she came back to earth.

But Amir had other ideas. Already he was pulling back, easing out of her grasp.

'That hardly touched the surface, did it, *habibti*? You're wound far too tight.' His mouth lifted at one corner in that sexy, wry smile of his, and Cassie's heart shimmied. 'And I still have to make up for my clumsiness before.'

Cassie swiped her tongue across her lips, ready to tell him that, far from being wound tight, she felt totally unravelled.

She didn't even get the first syllable out. Amir dipped his head and took her mouth in a slow kiss that drew deep, demanding a response. It came from a part of her she'd never known existed. A part of her that responded to every nuance of his caress, to each sure stroke of his hand over her throat, her shoulder, breast and hip.

Time and her thoughts blurred as Amir made love to her with his hands, his mouth, his whole body. He evoked slow, lush pleasure. He led her into another intense climax that shattered her soul into thousands of shards. Then he put her back together again with tender caresses and murmured endearments.

She never known such gentleness.

She felt…different. Born anew.

Cassie lay spent, gasping in air, her mind awhirl. This felt like something more than physical. But how could that be?

Through the haze of jumbled thoughts and sensations she felt him move. Heard a tiny sound and opened her eyes to find him tearing open a small square package with his teeth.

She was exhausted, too spent to move, her limbs weighted in the aftershock of bliss. She couldn't possibly want him now in this exhausted state, but she *did* want to hold him close, feel his heart beat next to hers.

Through slitted eyes she watched him roll on protection with dextrous movements. This was a man with lots of experience. In that moment, sated and revelling in the results of his loving, Cassie was glad. At least one of them knew what they were doing.

Nevertheless a tingle of anxiety tripped through her as he knelt between her legs.

She couldn't imagine giving or receiving any more pleasure. But the gleam in his eyes was unmistakable, as was the taut energy in his muscled frame and the erection straining towards her.

'I'm not sure I can.' Even speaking seemed too much effort.

Amir leaned close, his mouth whisper-soft on hers. 'You don't need to do anything. Trust me.'

Dazed, she watched him rise above her, his imposing shoulders blotting out the room. Yet it wasn't trepidation Cassie felt this time, only a sense of rightness.

He moved and her arms came around him, hugging him close as he surged with one easy thrust deep inside.

Home.

That was the word that spun in her brain as he lifted her knee a little, easing his way, then gathered her close.

She was enfolded, blanketed and at peace.

Amir tilted his hips and began a rhythm that was easy, gentle. The give and take lulled Cassie and a smile played about her lips.

'You feel good.'

'So do you.' He kissed her fluttering eyelids and cheeks, then her mouth. He stroked his tongue along the seam of her lips and a tremor of awareness passed through her.

Cassie's eyes popped open.

He cupped her breast, stroked her nipple in a slow arc and something tightened in her belly.

'You know what you're doing.' Her voice was husky.

He dipped his head and favoured her with a long kiss that left her pulse racing. Out of nowhere adrenalin charged through her lax body.

'And you're still in control,' she added.

'Do you mind?' One black eyebrow arched devilishly as he pushed higher, cupped her breast a fraction tighter.

Cassie caught her lip between her teeth in a gasp of surprise and delight.

Somehow she found enough energy to speak. 'No.' Her hands slid to his buttocks, tight and gloriously rounded, and pulled him higher. The resulting sensation almost knocked the breath from her lungs. She lifted her knees, feeling each measured thrust more deeply. 'You won't be for much longer.'

Then she gave in to the desire to taste him. Following instinct, she bit gently on the curve of straining flesh where his neck joined his shoulder.

A shudder ripped through Amir and his movements grew sharper. Suddenly Cassie was no longer teasing. Her body echoed his movements, maximising their impact as he took them both to unbearable heights.

What had started as a lazy game became a headlong rush towards completion. It overwhelmed them both. So sudden, so intense. It was fierce and fulfilling and indescribably wonderful for being shared.

Amir. His name was a shout of ecstasy. An exultation and a plea. Whether she called his name out loud Cassie didn't know, but his name was in every pounding beat of her blood, in each spasm of pleasure and every gasped breath. It was as if she'd absorbed him into herself, become one with him not just bodily but at some deeper level.

The last thing she remembered was Amir holding her tight, rolling onto his back so she sprawled across him.

His breath was hot on her face. His arms held her safe against the cataclysmic force that buffeted them. The sure rhythm of his heart was beneath her ear. It lulled her till exhaustion claimed her.

Dawn. From outside came the sound of the camp stirring: a shout, a jingle of harness. Amir surfaced from the soundest sleep he could recall. Sound and satisfying.

Almost as satisfying as the woman in his arms. She was a bundle of delight. Lushly curved instead of emaciated-chic. Warm, responsive and surprisingly addictive.

Cassie approached sex with wholehearted enthusiasm, as if it were a wondrous new world to explore. Not a battlefield where favours were traded for gifts or prestige or for more of Amir than he chose to give.

She met him as an equal. Asked for nothing save shared pleasure. There was something innately honest about her. Something that snagged his interest in ways other than the physical.

Right now it was the physical that interested him. With her body pressed close she was one hundred percent temptation. He stroked a possessive hand over her.

Still she slept. Could she really be so deeply asleep? There was a clatter outside but she didn't twitch. Did she feign sleep to tempt him to rouse her?

He *was* tempted. He grabbed the covers to slide them off her shoulders, then stopped.

A smear of blood stained the sheet.

Amir frowned. Where was it from? Neither he nor Cassie was injured.

He could have sworn this top sheet had been pushed way down the bed. Hadn't it been under their hips? It couldn't have been. There was only one explanation. Cassie had scored him with her nails.

He smiled. There was an untamed element to Cassie when roused. He couldn't wait to experience it again.

Last night *had* been intense. Witness the way Cassie had clawed at him, and those mind-numbingly powerful climaxes. She was dead to the world—unlike earlier nights when she'd slept restlessly, disturbed by dreams.

His hand slipped from the covers and away from the heat of her body.

Only with Cassie did Amir refrain from initiating sex when

he wanted it. In the past, to desire had been to act. To act had been to satisfy.

After what they'd shared he knew she'd welcome his touch. Yet he restrained himself. There was a strange satisfaction in putting Cassie's needs before his own. He stroked a lock of hair from her face. Watching her curled trustingly close, an unfamiliar peace filled him.

For the first time since boyhood he almost regretted that life had made him a loner. That he'd never had an intimate relationship except on the physical level. For a fleeting moment he experienced something like that old boyhood yearning to *belong* to someone, to be special to someone and have someone special to care for.

As a child it had been a secret craving, hidden deep in the belief that such emotion made him weak when he had to be strong to survive. As a man such sentimentality had no place in his world.

Now he wondered if there could be more in his life.

He shook his head, clearing it of half-formed imaginings.

Yes, he'd marry. Arrangements were already in progress. But, while his bride would provide comfort and pleasure, this would be no love match. No partnership based on attraction or volatile emotions. As a kid he'd learnt what an unstable foundation that was.

He'd marry to ensure a line of inheritance. For the stability of his nation. To shore up the prestige and reputation of his dynasty after so much notoriety and disharmony. His bride had been chosen for her impeccable breeding, her connection to one of the wealthiest, most powerful families in Tarakhar, as well as for her beauty and docility.

Not for him a wife who, like his mother, was a magnet for scandal. *His* children wouldn't know the disgrace of living in the shadow of outrageous parents. They'd bask in the care of a beautiful, calm, respectable mother. They'd have their father's unflinching support and protection.

Never would they suffer because of their parents' behaviour. There'd be no sidelong looks of distrust as a nation waited for them to go the same way as their parents.

A wedding was necessary. But that didn't stop his desire for Cassie.

He stroked her hair. There was something about this foreign woman, something utterly missing from the paragon of female virtue he planned to wed. He needed time to explore it, savour and enjoy it.

Amir smiled and drew Cassie closer.

He'd refrain from sex this morning, but he had no intention of denying himself in the longer term. Cassie would return with him to Tarakhar as his guest, his lover, till their passion was spent.

One last affair before the business of marriage began.

Arranging the betrothal and then the wedding would take time. Time to sate himself with Cassie's unique brand of sexual allure. A mutually enjoyable interlude beckoned.

CHAPTER ELEVEN

'No, no more!' Cassie stared at the clothes spread across the embroidered coverlet and shook her head. 'Thank you, but I can't accept these.' The garments had been reverently laid out for her approval in a kaleidoscope of sumptuous fabrics, a shopaholic's dream come true.

The palace maid frowned. 'Are you sure, ma'am? There is more to come.'

'Absolutely sure.' Registering her concern, Cassie softened her words with a smile. She didn't want Amir's staff thinking she was ungrateful. 'It's all lovely, but there's more than I need. Far more.'

And more beautiful than the hard-wearing cotton and denim she'd carried in her backpack when she came to Tara-khar. Who ever heard of a volunteer teacher wearing gauzy rainbow hues spangled with semi-precious stones or edged in silver?

Though there was more to her refusal. Seeing the finery reminded her of one of the few times she'd been allowed home to her mother's chic apartment during the holidays. Her mother had been shopping with her newest lover's platinum credit card. Her bedroom had been awash with silks and lace, teetering high heels and designer handbags. Yet they'd satisfied her only for a few days, till she'd discovered some woman wearing an even newer, more expensive fashion item that she craved.

Cassie had shrunk from her mother's blatant greed even

as she'd guessed it was a sign of discontent. That her much vaunted emotion-free life hadn't made her happy. Though she'd never admit it or accept Cassie's overtures for a closer relationship.

'I only need a few things,' Cassie explained to the maid. 'This just isn't me.'

Even after bathing in a marble bath the size of a plunge pool, being anointed with attar of roses like a princess from the Arabian Nights and wearing a caftan of finest silk, Cassie knew she didn't fit in this luxurious palace.

Prisoner in that isolated mountain camp, it had been one thing to hear Amir was a king, to read in his actions and attitude that he was used to command. It was another to see evidence of his position all around her. From the servants' deep bows to the excitement of people in the street as their air-conditioned four-wheel drives passed by.

Medics had awaited them as they'd crossed the border from Bhutran. It had taken just one phone call as they rode down the mountains and out of the telecommunications black spot for a team of professionals to be on the ground.

All for her.

Amir's consideration touched a part of her that she'd learned to guard close.

Impulsively she'd turned, reached out a hand to touch him, then stopped as she'd read the carefully blank expressions on his attendants. He'd worn a mantle of aloof authority that distanced him from everyone, even her.

Especially her.

Last night's lover might never have been.

All morning he'd been reserved. A gulf had yawned between them, unbreachable and forbidding. Loss had welled in Cassie, sideswiping her with its ferocity.

Yet she'd walked into the medical tent telling herself it was for the best. Last night had been madness.

She should be grateful Amir had made it easy to put the

madness behind her. Stupidly she hadn't felt grateful. She'd felt bereft. As if something vital had been severed inside.

The thought had made her square her shoulders. Cassie didn't *do* needy.

So she'd kept her head up as she'd been escorted through the palace. Despite the dusty camel-hair cloak, she'd carried herself like a queen through elegant marble corridors and porticoes, past glimpses of richly furnished apartments and picture-perfect gardens.

Now, in this exquisite suite, she gave up pretending.

'Are you all right, ma'am?' The maid hurried over as Cassie sank into a gilded chair.

'I'm fine.' She smiled up and tried not to notice how the woman's dark eyes reminded her of Amir. They were a softer, lighter brown, not the incredible midnight-dark hue of Amir's. They didn't sizzle as his did. But—

Cassie couldn't stop thinking about him!

'I'm just tired, and probably a little too relaxed after that long soak.'

'That's good. His Highness was concerned that you rest.' She clapped her hands. Instantly a couple of women hurried in. After some brisk instructions they cleared the bed.

'If you'll permit, ma'am, I'll have a smaller selection put in your dressing room. When you're rested you can choose which you'd like to keep.'

'Thank you.' Cassie smiled gratefully. It was stupid even to think it, but for a moment, looking at the display of beautiful clothes laid out, the suspicion had crossed her mind that Amir was paying for her services last night. A preposterous idea, but unsettling.

'Is there anything else I can get you?'

'No, thanks.' There was a myriad of things Cassie should be doing—organising a passport to replace the one she'd lost, accessing her bank account and letting the volunteer pro-gramme people know where she was. Yet it seemed too much effort. 'I think I'll rest now.'

Moments later Cassie was alone. She was safe and cared for. It was absurd to feel a sense of loss. Yet it pooled within her, grim and undeniable.

For the man who'd been her lover such a short time.

A prickle of sensation spread under her skin. Amir had been fierce yet gentle, demanding yet considerate. They'd shared things she'd never dreamed of.

Flattening her lips as they began to curve into a besotted smile, Cassie shot to her feet.

Probably most women felt this...*yearning* for their first lover. It *had* only been last night. She'd barely had time to assimilate what had happened before she was chivvied out of the tent for their perilous descent down the mountains.

She should be thankful there'd been no time for awkwardness. Much easier to act as if nothing had happened, as Amir did.

Cassie folded her arms and paced to the window.

She'd initiated their lovemaking. Sex was what she'd wanted. An antidote to the crawling tension that had filled her for a week, and to the stirrings of desire she'd felt for the first time. A way to overcome the murky fear that had surfaced at the idea of being intimate with a man.

So why was she battling distress because Amir kept his distance? Why did she long for a tender look?

She should be pleased he realised what they'd shared was over. That he didn't press for more.

The idea of Amir wanting more made her breath hitch. Her hand shot out to the window frame for support. For a split second she let herself imagine her and Amir together as a couple, not for a night but for much more.

'No!' Cassie spun on her foot and headed into the garden. She was strong and independent. She'd weave no foolish dreams about any man.

Dusk had fallen when Amir went in search of her. His spurt of anxiety on discovering her rooms empty disturbed him. The bottom had dropped from his stomach till he'd seen the open door and realised she'd gone into the garden.

Now, watching her sleep, he assured himself it was normal to feel relief that she was OK. She was his guest, his responsibility.

His lover.

His gaze trailed over her sinuous curves as she sprawled on the day bed in a secluded garden pavilion. The air was heavy with the scent of roses and she lay like an innocent seductress, one hand beneath her cheek, the other flung wide so he had an unimpaired view of her perfect breasts rising and falling beneath fine silk.

He closed the door and paced close.

On his return he'd been sucked into the business of ruling. Agreements, agendas and annotations. He'd met officials and dealt with a few crises.

Yet his mind had been fixed on her. It had taken all his effort not to shove aside his work and go to her. He told himself it was the novelty of their relationship. Lust, in the early stages, was incredibly distracting.

Yet how long since he'd felt one-fifth of this fascination for a woman? His interest in affairs had waned as boredom with his partners' over-eagerness took over.

In his early thirties and he'd grown jaded with the predictable!

In some ways he *was* like his father. But whereas his father had sought distraction in vice and mindless pleasure, Amir could control temptation.

Amir sank onto the bed, one arm braced over Cassie's hip. He lifted his hand and delicately circled one nipple with the tip of his finger. It peaked and he recalled her responsiveness last night when he'd taken that taut bud in his mouth.

Smiling, he touched his lips to that sensitive peak.

She stirred. Drowsily her eyes opened, dark violet and velvety with pleasure.

* * *

Amir was here. The laxness in her muscles, the heat in her blood convinced her it was no dream, even as her eyes opened and she found him, black eyes riveted on hers.

'Amir!' So right did it seem, it took a moment to shake the cobwebs of sleep away. When she did, Cassie shot a horrified look towards the door. 'What are you doing? Anyone might come in!'

She surged up, pushing him away, swinging her legs over the edge of the divan and rising on unsteady legs.

'No one will intrude, *habibti*, not without permission. These grounds are for my exclusive use and yours.'

Something about the deep, proprietorial tone made her brow pucker. He hadn't been so interested in her this morning when she'd sought his reassurance.

'As for what I'm doing.' His mouth lifted in a rare smile and, despite her misgivings, Cassie felt its impact deep inside. 'I was caressing my lover.'

My lover. In that resonant drawl the words stirred magic in her soul.

Till she reminded herself he'd withdrawn from her all day. He'd been aloof, not sparing her a private word, and acting as if last night hadn't happened. Despite her determination to treat it as a one-night stand, his behaviour hurt. It smacked of off-hand dismissal.

It reminded her of the cool attitude of her mother's lovers. Each had expected his mistress to be available on tap, but had never bothered to think about her needs.

Cassie moved away.

'I'm not your lover.'

Amir stood and Cassie's gaze clung to his rangy form, clad this time in tailored trousers and shirt. He looked mouthwateringly gorgeous with his sleeves rolled to reveal the corded muscle of his forearms. His collar was undone, drawing her eyes to the V of golden skin against the pure white cotton.

'Are you not?' Sleek brows pinched in disapproval as he stalked closer.

If she hadn't experienced Amir's tenderness she'd have retreated in the face of what looked like searing anger. As it was, trepidation shivered through her.

Her chin shot up. 'We had one night together. That's all.' She told herself that was all she wanted. One night out of time to experience such heady delights. Any more would be too dangerous. Too addictive.

He paced closer, stopped when his breath hazed her cheek and her skin contracted in response. Her nipples stood proud and pouting, as if inviting his touch, and between her thighs moist heat bloomed.

Her cheeks flamed as she registered how her body prepared itself for his possession. As if he only had to touch her and she'd give herself to him!

'Why not share more than a single night?' The words, pure temptation, swirled soft as thought on the air.

Because Amir scrambled her brains. He uncorked longings she'd barely known she harboured.

Because she was scared if she didn't make the break now it would be impossible to drag herself away.

Because she'd had a taste of what it was like to be dismissed by him. It made her feel...vulnerable.

'You didn't seem so interested in me this morning!' She kept her voice cool, but inside shreds of hurt whirled and accumulated, weighing her heart. 'There was no private discussion. Not so much as a look. For all I knew I'd never see you again!'

That had frightened her far too much.

'Cassandra.' His voice was seductively low. 'I'm sorry.' He lifted his hand towards her cheek but checked himself, his fingers mere centimetres from her face.

Yet she *felt* him as if he'd touched her!

'I sought to protect you from gossip and discomfort. Bad enough that my staff know you were given to me as a sex slave.' His look was grim. 'I tried to counter that by ensuring Faruq knew how things were between us until last night. He would have made that known to rest of my staff. My aim today was to reinforce that. To treat you with respect so others would too.'

'Really?' The notion hadn't entered her head. All she'd known was lacerating pain and a sense of shame she couldn't quite suppress when he'd seemed to spurn her. The possibility he'd attempted to protect her took a lot of assimilating.

Yet hadn't he cared for her? Hadn't he kept his distance as much as he could till last night?

'The people of Tarakhar are good people, but they are easily influenced in matters of reputation. Believe me; I know what I'm talking about.'

The steel in his words grabbed her attention and threatened to divert her.

'Besides, what's between us is private.'

The gleam in his eyes was nearly irresistible and Cassie's heart flipped over.

'You could have said something. Given some indication.'

Slowly he nodded, his gaze never wavering. 'Would it surprise you to know I was scared of what would happen if I did? The compulsion to touch you, kiss you and hold you close has driven me insane all day.'

Fingers of heat spread through Cassie as she heard truth ring in his words.

Logic told her to break this relationship, such as it was, before she got in too deep. Yet her overwhelming feelings were relief and excitement. He wanted more, as she did. She wasn't alone in experiencing this overwhelming need.

'I can't imagine you scared.'

His lips twisted wryly. 'A man doesn't like to lose control. Especially a man like me. And you, *habibti*, are too dangerous a test of my restraint.'

Cassie followed his look to where his hand hovered close to her face. It was unsteady.

Like her limbs that trembled from his nearness.

In that moment, like the single powerful stroke that sliced the Gordian knot, Cassie felt tension and doubt disintegrate in a violent rush of relief.

This was mutual. Amir wanted her as she did him. More, he was honest about it, treating her as an equal. He'd been genuinely considerate in attempting to prevent gossip.

'I want you, Cassie.' The words devastated thought. 'Do you still want me?'

Silently she nodded.

'Then why not share this passion a little longer?'

His eyes flared, reminding her of the conflagration that had consumed them last night. A delicious shudder racked her body.

She wanted to. How she wanted to.

Yet was it wise?

Suddenly it struck Cassie that, far from being strong all these years, she'd lived in fear. She'd let the past dictate her life, scared of repeating her mother's mistakes or laying herself open to manipulation. Had she used that as an excuse to hide from her own sexuality?

The disturbing notion wouldn't shift.

What Amir offered wasn't manipulation. It was mutual pleasure and respect.

How could that be bad?

'I'm here in Tarakhar for a reason. I can't just forget that.' It was a last-ditch attempt to resist the irresistible.

Amir's eyes narrowed as if displeased. Then he shrugged. 'I'm sure that can be accommodated. After all, you'll need time to sort out your travel documents and so on. There's no rush to leave, and you're welcome to enjoy my hospitality for as long as you desire.'

Desire. The word shivered through her very bones.

The evening air hung still. Even the end-of-day chatter of the birds faded as Cassie tried to weigh this sensibly. But it wasn't logic that dictated her response. It was something far more visceral.

'I'd like to stay.' She paused and swiped her tongue around suddenly dry lips.

Relief was the warmth of his hand cradling her jaw, his thumb brushing her cheek. It was the sight of his rare smile and the answering sunburst of sensation within her.

Amir stepped in, his body hard against her, his head swooping in a kiss that claimed her breath and her mind.

It felt like hours later that Cassie lay, sated and dreamy, within the circle of Amir's embrace. The cushions from the day bed had fallen to the floor and their clothes were strewn there too. But here in her lover's arms she felt content, warm and happy.

Despite the lingering niggle that she'd jumped into a situation without due thought, she sensed she'd made the right decision. All her life she'd let instinct guide her, and she prayed it wouldn't lead her astray now.

Something tickled at her waist and she stirred. It took a moment to realise it was Amir, stroking her skin. Lazily she smiled. He couldn't seem to get enough of touching her and she loved it.

She opened her eyes. In the gloom of early evening she could make out the avid glitter in his gaze as he traced the line of the chain still encircling her.

'You promised to help me get rid of that when we got back to civilisation.'

'Did I?'

Concentration pleated his brow as he slipped his hand under the links, palm flat to her skin.

It was impossible after their tumultuous lovemaking that Cassie should feel arousal stir, yet she did. The intensity of his regard and the languid sensuality of his touch awoke an instantaneous response.

'Yes. As soon as we got here, you said.'

Amir breathed deep and met her eyes.

'As you wish.' He didn't sound enthusiastic.

Puzzled, Cassie tilted her head. Then understanding struck. 'You *like* it! You enjoy seeing it there!'

At her accusing tone he shrugged. 'It accentuates your waist and your curves.' He paused. 'It's very sexy.'

She shook her head. 'It's a slave chain! It's a symbol that I'm not my own woman. That I—'

'That you're mine.' At her shocked stare he smiled gently and lifted his hand to skim his knuckles across her cheek. 'Don't worry, Cassie. I understand how you feel. I know it's untenable.' His eyes darkened. 'But I'm man enough to respond to it even though it's not politically correct. I love the idea that, for now, you're mine.' His voice vibrated with a possessiveness that echoed to her core. 'Not by force but by choice.'

Shocked, Cassie stared up, reading the truth in his lazily lidded eyes.

'You wouldn't feel that way if I suggested roping you to my bed so you couldn't get away.'

Heat glazed his eyes as he stared at her mouth, then at her breasts. His lips lifted in a smile of devastating sensuality.

When he looked up Cassie's pulse hammered out of control. Her skin tingled as if he'd trailed his fingers over every erogenous zone in her body.

'I don't know about that.' Amir leaned close and his words were hot on her sensitive flesh. 'I've never been into bondage. Yet I have a feeling I might enjoy it. With you.'

Cassie swallowed hard at the image he conjured. That oh-so-lazily sexy smile and his deep, deep voice tugged at places inside she'd barely been aware of.

Far from being horrified or outraged, she knew it was excitement that thrilled through her.

The idea of being *possessed*, of being claimed so blatantly by a man, should be anathema to her. In the camp the idea had made her skin crawl.

Yet now with Amir it was different—and not solely because

he spoke of her choosing to be his. Perversely she discovered a sense of power in the fact he wanted her so much. To her shock, the idea of having him at her mercy sexually held a forbidden allure she'd never thought possible.

Cassie's eyes widened. In agreeing to be Amir's lover she'd stepped from safety into the dark unknown.

She couldn't pull back. The allure was too strong. Her need was too intense. *She wanted everything he offered.*

'I see you understand,' he purred against her mouth, then swiped the tip of his tongue between her parted lips in a sensual promise of pleasure to come.

Too soon he pulled away.

'Dinner,' he said huskily. 'Our meal has no doubt been waiting for some time and you need your strength.' The twinkle in his eyes warmed her. 'Then I'll find something to cut those links.'

CHAPTER TWELVE

'AMIR?'

'Hmm?' Long fingers tangled with hers even as Amir focused on the chessboard. As ever, he threatened to distract her with the lightest touch, reminding her of the bliss they'd shared.

In the late-night stillness they might have been the only residents of the sprawling palace.

Cassie loved this time. Precious hours together when Amir finished his work and she came alive to his lovemaking. Sex with Amir had gone from spectacular to spellbinding as under his tutelage, she'd learned to listen to the needs of her body, and his, enjoying both to the full.

Yet, more than sex, Cassie enjoyed these times when, not driven by desire, they lounged, relaxed and companionable.

It was something she'd never before experienced—sharing.

They played chess or talked of anything from politics to town planning, about the theatre or music. They swam by moonlight in Amir's private pool lined with exquisite handmade mosaic tiles. Once Amir had driven her out to a lookout from where she'd seen the lights of the capital spread below her, like a glittering reflection of the starry sky above. On the way back she'd been enchanted by glimpses of the colourful night markets in full swing and vowed to revisit during the day.

Amir lifted her hand and pressed a kiss to it, sending her

thoughts spinning just as he moved his queen across the board. 'Check.'

Cassie laughed, albeit breathlessly. 'You're trying to distract me so you'll win.'

His eyebrows rose in mock surprise, belied by the glitter in his eyes. 'Will it work?'

She struggled against the tide of tenderness that rose when he teased her. 'Of course not.' She straightened and concentrated on the board, pulling her hand free.

'I spoke to the volunteer agency today. I told them I'm not ready to go to that school just yet.'

'Good.' Amir moved to sit beside her. His arm slipped around her waist.

Amir had been adamant she wasn't ready to leave the city and she'd agreed. Not because of lingering trauma, but because she didn't want to leave him.

'But there's work here in the city. Tomorrow I'll begin with a small English-language class.'

'Tomorrow? Impossible!'

Cassie turned and looked up at him. His aristocratically honed features looked tight.

'Why?'

He frowned. 'You've had a traumatic experience.'

Cassie smiled and lifted her hand to his face, stroking the deep groove that had formed at the corner of his mouth. It always struck her as incredibly sexy.

'You've helped me get over it.' Still he didn't smile. 'I'm *fine*, Amir. You know that.'

'You can't *want* to go there.'

She tilted her head as she surveyed him. 'Of course I want to go. What have I got to do here?'

'Am I not enough for you?'

Instantly Cassie stiffened. The smile bled from her face as she saw he was serious. With an effort she stifled her rising temper.

'I see you at night, Amir. That's all. During the day I've

nothing to do. I've got no occupation. I've got no companions. Even though your staff are friendly that's not the same.' She paused and drew a deep breath, focused on keeping her tone reasonable.

It didn't help that an insidious voice inside whispered that he wanted her at his beck and call, reminding her that her mother had lived solely to service a man's desires. This was different. *Wasn't it?*

'I don't see you giving up your work to spend all your time with me.'

'Of course not.' Some of the tension in his face eased, yet he didn't look happy.

'Of course not,' Cassie echoed. 'I wouldn't expect it.'

Her soft fingers stilled against his cheek and Amir covered them with his, revelling in the feel of her here, where he wanted her.

Where he needed her.

Where had that come from?

Amir ibn Masud Al Jaber didn't need anyone. He never had.

Yet the denial didn't ring true. At this moment he needed the reassurance of Cassie's touch, her warmth, as he'd never remembered needing anyone.

The realisation crashed through him.

He drew a breath, centring himself after the shock. Not at her statement that she wanted to work, but at his intense visceral reaction. What he'd felt in that moment was a possessiveness so crude, so primitive, it made a mockery of his claim to be a modern civilised man.

'This is important to you?'

Amir felt her tension ease as the militant light in her eyes faded. How often had he let himself fall headlong into those pansy-dark depths, transfixed by Cassie's unique passion? A passion for life as well as for pleasure.

'Of course it's important. That's why I came to Tarakhar. I want to do something useful. I love acting but right now it doesn't seem enough. I want something more tangible, at least for a while.'

Fleetingly Amir thought of the many women he'd known only too eager to live off his generosity in idle luxury.

'You want to leave your mark?'

She shrugged. 'You could put it like that. It just seems a shame not to contribute more. I like the idea of being part of something bigger than myself.'

Amir remembered what she'd said about her childhood, not being wanted by either parent. Cassie talked blithely of friends, and with her outgoing personality he was sure there were plenty, but she'd never spoken of anyone especially close. Was her determination to work in a foreign language and literacy programme spurred by her desire to belong? To be needed?

He pursed his lips. Why was he delving so deep, puzzling out every nuance?

Because Cassie was important to him.

A frisson of premonition feathered through him. Or was that warning?

These days he thought of Cassie more and more, even when he should be concentrating on the mass of royal work. His thoughts lingered not only on sex, but on how he enjoyed her company, the way she made him feel.

He stiffened, uneasy with the direction of his thoughts.

Having her occupied elsewhere would be good for them both. He didn't want her getting notions about a permanent place in his life.

What they had was perfect while it lasted. Mutual pleasure with no strings attached. He shoved to one side the lurking suspicion that soon he might want more. Such an eventuality would not occur.

'What's important to you, Amir?'

Startled, he focused on Cassie's upturned face. She looked so earnest.

'No one's ever asked me that before.'

In truth, he'd rarely considered it himself—except as a child, when he'd craved...love, he supposed. Then as an adolescent all he'd wanted was to prove himself and *belong*. Carve a place for himself in this new world of Tarakhar where, despite the frowns and misgivings over the son of a scoundrel, he'd discovered stability and honour and finally a home.

It struck him that perhaps he and Cassie had been driven by similar demons.

Though of course he'd vanquished his. As sheikh of a populous and prosperous country he had other concerns than the shadows of his past.

Cassie watched Amir's eyes flicker as if processing memories. What was he thinking?

'Let me guess what's important to you.' She leaned across and moved one of the beautifully carved antique pieces on the chessboard. 'Winning at chess.'

'Winning at everything.' A smile softened his words but they had the ring of truth.

'Really?'

He nodded. 'If anything's worth doing, it's worth doing well.'

Cassie's breath snagged as her brain diverted to what they'd been doing half an hour ago. She remembered his absolute concentration on giving her pleasure, the way he'd drawn out each caress till she was almost screaming with the pleasure-pain of arousal and need.

If something was worth doing...

No wonder he was such an exquisitely generous lover.

'What else?' Her voice was husky and she cleared her throat.

Amir moved a piece to corner her king. 'My people. My country.'

'But it wasn't always that way? Didn't you say you rebelled at one time?'

He shrugged. 'When I was young and impatient I had other

interests. At first I tried to be all they expected and more. I had to work twice as hard as anyone else. To be accepted I had to be not only competent but perfect at every task. And still everyone waited for me to run riot, just like my notorious parents.'

Cassie knew what it was like to be the child of notorious parents. School had often been hellish because someone had seen Cassie's mum at the races or the theatre on the arm of her latest paramour. Everyone knew she'd been bought and paid for, just like a new watch or a car.

'Finally I'd had enough. I decided I might as well fulfil everyone's expectations.' Amir's voice dropped to a pitch that made something quiver inside.

'What did you do?'

'I devoted myself to pleasure and nothing else. I went on a binge of parties, gambling and overindulgence of colossal proportions. I doubt I was sober one day in four.'

'And?'

'And what?'

'What changed?'

Amir's eyebrows rose and he pulled her hand towards him, bending to draw his tongue along her palm till she trembled and edged closer.

'Persistent, aren't you?'

'I want to know.' It surprised her exactly how much she wanted to know about Amir.

He shrugged, and she hated the hard edge of cynicism in his voice when he spoke again. 'At first it was exciting, satisfying, even. No rules, no regimen. Just pleasure.' His lips thinned in a tight smile. 'Then I woke one morning with a woman I couldn't remember. Her body was a testament to surgical enhancement in too many places to count. She had a plastic smile, eyes that flashed dollar signs, and a laugh like an asthmatic mule, guaranteed to tip a man into insanity after twenty-four hours.'

Cassie curved her mouth in a perfunctory smile at his

humour, but inside sadness carved a hollow. What a waste of a man like Amir.

'I had no idea whose apartment I was in, much less which country. I couldn't remember the previous week, but I had no trouble realising I was utterly, irredeemably bored.' He shook his head abruptly. 'I looked in the mirror that morning and for the first time ever saw my father's face looking back at me.'

'You didn't like your father?' She could relate to that.

Amir threaded his fingers though hers and looked down at their joined hands as if they held some great truth.

'You have to know someone to dislike them, don't you?'

When she didn't speak he shrugged again, and his breath escaped in a low rush.

'I never knew my parents. They were strangers to me. I was cared for most of the time by the staff at whatever resort they were staying at.'

'And the rest of the time?'

Amir lifted his gaze and Cassie was shocked by the fierce blankness she read there.

'The rest of the time I wasn't cared for.'

She flinched with shock and he turned his attention back to her hand, trailing his index finger over each of hers in a deliberately erotic caress, as if to distract her from his words. It didn't work, though deep inside the flicker of awareness that was ever-present near Amir burst into pulsing life.

'One of my earliest memories is waking to find my room being made up by an unfamiliar maid who didn't speak any language I knew. My parents had been invited to a party weekend in the Alps and had left instantly. Unfortunately they'd forgotten, till they got a call on arrival in Switzerland, that they'd left me behind in Rio de Janeiro.'

'Oh, Amir!' She curved her hand into his, cupped her other hand around them as if she could somehow erase the pain of such neglect. She'd never felt wanted, and had been told time and again she'd ruined her mother's life, but her mother had never forgotten she existed! How could his parents have cared so little? 'How old were you?'

'I don't know. Three? Maybe four?'

Cassie's heart thundered with outrage and distress at what such a childhood must have been like.

'It's all right, Cassie.' With his free hand he brushed his knuckles over her cheek. 'I survived. And when they died I came here to my uncle.'

The uncle who'd spent his days watching his nephew like a hawk, waiting for the day the telltale weakness of his parents would reveal itself.

What sort of life was that for a child? The fire burning in her belly had nothing to do with arousal, but with a fierce need to protect the boy Amir had been.

'After my taste of reckless living I ended up back here,' Amir continued. 'Not because I was ordered to but because I knew I'd do anything rather than turn into my father. Because this was what I wanted—this place, these people. I needed purpose and stability. I turned my life around and made a place for myself. I faced down the doubters and proved myself so well that when my uncle died the Council of Elders turned to me rather than my older cousin to lead the country. This is my destiny.'

His hand dropped from her cheek and he withdrew his other hand from her grasp.

She missed his touch so much it frightened her.

'My sons will grow up with a father to be proud of. A respectable mother, not a notorious one. There'll be no taint of scandal marring their lives. They'll be cared for and cherished, accepted by everyone.'

His words rang with a certainty she almost envied.

For a moment, before she realised where her thoughts had strayed, Cassie found herself wishing he'd look at *her* as he spoke of his wife and future family. How wonderful it would be if…

No! Such thoughts were dangerous.

Amir knew exactly what he wanted. He'd planned it all out. Whereas Cassie knew what she *didn't* want. A life without respect or choice. A life dependent on the whims of a man who didn't love her.

Yet surely now she was taking steps towards a more positive focus? With Amir's help she'd banished the dark demons of fear. She enjoyed to the full every moment with this remarkable man. A man so strong and honourable he banished her preconceived biases. A man so honest and forthright she could share anything. A man so tender he opened new worlds of delight.

Plus she felt so good about this new work she was planning. If she could make a difference in someone's life maybe that would give her the purpose she'd lacked.

What more could she possibly want?

'There's one more thing, Highness.'

Amir heard the hesitation in Faruq's voice and looked up sharply. His aide was anything but comfortable.

'Everything's in place in Bhutran, isn't it?' It had been weeks since they'd left the mountains and Amir grew impatient to conclude his unfinished business with Mustafa. The memory of what had been done to Cassie made him long for retribution.

'Yes. The situation will be dealt with in the next few days.'

'The situation' being Mustafa.

Despite the negotiations, and Mustafa's promises, the old renegade showed his true colours with continued incursions into Tarakhar, breaking every promise.

If necessary Amir would put an end to that with an incursion of his own that would topple Mustafa from his comfortable mountain perch.

But it seemed that wouldn't be necessary. Changes in Bhutran meant that a newly energised central government, eager to maintain peace with its neighbours, was moving against Mustafa and others like him.

Amir had conveniently supplied information on the size and location of his camp, and offered back-up should it be necessary.

Soon there would be peace on the border and Mustafa would be a spent force. Satisfaction filled Amir.

'Good.' He nodded and stood, stretching, behind his desk. It had been a long day and he'd promised himself the pleasure of an early visit to Cassie. Strange how her allure grew with each passing day instead of diminishing.

'It's about Ms Denison, Sire.'

Amir's head whipped round. Cassie wasn't a subject he shared with anyone. 'What about her?'

Faruq stood straighter, as if preparing to defend himself.

'I wondered how long she would remain in residence.'

Amir's eyebrows shot up. 'As long as I wish her to remain.'

'Of course. It's just that…'

'Yes?'

'The betrothal negotiations are nearing completion.' Faruq spread his hands in a stiff gesture of appeal. 'Ms Denison's continued presence in the palace has become a matter of speculation.'

Amir strode from behind the desk to the far side of the room, his hands clenched in tight fists behind him.

'Ms Denison is my guest. She is recuperating from a violent assault.'

'Of course, Highness.' Yet the tone of Faruq's agreement wasn't convincing.

'What are they saying?'

Faruq shrugged. 'There is speculation that you and she…'

Naturally there was speculation. How could he have thought otherwise? A beautiful woman living unchaperoned in his palace, albeit on the other side of the building from his own suite.

He'd never invited a woman to stay in his home. He'd kept his liaisons discreetly away from the palace. He'd considered installing Cassie in a convenient apartment but that wouldn't do. Amir wanted her *here*.

Their affair had barely begun. He had no intention of denying himself. Cassie was a feast for the intellect as well as the body, with her active mind and her interest in everything. One minute she was mimicking the self-conscious pomp of his chamberlain strutting the corridors, and the next she was asking penetrating questions about the state of education in Tarakhar. Or sharing her body with an almost innocent generosity and delight that sometimes made him wonder if she could be nearly as experienced as her sassy attitude suggested.

'I do not concern myself with idle gossip.' Short of providing Cassie with a personal chaperon, which would be a farce as well as an inconvenience, there was little he could do to prevent talk. 'Ms Denison is a private guest, not a public figure.'

'Of course, Sire.' Faruq nodded but didn't move away. He drew a deep breath and Amir sensed his reluctance to continue.

'What is it, Faruq?' Impatience rose, but the man had a job to do. Barking at him wouldn't stop him. That was why Amir liked him, he took his work seriously. 'You'd better tell me.'

'I fear it's not quite that simple. While Ms Denison *is* your private guest, she's hardly invisible. With her colouring she draws attention wherever she goes in the old city. Far from being discreet, she's becoming something of a local celebrity.'

'Indeed?' This was the first Amir had heard of it.

'Yes. Instead of holding classes on the premises provided, she takes her pupils out. They hold impromptu lessons in the market or the park, at the library and in the new art gallery. Even at the railway station.'

Amir's lips twitched at the image of Cassie and her small group of women practising their English on a railway platform. Why didn't it surprise him? It was just like Cassie to ditch the stuffy classroom for places where language could be demonstrated in action.

'I hardly see this as a problem.'

Faruq spread his hands. 'By all accounts the students are enthusiastic and the classes are popular. But when forty people gather in a transport hub or at a public building, they attract a lot of attention. Ms Denison and her students are becoming well-known.'

'Forty people? I was told it was a small language class for women who hadn't completed school. Half a dozen participants.'

Faruq nodded. 'It's growing daily. There's talk of extra classes, with more teachers to spread the load.' He paused. 'It's a great initiative, Sire, but not designed to help her keep a low profile. In fact...'

'Well?' Amir frowned. He couldn't begrudge Cassie her success with the classes. She'd described them enthusiastically but in general terms, saying the students were coming on well and mentioning some of the language issues they faced. He'd had no idea how successful they were. Her dedication to the project was clear, and the benefits to his people were equally apparent.

'The gossip has spread as far as your intended's father.' Faruq shot him a hurried glance, then looked down at his hands. 'He has expressed a query, couched in the most delicate of terms, about the...*longevity* of the situation.'

'Has he indeed?'

Anger roiled in Amir's belly that the man had the temerity to query his Sheikh's intentions. He sold his daughter in marriage to the highest bidder. The fact that it was Amir who'd snared the prize only inflated the man's ego.

'Should anyone ask, Ms Denison is making an indefinite stay. You can take it from me this has no relevance to my marriage arrangements. It's purely a private matter.'

CHAPTER THIRTEEN

'I HEAR your classes are a raging success.'

Cassie spun round as Amir's deep voice broke her concentration. It was late afternoon and she was making notes for tomorrow's class.

'Amir! What are you doing here so early?' Her voice was breathless, as if his sudden appearance was the most important thing that had happened in her day.

If only that weren't true!

It shocked her the way she came alive in his presence, as if the rest of the day was sepia-toned and only burst into Technicolor when he was here. Even the satisfaction she got from her classes, from interacting with the other women and learning a little about this fascinating city, paled into insignificance against the thrill of being with Amir.

Every evening it grew harder to let him walk away. She wanted to hold him so he stayed the night. Wake in his arms to the sound of his low voice rumbling through her and feel the harsh caress of his stubble on her skin.

She'd never have thought it possible but she missed the tent they'd shared. The intimacy of waking with him.

The palace was so huge and she'd got lost more than once trying to find her way to Amir, only to meet his stuffy chamberlain who'd inform her with exquisite politeness that His Highness could not be disturbed.

'I'm visiting you.' As ever, something melted inside her at the rich caress of Amir's voice. 'If you'll permit.'

Cassie soaked up the sight of him, tall and magnificent even in a casual white shirt and worn jeans that emphasised his lean masculine strength.

He stole her breath every time! Her heart pounded a faster beat.

'Of course.' She tried to sound casual but failed. Her breath hitched when he strode across the room, his eyes alight like a marauding bandit spying booty. An instant later he plucked Cassie from her seat, roped his arms around her and dragged her close.

His kiss was an explosive mix of demand and hunger with a hint of seduction that made her weak at the knees.

Cassie grabbed his shoulders and hung on as her body softened into his, returning his kiss with a fervour that even after all these weeks hadn't abated one bit.

She *loved* his kisses.

She loved the way he made her feel when he held her close. She loved his strength and tenderness. His honour and his concern for her. The way he teased straight-faced so it took her a moment to read the humour in his gleaming eyes. She loved...

Cassie's brain fused as a blast of white-hot power surged through her. A blast of revelation.

Gasping, she pulled her mouth from his and looked up into those long-lashed eyes that saw so deeply.

Did they see what she was thinking now?

No! Panic buzzed through her and she stepped back, only to be stopped by Amir's arms, linked hard around her body. Her pulse raced and hectic colour seared her cheeks.

'Cassie? Are you OK?'

Quickly she nodded, her tongue glued to the roof of her mouth by shock.

Desperately she tried to convince herself she was mistaken. The thought that had frozen her brain was so earth-shattering it couldn't be true.

Could it?

Amir raised one hand and stroked his thumb over her bottom lip. Tiny shards of arousal zigzagged through her.

A physical response, she assured herself. They were lovers and sexual pleasure was what kept them together.

But not all.

There it was again, that unsettling idea zipping through her brain and sending her into turmoil.

The idea that she...*loved* Amir!

'Cassandra?'

Her heart flip-flopped at the way he said her name in full. It never failed to affect her. Would it still affect her in six months? In six years? In sixty?

Stupid to form the question. There was no doubt, Cassie realised as a strange serenity settled upon her. Of course it would. And she would still care for *him*.

She'd fallen for Amir. Not for the pleasure they shared but for the man himself.

Part of her brain tried to shout a warning, but it was overwhelmed by a rush of endorphins, a wave of warm delight that filled her at the thought.

Amir.

The man she loved.

'You look different.'

'I do?' She smiled up into his concerned expression and almost blurted her revelation. But even the euphoria of self-realisation couldn't blot out the knowledge that this complicated everything.

What, exactly, did Amir feel for her?

'Hmm, could it be the stylish new way I've done my hair?' She tried to distract him with a smile, pretending to primp as if professionally coiffed instead of wearing the lop-sided ponytail she'd quickly created as she'd pulled her hair out of her eyes to read.

'Undoubtedly, *habibti*.' He kissed her hand and, as ever, her knees weakened. 'You are the loveliest teacher in the whole of the capital.'

'Flatterer!' Yet her heart sang at the gleam in his eyes.

'Never.' He lifted her hand and pressed his lips to the fluttering pulse at her wrist. Cassie felt the kernel of warmth inside glow brighter and spread. Oh, she had it bad.

'I'd like to talk with you about your classes, but first, are you free for an excursion? There's something I want to show you.'

An outing with Amir? 'I'd love to. Where are we going?'

'It's tremendous,' Cassie declared. 'You must be very pleased.' In all honesty it was the thrill of being out with Amir, sharing something of his world, that excited her most, but this was spectacular.

Below this knoll wound a canal, its curve mimicking the sinuous course of a river. Mature trees had been planted in groves that would provide shade, and more were waiting to be set in place by earth-moving equipment.

Now, bathed in dusk's indigo shadows, it was easy to imagine the broad corridor of parkland as it would be when complete.

'There's the site of the new hospital.' Cassie followed Amir's gesture to the right, where the building site was almost encircled by what would one day be public parkland. 'Over there is the medical research facility completed last year, and there—' he pointed to an area on the other side of the water '—the route of the new light railway that will give access to the medical precinct and pleasure gardens.'

Cassie surveyed the kiosks dotting the parkland, the massive adventure playground, swimming centre and the intriguing foundations of a maze.

'It will be a perfect place for families.' She could imagine coming here in the cool of morning or late afternoon. Listening to children's laughter and excited shouts as they explored. One day she'd love to picnic here, watching her children play.

It took a moment to absorb where her thoughts had strayed. To realise it was Amir she imagined sharing the picnic blanket with her. That the toddlers in her mind's eye had laughing dark eyes and golden-toned skin like the man beside her.

Cassie's heart lurched. Did Amir want children? Or marriage? This project, funded from his personal coffers, seemed to indicate an interest not only in modern infrastructure but in providing amenities for families.

Perhaps one day—

'I'm glad you approve, Cassie.' His hand on hers cut across her thoughts and she struggled to compose herself. 'It's been one of my pet projects.'

When she turned it was to see him pull a small pouch from his pocket.

'I have something for you, *habibti*.'

He extended his hand. On his palm lay a large teardrop stone of deep blue-violet that seemed to glow inside. Cassie's breath escaped in a hiss and her hand crept to her throat.

'You like it?'

Silently she nodded, stunned by its beauty. The stone was faceted to catch the light, and even in the dimming afternoon it sparkled with a thousand stars.

She couldn't shake the conviction this was some priceless gem he'd spied in the palace treasure house or, given the streamlined modern chain, a high-class jeweller's showroom. Yet surely not even a royal sheikh would give a real gem of that size on a whim?

Nevertheless, a sour taste tainted her mouth as she remembered the expensive diamond brooch of which her mother had been so proud. Given not with love but as part of her purchase price. Pricey gifts had been part of her arrangement with each new protector.

Cassie shivered. Instantly Amir's hand gripped her shoulder. 'Cassie?'

'It's not…?' She swiped her tongue over dry lips, needing to know but not wanting to chance the possibility she was right. 'It looks very expensive, Amir. I don't feel comfortable accepting it.'

Strong fingers tilted her chin till she was looking up into eyes that glittered brighter than the dazzling stone.

'Your scruples do you credit.' He smiled and the sombre lines around his mouth vanished. 'But you're mistaken if you think this some family heirloom. It's just a pretty stone, a trinket that caught my eye.'

'It's kind of you, Amir, but I can't take it.'

'It's not kind at all.' Something flashed in his eyes. 'I saw it and it reminded me of you: its colour, its vibrancy.' His words, like caresses, curled around her eager heart. It grew harder every moment to resist.

'You accept nothing from me but the roof over your head and the meals provided by my kitchens. You spurn every gift I try to give, even something as trifling as a chess set.'

Amir's voice echoed with disappointment and what she could almost convince herself was hurt.

'Even the clothes to replace the wardrobe you lost were too much to accept without limitations.' His hand slashed impatiently. 'Most of it you sent back.'

Cassie stared, stunned by the intensity of his feelings. Had she been churlish with her continual refusals? 'I didn't mean to offend you.'

Amir nodded, the militant spark fading as his expression softened. 'No offence taken.' He stroked her cheek with his knuckles. 'Wear it for me? It would make me happy.'

'It's utterly gorgeous.' She summoned a bright smile for Amir, firmly banishing the shades of the past and focusing on the man she loved.

Amir wasn't buying her with expensive jewellery, as her mother had been bought. He'd found a trinket of costume jewellery that to her untutored eyes looked stunningly expensive. But what did she know of gems? He'd thought to give her pleasure. *That* was what counted.

Happiness surged anew as she looked into his face. This time her smile was completely genuine.

His mouth brushed hers and she leaned in close, but too

soon he pulled away, mischief lurking in his eyes. 'Let me put this on you.'

Amir had chosen a long chain, so the stone nestled low between her breasts, which entailed undoing buttons on her silk shirt so the necklace could be appreciated properly.

Fortunately they were completely alone. There was no one to see as Amir bent to feather kisses across the top of her breasts, or as she clung needily to his shoulders.

Amir pressed another kiss to Cassie's sweet skin, then centred the pendant carefully between her breasts, enjoying the perfection of it against her gleaming satin flesh.

He wanted her to wear the gem always. Not because it was worth a fortune, but because he liked the idea she wore *his* gift so intimately.

'You'll wear this for me?' The words came out husky and he swallowed an unfamiliar constriction in his throat.

'If you like.'

'I like.'

'I like too. It's beautiful. Thank you.' Her smile warmed his soul as she lifted her hand to stroke his cheek.

Desire stirred. He clamped her hand in his and pressed a kiss to her palm, surprised at the fervour in his blood.

It was more than simply his libido stirring. It was something new, this feeling that swelled within him.

As if sensing a change, Cassie shifted a fraction and tilted her head, trying to gauge what it was.

'What were you saying about my English class earlier? You said you wanted to talk about it.'

'Did I?' Amir stroked his index finger along the platinum chain, between her breasts to the low-cut lace of her bra.

'Amir!' He grinned, but she pulled free. 'You're incorrigible.'

'Don't you mean irresistible?'

'That too.'

For long seconds he stared into the beckoning softness of

her violet eyes. Such warmth he read there. Such happiness and admiration. It cloaked him, making him feel more like a king than at any time since his coronation. As if he was invincible.

Anyone looking at Cassie now would mistake her for a bride, just discovering passion and dreaming of love.

Amir stiffened, appalled at where his mind had wandered.

Cassie would one day marry a man of her own culture. A man who would give her everything she desired. Everything she deserved. Even love—the one thing above all else Amir could give no woman. How could he when he knew nothing of it? Love for a child, yes, he could imagine that growing as he held his babe in his hands. But love for a woman?

What were the chances he'd ever love the woman chosen to be his bride simply because she fitted his requirements for the position of queen? Instantly he rejected the idea.

Amir's hands clenched as he fought surging nausea at the idea of Cassie in love with another man. Touching another man. Even smiling at one!

Still this possessiveness lingered, growing stronger each day. Was there no cure for it?

'I said I'd heard your classes were a great success.' He forced himself to concentrate. 'You should be proud. The idea of classes on the move was an inspiration.'

'Thank you. We enjoy them.'

Amir reached out to touch the priceless sapphire, watching it quiver with every breath Cassie took. His primitive self basked in the way it marked her as *his woman* just as surely as if she still wore the slave chain.

His woman.

He'd never felt so proprietorial.

Even after all this time he was as eager for her company as ever. More so. The thought of her strong yet softly yielding body beneath him was a constant distraction as he battled to concentrate on affairs of state.

Surely the novelty must pall soon? Yet he couldn't imagine

tiring of Cassie, so intoxicatingly erotic in his arms. Nor could he imagine growing bored with her company, her quick, irreverent wit and her mulish, endearing independence. The joy of just being with Cassie.

The thought brought him up short, alarm bells ringing. It gave him the strength to say what must be said.

'You might want to consider keeping your students in the classroom for a few weeks.' A rough note edged his voice. 'Let one of the other teachers take the group around the city.'

Deep inside pain needled his belly. Guilt?

'Why? That's part of their success. It's why they work so well, and the women are enthusiastic.'

'I'm sure a lot of it is to do with you, Cassie, not just the location.' He paused, wishing he hadn't raised this. 'But Faruq tells me you're attracting a lot of attention.' He raised his hand when she made to respond. 'I know it's great publicity for the programme, but from what Faruq says it won't be long before local journalists sniff around for a profile piece.' He held her bewildered gaze. 'My staff are discreet, Cassie, but once the press gets interested they'll dig up the fact you spent a week as my sex slave.'

'I didn't!'

The jab of pain in his belly became a searing dagger-slash as he watched her bright eyes shadow. Her mouth tightened and she swallowed as if in pain.

He'd done that to her.

'You and I know the circumstances. But imagine the salacious stories once they hear you were given to me and what our accommodation consisted of.'

It would be no time at all before the press shouted what now was only whispered in inner circles: that Cassie was his lover, flaunting herself in the palace even as arrangements proceeded for a royal betrothal.

Never before had Amir installed a lover in the palace. At this delicate time especially the furore would be tremendous.

'That might be a good idea. I'll think about it.'

Amir's heart clenched as he watched pride replace pain on her face. She really was a woman in a million.

He was desperate to buy them more time.

His only hope lay in the belief that soon he would grow out of this…need for her.

One day he'd take in matrimony the woman his country expected him to wed. The woman approved by the Council of Elders, who matched every one of Amir's own criteria in a wife. The woman who would give him and his children the stability he demanded. What he needed.

If only he could imagine ever wanting her as much as he did Cassie.

'Thanks. I'll be fine from here.' Cassie closed the car door and waved to the director of the language school.

This afternoon's class had gone better than expected, given they'd stayed in the classroom. The women had been as enthusiastic as ever, and there'd been a lot of laughter as well as an encouraging amount of progress.

Yet Cassie had felt hemmed in and unsettled. Amir's comments about the press had persuaded her to stop for now the roving class that had been such a success. The small school could do with the support publicity could bring, but not the notoriety of gossip about her and Amir. Sex slave, indeed!

Distaste shivered along her spine.

That tag pushed every sensitive button she had. Not surprising since she'd grown up watching men swagger in and out of her mother's life, and how the role of kept woman had brought out a calculating, hard-heartedness in her mother Cassie aimed never to emulate.

She walked through the enormous palace gates, determined to put all that from her mind.

Normally she used another entrance, marginally less grand, on the other side of the royal complex. But she'd enjoyed the chance to chat with the director rather than sit in a silent state in the back of one of Amir's gleaming vehicles that usually delivered her to her part of the palace.

Despite the noisy enthusiasm of the classes, Cassie realised she missed the chance for a chat with another woman. Amir's employees kept a discreet distance.

She smiled and nodded to a pair of uniformed guards, and made her way up the wide steps to the entrance.

The splendour of the grand foyer stopped her in her tracks. She'd never been in this part of the palace and its magnificence took her breath away.

A towering domed ceiling of gilt and azure mosaic work drew the eye from a forest of slender supporting columns. The marble floor was inlaid in an intricate geometric design that must have taken years to complete. Tiny in the immense space were clusters of antique furniture, silk rugs and enormous jardinieres filled with exotic blooms.

An army of staff was busy under the eagle-eyed direction of the palace chamberlain.

Slowly Cassie approached, loath to ask directions of the only one of Amir's employees who'd made her feel not unwelcome but uncomfortable. His piercing grey eyes never warmed and there was a cool punctiliousness to his manner that made her wonder if he disapproved of her.

'Miss Denison.' He bowed. 'How are you?'

'Fine, thank you, Musad. And you?'

'Well, thank you.' He folded his hands, watching her with a complete lack of expression she found unnerving. 'Can I assist you?'

Cassie smiled. 'If you would. I'm afraid I'll need directions to my rooms. I'm bound to get lost from here.' The sprawling palace covered hectares.

Musad didn't smile in response, merely inclined his head. 'Of course. The way to the harem is not easy from these public areas. Deliberately so.'

'Harem?' She was staying in a *harem*? It sounded so antiquated. So *suggestive*.

Something flickered in his cool eyes. 'Yes. That is the name given to the place where the women of the King live.' He lifted his hand and one of the servants cleaning a nearby chandelier hurried towards them. 'I'll have someone show you the way.'

The women of the King. Cassie supposed that meant the monarch's female relatives, yet she couldn't banish a trickle of horror, remembering stories about concubines immured in harems for some man's pleasure. That didn't apply to her. She was Amir's guest, not his possession.

'You're having a spring clean, are you?' she asked brightly, changing the subject.

Musad nodded. 'Preparations for the forthcoming celebrations will take weeks. It's a massive undertaking.'

'What are you celebrating?'

His head jerked up as if struck, and Cassie read what looked like shock in the chamberlain's stiff features. His eyes rounded and his jaw slackened.

The servant he'd summoned stopped before them. Musad waved him abruptly away before gathering himself and wiping his face clear of expression once more.

His reaction to her question confused and disturbed. What was going on?

'Come, Miss Denison, I'll show you to your rooms myself.' He turned and gestured for her to accompany him across the vast space.

Intrigued at the change in him, Cassie followed his lead, nodding vaguely as he spoke of the dimensions of the grand hall, the age of the wall paintings and the jewels embedded in the walls, designed to glitter by lamplight and remind visitors of the royal family's immense wealth.

His patter continued as they proceeded past vast reception rooms and wide hallways, each more splendid than the last, till Cassie was filled with a numb sense of dismay at how incredibly rich Amir was.

Her lips curved in a mirthless smile. Of course he was

wealthy. She'd known it from the start. But walking endless corridors filled to the brim with treasures only reinforced the enormous gulf that existed between his world and hers.

How had she ever hoped they might—?

What? The cynical voice deep inside probed her sudden pain, like a tongue seeking out a sore tooth. *What did you hope? That he'd want more than an affair? That he'd want something long-term?*

You've fallen in love with a king, not an ordinary man.

Yet hope lingered. The fragile dreams she'd harboured refused to die.

'You never did tell me, Musad.' She broke into speech—anything to silence the knowing little voice in her head. 'What celebration is it you're preparing for?'

Musad stopped and regarded her gravely. Again she caught a flicker of something in his eyes. She would almost swear it looked like sympathy!

'A royal event,' he murmured slowly, as if reluctant to speak. Fascinated, Cassie watched him draw a deep breath. 'It will mark the formal betrothal of our Sheikh.'

'The formal…?' For the life of her Cassie couldn't force out the next word. Desperately she groped for a near pillar, clutching at it for support as her legs wobbled alarmingly.

Musad nodded. 'Our Sheikh is to marry a woman from one of the most prominent Tarakhan families.'

Dimly Cassie registered Musad's gentle tone, as if he regretted breaking the news. In slow motion she saw him raise a hand to fiddle with his perfectly arranged headcloth. Her pulse decelerated to a heavy thump and for a moment she wondered idly if she might faint as the world spun around her and nausea rose in an engulfing tide.

Amir was to marry. Betrothal celebrations were imminent. Which meant he'd been planning his wedding while keeping Cassie here as…what? His mistress?

Cassie's fragile dreams shattered in a moment that stretched out to accommodate infinite pain.

CHAPTER FOURTEEN

'Fool, fool fool!' Cassie paced her room, allowing anger to surge, hoping it might relieve the gaping ache that filled her soul. The emptiness where hope and happiness had resided.

Amir hadn't promised for ever. He hadn't promised anything. Nor had she demanded any assurances from him. She'd told herself it was enough that they shared their bodies, shared themselves with no strings attached, because they weren't hurting anyone. That what they had was open and honest. In her innocence she'd believed their relationship was special, that eventually Amir would come to feel what she did. That at least there was a *chance*.

But there'd been nothing honest about what Amir had done. He'd kept her in his house, in his *harem*, while he arranged to marry to another woman!

Pain ripped through Cassie and her pace faltered as she doubled up, her knuckles pressed to her mouth to stop a cry of distress.

She felt…betrayed. She felt cheapened by what she'd allowed Amir to do to her.

She felt disgust, reliving the moment when as a child she'd realised what her mother did for money. Yet now it was *self*-disgust Cassie felt. Its taste was bitter gall on her tongue.

What she'd thought wondrous had merely been Amir using her to satisfy his physical needs until he settled down with his wife.

Needle-sharp pain splintered through her belly.

No wonder Musad had looked concerned. He hadn't wanted to be the one to break the news. At least he'd had the decency to take her somewhere private first.

How could she not have realised Amir played a double game?

She'd given herself to him believing they shared as equals. That this passion, this rare sense of connection, was real and worth pursuing. That he respected her as she had him. The man who'd protected her when she'd had no one else but herself to rely on. The man who'd held himself back from her, night after night, because she was so vulnerable.

His honour, his restraint, his caring had broken down the barriers she'd spent a lifetime erecting.

What had happened to that man? When had he changed?

Or had that all been a ploy to suck her into the heady spell of sensuality he wove around her?

Had he seen how needy she was for affection when she hadn't realised it herself? Had he deliberately worked on her weaknesses?

Her breath sawed as she recalled that moment today when she'd bent to pick up a pen she'd dropped in class and the women had murmured appreciatively over her new pendant as it slipped loose. One woman had claimed the blue stone was a sapphire, a rare stone of superb quality only found in a single mine in a remote part of Tarakhar. She'd claimed it was worth a fortune.

Cassie had smiled and tucked the pendant under her shirt and forgotten about it, knowing the woman was mistaken.

What if she wasn't?

Had Amir's gift been payment in kind for services rendered?

What had Cassie allowed herself to become?

She sagged against the wall, knees trembling, as the truth hit her. That necklace: the sort a rich man gave his mistress. The gossamer-fine silks and barely there underwear he provided instead of the sturdy cotton she'd once worn. The way

Amir kept her in his harem but never invited her to the other parts of the palace. He came to her bed. She'd never so much as *seen* his bedroom, and he took care to leave her before dawn each morning. He came to her at night or dusk, never in the day. Nor did he invite her to participate in any of the events he attended. She hadn't been introduced to his friends or family.

Because he was ashamed of her?

No! It was left to Cassie to feel shame.

The truth was so blindingly obvious she couldn't believe she'd never seen it. Amir didn't care enough to feel ashamed of her. He simply kept her in exquisite isolation where she could pander to his wishes and pleasure him.

Like a harem girl of old.

Bile rose in her throat but she forced it down. She had to face this.

Cassie thought of the daring way she'd caressed him with her mouth last night. She'd been so aroused by his response, revelling in the sense of power, having him so blatantly at her mercy. Now she felt sick, realising what a sham it had all been. Had he thought her enthusiasm manufactured because of his generous present?

All the time she'd given herself to him, loving him, Amir had seen her as little more than a prostitute, paying for her favours with jewellery and rich clothes and this luxurious accommodation.

No wonder he'd been so insistent she accept the pendant! It was an unspoken but necessary part of the bargain she hadn't realised she'd made.

And all that time he'd planned his future with another woman.

Air. She needed air.

Cassie stumbled to the doors that opened onto the private courtyard. As she went she scrabbled at the catch on the necklace he'd given her. The heavy stone burned like ice between her breasts, reminding her of the intimacy they'd shared and the price Amir put on it.

She yanked the chain free and flung it across the room.

Amir pushed open Cassie's door, anticipation fizzing in his veins.

He'd reorganised his schedule so he could finish early and he'd planned a surprise for Cassie: a sunset picnic at a renowned beauty spot.

He loved surprising her. The way pleasure lit her face and her eyes glowed brighter than stars. The way she turned impulsively to him, touching, talking, sharing her excitement at the smallest of things, from a moonlit swim in dark velvety water to a perfect rose.

Amir found the intimacy of that shared pleasure addictive.

Striding across the room towards the open courtyard doors, he stepped on something and frowned. It was the necklace he'd given her just last night. The gem that was such a perfect match for her lustrous eyes. Was the catch faulty? He paused to examine it but could see nothing amiss. He pocketed it and moved on.

'Cassie?'

A flash of movement caught his eye. There she was, walking in the shaded colonnade that rimmed the courtyard.

Amir stepped outside, drinking in the sight of her as a man who spied water after days in the desert. Something lifted inside him as he watched her pace quickly, all vibrant energy. She wore loose-fitting trousers that clung in all the right places and a shirt of gauzy violet that matched her eyes.

His pulse quickened.

'Cassie!'

She swung round, but instead of hurrying to meet him she stood where she was. He couldn't read her expression in the shadows but her stillness spoke of wariness, of tension.

'What's wrong?'

He covered the distance between them quickly. As he

approached she crossed her arms, accentuating the thrust of her breasts. His eyes lingered on the taut fabric even as his brain began calculating how long they could afford to linger here in pleasure without missing the spectacular sunset. They might just have time—

His eyes met hers and shock hit him.

Where was his sweet, warm lover? The engaging woman who'd stolen his attention these last two months?

Cassie's eyes flashed fire and her mouth was set mutinously.

'What's happened? Did something go wrong at school today?'

Silently she shook her head. Amir stepped forward, his hand lifting to caress her cheek.

Cassie moved back, further into the shadows.

Something slammed into him. Shock. Dismay. Why did she withdraw?

'I found this on the floor.' He dug the sapphire from his pocket and held it out.

Instead of reaching for it Cassie backed up another step, putting her hands behind her as if touching it might contaminate her. His belly tightened as something like nerves hit him. What was wrong with her?

'You can keep it. I don't want it.' Emotion vibrated in her words.

'What do you mean?' Amir paced towards her and was immeasurably relieved that she stood her ground. He wanted her close, where she belonged. 'Last night you were thrilled by it. You promised to wear it for me.'

He wanted her to wear it now. The fact that she'd dropped it on the floor sent a dart of dismay spearing through him.

'I didn't know what it was then.' Her fine brows drew together. 'It's a real gem, isn't it?'

Amir frowned at her accusing tone. 'It is. A sapphire from—'

'I don't care where it's from. I don't want it!'

'And you wonder why I didn't tell you all about it last night?' This woman drove him crazy. How many others would have leapt on the extraordinary piece just for its monetary value? He spread his hands. 'I realise you're not comfortable with expensive gifts, so I—'

'Lied.'

Amir stiffened. 'I didn't lie. I just told you it was a trinket.' That was true. With his wealth, the cost of it was trifling. 'I saw it and wanted it for you. Is that a crime?' Her attitude rankled. The way she glared up at him, as if he'd done something wrong, was ridiculous.

'I don't like being lied to.'

Angry, Amir shoved the necklace in his pocket. 'If it offends you so much I'll take it away.' What had got into her?

'I don't want *anything* from you.'

Amir frowned. 'What does it matter? I'm a rich man. It pleases me to give you pretty things.'

Her chin tilted up. 'Like it pleases you to keep me as your mistress?'

Cassie's words sent a prickle of warning down his nape.

'I wouldn't use the word *mistress*.' There'd been other women—plenty of them—he'd put in that category. But not Cassie. She was different. This wasn't a mercenary arrangement.

'What term *would* you use? Kept woman? Bit on the side?' The words snapped like staccato bites eating into his skin.

'Don't talk like that! We're lovers.'

Slowly she shook her head. 'No. Lovers share. Lovers are equals. But we're not, are we? I thought we were. But it's impossible.'

'Why?' He stepped closer still, driven by an urgency he didn't comprehend. All these weeks they *had* been equals, sharing a gift so precious he'd never experienced anything like it. He'd told himself at first it was purely sex, but denial could only last so long. This was about far more than satisfying the libido.

With Cassie he felt…

'Because you're getting married.'

The words fell like blocks of ice into a surging sea.

'Because you've made me into your prostitute, your private whore, buying my favours while you plan to marry another woman.'

Horror froze Amir as he looked into her pale, set face and read the anguish in her eyes.

'Now, stop right there! It wasn't like that.' How could she talk about herself in that way? His stomach churned in fierce denial.

'No?' One eyebrow arched in magnificent disbelief. 'What was it like, then?'

Amir's hands clenched at his sides. He smarted from the insult she offered them both.

'You know it wasn't like that. I didn't pay you. This—' his gesture encompassed the secluded garden and her private suite '—has been about us alone, no one else. What has happened between us is genuine, Cassie. I…care for you.' The words were out of his mouth without conscious decision, stunning him as he realised his feelings ran bone-deep.

For a moment she stared up with a look in her eyes that told him she wavered.

'Yet you conveniently forgot to mention you were going to marry soon. That our relationship was doomed before it started.'

Amir frowned. 'I never spoke to you of marriage. You can't have expected—'

Her bitter laugh cut him off. 'No, I couldn't have, could I? That would have been the act of a naïve fool, wouldn't it?'

Yet her voice betrayed pain as well as anger.

How could she have imagined he'd marry *her*? She was passing through, a foreigner with no lasting interest in his country. How could he marry a bride who'd been given to him as a sex slave? Who, albeit through no fault of her own, would create almost as much scandal as his own mother had when those circumstances became known? Tarakhar needed an accomplished woman of good repute as its queen. A woman who would bring his carefully nurtured plans to life.

He needed that.

Cassie and he…it was lust, desire, hunger between them. And liking. Respect too. He cared for Cassie. But that wasn't enough to build a successful royal marriage.

'You lied, Amir.' She almost spat the words and he stiffened. 'You lied by omission. You owed it to me, and to your fiancée, to tell the truth about your marriage plans.'

'She's not my fiancée.'

Cassie shook her head, fire dancing in her eyes.

Despite her accusations and the roiling mix of emotions churning inside an urgent need consumed him—to reach out and pull her close, stop her mouth with his kisses, stroke the tender skin of her throat and lose himself in shared passion. His need for her weakened him.

'Not yet. But the deal's as good as done, isn't it? Your staff know about it. How many others?'

Amir shrugged, disliking the sense of being pushed onto the back foot.

'My plans to marry don't impact on what we have. I told you I intended to wed.'

'So you did.' Her voice was saccharine sweet as she folded her arms again. 'But I thought you were talking about some day in the future. How was I to know you'd already picked a bride and made arrangements to marry her?'

'It's not relevant to us.' Desperation stirred that he couldn't make her understand. And that it mattered so much that she did.

'No?' She lunged forward and prodded him square in the chest with her index finger. 'And what about when you're married? Would it have been relevant then? Or would you have kept me on after the wedding? Does the idea of having both a wife and a concubine turn you on?'

'Don't be crude.' How could she even *think* he'd treat her that way? Nausea curled in his belly at her words.

But what was his excuse?

She'd honed in on the one flaw in his plans. For weeks he'd told himself he'd end their liaison as soon as it began to pall. That there'd be plenty of time to break it off before the wedding. That this was one final fling before he settled down to domesticity. Yet there'd been no sign of it palling. No ennui, no predictability. Instead his need for Cassie grew stronger each day.

Amir had refused to face the fact that one day soon he'd have to give her up. That this liaison which brought him such satisfaction had to end before he took his bride.

'You call *me* crude when you install me as your mistress? When you pay me in jewels and fine clothes and think that will stop me caring about the fact you're promised to someone else? When you decide I'm not good enough to meet your friends or to present in public? That I'm only good for—'

'Enough!' The roaring sound of his voice echoing through the portico shocked him. His pulse thrummed heavily, almost blotting out the sound of his laboured breathing. Fire scorched his chest and belly as he fought a turbulent tide of emotion. 'There was no insult intended, Cassie.'

She blinked, and for a moment he could have sworn he saw the glitter of tears on her lashes. The sight gutted him.

'And when you warned me off going out with my class in public?' Her voice was low now, and husky, as if her throat were tight like his. 'Tell me that was solely for my benefit. Tell me you weren't worried the publicity would interfere with your marriage arrangements.'

Guilt engulfed Amir. She was right. He'd thought of himself, smoothing things over till the time came to put Cassie away from him.

'Don't bother answering that. I can see it in your eyes. You weren't protecting me. You were protecting yourself.' She huffed out a laugh that wrenched at his heart. 'You know, I thought you different from the rest. A man of honour. A man I could respect. Naïve, wasn't I?'

The raw anguish in her husky voice pierced him and pain surged as if from a gaping wound. He reached out to her cheek. How had something so perfect gone so horribly wrong?

'*Habibti*, I—'

Cassie knocked his hand away and swung round to stare out over the darkening courtyard. But not before he'd seen tears well in her eyes. Razor-sharp talons tore at him. He'd never felt anything as intensely as this torture, watching her distress.

'I'm *not* your beloved! I may have given you my innocence but I'm not a fool. Don't insult me like one.'

Her innocence?

Amir swayed with shock. She couldn't be serious. No innocent would have blatantly seduced him the way she had, demanding he make her his. She'd been like flame in his hands, all hot energy and enthusiasm. She'd been no shrinking violet but had enjoyed sex with an honest delight that had shaken him to the core.

A delight mixed with wonder, he now remembered. And moments of hesitation that he'd convinced himself he'd imagined.

That smear of blood on the sheet! The stain that had been beneath their hips after he took her that first time. Amir recalled the ecstasy of that joining, how incredibly tight she'd felt as she gripped him and sent him over the edge.

He stared, dumbfounded, and saw the fine tremors racking her body.

What had he done?

'Cassie.' His voice was unsteady. His vocal cords paralysed. 'I didn't want it to be like this. I just wanted *you*.'

He'd thought about nothing else. For the first time he hadn't planned ahead. He'd acted on instinct, grabbing greedily at this woman and not relinquishing her. Now she was paying for his selfishness. He'd never felt so helpless in his life.

'But it *is* like this.' She sounded drained, her voice empty. 'I let you make me your mistress. I didn't even realise I was turning into the very woman I'd vowed never to become.'

Again that huff of laughter that sounded more like pain. Something twisted in his chest at her anguish.

'How's that for blind? That I of all people didn't realise what I'd become till today. That while I hoped for something else, you'd turned me into the other woman.'

'Of all people?'

She swung round, and the sight of tears trickling unheeded down her pale cheeks hit him like a sledgehammer to the solar plexus. Even in the mountains when she'd feared for her life Cassie hadn't cried.

For the first time in his memory fear overwhelmed him.

He wanted to hold her close, soothe her with gentle caresses. But the pain in her eyes, the memory of her accusations, stopped him.

Her mouth twisted in an ugly grimace. 'All my life I've fought for my self-respect. Don't think I didn't see the look in your eyes when I said I did whatever I could to make ends meet when acting jobs dried up. But I never sold myself!'

Amir opened his mouth to assure her he hadn't thought she had, but she was speaking again, her eyes glazed as if she looked inwards and didn't see him.

'I told myself I'd never be like her, and now I am, and it feels…' She shuddered and wrapped her arms around herself.

'Like whom, Cassie?' He lifted his hand to her shoulder and then dropped it, helpless in the face of her distress.

Huge bruised violet eyes lifted to his. 'My mother. I didn't tell you much about her, did I?' Her chin tilted up gallantly even as she swallowed convulsively. Pride and shame and hurt flitted across her drawn features.

'She was a rich man's mistress. She was married to someone else when she got pregnant by my father. When her husband kicked her out because he discovered the affair she moved to Melbourne and lived as my father's mistress for years. Living off his bounty and the crumbs of his attention. When he'd had enough of her she found herself another protector. Then another. One of them even decided that since he'd bought my mother he could have me too.'

Amir rocked back on his heels. At his gasp of horror her lips tilted in a vague smile.

'He didn't succeed. After that I never went home for holidays. But watching my mother prostitute herself, seeing the woman she became, I vowed never to be like her. Till you, I avoided getting close to any man.'

She shook her head, arms wrapped tight around her torso as if to hold in pain.

'And look at me now!'

Her pride, her distress, evoked a surge of emotions such as he'd never known.

Amir could stand no more. He dragged her to him, his hold careful yet unbreakable, as if he held the most fragile substance in the world. Her fragility scared him. Within the circle of his embrace Cassie stood stiff and unyielding, yet her tears wet his shirt and her gasping breath was hot against his chest.

Guilt carved a dark cavern in his soul. How had he thought himself honourable when his selfishness had wounded her so? What sort of man was he?

Never had he felt such shame and regret. Her despair and self-loathing vibrated in each word, every stifled sob. Every tremor racking her body was a blow straight to his heart. How could he ever—?

'Amir?' The tears had stopped and her voice held barely a wobble.

'Yes?' He just prevented himself adding an endearment and his hand itched to stroke her, ease her torment.

'I want to leave now. I never want to see you again.'

CHAPTER FIFTEEN

THREE weeks later Cassie looked out of the window of her rural classroom. Mountains rose in the distance. She tried not to think about that week she'd spent in Bhutran. Or about the man she'd met there. The man who'd stolen her heart when she wasn't looking and shattered it.

How could she love him still?

It was ridiculous. Pathetic.

After what he'd done to her he should mean less than nothing to her. After what she'd done to herself.

Amir wasn't solely to blame. Cassie had allowed herself to be swept on a tide of desire, enthralled by what he made her feel not just physically, but emotionally. For the first time Cassie had felt whole, content and joyously happy sharing her life with Amir.

Was this how her mother had felt all those years ago? Could it have been love after all that had driven her to follow Cassie's father and give up everything in the process?

Once, the idea had seemed preposterous, knowing the calculating, self-absorbed woman her mother had become. But now Cassie knew how devastating love could be. How dangerously strong its pull.

How could she still long for Amir's touch? How could she miss the deep rumble of his voice, or the glitter in his eyes when he teased her over a game of chess? She even missed listening to him talk about plans for urban renewal!

It scared her that, though she felt pain and shame at having allowed herself to become 'the other woman' in a relationship triangle, her main emotion was grief. Grief at the loss of Amir.

She had to get a grip!

Behind her came the sound of women's voices, her students practising in pairs the simple conversation she'd taught them. She needed to forget these daydreams and stop feeling like a victim.

Cassie moved to the nearest pair, nodding encouragement and automatically helping when the new English vocabulary eluded them.

Classes kept her sane. They gave her purpose and even a measure of happiness, seeing the difference even she, with her minimal qualifications, could make to the lives of these women. She even got to use her dramatic skills sometimes, miming concepts to help the class understand and breaking down language barriers with laughter.

She didn't miss acting as she'd thought she might. She'd even begun to think of teaching English long-term. Not here in Tarakhar. That would be prodding an open wound, knowing she was so close to Amir and his carefully chosen perfect bride.

Cassie moved between the groups, assisting when needed and praising the women who a couple of weeks ago had been too shy to speak English aloud.

How far they'd come. Their determination to improve made her ashamed of how she kept dwelling on her time with Amir rather than the future.

It didn't matter that the future was a grey, foggy place she couldn't see clearly or be enthusiastic about. She had to push herself.

The door opened and she turned to see the principal enter, excitement bright in her eyes and quick gestures.

'Ms Denison.' The principal nodded to her. 'Excuse the interruption. We have important guests, here on an impromptu visit. Such an honour!' Already she was turning to the class and addressing them in their own language.

Cassie watched as the women sat straighter, their chatter dying into a hush of expectant silence. Discreetly clothes were straightened and hair smoothed as they turned towards the door, their faces alight with excitement.

In this rural area visitors were a source of endless interest. Look at the fuss *her* presence had caused, the sole foreigner for half a day's travel.

She turned, a polite smile on her face, then froze, appalled, as her blood congealed in her veins. The words of welcome dried on her lips as she took in the tall figure in white, his stern, proud face so frighteningly familiar.

She hadn't seen Amir in weeks, yet he visited her dreams every night. She discovered she'd forgotten nothing of his austere, masculine beauty.

Just looking at him hurt as she remembered the profound joy they'd once shared.

A gasp penetrated the silence, drawing all eyes to her.

'And this is our volunteer teacher, Ms Denison.'

'Ms Denison.' He bowed, his penetrating dark gaze unreadable as it flicked her from head to toe. Instantly her body heated to tingling awareness that even shock couldn't douse. He looked so *good*, his features as magnetic as ever, though his mouth was grim and she noticed new lines bracketing his lips as if he'd given up smiling.

'Your Highness.' Her voice was husky. She was surprised to discover it worked. Her feet were rooted to the spot and her heart catapulted against her ribs as if trying to break free. A dull queasiness stirred and for one horrible moment she thought she'd be sick.

She dragged her gaze from Amir's and the unbearable tension snapped down a notch.

'Faruq.'

'Ms Denison. It's a pleasure to see you.' Faruq shook her hand and smiled as if genuinely glad to be here.

But *why* were they here? Amir was a great one for meeting his people and monitoring local issues, but she knew his life was planned to the nth degree. No spur-of-the-moment visits for him.

Unless... Could he be here to see *her*? Unbidden, the thought rose and refused to be banished. Excitement and anxiety filled her as she listened to the interchange between Amir and the suddenly shy group of women.

Tension crawled through her, tightening every nerve.

What could he want? What was there to say between them? Even here in the provinces she'd heard about the approaching betrothal celebrations and the wedding to come.

Amir had let her walk away, never attempting to detain or persuade her. Her presence in the palace was a potential embarrassment, and it was obvious nothing was more important than his carefully arranged marriage to his suitable wife.

The bottom dropped out of her stomach.

She'd had weeks to get used to the idea of him with another woman and still it made fury scream in her blood and despair weight her soul.

When would she get over him?

Cassie clenched her hands and stood still, calling on every vestige of her theatrical training to project an image of polite interest.

If he could stand being here with her, then she could do the same. He would *not* see her buckle under the weight of distress.

By the time they'd finished Cassie's knees were shaking so badly she had to grope for the wall beside her, surreptitiously propping herself up as she struggled to breathe normally through lungs cramped impossibly tight.

If only they'd leave.

At last they were moving. No, they'd paused. Through her haze of shock Cassie saw the principal's surprised stare in her direction. Then, next thing she knew, the whole class was rising and filing out through the door. Furtive glances were shot her way, but they couldn't pierce the bubble of disbelief that held her in stasis.

Faruq bowed low and followed the rest, leaving only...

Without conscious thought Cassie started forward. She couldn't stay here with Amir. She just couldn't!

Each step was an achievement on legs turned suddenly to jelly. She'd almost made it to the door when a hand shot out as if to take her arm. She shied away, banging against the wall.

'Cassie.' His voice was hoarse and low, as if stretched. She felt it in every cell. 'Don't go.'

How she'd longed to hear him say that weeks ago. Despite her outrage and hurt, she'd hoped against hope he'd stop her leaving, tell her he'd changed his mind and he wanted her as more than his mistress, that he wanted her—

'No!' She didn't know if she was shouting at him or her own vulnerable self for harbouring such foolish thoughts.

The door closed quietly, his hand spread wide to hold it shut.

She didn't have to meet his gaze to know she had no hope of leaving till Amir was ready for her to go.

'How dare you keep me here against my will? How dare you show your face here? Haven't you done enough?' Her voice cracked on the last word and her lips wobbled. 'Or are you here to send me away? Is that it?' Valiantly she tried to whip up pride to counter the traitorous weakness that undermined her. 'Is it too embarrassing having an ex-mistress in the country with your wedding so close?'

'Of course not!'

His voice was tight, as if with unspoken anger, but all she registered was that he wasn't here to exile her. How stupid and self-destructive to feel relief.

'Cassie—'

'No.' She spun away on a surge of energy. 'I don't want to hear it. There's nothing to say.' She folded shaking arms and straightened her spine, focusing on the distant view of the mountains.

'You're wrong.' His voice came from just behind her. She felt the warmth of his big frame raying out to her chilled body.

Part of her wanted to sink back against him and pretend, for a moment, that everything was as it had once been.

Except it had never been as she'd imagined. What she'd thought a glorious adventure had been a tawdry affair.

'There's a lot to say,' he murmured, his low voice insinuating itself into her blood, curling deep and powerful within her.

'How is your fiancée?' She couldn't let herself weaken.

'She's not my—'

'OK, then. Your soon-to-be fiancée?'

'She's not that either.'

His words hung in the silence. Her eyes widened. Had she heard right?

Slowly she turned. He stood, shoulders squared and jaw tight, before her. His eyes wore that shuttered look she remembered so well. The one he'd worn whenever he didn't want her to know what he was thinking.

'What are you saying?'

'The betrothal will not proceed. I will not take her as my wife.'

Cassie blinked as the walls seemed to dip and sway around her.

'Cassie!' He reached out to her and she stumbled back, coming up against a desk and leaning heavily on it.

'Are you telling the truth?' But why would he lie? Cassie held no place in his world now.

His lips thinned, but the expected flash of anger was absent. 'There will be no lies between us again, even by omission.' He lifted his hand to the back of his neck, then dropped it again in a gesture that made him look almost unsure of himself.

Cassie didn't believe that for an instant. What did he want?

'What about your wedding? Even here people are talking about it.'

'It's cancelled.' He held her eyes and heat shuddered through her.

Cassie shook her head. 'It can't be. The way Musad spoke,

it was public knowledge. You said it was expected you would marry. There were contracts being drawn up and—'

'Nevertheless, it's done.' Amir lifted his shoulders in a dismissive gesture. 'There will be restitution to her family, of course. A large restitution even though the betrothal wasn't formalised. It's over.'

At first she couldn't believe the stunning news, but there was no mistaking the grim honesty in his eyes. She felt queasy with shock.

'But what about *her*? The woman you were to marry?' Was she broken-hearted? Crazy to experience fellow feeling for a woman she'd never met, a woman she'd resented and envied.

'It was an arranged marriage, Cassie, not a love match. Another husband will be found for her.'

But not a king. Not Amir. What must she be feeling?

'The news will break publicly today.' He said it so calmly.

'But won't there be a scandal?' Cassie rubbed a finger across her forehead, as if that would help her brain chug into gear. None of this made sense. 'You said you wanted to avoid that at all costs.' It had been one of the reasons he hadn't wanted *her*. Because her past was too scandalous!

'I'll ride it out.' His look told her he had other things on his mind.

Cassie sagged lower onto the table, shaking her head.

'Don't you want to know why?' He stepped closer, and Cassie had a sense of the room crowding in around her, yet she didn't have the energy to move.

Silently she nodded. Of course she did.

'I couldn't marry her. I couldn't marry anyone, I discovered, simply for the sake of my country and because it was expected. Not even a stable, sensible partner of impeccable breeding and excellent reputation who fitted my plans exactly.'

'I don't understand. Why are you telling me this?' Disjointed thoughts tumbled through her brain, yet Cassie couldn't make sense of them.

'I couldn't marry her when it's someone else I want.'

His voice rang clear and strong, jerking her gaze up to his. He stood so close she could see the fire kindling in his dark eyes. It made her skin prickle and shrink over her bones. It made her feel...

Finally his words sank in and she shot to her feet.

'No, you can't mean—'

'I do, Cassandra.' He spoke slowly and clearly, as one might recite a vow. The idea stirred silly, vulnerable longing in her. 'I want you.'

'Well, you can't have me!' When would this torture end? She'd taken herself to the other side of the country, hoping to find some sort of equilibrium, and here he was, tempting her with some devil's bargain.

'I won't be your mistress!'

'I don't want you as my mistress.' Another pace brought them toe to toe. 'I want you as my wife.'

For a second, then another and another, she stood gawking, processing his words. Then her hands slammed into his chest and she shoved with all her might.

He didn't budge. Desperate fury rose.

'Don't you *dare* play such games with me!' Her voice was a hoarse rasp of agony.

Large hands clamped on hers, pressing them against his chest. The rapid thud of his heart pounded beneath her palm like a runaway horse.

'It's no game.' He drew in a mighty breath and her hands lifted with the movement of his torso. 'You left and nothing was the same.' His fingers tightened on hers. 'The colour leached from my world when you went, Cassie. I hadn't re-alised till then how much you mean to me.'

She shook her head. 'I don't want to hear this.' It had to be some sort of trick. She didn't have the strength to pick herself up a second time.

'Please hear me out.'

Cassie's eyes rounded at the desperation in his voice. She

looked up into sober eyes that shone with…*anxiety*? Was it real or did she imagine it?

'All those weeks together I told myself it was infatuation. That once lust was sated I'd move on, do my duty and marry a suitable wife. It was what I'd spent so long planning, after all. I was a coward—telling myself I acted to protect my country and my unborn children when really I hid from the possibility of true intimacy. Of caring.'

His mouth twisted grimly.

'I was thoughtless and self-absorbed. But what I felt didn't pass. I was drawn deeper. That day I urged you not to go out with the class? Yes, I wanted to avoid publicity, but it wasn't so much to protect the marriage arrangements but so I could keep you to myself for as long as possible. Because I couldn't let you go.'

Cassie's mouth dropped open, not only at his words, but at the tension in his stance, the vehemence of his tone.

'It wasn't till you confronted me that I realised what that meant.'

She licked her dry lips, watching emotions flicker across Amir's face, unable to look away.

He lifted one hand to cup her jaw, his fingers splayed over her cheek, and her eyelids fluttered at the thrill rioting through her dormant hormones.

How could his touch awaken her? She should stop him, but for the life of her she couldn't move.

'I told you that day I cared for you, Cassie. The truth is I love you.'

Her eyes blurred and heat slammed into her chest, crushing it tight as she fought to hold on to sanity. They were just words designed to tempt her. Yet she longed so much for them to be true. How could he be so cruel?

She opened her mouth to speak but nothing emerged. In that instant his head dipped low. Cassie stiffened and tried to pull back, but he held her remorselessly, ignoring her gasp of distress as he took her lips.

It was a gentle, tender caress so piercingly sweet she almost wept.

'It's not true,' she whispered when he lifted his head. Yet he surveyed her steadily, his expression unlike any she'd read before. Determined yet uncertain.

Inside her poor, bruised heart leapt.

'On my life it's true, Cassie. I was never more serious.'

Long fingers cupped her jaw, then caressed her cheek. Was that her trembling or him? Her eyes widened. The sincerity in his voice sounded real, as if it was dredged from his very soul. Was anyone that good an actor?

'I think I've loved you almost from the first,' he confided. His hand slipped gently into her hair to massage her scalp, making whorls of pleasure spiral through her. 'You were so strong, so determined, so beautiful. Your courage alone made me yearn to understand you.'

'You didn't want me for my courage.' Cassie tried to pull her defences close, still not ready to believe his easy words. 'You wanted my body.'

'Of course I did. What man wouldn't? You're beautiful, sweet Cassie.' His smile was bittersweet. 'That was the trouble, I couldn't see past that till the day you confronted me with what I'd done. I couldn't see that this wasn't simply lust. That it was much, much more.'

Staring up into his eyes, Cassie wanted to believe him so badly. Already something melted inside at the urgency of his words and the yearning in his gaze.

'Then I saw what I'd done to you.' He clasped her tight. 'Cassie, can you forgive me? I had no idea until that evening. I didn't *let* myself think about it, though Faruq and Musad tried to persuade me to break with you.'

'They did?' She'd known Musad didn't approve of her, but Faruq too?

He nodded. 'Musad fretted over the potential scandal, but Faruq feared what the situation would do to *you*. He saw what

I was too blind to see. I was too wrapped up in my own selfish pleasure to listen.'

Amir lifted her hands, pressing kisses on each.

'It wasn't love you felt. Just lust.' Desperately she tried to shore up her defences against insidious temptation. She wanted Amir's love so desperately.

'It *was* more, Cassie. But I've had a lifetime believing love doesn't exist because I'd never known it. Never seen it up close. I didn't believe it could hit me like it has. I wanted you so badly I didn't think past my needs. I wanted you happy and I let myself believe you were.'

There was anguish in his eyes and Cassie's heart lurched. A spark of warmth flared. 'I *was* happy.'

'Really?'

'Yes.' Stunned, she watched light blaze in the velvet blackness of his eyes. Could this possibly be real?

'So you...care for me?'

The uncertainty in his voice tore at her. The Amir she knew was always sure of himself. That, above all else, convinced her. She drew a shaky breath and the cramped tension in her chest eased.

'Of course I care. How could you not realise that?' Her voice was gruff.

Slowly Amir smiled. The tightness around his mouth disappeared as he grinned down at her. The warmth of that grin wrapped around her like an embrace.

'You do? Enough to forgive me?'

'I...' Cassie tried to be sensible, to remind herself of the pain he'd wrought. But suddenly being cautious didn't seem sensible—not with Amir here, looking at her as if she was the most precious thing in his world. Not when her dreams were coming true.

She swallowed hard, dredging her courage. 'I love you, Amir. I—'

The rest of her words were obliterated as his head swooped down and he took her lips in an open-mouthed kiss that tore the last shreds of thought from her. This was no tentative foray but a bold, demanding caress that heated her blood and made her shiver in delicious anticipation.

Cassie kissed him back, holding his face in her hands and tugging him lower as she stood on tiptoe, pressing herself against him with the urgency of a woman who'd found her man against all odds.

'It's not real,' she gasped when the kiss ended.

Amir tucked her close, arms wrapped tight round her. 'It's real, sweetheart. Believe it.' He drew a shuddering breath. 'I couldn't bear to lose you. I want you with me always.'

He drew back enough that she could see his face.

'Can you forgive me, Cassie?'

She saw the shadow of fear in his eyes and her heart swelled, blanking out the last of her doubts. 'Yes.'

He smiled and it was like the sun emerging from behind clouds. His hold firmed. 'Will you marry me, Cassie?'

A world of hope and love lay in those words, yet she hesitated. 'You didn't want a wife who was notorious. You wanted someone with an unblemished reputation—'

'When I lost you I got a short, sharp lesson in what *really* matters. No gossip could stop me making you mine. Besides, nothing you do could come close to the antics of my parents. They filled the tabloids for years. Yet I survived. Our children will be fine.'

For a dizzying moment Cassie's brain stuck on the notion of having children with Amir.

'But there'll be an awful fuss. The story of me being given to you will get out.'

'And we'll survive the headlines. Besides, when people come to know you it will be water under the bridge—especially when they see how devoted we are to each other.'

It sounded like heaven.

'But I'm a foreigner. I don't speak the language.'

'You're intelligent. You'll learn. The fact you've already spent time teaching here will stand you in good stead.'

'And what if it comes out who my mother was? How she lived?' She forced the words out, old shame clogging her throat. 'I can't do that to you, Amir.'

His hands tightened and his mouth turned grim. 'You are not your mother, Cassie. Any more than I am my parents. I'm tired of worrying about public opinion. My people have accepted me and they'll learn to love you too.' He stroked his palms over her face, into her hair, and held her while he pressed a gentle, loving kiss to her parted lips.

The perfection of it brought tears to her eyes. Love welled in her heart for this man who understood her so well. The one man in the world for her.

'The past is the past, sweetheart. I refuse to let it destroy what we've got. This is too precious. *You're* too precious.'

She gazed up into that beloved, familiar face, devoid now of any trace of arrogance. Instead Amir looked determined and endearingly vulnerable.

A shadow flickered across his face. 'You still haven't answered me.'

Cassie smiled, feeling the answer deep inside and knowing it was right. She let everything she felt show in her eyes. 'I'll be your wife, Amir. You're the one man in the world for me.'

Happiness and love blazed in Amir's face. The sight stole Cassie's breath.

'I couldn't ask for anything more.' He raised her hand and pressed a fervent kiss to her palm. 'Now, let's go and break the news to the crowd outside. The sooner we announce our engagement, the sooner we can be together always.'

EPILOGUE

In the end Amir refused to wait long for the wedding. betrothal celebrations were barely ended when the nupt. began.

Secretly Cassie wondered if it was abstinence that mot vated his desire for an early wedding. Instead of installing her in the harem on their return to the capital Amir had taken her to the house of his cousin, an academic whose claim to the throne had been bypassed when Amir had been made Sheikh.

If Cassie had had worries about jealousy between the cousins, or not being welcomed, they were dispelled within minutes of arriving. Within an hour she and Amir were the centre of an impromptu party with Amir's cousin, his wife, his wife's sister and husband, and a gaggle of excited children.

Cassie remembered what Amir had said about being isolated as a boy. But if Amir the loner felt any qualms about the lively family gathering they didn't show.

At the end of the afternoon she saw him holding the hands of a toddler while the little girl jumped up and down on his knees. The tender look in his eyes made Cassie's heart melt, especially when he looked up and held her gaze.

The world fell away and there was only them, and the promise of their future to come. It took her breath away.

It made her hope that maybe they, a pair who'd never known the love of family, would one day create their own.

For three weeks Cassie stayed with Amir's relatives, fussed over and cosseted. Finally the wedding day arrived.

That was when she truly understood how popular Amir was, how much his people wished him well. Not by a whisper or sideways glance did anyone hint at disapproval or doubt. Instead there were smiles, cheers, and an abundance of goodwill. Cassie was overcome.

There had been speculation in the press, of course, and her story had caused a sensation in the foreign media. But instead of dwelling on titillating details most were captivated by the romance and drama of their story.

Cassie suspected Amir's masterful handling of the press had been a significant factor in the slant taken.

'Are you all right, *habibti*?' Amir's voice at her shoulder betrayed concern as they stood now before his people, receiving applause and good wishes. 'What's wrong?'

'Nothing.' She blinked rapidly. 'I'm just happy. So very happy.'

'Because of this?' He gestured to the crowd.

'That too,' she murmured, turning to face him. 'But mainly because of you.'

His eyes lit with that special fire she knew was just for her, and her heart tumbled over once more. Would she ever get used to seeing Amir's love? Hearing it in his voice? Feeling it in every touch?

Never.

He raised her hand and pressed a kiss to its centre, then turned it over and kissed her palm, lingering while his tongue swirled. She shivered with delight.

'Amir! You can't! Not in public.'

'Then we'll go somewhere private.'

'But doesn't the wedding reception have hours to go?'

He shrugged, and the devil was in his eyes. 'It does. Traditionally such occasions don't end till the early hours. But our guests will understand our absence.'

'That's what I'm afraid of.' Cassie tried to inject reproof into her voice, but instead she sounded breathless with anticipation.

'Do you mind?' Suddenly he was serious.

Cassie shook her head. 'I think it's obvious to everyone that I'm smitten.'

'That makes two of us.'

He made a deep, courtly bow, then held out his hand. Cassie placed hers in his, feeling Amir's strength, his tenderness, and knew that whatever the future held their love would last a lifetime.

Amir paused and waved to the crowd before leading her away to their private apartments.

Behind them spontaneous cheers rang out for the Sheikh and his bride.

* * * * *

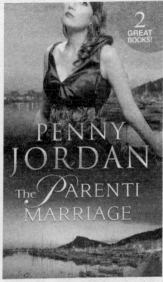

Two fabulous stories full of drama and passion
from Mills & Boon® favourites

Lynne Graham and
Penny Jordan

Now available from:

www.millsandboon.co.uk

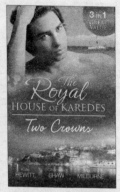

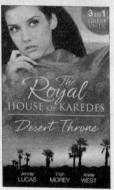

When five o'clock hits, what happens after hours...?

Feel the sizzle and anticipation of falling in love across the boardroom table with these seductive workplace romances!

**Now available at
www.millsandboon.co.uk**

Discover more romance at

www.millsandboon.co.uk

- ❤ WIN great prizes in our exclusive competitions
- ❤ BUY new titles before they hit the shops
- ❤ BROWSE new books and REVIEW your favourites
- ❤ SAVE on new books with the Mills & Boon® Bookclub™
- ❤ DISCOVER new authors

PLUS, to chat about your favourite reads, get the latest news and find special offers:

- Find us on facebook.com/millsandboon
- Follow us on twitter.com/millsandboonuk
- ❤ Sign up to our newsletter at millsandboon.co.uk